Last One To Know

BARBARA FREETHY

Fog City Publishing

PRAISE FOR BARBARA FREETHY

"Barbara Freethy's suspense novels are explosively good!" — *New York Times bestselling author Toni Anderson.*

"A fabulous, page-turning combination of romance and intrigue. Fans of Nora Roberts and Elizabeth Lowell will love this book." — *NYT Bestselling Author Kristin Hannah on Golden Lies*

"Powerful and absorbing...sheer hold-your-breath suspense." — *NYT Bestselling Author Karen Robards on Don't Say A Word*

"Barbara Freethy delivers riveting, plot-twisting suspense and a deeply emotional story. Every book is a thrilling ride." *USA Today Bestselling Author Rachel Grant*

"Freethy is at the top of her form. Fans of Nora Roberts will find a similar tone here, framed in Freethy's own spare, elegant style." — *Contra Costa Times on Summer Secrets*

"Freethy hits the ground running as she kicks off another winning romantic suspense series...Freethy is at her prime with a superb combo of engaging characters and gripping plot." — *Publishers' Weekly on Silent Run*

"PERILOUS TRUST is a non-stop thriller that seamlessly melds jaw-dropping suspense with sizzling romance, and I was riveted from the first page to the last...Readers will be breathless in anticipation as this fast-paced and enthralling love story evolves and goes in unforeseeable directions." — *USA Today HEA Blog*

PRAISE FOR BARBARA FREETHY

"Barbara Freethy is a master storyteller with a gift for spinning tales about ordinary people in extraordinary situations and drawing readers into their lives." — *Romance Reviews Today*

"Freethy (Silent Fall) has a gift for creating complex, appealing characters and emotionally involving, often suspenseful, sometimes magical stories."— *Library Journal on Suddenly One Summer*

"If you love nail-biting suspense and heartbreaking emotion, Silent Run belongs on the top of your to-be-bought list. I could not turn the pages fast enough."— *NYT Bestselling Author Mariah Stewart*

"Hooked me from the start and kept me turning pages throughout all the twists and turns. Silent Run is powerful romantic intrigue at its best."— *NYT Bestselling Author JoAnn Ross*

"An absorbing story of two people determined to unravel the secrets, betrayals, and questions about their past. The story builds to an explosive conclusion that will leave readers eagerly awaiting Barbara Freethy's next book."—*NYT Bestselling Author Carla Neggars on Don't Say A Word*

"A page-turner that engages your mind while it tugs at your heartstrings ... DON'T SAY A WORD had made me a Barbara Freethy fan for life!" —*NYT Bestselling Author Diane Chamberlain*

"*On Shadow Beach* teems with action, drama and compelling situations... a fast-paced page-turner." —*BookPage*

ALSO BY BARBARA FREETHY

Mystery Thriller Standalones

ALL THE PRETTY PEOPLE

LAST ONE TO KNOW

Romantic Suspense

Off the Grid: FBI Series

PERILOUS TRUST

RECKLESS WHISPER

DESPERATE PLAY

ELUSIVE PROMISE

DANGEROUS CHOICE

RUTHLESS CROSS

CRITICAL DOUBT

FEARLESS PURSUIT

DARING DECEPTION

RISKY BARGAIN

PERFECT TARGET

Lightning Strikes Trilogy

BEAUTIFUL STORM

LIGHTNING LINGERS

SUMMER RAIN

For a complete list of books, visit Barbara's Website!

LAST ONE TO KNOW

For more information on Barbara Freethy's books, visit her website:
www.barbarafreethy.com

PROLOGUE

New Orleans, Louisiana

The weather had changed since I'd landed in New Orleans twenty-four hours earlier. There was a hurricane stirring up trouble in the Gulf, but it was supposed to miss the city. But even if it didn't, I'd be gone before the storm made landfall.

As I walked through the busy French Quarter on a Saturday night in mid-September, I wouldn't have guessed that anyone was worried about the storm. The bars and restaurants were full, with crowds spilling out into the street. The weather was balmy, humid at seventy-five degrees at eleven fifty at night, and I could feel the sweat beading up on my face, my dark-brown hair getting thicker by the minute. I wished I could leave right this second, hop in a cab, and take a plane back to my normal life. But normal had never lasted long for me, which was why I was here now when I should have been home.

I took a turn at the next corner, walking down a much quieter side street, where the music faded into the distance and the shadows grew longer and darker.

I paused in the doorway of a tattoo shop that was closed for the night and checked my phone. The last text I'd sent sat there with no reply, and my stomach turned over again. I'd been fighting fear and nausea ever since I'd left Los Angeles, ever since I'd lied to the people who loved me.

Looking up from the phone, I saw a cluster of drunken twenty-somethings coming in my direction. They passed by, barely giving me a second glance, too interested in trying to remember the lyrics to a song they were singing as they stumbled down the street. I was twenty-nine years old, not that much older than them, but I felt like an old woman in comparison. I couldn't remember the last time I'd felt so carefree, so confident, so young, and so free.

Maybe I'd never really been any of those things. I'd just pretended to feel like that, so I would be like everyone else. But I had never been like everyone else.

The bells on a nearby church suddenly rang…twelve long, penetrating, clanging bells that were echoed by my pounding heart. I hurried down the street. We were supposed to meet at the cemetery next to the church. Even though I hadn't gotten a text to confirm, I needed to be there, because that's why I'd come.

As the wind lifted my hair, I felt drops of rain. Maybe the city wouldn't take the full force of the hurricane, but the incoming storm only deepened my sense of foreboding. It didn't help that I was heading into an old cemetery with overgrown trees and bushes or that the black iron gates squealed as I opened them, like a painful ghostly scream. This cemetery had been full for decades and as I walked around the crowded, sometimes broken gravestones, my bad feelings increased. I told myself it wasn't evil spirits I had to worry about. If I ran into danger, it would be from someone who was very much alive.

When I reached the mausoleum, a stone building in the middle of the property, I paused under an overhang, happy to have shelter from the increasing rain. Every crack of a twig had my head turning in fear. It felt like someone was watching me, but everyone here was dead. I paced back and forth. The adrenaline surging through my body needed somewhere to go.

This was a mistake. I shouldn't have come.

But I'd had to come. I'd had no choice.

Finally, I heard the gate open again, then footsteps. I held my breath until one of the few nearby lights in the cemetery illuminated a familiar face. Relief ran through me. "You're late," I said. "But it's good to see you."

"I wasn't sure you'd come."

"Yes, you were. I've never not come. But why are we here in this spooky place?"

"The past has caught up to me."

The words were haunting and terrifying, and an icy shiver ran down my spine. "What happened?"

"I was seen. I need to get away. Did you bring what I asked?"

"Yes."

"Good. My...friend should be here soon."

"I hope so. The weather is turning bad," I said. "Is this person someone you can trust?"

"I hope so."

That answer didn't make me feel better. My heart sped up. "The rain is getting worse."

"The storm changed directions. It's heading straight for us. But it might be helpful. It might provide cover for us to leave the city. There will be chaos and confusion."

"I don't need cover." I held out the bag I was carrying. "I brought what you asked. Now I'm going home." I said the words as forcefully as I could, even though I was torn up on the inside as to what I should do.

Headlights from an incoming car lit up the street next to the cemetery, and then they went off. Car doors opened and closed.

"Is this who we're waiting for?" I asked.

"No. It's not. Oh, God! They've found us."

The gate screeched opened again. Two figures were heading straight toward us. "Is there another way out of here?" I asked.

"There's a back gate on the other side of the cemetery that leads to Washington Street. That's where my friend was supposed to enter."

"Lead the way," I said.

We ran around the back of the mausoleum, moving deeper into the cemetery. I thought we might be able to get away. Then I heard a shout behind us. The beam of a flashlight lit me up.

Fear drove me to run even faster, but as we dove into the shadows, it was hard to see where we were going. I stumbled, hitting my knees on a protruding gravestone that tumbled me to the ground. I scrambled back to my feet, ignoring the searing pain in my leg, as I prayed for a way out.

A gunshot rang out, the blast instinctively making me duck my head. Swearing, I ran faster, flying over the ground, desperate to get back to my life. "I'm not dying tonight," I swore. "Not here. Not now."

A flash of lightning and an earth-shaking roar of thunder followed my words, the skies opening up with torrential, windy rain. Maybe the storm would provide the cover we needed to escape.

I had to survive this night. I had to get home. I had to...

CHAPTER ONE

CARMEL, *California*

The biggest call of my life came at three o'clock on a Thursday afternoon in the middle of September. I'd been working at my sister's clothing boutique in downtown Carmel when Ray Price's name flashed across my phone screen. I couldn't take the call in the shop, so I'd jumped into my car and driven a half-mile to the beach where I'd parked along the coastal trail and called him back.

"You're in," Ray said, his voice filled with excitement. "The Pacific Coast Orchestra wants to hire you as a second chair violin for our upcoming European tour. It's the chance of a lifetime, Brynn. We'll be touring for eight weeks starting in November and ending just after the New Year. You'll get to play in eight major cities, ending in Paris."

My heart pounded hard against my chest. "Are you sure? I can't quite believe it's real."

"That's because you've never really believed in how good you are."

"You've always been one of my biggest supporters," I said

gratefully. I'd met Ray nine years ago in a music class at UCLA. Ray also played the violin, and we'd become instant best friends. But while we'd started out on the same path, mine had diverged after college, when I'd given up my goal of playing in a world-renowned orchestra and decided to run a clothing boutique with my sister. That goal had seemed far more practical and attainable than the other.

While I'd played for community orchestras on the side and earned extra cash giving lessons, I'd thought it was too late to go back to that childhood dream of mine. But then, last week, Ray had asked me to audition for a last-minute opening with his orchestra, and I'd given it a shot, thinking the odds were very much against me.

"Rehearsals won't start until the first of October," Ray continued. "But they'll need your answer by Monday. Not that I think you need that long to decide. You can't turn this down."

"I don't want to turn it down, but I need to talk to my sister," I said, dreading that conversation.

"I'm sure Dani will be thrilled for you."

"I'm not sure about that," I replied. I was going to bail on our business and that would not make Dani happy. Although it wasn't really *our* business; it was Dani's store. But I'd been by her side since she'd first opened the clothing shop four years ago. I'd helped her grow the business and managed the store when she'd gone through difficult personal trials.

"Why wouldn't she be happy for you?" Ray questioned. "You have a gift, Brynn, and you're not using it. Your sister can find someone else to help her run the store. She'll want you to take this job. Just say yes."

"I'll call you back as soon as I talk to Dani, but since they are giving me until Monday, I'm going to take the weekend to get things organized here."

"All right. Congratulations, Brynn."

"Thanks, Ray. I know you put in a good word for me."

"I just told them the truth. You're one of the best violinists I've ever had the pleasure to play with."

"Right back at you. I'll call you soon."

As I set down the phone, I looked out the window at the crashing white-capped waves of the Pacific Ocean. There was a storm blowing in, and I felt like the sea echoed the turbulent emotions running through me. I liked my life best when everything was relaxed, on an even keel. I didn't like highs because they were usually followed by painful lows. Today was one of those days that seemed too good to be true.

But it was true. I had an offer to play with an incredible orchestra touring across Europe. It was an unbelievable opportunity. I wanted to believe that my sister would be happy for me. We'd always been there for each other, but the last several years had been more about me being there for her.

I'd moved to Carmel with her after college, when her very serious boyfriend had popped the question right after graduation. Steve had just finished law school and was about to join his parents' firm in Carmel. Dani hadn't wanted to move there without me. So, I'd gone to help her get settled and plan her wedding. It wasn't supposed to be forever. But after the wedding, she'd wanted to open the boutique, and she needed my help again. Then had come her issues with pregnancy, miscarriage, and sadness. My sister had needed me, and I couldn't say no to her, because when I'd needed her, she'd been there.

It had been the two of us against the world since my mother had died when we were seven. Our dad had been around, but his grief had taken him away from us, mentally and emotionally. He hadn't come out of that grief until he'd remarried, and then it was all about his second wife, Vicky.

But even without the attention of my father and stepmother, I'd always had Dani. Born twenty-two minutes before me, Dani had taken on the role of big sister from the minute she was born. She'd been the bossy one, constantly looking ahead, making sure

I wasn't breaking any rules and acting like my second mother. I'd needed her to fill that role. I owed her a lot and leaving now would hurt her. Not just because she'd need to hire someone at the shop, but because after a couple of unsuccessful attempts, she was now four months pregnant, and the last thing she needed was stress in her life. It wasn't the best time to leave.

But would there ever be a good time?

Once she had the baby, Dani would want to be home with her child. She'd want me to keep the boutique running. I couldn't keep putting my own life on hold no matter how much I loved her, no matter how much I didn't want to disappoint her.

My phone rang, and Dani's name flashed across the screen. I felt almost panicked at the sight of it. I knew she was wondering where I was. I couldn't talk to her on the phone. This conversation had to be done in person. I sent her a text, telling her I was on my way back, and then I started the car.

A few minutes later, I pulled into the small lot behind the store, drew in a deep breath and headed inside. I dropped my bag in the office and made my way through the dressing-room area, where all three stalls appeared to be full. That wasn't surprising. This weekend should be especially busy as there were a ton of tourists in town for a big celebrity golf tournament.

Dani was ringing up a customer while our other clerk, Maddie, a local college student was hanging up clothes. I smiled at Maddie, then made my way over to Dani. The customer she was helping gave a double take when she saw me.

"There's two of you," she murmured in bemusement.

I smiled, used to the surprised reaction, although it hadn't happened as much in recent years. Dani and I were identical mirror twins. While we looked alike, she was right-handed, and I was left. She had a freckle above her right eyebrow, while I had the same freckle on the left. But we shared the same brown hair and dark blue, almost purple, eyes.

Beyond that, we'd made some changes to distinguish ourselves over the years. Dani had cut her brown hair to collar length and wore it straight, while my hair fell below my shoulders in tangled waves. Dani's fashion style was trendy and modern, while I was more casual and liked a bohemian look.

"Sorry for staring," the customer continued.

"No worries," Dani said. "Brynn is my twin sister, and we've had some fun over the years confusing people until we changed our hair and the way we dress."

"It must be odd to look at each other and see your own face," the customer said.

"It feels normal to us," I said.

"Enjoy your dress," Dani added, as she handed the customer her bag.

"Oh, I love it already. It will be perfect for my best friend's wedding. Thanks."

As the woman left, Dani's sales smile faded as she gave me an annoyed look. "Where have you been? I told you I need to leave early to get to my doctor's appointment. Steve will be here any second to pick me up."

"Oh, right." I realized my plan to shake up both our lives was going to have to wait. "Sorry, I forgot."

"You've been preoccupied lately. Are you thinking about Jeff?" Dani asked, referring to the man I'd been dating the past month.

I started at the question, realizing I hadn't given Jeff one thought in the last week.

"Are you two getting serious?" Dani asked with a hopeful smile.

"It hasn't been that long. He's a nice guy, but I don't know…"

"You're so picky, Brynn. Jeff has a good job, and he's Steve's best friend. Think how great it would be if the two of you fell in love. Jeff is already part of the family. He's a good catch."

"I'm not looking to catch someone."

"I wish you would change your mind. I want our kids to grow up together."

"Dani, slow down," I said with a laugh. "Nothing would happen that fast, even if I keep dating Jeff."

"I know. I just like it when we're both happy. And it doesn't feel like you've been that happy lately."

Her words seemed like the perfect opening to say I'd found a way to make myself happy. But then Steve walked through the front door. Dani's husband was an attractive man with blond hair and blue eyes. Steve was dressed in a navy-blue suit. His glasses framed a pair of tired brown eyes. Dani had told me earlier that he'd been putting in long hours at the office and in court as a trial was just getting underway.

He gave me a friendly smile, then walked over to Dani to give her a kiss. "Are you ready to go?"

"I am," she said. "I'm a little nervous."

"It's going to be fine," he told her.

"Just what I wanted to hear you say."

I envied the look of intimacy that passed between them. They'd been through a lot of heartache since their wedding, but they seemed to have grown stronger because of it. I hoped today's exam would provide nothing but good news. They deserved a break.

"I'm going to grab my purse. I'll be right back," Dani told Steve.

As she went into the back room, Steve moved over to the counter. "Have you talked to your dad lately, Brynn?"

"No. Why?" I asked curiously.

"Vicky just called me. She wanted to know if I knew where Ross had gone on his business trip. His assistant told her he'd gone to Portland, but he's not staying at his usual hotel there. Nor is he returning her calls."

"Why would she call you?"

"Ross and I are supposed to play golf on Sunday."

"Oh. Well, my father doesn't check in with me. Dani would hear from him before I would."

"I'll talk to her about it." He paused. "Don't say anything

about your dad right now. Dani might worry, and I want her to go into this appointment with a relaxed, positive attitude."

I could see by the tension in his eyes that he wasn't feeling at all relaxed. "I won't say anything, and I hope it goes well today."

"Me, too. It has been a lot to get to this point."

"It's all going to be good from here on," I assured him. "I wouldn't worry about Dad or Vicky. She lives for drama. She has always been insecure, imagining the worst whenever Dad isn't giving her a hundred percent of his attention. But he gets distracted by work, and he doesn't always check his phone when he's with clients. I'm sure he's fine."

"I hope so. I don't want Dani to be stressed about anything right now. Whatever you can do to take pressure off her, I'd really appreciate."

My heart sank at his words. I couldn't promise him I'd be taking pressure off Dani, not with what I needed to talk to her about. But first things first; they needed to see the doctor and find out everything was exactly as it should be.

Dani came back into the shop and gave me a smile. "Thanks for taking over, Brynn. I don't know what I'd do without you."

Her words lingered in the air long after she and Steve had left. She was going to have to do without me if I took my dream job. *When* I took my dream job, I silently amended.

It was a risk. I could play horribly and get fired within a week, and that might hurt worse than not playing at all. But I'd been playing it safe my entire life.

Growing up, Dani had never let me stray too far. If I got close to the street, she'd take my hand and yank me back. I hadn't always appreciated her tight grip on me, but I had relied on it. She had kept me safe over the years. But I couldn't let my sister's needs dictate the rest of my life. I was twenty-seven years old, and Dani and I both needed more than each other. She had Steve and the boutique and a baby on the way. It was my turn.

But for now, I needed to finish the day. For the next hour, I did everything I could do to keep myself from thinking too much. As the clock ticked toward five, the customers petered out.

Maddie left to get ready for a date, and I was about to turn the sign to *Closed* when the door opened, and Jeff Dunbar walked in with a smile on his boyishly handsome face. He wore gray slacks and a light-blue shirt with a tie loose around his neck. Jeff was a lawyer at Steve's firm and one of my brother-in-law's best friends. We'd been dating the last few weeks, and I liked him, but I didn't see it going anywhere.

There was nothing wrong with Jeff. He was attractive and nice. There were a few sparks, but I rarely thought about him when we weren't together, which wasn't the best sign. He was also five years older than me and far more interested in settling down than I was. With my change in career looming, I couldn't imagine where he would fit into my life, or if he would even want to. But I couldn't get into anything with him before I spoke to Dani.

"Hey, Brynn," he said with a smile. "How about Happy Hour at Casa Maria tonight? Margaritas, chips, and guacamole are calling my name."

A drink didn't sound bad, but I felt in too much emotional turmoil to fake being a good date tonight. The sound of my phone ringing gave me a reason to stall. "Hold on, I need to get my phone. Dani is at the doctor." I dashed into the office to retrieve my phone from my bag. I really didn't want this to be Dani calling with bad news.

Jeff followed me into the office with concern in his eyes. But it was an unknown number flashing on my screen.

"It's not her," I said. But I answered the call just in case it was the doctor's office. "Hello?"

"Brynn Landry?" a woman asked.

"Yes."

"I'm Kendra Miller, a nurse at St. Mary's Hospital in San Francisco."

"Okay." When she said *hospital*, my brain went straight to

Dani, but my sister wasn't in San Francisco. "What do you want?" I asked.

"I have some bad news," the woman replied. "Your mother is in critical condition."

My breath caught in my throat. "What?"

"She was brought in thirty minutes ago," Nurse Miller said.

"That's impossible." I felt suddenly dizzy. I put a bracing hand on the desk in front of me. "My stepmother is in Los Angeles."

"The woman told me her name is Kim Landry. Although, there is some confusion, because her ID gives her name as Laura Hawthorne."

My stomach flipped over. "I don't understand." Kim Landry was my mother's name. But I didn't know a Laura Hawthorne. "Why are you calling me? How did you get my number?"

"It was in her phone. I spoke to your mother briefly when she was brought in. She said to tell you and your sister she's sorry and that she always loved you."

My breath started coming too fast. My mother had died twenty years ago, when I was seven years old. "There must be some mistake. You have the wrong person."

"I don't think so. There's a photo in her wallet of her with two little girls, Brynn and Dani. You're Brynn, right?"

"Yes, but…"

"I just took a picture of the photo. I'm texting it to you," the nurse said.

I opened the text, and the image sent a stabbing pain through my body. I was looking at the same photo that sat on my night-stand, that sat on Dani's nightstand—the last one taken of my mother with Dani and me at a park a month before she died.

"Is that your mother?" the nurse asked.

"Yes," I said, barely able to get the word through my tight lips.

"You should come to the hospital, Ms. Landry."

"What—what happened to her? Was she in an accident?"

"No. She was shot."

Her answer shocked me again. "Shot? Who shot her?"

"I don't know. You can talk to the police about that. I just wanted to let you know that if you want to see your mother, don't delay. Her condition is grave."

The call disconnected, and I struggled to draw a breath.

"Brynn? What's wrong?" Jeff asked, walking toward me with concern. "You look like you've seen a ghost."

"I just heard from one."

"What does that mean?"

"My mother," I said shortly.

"Vicky? Is she all right?" he asked.

I shook my head. "Not my stepmother. My mother."

"I thought your mom died when you were a child."

"I thought so, too. But a nurse from a hospital in San Francisco just called me. She said my mother was shot, and she's in critical condition. She wants me to come right away."

Jeff gave me a disbelieving look. "She must have the wrong person."

"She sent me a photo of my mom with me and Dani. It was in the woman's wallet. And she said her name was Kim Landry, although she had some other name on her ID. But she had my name in her phone. That's why they called me. She wanted me and Dani to know she was sorry." The words poured out of me before I could even process them.

"There has to be an error." His brows furrowed together in a frown. "You should call Dani."

Dani was always my first call when I had a problem, but she was at her doctor's appointment. She was going to find out if her baby was okay. I could not drop this bomb on her, not until I knew what was going on. "She's at the doctor's office with Steve. They're doing an ultrasound. I can't call her right now."

"What about your father?"

"I could call him." I grabbed onto the idea like a lifeline. I punched in my father's number, but it went straight to voicemail, and I remembered Steve telling me that my father had been out of touch. I hung up without leaving a message because I had no idea what I would say. "He didn't answer."

"What about Vicky?"

"No," I said. My stepmother was the last person I wanted to talk to right now.

Jeff gave me a troubled look. "What do you want to do?"

My mind was spinning, but there was only one answer to that question. "I have to go to San Francisco, and I have to leave now."

"That's a three-hour drive, maybe longer at this time of day."

"Then I better get started."

"This is a bad idea," Jeff said. "You should talk to Dani."

"No. I need to find out what's happening. Then I'll talk to her. Please don't tell her, Jeff. Don't tell Steve, either. Promise me."

My demand made him uncomfortable. "I don't know. You're acting on emotion, Brynn. This could be a bad decision."

"Well, it's mine to make," I snapped. "I need you to give me a day before you say anything to my sister or her husband. I want her to have a night to celebrate. This could all be nothing, so the last thing I need to do is cause her undue stress."

"All right. I won't say anything," Jeff said with an unhappy glint in his eyes. "I wish I could go with you, but I have a lot of meetings tomorrow."

"I'll be fine." I ushered him out the front door, then locked up, and ran to my car. As I started the engine, I knew I wasn't anything close to fine. My world had just turned upside down. I'd thought the call I'd gotten from Ray earlier was the one that would change my life. But I had a terrible feeling it was going to be this one.

CHAPTER TWO

THE THREE-HOUR DRIVE to San Francisco passed in a blur of anxiety and confusion. It didn't help that it started raining an hour into the drive, because the rain reminded me of the storm that had taken my mother's life.

Or maybe it hadn't…

But her being alive seemed impossible to believe. She had a different name, I reminded myself. Laura Hawthorne. Maybe I should have taken a minute and searched for Laura Hawthorne online instead of jumping in my car, but it was too late now. I was going to San Francisco no matter what.

As the windshield wipers wiped away the constant splatter of rain, I thought back to the night my mother died.

We'd been living in Los Angeles. My dad had tucked us into bed after reading one of our favorite stories. He didn't normally do the bedtime books; that was my mom's job. She'd snuggle into bed with us, and we'd talk our way through the stories. But that night my mother was out of town. She'd gone to New Orleans to visit a friend from childhood. My dad had made us dinner, which consisted of hot dogs and mac and cheese out of a box. Then he'd read us a story as quickly as possible, tucked us in, turned off the light, and closed the door.

Only a minute passed before I got out of bed and asked Dani to play horses with me. Dani said we were supposed to go to sleep. She loved to follow the rules. I ignored her and started playing with our horse farm. Eventually, she got out of bed to join me. It wasn't the first time we'd stayed up past our bedtime. We'd loved playing in the shadows of our nightlight, in our own little world.

At some point, I heard my dad's phone ring. It was loud and close by. He was out in the hall. Dani and I froze, thinking we were going to get caught for playing after bedtime. But then he shouted, "Oh, my God! Oh, my God!"

We stopped playing and stared at each other. Something was terribly wrong. My father wasn't the kind of man to raise his voice. When he got angry, he got quiet.

The phone rang several more times after that, and each time, my father's voice grew louder. Dani and I crept to the door. I put my hand in hers. I was scared. I knew something bad had happened.

We heard the front door open and close. We snuck into the hallway, hoping my mom had come back early. But my dad was talking to the neighbor, a woman by the name of Mary Carpenter. She put her arms around my father. He was shaking.

I started shaking, too. Dani squeezed my hand. "It's going to be okay, Brynn," she told me.

I cried in response.

That's when my dad saw us.

"You're supposed to be in bed," he said, tears in his eyes, as he walked toward us.

"What's wrong, Daddy?" I asked.

He dropped to his knees and opened his arms, taking both of us into his warm, safe embrace. "It will be okay. You need to go back to bed. I have to go out for a bit. Mary will stay with you."

"I want you to stay, Daddy," Dani said.

"I'll be back soon," he promised. "Take care of Brynn."

"I will," Dani replied, always happy to be in charge.

"I want to go with Daddy," I said when he walked away.

"You can't," Dani told me.

"I want Mommy," I added.

"Me, too," Dani said, meeting my gaze. "But we have to be strong, Brynn. We can't cry. Let's go to bed."

We went into our room. Instead of getting into her bed, Dani got into mine. I needed her near me, because the fear was overwhelming, and I didn't want to be alone.

As memories of the past swamped me now, I felt tears gather in my eyes. I'd never seen my mother again.

For almost a week, Dani and I thought our mom was just delayed in New Orleans because of the horrible storm that had hit the city. Eventually, we'd been told that our mom had been caught in the hurricane, and that she'd gone to heaven.

I hadn't known what that meant. I just knew she wasn't going to be around anymore, and nothing would ever be the same.

I was right. Our lives changed drastically after my mom passed away. My father withdrew into a sad shell. He hired a nanny to take care of us and buried himself in work. Dani and I were the last people on his mind.

Four years later, Vicky married my dad. For a moment, I'd thought I might have a family again. But within six months, Vicky had talked my father into sending us to boarding school.

Neither of us wanted to go, but in some ways being away at school had been a relief. We didn't have to tiptoe around my dad or be super nice to Vicky. We could just be ourselves.

It was at boarding school where I'd really honed my musical skills. My mother had been a violinist, and I'd learned the basics from her before she'd died. But at boarding school, playing the violin had become my escape from reality, and I became very, very good at it.

After graduating from high school, Dani and I moved on to UCLA, where I started out in the music program but eventually changed my major to business, because Dani convinced me we needed to be practical and to be able to make our own way in the world. Dani and I were different in a lot of ways, but one thing we both hated was unpredictability, probably because of how drastically our life had changed in one night. We never wanted to feel out of control again.

But I felt that way now, and it was terrifying.

I would love for my mother to be alive.

On the other hand, if she wasn't dead, where the hell had she been all these years?

Did my dad know she was alive? Did Vicky?

The questions ran around in my head, the anxiety making me press down harder on the gas. Maybe when I got to the hospital, the answers would be right in front of me. I would see that the woman who had been shot was not my mother, that it was all a bizarre mistake, and my life could return to normal.

When I finally drove into the hospital parking lot, it was eight thirty at night. The rain had stopped, but it was cold and foggy, adding an eerie atmosphere to an already scary destination. Before getting out of the car, I checked my phone, seeing a stream of messages from Jeff, Ray, and my sister. There was also a voicemail from an Inspector Alan Greenman with the San Francisco Police Department asking me to call him back as soon as possible. That had to be about my mother, or the woman who people thought was my mother.

I left all the messages for later. I got out of the car and walked toward the lobby doors. Once inside, I was directed to the Intensive Care Unit on the fourth floor. The smell of medicine and bleach made my already queasy stomach turn over, but I pressed on.

When I reached the nurses' station, the woman who'd called me earlier, Kendra Miller, told me that my mother had come out of surgery and had been placed in a medical coma to give the injury to her brain a chance to heal. Apparently, she had been shot in the head and in the shoulder. Her condition appeared to be stable at the moment, but it was too early to know whether she had suffered any brain damage.

While I listened as carefully as I could, my heart was beating so fast that I could barely concentrate. And when Nurse Miller led me down the hall, panic rose within me.

With every step I took, my need to run increased. I didn't know what I was doing here or why I was by myself. I couldn't do this on my own. I should have told Dani. I could feel my fingers tingling. I wanted to reach for my sister's hand. I wanted her to be at my side. I wanted us to face this together. But I'd left her out of it. I'd chosen to protect her from this stressful situation. It had been the right decision, but still…

The nurse waved me into the room. I drew in a breath and moved forward. The person in the bed was hooked up to machines and tubes. It took a long minute for me to let my gaze slide up her body and settle on her face.

She didn't really look like my mother, at least not the woman I remembered. Her once long, brown hair was streaked with gray and cut short to her shoulders. A wide bandage wrapped around her head. Her face was very pale, and her breath barely a whisper. Her eyes were closed so I couldn't see if they were the deep-blue violet I remembered. But as I stared at her for a long minute, her features resonated deep within me. I knew her face. I knew her nose and her mouth. I knew the freckle under her left eye that matched mine.

The truth hit me like a punch to the gut.

This woman was my mother.

The woman in this bed had once loved me and sang to me and laughed with me. She'd told me she'd always be there for me, but that had been a lie. She'd left me. She'd left Dani. We'd thought she was dead. My father had told us she had died.

Had he lied? Was he in on the secret? Or did he think she'd died, too?

I suddenly felt dizzy, overwhelmed with shock and emotion.

I didn't know what to think. It was difficult to process the fact that my mother was alive...but barely.

That realization created another wave of conflicted feelings. My mother might not have died twenty years ago, but she might die before I had a chance to ask her why she'd left and why she'd stayed away.

I put a steadying hand on the bed rail. Looking at the face of a woman who was my mother but also a stranger made me shaky. I didn't know where to look. I couldn't focus. Her face was blurring in front of me.

"Are you all right?" Nurse Miller asked, her sharp voice snapping me back to reality. "Ms. Landry?"

"I don't know," I murmured helplessly.

"Why don't you sit down? I'll get you some water."

I nodded, then stumbled toward a nearby chair, taking the weight off my weak legs. The nurse poured me a cup of water, and I drank it down, needing something to take the edge off, even if it was just water.

"Do you need anything else?" the nurse asked, compassion in her eyes.

She was an older woman with a kind but weary gaze. She must be used to people falling apart in front of her.

"Is my mother's doctor around?"

"Dr. Ryker has gone home for the day, but she didn't expect any change in your mother's condition this evening. She'll be in to check on her tomorrow morning."

"Do you know where my mother was shot?"

"I believe it was on the sidewalk outside her home. There was a detective here earlier. I told him I had notified you. I'm sure he'll be in touch."

"He left me a message. I haven't had a chance to call him back yet." I paused. "You said you had my mom's phone and her wallet?"

"I did, but I turned everything over to the police. You'll have to get whatever you want from them."

"All right. You also said that my mother asked you to tell me and my sister that she was sorry, that she loved us. Did she say what she was sorry about?"

"No, she didn't, but she was in terrible shape. She wasn't able to speak more than a few sentences."

A knot grew in my throat. "I guess she didn't completely forget about us." I drew in a shaky breath. "I was told my mother died twenty years ago. We had a funeral for her. That's why I was so shocked to get your call."

Surprise ran through her gaze. "I had no idea. I hope you'll get the chance to speak to your mother directly."

"I hope so, too. Can I sit with her for a few minutes?"

"As long as you like. I'll be going off shift at eleven. But I put your number on the chart. If there's any change, someone will notify you. I'll also leave a note to have Dr. Ryker call you in the morning."

"Thank you." As she left, I got to my feet and gave my mother another long look. I was shocked she was alive but also scared she might die. There were too many emotions running through me. I felt overwhelmed, and I needed to think. I turned away from her and walked out of the room.

When I left the hospital, the cold, damp air hit my face, and I drew in a breath of relief. It felt better just to be outside, away from the woman who was my mother and the machines that were keeping her alive. I got into my car and debated my next move.

Clearly, I had some calls to make. I just didn't know who to call first. The more information I could get, the easier it would be to talk to my sister and my father.

I punched in Inspector Greenman's number, relieved when he answered. "This is Brynn Landry. You called me earlier."

"Yes," he said. "I have some questions for you about your mother, Laura Hawthorne. Can you come to the station?"

"Uh, I guess. I'm at St. Mary's Hospital. I'm not from this area. Where's the station?"

"Less than ten minutes away."

"All right," I said, texting myself the address he rattled off. "I'll be there soon."

As I set down the phone, it vibrated with an incoming call. Danielle's name flashed across the screen. I wasn't ready to talk to my sister, so I let it go to voicemail. Then I played her message back.

"Everything is perfect with the baby," Dani said with excitement. "And it's a boy. Can you believe it? I'm going to have a son."

I smiled at her words, tears filling my eyes.

"I'm a little sorry I'm not carrying twins," Dani continued. "Growing up with you was so special. But everything is good, so I can't be greedy. Steve and I just got back from a celebratory dinner. Call me when you can. Love you."

"Love you, too," I whispered.

I wanted to call and congratulate her, to share in this moment that had taken so many years to get to. But Dani would ask where I was, what I was doing, and I didn't want to tell her tonight, not while she was feeling so good about everything. I'd call her tomorrow. Hopefully, by then, I'd have more answers.

I sent her a quick text. *So happy for you. I'm in a movie now. I'll talk to you tomorrow. I can't wait to celebrate with you.*

Dani sent back a smiley face in response, and I put down the phone.

Then I drove to the police station, hoping the bad news wasn't about to get worse.

CHAPTER THREE

INSPECTOR ALAN GREENMAN looked like a man who had once been on a football field. He had broad shoulders and a stocky build that strained the fit of his gray suit. His face was square, his hair and beard were brown and peppered with gray. He ushered me into an interview room, which made me nervous. I felt like I was guilty of something instead of just wanting to get information about a victim. As we sat down across from each other at a long, narrow table, he gave me a speculative look, then said, "How is your mother doing?"

"I'm not sure. She's unconscious. The nurse said she's in critical condition. They'll know more tomorrow."

"I'm sorry to hear that."

His comment seemed more polite than heartfelt, but then everything about him seemed jaded and weary from his tired eyes to his somewhat wrinkled shirt.

"Do you know of anyone who might have had a motive to shoot your mother?" he asked.

"No. I can't tell you anything about my mother. I thought she died when I was seven, that she lost her life in a hurricane in New Orleans twenty years ago. Then tonight, a nurse called and told me that my mother was alive, that she'd been shot. To say I was stunned would be an understatement. I thought it had to be a case of mistaken identity. The woman's ID says her name is Laura Hawthorne, but my mother's name was Kim Landry." I drew in a breath. "But when I got to the hospital, and I saw her face, I knew it was her. It was my mother. She didn't die twenty years ago, but I guess there's a chance she could die now." I blinked away the angry and frustrated tears gathering in my eyes.

Inspector Greenman sat back in his chair, folding his beefy arms across his chest. He gave me a long, thoughtful look. "That's quite a story."

"It's not a story; it's what happened. Where was my mother shot?"

"On the sidewalk in front of her residence. The doorbell camera across the street showed her walking away from her home at three ten. She was about fifteen yards away when she collapsed."

"And the person who shot her?"

"Not caught on camera—yet. We're canvassing the neighborhood for more security footage. It appears that the shots may have come from in between houses across the street, but we're still investigating."

"The shooter was on foot? Does he live in the neighborhood?"

"I wish I could answer those questions, Ms. Landry."

I frowned as I went over the few facts he'd given me. "There was no one else around? It was the middle of the afternoon."

"Unfortunately, we have not located a witness. A woman walking her dog said she heard shots, but she didn't know where they came from until she walked around the corner and saw your mother's body on the ground."

I winced at the mention of my mother's body. It made her sound like she was already dead. But she wasn't, I reminded myself.

"What about the neighbors? Did you interview them?" I asked.

"We've talked to several of them. Most weren't home or didn't see anything. Your mother is employed at the Harding School for the Arts as a music teacher. I spoke to the principal, Joanne Hunt. She told me that she couldn't imagine who would want to shoot your mother, that Laura is a kind, thoughtful teacher and very well-liked by both students and staff. She was not aware of any incidents at the school that would suggest someone had a problem with your mother."

His words were filling in a couple of blanks but also creating more questions in my head. "Is she single? Is she married? Does she have kids?"

"Mrs. Hunt said that Ms. Hawthorne is single and to her knowledge has not been married, nor does she have children. Clearly, that may not be the case since you're here and your name is in Ms. Hawthorne's phone with the designation of daughter."

"You have my mother's phone, don't you? Were there a lot of people on her contact list? I'm wondering if she had my sister's number or my dad's."

"There were ten contacts on the phone besides yourself. Three of them were teachers at the Harding School, two were friends who said they were part of your mother's book club, one was for her dentist, another for a local restaurant, and three numbers had no names. We called those numbers but didn't reach anyone. One of them had a voicemail for a man named Tom Wells. I don't suppose you know that name?"

"No. I wouldn't know the names of anyone in her current life. It's possible I might recognize one of the undesignated numbers. May I see the phone?"

"I'll get it."

I sat back in my chair as he left the room, my brain spinning as I thought about what I knew. My mother had a job as a music teacher. She had neighbors, friends, a book club, maybe even a boyfriend. That didn't sound like someone who was hiding. On the other hand, she was using the name Laura

Hawthorne. *Was that her real name? Was Kim Landry the fake name?*

Inspector Greenman returned to the room with a large plastic bag. Inside was a brown leather purse. Next to that was a smartphone. He took it out and handed it to me.

"What's the code?" I asked, seeing the numbers pop up as the phone came on.

"0413. Your mother gave the code to the nurse when she asked her to call you. That saved us the trouble of trying to get into the phone."

My heart jumped. "That's my birthdate."

"Not surprising," he said with a nod. "Most people stay close to meaningful numbers."

I looked back at the phone, scrolling through her contacts. Dani's number was not there, which I once again found odd. I didn't recognize any of the other numbers. She hadn't put my dad's number on her contact list or Vicky, who had been my mother's friend before she'd become my stepmother.

"Anything jump out at you?" Inspector Greenman asked.

I shook my head. "No." I clicked on text messages, scrolling through those, but there were very few and most seemed to be about work or book club. "She didn't text a lot."

"Nor did she have an online presence," he said. "She lived a very quiet life." He glanced down at his notebook. "Your mother's date of birth would make her forty-nine years old." "Her ID said her birthday is May second."

I shook my head. "Her birthday is February ninth. I don't understand how my mother could live an entire life as Kim Landry and then become someone else. How could she get IDs in a different name? How could she get a Social Security number to match that name? She works, so she must pay taxes. Does she have a bank account?"

"She does. She has a checking account with about twelve thousand dollars in it and a savings account with another ten thousand. She owns the building where she lives, which consists of her two-story flat and a studio apartment on the first floor. We spoke to a man who is renting that unit. He wasn't home at the time of the shooting and said he only moved in a month ago. He didn't know much more about your mother than what I've told you." He paused. "It's not impossible to create a fake identity, but it's usually expensive. Aside from your mother's home, we haven't discovered any other assets. But I didn't realize until this conversation that your mother's shooting may be more complicated than I originally thought."

"Because she used to be someone else?"

"Yes. Most people don't disappear unless they have a good reason, including being afraid for their life. Maybe her past caught up to her." He picked up a pen. "You said her name was Kim Landry. What else can you tell me about the woman you knew?"

"She was born in Los Angeles."

"What was her maiden name?"

I thought for a moment. "I think it was Sullivan. I can find out from my dad."

"Good. What about your father? What's his name?"

"Ross Landry."

"And where is he now?"

"I'm not sure. I haven't spoken to him yet. I haven't told anyone in my family that my mom is alive. I didn't think it was real. I thought the nurse had made a mistake, that the woman in the hospital was some friend of my mom's, someone who might have somehow had a photo of my mother and my sister and me."

"Right," he said with a nod. "I saw the photo. It's in the bag along with her house keys, which we used to enter her home."

"Did you find anything at her house?"

"Nothing of note. Who else is in your family?"

"My father remarried after my mother died—or disappeared. Her name is Vicky Landry. She was also a friend of my mother's. My sister, Dani, and her husband Steve. That's it. My grandparents on both sides were dead before I was born and neither of my parents had siblings." I took a much-needed breath. "Unless that's not true, either." I pressed my hands to my temples. "I'm so confused."

"We'll help you figure it out. What was the relationship like between your father and your mother?"

"I think it was good, but I was seven, so I don't know. He seemed heartbroken by her death. He grieved for years. He eventually got together with Vicky, but several years passed in between. I always thought he really loved my mom. He doesn't speak of her often, but when he does, I hear the love in his voice."

The detective made a few more notes.

"I don't believe my father knew she was alive all this time," I added.

"Okay," he said, but he didn't sound convinced.

I could hardly blame him. I didn't know what was true anymore.

"Where do you live?" he continued.

"In Carmel. My sister and brother-in-law live there as well. My father and Vicky live in Los Angeles. My father travels a fair amount for his job."

"And what does he do?"

"He's in sales for a technology company."

"I'll need his information and your sister's."

"I want to tell them first. This news should come from me."

He gave me another speculative look, then set down his pen. "If your mother isn't dead and your father told you she was, there's a good chance he lied to you, that he knows she was alive all these years."

It wasn't like that thought hadn't occurred to me but having him spell it out so succinctly sent a chill down my spine. I didn't want to believe my father could tell such a lie. I didn't want to believe my mom could, either. But someone had lied. That put a sinking feeling in the pit of my stomach.

"It's also possible your father is the reason she disappeared," the detective added.

"I don't believe that's true. My father is a good man. He's not dangerous in any way. I'll talk to my family, but I think the past is less important than the present. You need to find out who shot my mother."

"I intend to do that, but it's possible that the past is intertwined with the present. This attack appears to be personal and premeditated. The shooter waited for your mother to leave the house. He was able to vanish without being caught by any cameras in the neighborhood, which suggests he knew the area well."

"My father doesn't know this city. I don't think he's been here in years."

"Are you sure? You just said he travels a lot. Do you always know where he's going?"

I wished I could answer his question with a confident yes, but I couldn't. "No," I admitted. "But I don't want you to focus on my dad when he's unlikely to be involved."

"I follow the facts where they lead. Are you staying in the city tonight?"

"Yes. I'll get a room somewhere."

"Let's talk tomorrow. Once the shock has worn off, you may see things more clearly or remember information that might be helpful."

"I can't imagine what that would be, but all right." As he rose, I got to my feet. "Can I have my mother's bag?"

He hesitated. "I'm going to hang on to her phone, but we've already been through the bag and taken photos of its contents, so you can take that with you."

"I'd like the keys to her house, too. I want to see where she lives."

"They're in the bag."

Inspector Greenman ushered me out of the conference room and waved me toward the exit.

When I got back into my car, I locked the door, fastened my seat belt, and let out a breath. Then I opened my mother's handbag. There wasn't a lot to look at, but I started with a black wallet, which contained a driver's license with the name Laura Hawthorne on it and an address in San Francisco.

The face of Laura Hawthorne matched my mother's face. There was one credit card in the same name, and the photo of my mother holding me and Danielle. It was old and faded, ripped at one corner, and bent in the middle. There were two twenties in the billfold, along with a couple of quarters. In addition to the wallet, there was a lip gloss, a pair of reading glasses, sunglasses, a packet of tissues, and something that looked like a program for a musical concert. There were also a couple of keys on a ring that was shaped like a musical note.

A wave of disappointment ran through me. I had hoped to get more clues to her life.

I set down the bag and reached for my phone. I punched in my father's number. It rang four times and went to voicemail again. This time I left a message: "It's Brynn," I said, knowing that my dad couldn't always tell my voice from Dani's. "I have some strange news, something I need to talk to you about as soon as possible. Dani doesn't know anything about it yet, so don't call her, call me. It's urgent, Dad. Please, I need to hear from you as soon as possible."

I put the phone down and debated my next move. I should find a hotel, but there was no way I was going to sleep now. I felt too wired and amped up. I needed to know more about my mother's life. I pulled her ID out of her bag, put the address into the car's navigation system, and then started the car.

My mom lived ten minutes from the hospital and a few blocks from the infamous corner of Haight and Ashbury, where the sixties hippie movement had once flourished. Now it was an eclectic neighborhood of cafés, tattoo parlors, and vintage clothing stores. Mixed in with the old businesses were trendy juice bars, tea shops, an art gallery, and an organic market.

Almost all the businesses were closed, with the exception of a few bars and restaurants.

As I left the business area, I drove a few more blocks, then turned down my mother's street. My pulse raced as I parked in front of her house, which was a three-story Victorian-style building. There was a gray truck parked in the driveway. I wondered if that belonged to my mother or to her tenant, although I didn't see lights on anywhere in the house.

I grabbed her keys and got out of the car, a shiver running down my spine. It was quiet, almost too quiet. I didn't know exactly where my mother had been shot. The street was very dark now, the nearest streetlight twenty yards away. The thought of accidentally walking through her blood made me sick to my stomach, so I moved quickly toward the steps leading up to her property. As I neared the front of the building, I saw a door off to the left side. That must belong to the studio apartment. I went up another set of stairs to her porch.

When I reached the door, I hesitated. *What was I doing here? Was I really going to enter her house?* She might have once been my mother, but that had been a very long time ago. She was a stranger to me now.

On the other hand, she'd asked the nurse to call me. She'd wanted to apologize. She couldn't tell me why she'd faked her death, but maybe there were clues in this house. I took out the keys and tried them one at a time. On the third attempt, I got lucky. The door opened.

The interior was dark, and I was happy to find a light switch just inside the door. As the light went on, a long hallway was illuminated, with doors appearing to open to several other rooms along the way. Right next to me was the entry to the living room. I closed the door behind me and moved into the living room, turning on more lights as I did so.

The room was charming and filled with color. Three walls were light blue, while one wall was painted maroon. A white sofa and two floral-covered chairs faced each other on either side of a fireplace. Each piece of furniture had a bright pillow and a throw blanket over the back. There were lots of paintings on the walls, but no photographs.

I left the living room to explore the rest of the house. A guest bathroom was across from what appeared to be a guest bedroom, judging by the size of the room and the impersonal feel to the décor. Farther down the hall, I found a kitchen and family room as well as a staircase. I moved up the stairs and discovered the master bedroom and bath.

A window was open in the bedroom, a light breeze blowing the curtain in front of it.

The bed was unmade, a soft cocoon of blankets and pillows, but only one side of the bed appeared to have been slept in. There wasn't any evidence that a man lived in this house or even a roommate of any gender.

I walked back down the stairs and looked around the kitchen and family room. There were no photographs here, either. But there had to be some clues to my mother's life.

As my gaze drifted across the room, I let out a gasp. In the corner was a violin, and it took me back in time.

My mother had played the violin almost every night, and she'd taught me how to play before I was in kindergarten. The music had bonded us in inexplicable ways and seeing the instrument now sent a deep, aching pain through me. I'd kept on playing after she died because I'd wanted to stay close to her. When her face faded from my mind, it would reappear when I played. My music kept her alive. It had gotten me through the horrible days when missing her had consumed me, had made me feel like I'd lost a piece of myself.

I moved across the room and picked up the violin, running my fingers over the wood and the strings. It wasn't the violin she'd played with me. She'd left that behind when she'd gone to New Orleans, but this one looked old. It showed signs of wear but also signs of care.

More emotions swept through me as I remembered lying in

bed on hot summer nights with the windows open, the strains of music floating through the air as my mother would play in the garden. It had always soothed me, made me feel like everything was right in the world. I'd fall asleep to her music and then it had filled my dreams.

At the sudden sound of a click, I whirled around. *Someone was in the house!* The front door opened, then closed. Decisive, purposeful footsteps came down the hall.

A wave of fear ran through me. My gaze darted around the room. There was a back door by the kitchen that led into the yard, but the footsteps were getting closer. There was no way I could escape. I held the violin in front of me like a shield, gasping in alarm when a man came into the room with a baseball bat in his hand, a look of grim determination in his dark eyes.

CHAPTER FOUR

"Don't come any closer," I ordered as the man took a step forward, and I took another step back.

"Who the hell are you?" he demanded, a suspicious and threatening gleam in his gaze.

He had thick and wild brown hair that almost hit his shoulders and appeared to be in his early thirties. There was a shadow of a beard on a face that was strikingly attractive in a dark, intense kind of way. He wore faded jeans and a maroon T-shirt that was covered with splashes of paint, and his muscled arms were heavily tattooed.

"Answer me," he ordered, still holding the bat like a weapon. "What are you doing in here?"

"What are you doing in here?" I countered. "This is my mother's house. Who are you?"

"Your mother's house?" he echoed, surprise filling his gaze as he lowered the bat. "Laura has a daughter?"

"She has two daughters. But when she was my mother, her name was Kim."

"What do you mean—her name was Kim?" he asked in confusion.

"First, tell me who you are."

"Kade Beckham. I live downstairs."

I blew out a breath. "Oh, you're the renter the police told me about."

"Yes. I heard someone moving around up here and after what happened earlier today, I thought I better check it out."

"You should have brought a gun instead of a bat. My mother was shot."

"I know," he said tersely. "I heard."

"But you weren't here when it happened?"

"I was at the gallery. I arrived an hour after she was taken to the hospital. The police were here, conducting their investigation. How is your mother doing?"

"She's critical but stable for the moment."

"I'm glad she's hanging in there."

"You said you were at the gallery?" I asked.

"I'm an artist."

That explained the paint on his shirt.

"What's your name?" he continued.

"Brynn Landry." I frowned, wondering if I should just believe what he was telling me. "Do you have an ID?"

"Do you?" he countered.

"Yes."

"All right. Let's do it." He pulled out his wallet and handed me his license. The name matched his face, but the address was not downstairs.

"It says you live in New York," I pointed out.

"I was in New York City until last month. I haven't changed my driver's license yet."

"Or maybe you're just making all this up, and you don't really live downstairs."

"How else would I have a key?"

"You might have stolen it."

"I didn't. Let's see your ID."

I set down the violin and pulled my wallet out of my bag, handing over my license.

"Carmel. That's a few hours from here, isn't it?" he asked, as he handed the license back.

"Yes. I drove here as soon as the hospital called to tell me my mother had been shot."

"That must have been upsetting."

"Yes, but that's a massive understatement. I thought my mom was dead years ago."

Surprise ran through his gaze. "What? Why?"

"Because that's what I was told. Here's the deal. My mother's name was Kim Landry. She was married and had two daughters. Twenty years ago, she went to visit a friend in New Orleans when a hurricane hit the city. She was supposed to have died in that storm. We had a funeral for her. My father remarried. We moved on. When the nurse called me today, I believed it was a mistake, but it wasn't. Laura Hawthorne is my mother. She was alive all this time, living under another name, and I never knew."

"That's crazy," he murmured.

"It feels that way to me, too."

"How did the nurse know to call you?"

"Apparently, before my mother lost consciousness, she told the nurse my number was in her phone and that she wanted her to tell me she was sorry. Whatever that means," I added, unable to hide the bitter note in my voice. I suddenly felt overwhelmed by emotion. I stumbled to the couch and sat down.

Kade set down the bat and took the chair across from me, his gaze intent on my face. "Try to take some deep breaths," he advised.

"My chest is so tight."

"I know. Give it a shot. In and out, slow and easy."

I took his advice and felt a little better.

"The color is coming back into your face," he said approvingly. "I thought you were going to pass out for a minute there."

"Me, too." I drew in another breath. "Do you know anything about what happened today? Where my mother was shot? If she had enemies? Do you know anything about her? Or is she just your landlord?" The questions poured out of me.

"Slow down. I'll tell you what I know, which, unfortunately, isn't much."

"Start with today, with the shooting."

"I came home around four. The street was filled with police vehicles. A neighbor told me that Laura had been shot on the sidewalk, but they didn't know where the shots had come from. A bunch of people had called 911 while a few tried to render first aid. Help came pretty quickly from what I understand."

"Okay. What do you know about my mother besides what happened today?"

"She's a musician and teaches music. She loves art, and she's a big supporter of artists like me."

My brow shot up at that piece of information. "What do you mean?"

"She approached me a few years ago to buy one of my pieces. That's how we met." He tipped his head toward the painting on the wall next to us. "That's it."

My gaze moved to the stormy scene, a blend of blues, greens, and grays, a tiny boat bobbing on the water between giant waves. A distant speck of light called the boat home, but there was a sense that the boat wouldn't make it. "That's beautiful. It's also disturbing and dark." I swung my gaze back to him. "Sorry. I don't mean to be rude."

"That's exactly the way I want you to feel when you look at it —unsettled, unsure."

"Really? Does the boat make it to shore?"

"What do you think?"

"I have no idea. Sometimes bad things just happen. People don't always come home. Life can be a battle for survival."

"Exactly."

I looked back at the painting once more. It had many layers. I had a feeling I would see something new every time I looked at it. "You're really talented."

"That's one of my early pieces," he said, as I met his gaze once more. "I've now become interested in mixing paint and canvas with other materials. My work is constantly evolving. But getting back to your mother…"

"You said you met her when she bought your painting. Where was that?"

"It was at a show in Seattle. That was about two years ago. She contacted me after the show to say she loved it and wanted to buy it. She told me that the storm was a metaphor for her life. After selling it to her, we became friends. She was interested in seeing other pieces and supporting my work when she could. She talked me up to a local gallery a few months ago. They offered me a show, and she suggested I use the apartment downstairs while I was getting ready for it."

"That seems generous." I felt oddly resentful. "So, you're not just a renter?"

"No. And I thought it was generous, too. Do you remember your mother being interested in art?"

"Yes. She used to take us to museums on the weekends. It was always art and music, sometimes both at the same time. I loved the music more than the art. She played the violin, and she was my first teacher. After she died, I kept on playing. I felt like the music connected us." My gaze drifted to the violin I'd put on the table. "I guess she still plays."

"She's very talented," Kade said. "I don't know if she ever performs professionally, but I often hear her playing late at night. She's good."

"I used to hear her play at night, too. It was such a beautiful sound. But it also felt lonely, yearning… At least, that's how I remember it, and how I feel when I play."

"You're a musician, too?"

I didn't really know how to answer that question. "Sometimes. Did she ever talk about her family?"

"Laura told me she didn't have any family. She said she regretted that, that family was the most important thing in the world. She became quite sad, so I didn't pursue the conversation."

His words made me angry. "She had a family. She walked away from us. And we grieved for her. How could she hurt us like that? How could she let her husband and her children think she was dead?"

His expression turned grim. "I don't know. What about your father? What does he say?"

"I haven't been able to reach him. But he's the one who told me and my sister that our mother had died. I can't believe he wasn't duped, too. But I guess I don't know for sure." I changed the subject, not wanting to think about my father possibly being a liar, too. "What about my mom's friends? Did she have any? Did she have a boyfriend?"

"She has had people over a few times. I ran into a man leaving early one morning, but I don't know his name. Sorry. I wish I could tell you more. Do you have her phone? You could probably start there if you can access her contacts."

"I looked in her contacts, and she only had a couple of numbers, which seemed odd. I have hundreds of numbers in my phone, people I haven't seen for years. Why did she have so few?"

"I don't know."

"The police still have her phone. They're contacting everyone. They don't seem to have learned much in the hours since she was shot. The detective I spoke to said they don't have any witnesses or cameras showing the shooter, just my mother falling to the ground. They've spoken to her employer, but no one seems to know of any threats she might have received."

"Maybe it was random."

"Inspector Greenman doesn't think so. He believes the person was waiting for her and knew how to avoid the cameras." As I talked, I realized I was answering more questions than Kade was, and it gave me pause. I didn't know anything about this man. I didn't know what his relationship to my mother was. Hell, he could have shot her from this very building.

Anxiety ran through me as my imagination went into overdrive. I told myself to calm down. Kade hadn't been anything more than helpful, and he was the only person I could talk to who knew my mother, or at least knew the woman she was now.

"What's she like? Personality-wise?" I asked.

"Laura is friendly. She always has a smile on her face," Kade said. "She's easy to talk to, but she also seems private. Our conversations never go deep, unless we're talking about art, but that's not personal to her, only to me." He paused. "She doesn't seem like the kind of person who would pretend to be dead and run out on kids and a husband."

"But that's what she did."

"She must have had a reason."

"I can't imagine what reason could justify faking her death. But I need to find out why she left." I paused. "I was going to go to a hotel, but maybe I should stay here tonight."

"I'm sure your mother wouldn't mind. Not if she told the nurse to call you. So, what's your story?" Kade asked. "I know you live in Carmel. What do you do?"

"I run a clothing boutique with my sister." As I relayed that information, I realized that for the past several hours, I'd completely forgotten about the job offer and the big change my life was about to take.

"Why didn't your sister come with you today?"

"I didn't tell her what happened. She's in the early stages of a high-risk pregnancy, and I didn't want to upset her until I knew what was going on. I thought I would come here and find out it was all a mistake. But it's not. I should be happy my mother is alive, but then there are so many questions."

"That's rough," he said.

"You have no idea."

"I have some idea. Not the part about your mother coming back to life, but I know what it feels like to lose a parent. I was four when my father died."

"Oh, I'm sorry."

"I would be shaken to the core to find out he wasn't really dead," Kade added, meeting my gaze. "Maybe you should think of this as a second chance."

"I want to think that way, but to be honest, I feel anger more than anything else. Then I feel guilty because I'm not thinking it's a fantastic miracle that she's alive. It would make sense if she'd had amnesia for twenty years and had no idea that she'd left her family behind. But since she had my number in her phone, I don't think that's what happened." I ran a hand through my hair. "It's complicated."

"It is," he agreed. "You'll figure it out." He grabbed the bat and stood up. "I need to take off. I'll be downstairs if you run into any problems."

"Okay." As I got up and walked him to the door, I felt oddly disappointed that he was leaving. I would have liked to hear more about my mother. But he was gone before I could formulate any more questions. I wondered about his sudden and hasty exit. He'd seemed to be happy chatting about his relationship with my mother and then he'd just decided it was time to go.

I let out a sigh. I had enough to worry about without trying to figure out the darkly handsome man who lived downstairs. I locked the door behind him and returned to the family room. Moving to the bookshelves, I trailed my finger along the titles of dozens of novels. I wanted something more personal. I wanted photo albums. I wanted a diary or a journal. I wanted to know who my mother was and what she'd been doing for the last twenty years. But there was nothing on these shelves.

I walked over to the desk and opened her laptop computer. I put in the same password as her phone, but it didn't open. *That would have been too easy*, I thought with a sigh.

As I considered my next move, my phone rang. It was my stepmother, Vicky. "Hello?" I said, wondering why Vicky was calling me. We rarely talked unless it was about some family function.

"Have you spoken to your father, Brynn?"

"No. I left him a message, but he hasn't called back."

"That's not good. Ross hasn't returned any of my calls or texts since Tuesday. I'm very concerned. Dani and Steve haven't heard from him, either. I know your father is busy with work, but he usually responds to a text, especially from you or Dani."

"Not always right away," I reminded her. "I've waited days for him to return a text or a call. When he's working, he gets wrapped up in what he's doing and forgets about the rest of his life."

Vicky let out a troubled, angry sigh. "I don't appreciate being forgotten."

I knew that. Vicky had always needed a lot of attention, and for the most part my dad seemed to give her what she needed. "I'm sure he'll call you tomorrow."

"Probably. I just feel like something is off. I can't explain it. He's been...secretive lately. It started after he went to New Orleans for a few days. I thought maybe the trip brought back sad memories. It was the first time he'd gone there since your mother died, since he'd spent a week trying to find her."

My muscles tightened as I debated whether I wanted to tell Vicky my mother was alive. But I couldn't tell her before I spoke to Dani or my father. "Do you think my parents were happy?" I asked instead.

There was a pause at the other end of the phone. "That's a strange question. Of course they were happy. They were very much in love." Vicky paused. "I've always known that Ross could never love me the way he loved Kim. But that's okay because I loved her, too. I was devastated when she died."

I wanted to scream that she hadn't died, but Vicky could not be the first one I told. "I have to go, Vicky. I'm sure my dad is fine."

"Will you tell me if he calls you? Will you ask him to get in touch with me?"

"I will," I promised, then ended the call. It did make me uneasy that my dad had dropped out of touch with everyone. Maybe he did know something. Hopefully, it was just work that was preoccupying him, and he'd call one of us back soon.

With my phone in hand, I walked up the stairs to my mom's bedroom. I moved into the small walk-in closet and looked at her clothes.

As I sifted through the hangers of tops and dresses, my breath caught in my chest. Some clothes still had tags on them, and the tags bore a familiar logo...*Two Sisters Boutique.*

My mother had clothes from our shop. She must have ordered them online. I couldn't imagine she'd been into the store. *But how did she know about it?*

If she'd gone to the website, she would have read the section about Dani and me, about how and why we'd started the company, although it was really all about why Dani had started it. I'd just been there to fulfill the "two" part of the Two Sisters.

I drew in a shaky breath, feeling overwhelmed again with emotions. As I searched through the rest of the clothes, the new items were replaced by older tops and dresses. At the very end of the rack was a thick red sweater. An old memory flashed through my head. My mother had worn that sweater the day she left. She'd hugged me hard, and I remembered how soft and warm she'd felt.

Pulling the sweater off the rack, I pressed it to my face. I could still smell the scent of gardenias that came from her favorite perfume. It was a scent that had comforted me throughout the years. Tears filled my eyes. It was too much. It was all too much.

I took the sweater into the bedroom and laid down on the bed, wrapping it around me. I felt exhausted, emotionally spent.

I closed my eyes, and as the darkness enveloped me, I let myself think her arms were wrapped around me, the way they'd been when I was a little girl.

It was the only thing I would allow myself to think. Everything else had to wait…

CHAPTER FIVE

I WOKE up in the middle of the night to the sound of a dog barking. For a second, I didn't know where I was. Panic ran through me, but as the furniture in the room came into focus, I remembered everything that had happened. I rolled over in bed as the dog's barking got more frantic. I wondered where his owner was. I scrambled out of bed to look out the window. Then I heard a loud crash outside.

A moment later, I saw a figure running off to the side of the house.

My heart pounded fast as I raced down the stairs to grab my phone, which I'd stupidly left downstairs. I grabbed it on my way to the front door. I peered through the window next to the door, but I couldn't see anyone, and the dog had settled down.

Then I heard another door open, and Kade walked toward the sidewalk. He was barefoot and bare-chested, wearing a pair of black sweats. I opened the front door and saw a potted plant turned over on its side, broken into several pieces.

Kade turned around and spied me in the doorway. "Are you all right?" he asked as he returned to the house. "I wasn't sure if you had stayed here or gone to a hotel."

"I stayed. I fell asleep." My gaze moved to the pot. "Someone was on the porch, maybe trying to get into the house."

His lips drew into a grim line. "They made a hell of a lot of noise doing it," he muttered, running a hand through his messy hair, his eyes tired. "But they didn't get in."

"No," I said, my heart still racing. "The dog next door started barking. Maybe that scared them off."

"That's what woke me up."

"Me, too." I met his gaze. "This has to be connected to my mother, right?"

"It seems likely," he muttered.

"I should call the police."

He went downstairs to close his door, then came back up the steps and into the main house.

I called 911 and told the dispatcher that someone had tried to break into my house, and it could be connected to an earlier shooting. She said she'd send an officer out to check the property.

"Someone is coming," I told Kade. "But they won't find anyone. The person ran off. I saw a figure in the dark, but I couldn't identify the person. I assume it was a man, but I couldn't even say that for sure."

"The police can look around and make a report and let the detective on your mom's case know what happened. If someone was trying to get in here, they must want something."

My gaze clung to his. "Like what?"

"I don't know. Did you look around? Did you see anything odd?"

"Only odd to me. My mom had clothes from the boutique that I run with my sister. They were new. They had tags on them. She couldn't have come into the shop. We would have recognized her, so she must have bought them online." I tucked my hair behind my ears. "Sorry. That's not what you were asking. Anyway, I saw the clothes, I got tired and laid down on her bed, and I didn't look for anything else."

"Well, there's still time. I can help you," he offered.

"Really? You're not exhausted?"

"I was thinking maybe tomorrow," he amended.

"Oh, of course." I saw flashing lights through the window. "The police are here."

I moved to the door to let in a female officer. I told her what had happened while her partner looked around the house and yard. He returned a few moments later to say that the lock on the side gate had been broken, and it looked like someone had tried to jimmy the back door. He had noticed the same marks on the front door, where the pot had been broken.

I didn't feel better after hearing that information, although I was relieved that my mother's dead bolts had apparently been enough to keep the intruder away.

"We'll report this information to Inspector Greenman," the female officer said. "He'll probably want to talk to you in the morning."

"Thanks for coming out," I said.

"No problem," she replied.

As they left the house, I locked the door behind them, turning to face Kade once more. "You probably want to go back to bed."

"What are you going to do?" he asked.

I hesitated. "Maybe I should go to a hotel."

"It's the middle of the night."

"There must be something nearby."

"Not that close."

"I guess I could stay here. I don't think anyone will come back now, do you?"

"Probably not, but I can stay in the guest room, if that will make you feel better. If anyone tries to get in, they'll have to go through me."

"If they break in with a gun, they could go through you," I couldn't help pointing out. Although I had to admit he was a formidable-looking guy with more tattoos on his very sexy muscled chest. I licked my lips, forcing my gaze back to his face.

It was probably crazy to let him stay, but I didn't want to be alone. "I appreciate the offer," I said. "And I wouldn't mind if you stayed."

"Then I'll stay."

As we stared at each other, I became aware of a new kind of tension. I did not need to complicate my life any further. "I'm going upstairs then," I said.

"Goodnight."

"Goodnight." I walked quickly down the hall and up the stairs. When I got into my mother's bedroom, I locked the door, put my phone on the bedside table, and laid down on the bed once more. After another second, I grabbed the red sweater and wrapped myself up in it.

I felt scared and alone. I needed Dani. I needed my mother. I needed someone. But at least I had Kade downstairs. I didn't know anything about him. But my mom had known him well enough to invite him to stay in her house. She wouldn't have let someone she didn't trust get close to her, so I had to trust him, too. I hoped I wasn't making a mistake.

I hadn't thought I would sleep at all, but at some point, I drifted off. When I woke up, the sun was coming through the curtains and the clock said half-past eight. I scrambled out of bed, grabbed my phone, unlocked my door, and moved down the stairs. The house was extremely quiet. When I reached the kitchen, I smelled coffee. In fact, there was a full pot. And next to the coffeemaker was a handwritten note.

Went to work. Call me if you need me. Kade

He'd left his phone number as well. I appreciated that. Although it felt oddly intimate and strangely weird to feel such a strong connection to a man I barely knew. But then, everything that had happened since my phone rang yesterday afternoon had been strange and upsetting.

I filled a mug with coffee, feeling better and more in control with each sip. It was a new day. The sun was shining, which helped. Maybe it would give me some light, some insight into this world of secrets and lies that I'd landed myself in.

Taking my coffee with me, I wandered around the house. Everything seemed in order. Although the front door no longer had the dead bolt on as Kade had obviously left at some point. That made me wish he'd woken me, so I could have put it on. But at least the lower lock was still intact. I turned the bolt, then made my way back to the kitchen and opened the refrigerator, realizing I hadn't eaten since lunchtime yesterday. My mother's refrigerator was well-stocked, with a bowl of cut-up fruit and a Greek yogurt calling my name.

As I ate breakfast, I checked my messages. Dani wanted me to cover for her later in the day, because she had to leave early for a dental appointment. That was obviously something I couldn't do.

A text from Ray was next, asking me how it had gone with my sister, which reminded me I still had to have that conversation with Dani.

But how was I going to have that discussion after I told her our mother was alive? I could feel my dream job slipping away, which wasn't really all that surprising. Whenever my dreams got close to coming true, something happened to end them. It was the story of my life, a story that had started when my mom died just after the happiest birthday party Dani and I had ever had. Good was always followed by bad. I'd learned that a long time ago.

I still had a few days before I had to get back to Ray. First things first.

I took out my phone and punched in Dani's number.

"Hi," my sister said, a cheerful note in her voice. "Did you see my text? Can you cover the store this afternoon?"

"No, I can't."

"Why not? Do you have plans with Jeff?"

"No."

"Then what's the problem, Brynn?"

I could already hear the change in her tone. Dani didn't like it when I didn't go along with her plans.

"Brynn," she said impatiently. "What is going on with you?"

"A lot," I said. "So much, I don't know where to start."

Silence followed my words. Then she said, "Is it Dad? Vicky called me this morning. She thinks Dad is having an affair."

"That's not why I'm calling."

"Then talk," she said impatiently. "Whatever it is, just say it."

"I wish I could tell you this in person."

"Then let's meet. Where are you?"

"We can't meet; I'm in San Francisco." I licked my suddenly dry lips and told myself to just get on with it.

"San Francisco? What on earth are you doing there?"

"I got a call yesterday after you left to go to your appointment. It was from a nurse at a hospital here in the city."

"Oh, my God! Is it Dad? Has something happened to him?"

I really needed my sister to stop guessing, which meant I just had to tell her. I had to drop the bomb.

"The call was about Mom," I said.

"Mom?" Dani echoed. "What about her?"

"She didn't die twenty years ago, Dani. Yesterday, she was shot outside her house in San Francisco. The nurse told me I had to come right away if I wanted to see her." Silence followed my words. "Dani? Are you there? Did you hear me?"

"I don't think I did. You're not making sense, Brynn."

"Mom didn't die. She has been alive all these years."

"That's impossible. It has to be a mistake," Dani said slowly.

"That's what I thought until I walked into the hospital room and saw her. She was unconscious, but it was her. It was Mom. But now, she's in critical condition, and I don't know if she's going to make it."

"I don't understand."

"I don't, either, but she was living under another name. She has had à different identity the past twenty years. She has a house in San Francisco. She works at a music school. And she had my number in her phone. She told the nurse to call me and to say she was sorry and that she loved us."

"Sorry about pretending to be dead?"

"She just said she was sorry."

"And the nurse was supposed to call you, not me?" A hurt note entered her voice.

"She didn't have your number. Maybe because you changed your name when you got married."

"But she had yours? And she said to call you?"

"I don't know what her exact words were. You're focusing on the wrong thing, Dani. Mom is alive, but barely. She was shot in the head and the shoulder. She's unconscious."

"Who did it?"

"The police don't know, but they don't believe it was random. Once I showed up and told the inspector that Mom had another life twenty years ago, he wondered if she was in hiding for a reason and if that reason had caught up to her." I paused, thinking the always talkative Dani would jump in with more questions, but she was quiet. "I called Dad," I continued. "He didn't answer or call me back, even though I told him it was important that I talk to him."

"Did you tell him Mom was alive?"

"No. I didn't want to say that on a message."

"Why didn't you tell me yesterday when you got the call?"

"You were at your appointment, and you were happy. I didn't want to take that away from you, not before I was sure it was Mom."

"All right. Where are you now?" Dani asked.

"I'm in her house. They gave me her purse, so I had her address and her keys. I thought I could find some answers."

"Did you?"

"Not yet."

"Text me the address. I'll leave as soon as I find someone to cover the store."

"Maybe you should just wait, Dani. I can tell you what's going on. I don't want you to be under stress."

"Too late for that," she snapped. "And I need to see her for myself."

"Can Steve come with you?"

"He's in court today."

"I hate for you to drive here alone. I don't think Steve would like it, either."

"Well, it's not your decision or Steve's. I'm coming. You should have told me yesterday."

"I didn't want to ruin your night. I love you, Dani."

"I love you, too." She paused. "Maybe you're right, though. Maybe I shouldn't go to San Francisco. Perhaps you should just come home. Mom stayed away from us for twenty years. She didn't want us in her life, Brynn. You don't owe her anything."

"I have to know what happened. I need to find out why she left us. But I can do this on my own." I didn't want to do it on my own, but I did want to protect my sister.

There was another long silence. "No, I'll come. But Brynn, do you really think the truth will make it better?"

"It can't make it worse," I said. But as I ended the call, I wondered if that was true.

CHAPTER SIX

AFTER TALKING TO DANI, I refilled my coffee mug, cleaned up the kitchen, and then called the hospital. Several minutes later, I got Dr. Elizabeth Ryker on the phone. She was a sharp, fast-talking woman, who used a lot of medical terms that made little sense to me.

"Can you just tell me if she's going to recover, if she'll wake up today?" I asked when she finally took a breath.

"We're going to keep her sedated for another twenty-four hours," she replied. "We're monitoring her condition closely, and we're hopeful that tomorrow we'll be able to make additional decisions about her continuing care and prognosis."

"Hopeful?" I asked, grabbing on to that one word. "Does that mean she will recover?"

"I can't be more definitive, but your mother is holding her own, and that's good."

"Okay. Thank you. I'll be in later today to see her." After ending the call, I tapped my fingers restlessly on the kitchen counter, then went out to the car to grab my suitcase. I'd been in such a hurry to leave the day before, I had tossed random items of clothing into my overnight bag, not sure what I'd need or how long I'd be gone. Now, I was glad I'd probably over packed since I had no idea when I'd be leaving.

When I left the house, I saw the truck still in the driveway. I had assumed it belonged to Kade, although there were two garage doors, so maybe it was my mother's vehicle. It seemed strange that she would drive a truck, but then, what did I really know about her?

As I moved down the path to the sidewalk, I saw splashes of dark red on the pavement, and I knew instantly that it was blood, my mother's blood. I stopped abruptly, turning in one direction and then the other. I wondered where the shot had come from. Surely the police had some idea, judging from the way she'd been hit, the projection of the bullets. But if they did, they certainly hadn't shared it with me.

It was a nice neighborhood, with mostly three-story buildings that housed one or two units. I'm sure every house was expensive, which made me wonder how my mother had bought herself a home. Being a music teacher wouldn't pay that much. Just another question to add to the list.

As I opened my trunk, I glimpsed someone staring out the window at me from the home directly across the street. Then the curtain fell. It was probably nothing, but I felt uneasy after what had happened last night. Someone had clearly taken advantage of my mother being in the hospital to break into her house. I needed to be careful.

I grabbed my overnight bag, locked the car, then hurried back to the house, thinking I probably should have told Dani I would meet her somewhere else. But she'd ask a million questions why, and in the end, she'd want to see where our mom lived.

Back in the house, I took a brief shower, made quicker by the fact that my mom's shampoo smelled exactly like her and made me feel very emotional. At risk of sobbing my way through a long shower, I hopped out and changed into dark jeans and a cream-colored sweater, feeling significantly more alert and ready to take action. After considering my options, I left the house and headed to the school where my mother worked.

Inspector Greenman had spoken to the principal. I needed to do the same. I also wanted to see where my mom spent her time. I'd done a quick search on my phone for information about the school and had learned that it was a charter high school, offering specialized classes in music, dance, and theater for approximately four hundred students who had to audition to get into the program. While some of the staff had photos on the website, Laura Hawthorne did not, and I wondered if that was a deliberate choice.

When I arrived at the school, I parked in a visitor's space and made my way through the front door and into the administrative office. It was quiet in the building, although I could hear music wafting down the hallway. It was a Friday morning just after nine, so classes were clearly in session.

The school secretary, an older woman with sharp eyes, gave me a questioning look. "Can I help you?"

"I'd like to speak to the principal about my mother—Laura Hawthorne."

The woman's eyes widened. "You're Laura's daughter? I didn't think she had any children."

"She has two daughters, and I'm one of them. My name is Brynn Landry."

"I'm sorry. I didn't know. We're all very upset about Laura and praying that she recovers."

"Thank you. May I speak to the principal."

"Let me see if she's free." The secretary got up from her desk and disappeared through the door behind her. A moment later, she returned. "Mrs. Hunt will see you now."

I moved around the counter and followed her down the hall and into a large office with windows overlooking an interior courtyard.

The principal was much younger than the secretary, probably in her early forties, with red hair and brown eyes. She got up to shake my hand.

"I'm so sorry about your mother," she said. "I'm Joanne Hunt."

"Brynn Landry."

"How can I help you, Ms. Landry?"

"I'm trying to find out about my mother's life, and I understand she works here."

"Yes. She's been at the school for ten years." Joanne's gaze turned thoughtful. "She never mentioned she had a daughter."

"She left me and my sister twenty years ago, when we were seven."

Shock ran through her eyes. "I had no idea," she muttered.

"I guess that answers my first question, that you didn't know she had kids."

"She told me she didn't have any family."

"I guess when she left, she made that an accurate statement," I said bitterly. "Anyway, you've known her for ten years?"

"No. I've only been here for three years, but we have worked closely together. She's a wonderful music teacher. She has drawn brilliance from kids who had no idea they could be good."

I felt another wave of resentment. My mother seemed to inspire and take care of everyone but me and my sister. She'd supported Kade's art, and she'd been working at a school, encouraging kids to pursue their passions. But she had done nothing for me or for Dani except to turn her back.

There was a part of me that wanted to walk out the door and keep going. But there was another part of me that still wanted to know everything.

"Do you know if my mother had any enemies?" I asked. "Was anyone bothering her? Did she mention problems with friends or coworkers?"

Joanne gave me a sympathetic look. "The police asked me the

same questions. The answer to everything is no. Laura didn't mention any problems here or at home. I asked other staff members, and they all said the same thing. As far as anyone knew, she was a happy person."

"And a single person? Did she have anyone in her life?"

"I'm sorry. I don't know."

"She has worked here a long time. Is there another teacher who might have more information?"

"I asked around for Inspector Greenman. I gave him a few names, and he was going to follow up. You should probably talk to him. He'll be able to tell you more than I can."

"I am talking to him. But I'm not just interested in what happened to her yesterday but also who she is, what she likes, what she does for fun. I guess I want to know who she became after she left me."

"Well, let's see." Joanne paused for a moment. "Your mom is a terrific violinist and pianist. Her voice is beautiful. Occasionally, she sings in accompaniment to the students. She's very active here at the school. She puts on the concerts each quarter. There's one tomorrow night. She was rehearsing for that yesterday." Joanne's voice faded. "The kids are all devastated by what happened. We're going to have a vigil for your mother before the concert if you'd like to come. The kids want to show their support, and that seems like the best time. Of course, we hope your mother will be better by then."

"That sounds nice."

"I know you're probably not interested in the concert, but you're welcome to stay and see what your mother put together."

"I'd like to see what my mother was working on. She was my first violin teacher, too," I said. "I fell in love with that instrument because of her. I've played every day since she left. I actually became quite good. I'm going to play with an orchestra next month." I paused. "I'm sorry. I don't know why I told you all that."

Joanne's gaze filled with compassion. "It's a difficult situation. I can tell you one thing for sure. Laura is a good person. I don't know what happened in her past, but she's very generous with everyone at the school. She is always the first one to help if there's a problem."

"Well, that's good to know." The caring person Joanne was describing sounded exactly like the mother I'd known, but that same woman had abandoned her husband and children, and I didn't think I was even a speck closer to understanding why.

As the bell rang, Joanne stood up. "I'm afraid I need to go."

"Thanks for talking to me. I'll see you tomorrow at the vigil. Perhaps, I can speak to some of the other teachers then."

"Absolutely."

I walked out of the office and got caught up in a flood of kids heading out of the school. As I moved down the steps, I realized there was an impromptu concert going on outside. I paused to listen to the kids singing and dancing. They were so young, so free, full of optimism and hope. It made me feel a thousand years old.

I couldn't help wondering what it would have been like if my mom had stayed, if she'd supported my music, the way she'd supported these kids. I probably wouldn't have majored in business or gone into running a clothing boutique with my sister. I might have already been first chair violinist for a major orchestra.

I shook my head. I couldn't go down that road. I turned toward the parking lot. As I did so, a man stopped me. He had dark hair and an olive complexion and wore slacks and a gray wool coat. He looked like he was probably in his fifties.

"Excuse me," he said.

"Yes?" I asked warily.

"I'm sorry to stare, but you look just like a woman I know."

"You mean Laura Hawthorne?"

"That's the one. Are you related?"

"Yes. She's my mother."

"Your mother? Really?" he asked, surprise in his voice. "I had no idea she had a daughter."

"You're not the first person to tell me that," I said with a sigh. "Are you a friend of hers?"

"I am. I heard about what happened to her. I thought I'd come down here and see if anyone knew anything. I know her best friends work here at the school."

"They don't seem to know much of anything."

"What about you?" he asked. "Can you tell me how she's doing?"

"She's fighting for her life. That's all I know."

"Do the police know who did it? I can't get over the fact that someone shot her in the middle of the day. I looked online, but I couldn't find any information."

"I don't know anything. I'm sorry." My phone buzzed. I pulled it out of my purse and saw a message from Dani. She was about twenty minutes away from my mother's house. I texted back that I'd see her soon. "Sorry, I have to go, Mr. …"

"Harrison," he said. "Mark Harrison. I hope your mother will be all right."

"Me, too." I paused, giving him a curious look. "How do you know my mother?"

"We met here at the school a few months ago. My step-daughter goes here. She loves your mother. Says she's the best teacher she's ever had."

"That seems to be the consensus." I felt another twinge of envy for all the people who knew this version of my mother.

"To be completely honest," he continued, "I'm not just the stepfather of one of her students. I've also taken your mother out a few times."

"You're dating?" I was surprised and now even more curious about him. He was a good-looking older man with skin tones and dark hair and eyes that suggested he might be Spanish or Italian or some mix of cultures.

Mark smiled. "I'm not sure I'd call it dating at our age, but we've had dinner and gone to a movie."

"Sounds like dating to me. How long have you been going out?"

"A few weeks. We've just started getting to know each other, and now this. I'm in shock. Who would shoot your mother?"

"I can't imagine. She never told you about anyone who might have been bothering her or threatening her?"

"Not one word. She seems to have a lot of friends, and she doesn't get bothered by petty grievances. She doesn't look for drama, which I appreciate."

That sounded like my mother. I remembered her telling my dad once that she loved Vicky, but she hated how much Vicky liked to gossip and stir the pot. At the time, I didn't really know what that meant but as I got older and got to know Vicky, I could see where my mom had been coming from.

"Do the police have a suspect?" Mark asked.

"Not that they've told me."

"Well, I'm sure they'll find whoever did this."

"I hope so. You might want to speak to Inspector Greenman. I know he's interested in talking to my mother's friends."

"Do you have his number?"

"I do." I pulled out my phone and gave him the number. "Thanks for doing that. He needs all the help he can get."

"I don't know a lot, but I'm happy to share what I do know. Is your mother allowed visitors?"

"I'm not sure. She's in critical condition, so I don't think so. It might just be family only."

He shook his head, his gaze darkening as his lips tightened. "Well, please tell your mother I was asking about her and that I'll visit as soon as I can."

"I'll do that when she wakes up. She's not conscious at the moment."

"I'm sorry to hear that. I was hoping for better news. I'll pray for her."

I'd never seen prayer do much good, but I wasn't about to turn down the offer. "Thank you. It was nice to meet you, Mr. Harrison."

"Please, call me Mark. I didn't get your name."

"I'm sorry. It's Brynn. Brynn Landry."

He nodded. "I still can't believe your mother didn't tell me she had a daughter. You said you haven't seen her in a while, why is that?"

"We were estranged when I was a child," I said, not wanting to go through the whole story again.

"Well, I believe Laura will be all right," Mark said confidently. "She's a strong woman. You'll get your mother back."

"I hope so." I said goodbye, then hurried toward the parking lot. I was almost to my car when I saw a man walking across the street. He looked familiar, and when he turned his head, I let out a gasp.

My heart pounded against my chest. I had to be wrong. *It couldn't be my father. He couldn't be in San Francisco, at the school where my mother worked.*

Belatedly, I moved toward the street, but the man had disappeared.

I had to have imagined the resemblance. I'd been thinking about my dad. That's why I thought I'd seen him. But as the rationalizations filled my head, I had trouble believing them.

I'd seen what I'd seen. I pulled out my phone. I had no messages or voicemails. *Why hadn't my father called me back? Was it because he was here in San Francisco? Did he know about Mom being shot?*

The detective's words rang through my head. *Maybe your mother had a reason to leave you and your father.*

There was no way my father had hurt my mother. They'd always been so loving toward each other. It didn't feel right.

But did I even know what was right anymore?

I walked back to my car and got inside. I needed to go to the house, to see my sister, to talk to the one person in my life I could trust completely.

But as I drove away from the school, I couldn't stop wondering about my dad, and I couldn't think of one good reason why my dad would be in San Francisco, at the place where his allegedly dead wife now worked.

CHAPTER SEVEN

DANI DROVE down the street thirty seconds after I parked the car in front of Laura's house. I waved her into the driveway. She parked next to the truck and got out. We ran into each other's arms, hugging for several long minutes, the way we had a million times in the past. We'd always drawn upon each other for strength and for hope. I needed both right now.

Finally, we broke apart. "Are you okay?" Dani asked, her gaze searching my face for a truth that might not be in my words.

I'd never been able to lie to her. "No. Not even close." I blinked back tears. "I'm so glad you're here."

"I should have been here from the beginning. You should have told me, Brynn. I should have been your first call."

"Well, you're here now. I only called Dad before you, and I didn't even tell him."

"You told Jeff. He came by the house right after I talked to you this morning. He said he was worried about you, and he wasn't supposed to say anything, but he couldn't keep such a big secret from me."

Anger ran through me. "He had no right to tell you. I told him not to. He and I are done."

"Don't be ridiculous. The man was worried."

"He made me a promise, and he broke it. I am not going to have one more person in my life who can't keep a promise."

Dani's gaze went from irritated to concerned. "We're not talking about Jeff anymore."

"She had another life, Dani. Our mother has people who love her and who she presumably loves back, and none of them have ever heard about us. When she left, she erased us from her life. She walked away, and she never gave us a second thought." An odd shadow passed through Dani's eyes. I frowned. "What?"

"Nothing," Dani said quickly. "Let's go inside. I want to see her house."

There was something she wasn't telling me, but I didn't want to talk to her in the driveway. "All right. Follow me."

"Who lives there?" she asked, pointing to the door leading to the downstairs unit.

"Kade Beckham. He's an artist. Mom discovered his work a few years ago and helped him get a show at a local gallery. While he's in town, she's letting him stay in that unit."

"You seem to know a lot about him."

"We met yesterday." I unlocked the front door and opened it. "He thought I was breaking in, and I thought the same. But then I heard his story." My voice faded as I realized Dani wasn't listening to me. She was too busy looking around, searching for traces of our mother, the way I'd done when I first arrived. "There aren't any photographs or anything," I said. "But the shampoo in her shower smells like her."

"God," Dani breathed, giving me an annoyed look. "Why would you tell me that?"

"Because you want to know if it's really her. You won't be able to tell from this house. But when you see her, you'll know."

Dani wandered down the hall, and I followed, watching her pick up the violin. "She still plays, I guess."

"Yes. She also teaches music at a high school for the arts. Everyone loves her, especially the kids. She inspires them to follow their passions and to be great. I guess that desire to inspire children didn't extend to us."

Dani put the violin down on the coffee table. "I don't think she completely forgot about us, Brynn."

Her words surprised me. "Why would you say that? She faked her death, Dani. Maybe that hasn't sunk in yet. You haven't had as much time to process the situation as I have. But she hasn't had amnesia for twenty years. She wasn't lost. She chose to live another life. She has IDs in the name of Laura Hawthorne. She has a credit card, a bank account, and this house," I said, waving my hand in the air. "She has a job and belongs to a book club. She has a man she's apparently dating named Mark Harrison. I met him at the school."

"Seriously? She's dating someone?"

"Yes. And she never told him about us. She never told the principal or her coworkers or the guy who lives downstairs."

"You're really angry, Brynn."

"I am. Why aren't you?" That odd gleam moved through her eyes again. "What aren't you telling me, Dani?"

Dani hesitated. "I just don't think she forgot us, that's all."

"What are you basing that on?"

"I don't know."

I didn't believe her. "You do know. Talk to me."

She stared back at me, then licked her lips and said, "I think —I think I saw her once."

Her words shocked me once again. "What do you mean, you think you saw her? When was this?"

"High school graduation. You went to fix your hair. I was standing in line, getting ready to go on the stage, and there were a lot of people milling around. I was looking through the crowd, and I saw a woman off to the side, under the trees. She was staring at me, and—"

"It was Mom?" I asked in disbelief.

"Our eyes met for a second, and then someone moved in

between us, and I couldn't see her anymore. When they'd passed, she was gone."

I stared at her in amazement. "Why didn't you tell me?"

"I thought I imagined her."

"Dani," I breathed. "You should have said something."

"I didn't want to say something that would upset you when I didn't know if it was even true. You didn't tell me when you got the call last night," she reminded me. "It's the same thing."

"It's not. You're pregnant. You've been having problems and need to stay stress free. I wasn't any of those things in high school. I could have handled it."

"It probably wasn't her. Even if it was, she was gone in a flash."

"Knowing that she's alive now, I'm pretty sure it was her." I paused, thinking that Dani was right. Our mother hadn't forgotten completely about us. "She also has clothes from the boutique in her closet upstairs. Clothes with tags on them. She must have ordered them online."

"Are you serious? She has our clothes?"

"Yes. You're not going to tell me you also saw her in the store one day, are you?"

"No, of course not. I can't believe she bought some of our clothes." Dani shook her head in bemusement. "I wonder if Dad…"

"What about Dad?" I asked when she didn't finish her statement.

"I'm just wondering what he knows."

"Me, too. Did you tell him you thought you saw Mom at graduation?"

"Yes. He just gave me a hug and said he was sure she was watching down from heaven, that she was with me in spirit. I said I didn't see a ghost; I saw a real person. He said I was wrong, that I was just being hopeful. I don't believe he knew she was alive."

"I'm not so sure. I thought I saw Dad at Mom's school earlier today. He disappeared before I could catch up to him. I told myself that I imagined him, too, but I don't think I did. I think he's in San Francisco."

Dani's eyes widened. "That doesn't seem possible."

"At this point, anything is possible." I took a breath. "I told you the police are wondering if her past life caught up to her. What if it was Dad who caught up to her?"

"He wouldn't have shot her," Dani said. "My God, Brynn. How could you suggest that?"

"I didn't say that. But it's weird that he's not calling any of us back. We need to talk to him, Dani."

Dani took out her phone. "I'll call him again."

"What are you going to say?"

"I don't know. Let's find out." She put the phone on speaker. It rang four times and then went to voicemail. Dani frowned, then said, "Dad, it's Dani. Call me back. It's urgent. Something is terribly wrong. Brynn and I need to talk to you."

As she ended the call, our gazes met once more, and it felt like we were sharing the same thoughts, the way we had done so many times in our lives.

"Just because he's not calling us back doesn't mean he's guilty of anything," Dani said.

"I don't want him to be guilty of anything. I want all of this to be a mistake, but it's not."

"I need to see her, Brynn."

"I know. But are you sure you can handle it? I don't want the stress to hurt you or the baby."

"I can handle it. I've always taken care of you, haven't I?"

"You have." Dani had always been the strong one, and I was relieved to see that strength now. I needed it to flow into me. "It will be a lot easier to get through this with you at my side."

"Then let's go to the hospital and see this woman. After that, we'll drive back to Carmel."

I stared at her in amazement. "We can't just see her and leave."

"What are we going to do here?" Dani challenged.

"Find out the truth. I know you think the truth might hurt, but I'm already hurting. I have to know what happened."

"It was twenty years ago, and if she dies without waking up, her secrets will die with her."

I met Dani's hard gaze. "Maybe that's why someone shot her, to protect their secrets."

"If they did, then the last thing we should do is try to find out those secrets."

"Dani—"

She put up a hand. "Let's talk about it later. I can't decide until I look at her face."

CHAPTER EIGHT

WE ARRIVED at the hospital just before noon. There were several people gathered around the nurses' station including Inspector Greenman and a couple of security guards.

"Something is wrong," I told Dani.

"What do you mean?" she asked.

I didn't have time to answer. Inspector Greenman broke away from a conversation he was having with a security guard and walked over to us.

"Ms. Landry. I was just going to call you." As his gaze moved from me to Dani, his eyes widened. "Wait a second. There are two of you? Who did I talk to last night?"

"That was me," I said. "This is my sister, Dani. What's going on? Why are you here? Is my mom all right?"

"Someone attacked your mother about an hour ago."

"What?" I asked in shock. "How could that happen?"

"The man was in scrubs, with a head covering and a mask," the detective replied. "He was trying to disconnect the machines when a nurse entered the room. He shoved her and got away. Fortunately, your mother's condition is unchanged. We're putting security on your mother's room now."

I had trouble processing his short, clipped words, but one thing was clear. Whoever had tried to kill my mother yesterday had come back today to finish the job. "It wasn't random," I muttered.

"No," he said grimly.

"I don't understand," Dani interrupted. "Someone tried to kill our mother here in the hospital with all these people around? How could he get away? There's security. There are cameras."

"Yes, but it's difficult to identify him with his face covering. He got out of the building through a back stairwell and disappeared into the parking lot. But we're just starting our investigation. We'll find him."

"Do you think it's the same person who shot her?" I asked.

"That would be my guess." His gaze narrowed. "I also heard from one of my officers that there was a problem at your mother's house last night."

"Problem? What problem?" Dani asked, giving me a sharp look.

"Someone was outside," I said. "They knocked over a plant on the porch. It looked like they tried to get in, but they didn't. Everything was fine."

"You should change the locks and stay somewhere else," the detective said. "Whatever is going on is not over."

"I spoke to someone she's been dating—Mark Harrison. I gave him your name and number. He said he would call you. He's a parent at my mom's school."

"I appreciate that."

"Can we see our mother now?" I asked.

He nodded and took us down the hall, introducing us to the security guard. Then he said, "I'll be in touch. In the meantime, we'll do everything we can to keep your mother safe."

"Thank you." I opened the door and walked into the room.

Dani stopped just inside. I could see the panic in her eyes.

"Are you okay, Dani? You don't have to do this," I said.

"I do have to do this. I just don't want to." Dani lifted her chin, drew in a breath, then said, "Okay, I'm ready."

I took her hand in mine, and we walked over to the bed together.

My mother looked the same as she had last night. Whatever had happened to her an hour ago hadn't visibly changed anything. She was still, pale, and lifeless.

"It really is her," Dani murmured. "All this time, a part of me thought you were mistaken."

Her words irritated me, but I also knew how difficult it was to accept the truth—that our mother had not died, she'd just disappeared.

Dani turned to face me. "Do you think she's going to wake up?"

"Not today. The doctor said they're sedating her so her brain can heal. But she's holding her own, and we should be hopeful."

"I still can't believe it's her or that someone tried to kill her," Dani mused.

"Twice," I said. "She must have some dark secrets. Maybe that's why she left us. She didn't want us to be in danger."

"That would be the best reason. But it might not be the real reason."

"I know, but I want to believe she loved us, that she didn't forget about us."

Dani bit down on her lip, her eyes filling with tears.

"What's wrong?" I asked.

"This is my fault."

"Your fault? Why would you say that?"

Guilt ran through her eyes. "I didn't tell you the whole story about graduation."

My stomach twisted. "What didn't you tell me?"

"When I saw her, the woman under the trees, she waved to me, like she wanted me to come over, but I was too scared. I turned away. She didn't stop looking at me. I stopped looking at her."

I felt betrayed by her words. Dani was my best friend, my sister, my other half, but she'd kept something huge from me all these years. "Is there more to this story? Because it seems to get longer every time you tell it," I said, anger in my voice.

"I didn't tell you because I was trying to protect you, Brynn. You were so sad when Mom died. You cried for weeks."

"So did you."

"Not like you did. You were Mom's favorite. You had more in common with her than I did."

"That's not true."

"You had music. I didn't have anything with her."

"I barely remember what we had, Dani. But I do remember that she loved both of us." I paused. "So, tell me the truth. Did you know it was her at graduation?"

"I didn't think it could possibly be her. And Dad didn't, either. He told me I just wanted her to be there because I missed her."

"You should have told me."

"I didn't want you to get hurt. I still don't. I think you should come back to Carmel with me today."

I immediately shook my head. "I can't go back yet. We don't know what happened."

"We know someone is trying to kill her. You should have told me that someone tried to break into the house last night. You were all alone. You could have been hurt."

"Well, I didn't want to worry you, either. Kade stayed the night, so I wasn't alone."

"Kade?"

"The guy downstairs."

"You let some guy you didn't know spend the night after someone tried to break in?" she asked in disbelief. "What were you thinking?"

"That it was the middle of the night, and I was scared." I paused. "Mom trusted Kade."

"You don't know that."

"She was supporting his art. She got him a showing at a gallery. She let him live in her downstairs flat. She had to trust him."

"I don't know," Dani said doubtfully.

"Well, what I do know is that I'm not going back to Carmel until I know what happened to Mom, not only yesterday but also twenty years ago."

"It's too dangerous, Brynn. You heard the detective. He told you not to stay at Mom's house."

"Then I'll get a hotel room, but I'm not leaving San Francisco. Not yet."

"That's crazy. You can't just stay here. I need you at the shop. Mom doesn't deserve for you to turn your life upside down for her. You need to think of the bigger picture."

"I can't leave today." I knew I should tell her about the job offer, about my long-term plans, but there was so much else to deal with it, I just couldn't get the words out.

"I'll worry about you if you stay," Dani argued. "And I can't stay with you. I can't put my baby in danger."

"I would never ask you to do that."

"But I don't want you to be in danger, either. And you will be. Mom had to be mixed up in something terrible. I don't want you to pay any more than you already have for whatever she did in her life. I love you, Brynn. We're sisters. We have to stick together."

Dani's words were persuasive, as they always were. Whenever I'd tried to put distance between us, she'd remind me how much we needed each other. And I did need her. I loved her. But at one time, I'd also loved my mother. My gaze moved past Dani to the very vulnerable and helpless woman in the bed. I wondered if she could hear us fighting about her. It probably wouldn't help with her recovery. No matter what she'd done, I wanted her to live. And I couldn't leave her here with no one to look out for her. The police would do their job, but I was her family, even if it was a family she didn't acknowledge.

I looked back at Dani. "I'll be careful."

"I'm sure she was being careful, too," Dani said harshly. "I know this sounds cruel, but she left you, and you're forgetting how much she hurt you."

"I'm not forgetting anything. Everything changed when she died, the way we grew up, our relationship with Dad, our sense of safety. I have to know why it happened."

"It's only going to hurt you more. There's no reason for her leaving that will be good enough," Dani argued. "You're setting yourself up for more pain."

"You might be right, but I still need to know." I blew out a breath, feeling like I'd just made a momentous decision. "Are you ready to leave? I'll drive you back to the house so you can get your car and go home."

"I don't like this, Brynn."

"I know you don't. But this is what's happening. Do you want to say anything to Mom before we leave?"

Dani shook her head. "No. I don't have anything to say to her. I hope she doesn't die. But if anything happens to you because of her, I'll never forgive her for having that nurse call you. I don't know what she was thinking. She stayed dead all these years. Why bring you here now? And why didn't she call me?" Dani bit down on her lip. "She didn't care to call me, so I'm ready to go."

"I think she only had my number. She knew I would tell you."

"Or she thought I wouldn't respond. That I'd turn my back, the way I did before."

Her words didn't make me want to offer comfort, because I didn't like that Dani had kept the secret from me.

"We don't know why she did anything," I said. "There's no point in arguing about it. You need to go home, and I need to stay. I'll be fine. I promise."

"I wish you could make that promise, Brynn, but I don't think Mom expected to end up where she is. I'm sure she thought she'd be fine, too."

I didn't know about that. I had a feeling that she'd run away because she was very much afraid that she was going to end up exactly where she was.

CHAPTER NINE

DANI and I didn't talk on the drive back to my mother's house. It was the first time in forever that I felt disconnected from her. Of course, we'd fought over the years. We were sisters with different personalities, but we'd always had a bond that was unbreakable, a connection that was ridiculously close.

I didn't feel close to her now. Some of that had to do with her keeping a secret from me for so long. I still didn't know how to feel about that betrayal. Maybe she had talked herself into thinking she'd just imagined seeing our mother, but we still should have discussed it.

A car horn beeped behind me, and I realized the light had turned green. Several minutes later, I pulled up in front of my mother's house. As we got out of the car, Dani saw the bloodstains on the sidewalk and froze.

"Is this where…" she asked, her voice falling away.

"I think so," I said. Footsteps drew my attention away from my sister. An older man approached us with a vase of flowers in his hand. He was of medium height, with thinning blond hair and pale skin. He wore beige slacks and a blue polo shirt that matched the blue in his eyes. When he reached us, his jaw dropped in surprise.

"Who—who are you?" he stuttered. "My God! You both look just like Laura."

"She's our mother," I replied. "I'm Brynn. This is Dani."

"She's your mother?" he echoed. "She never said she had children."

"Well, she did." I was getting tired of hearing how my mother had erased us from her life.

"How is she?" he asked. "I just went by the hospital, but they said there were no visitors allowed. I wasn't sure she'd get the flowers if I left them at the desk, so I thought I'd drop them off here, hoping someone might take them to her."

"I can do that," I said.

"Who are you?" Dani asked.

"I'm Tom Wells. I live up the street. Your mother and I are... friends." He paused slightly before the word friends.

"You live on this block?" I asked. "Did you see what happened yesterday?"

"No. I wasn't home, but I heard about it from the neighbors. Everyone is really shaken. This is a safe area. We don't have problems like that here. It's just terrible. Can you tell me how your mother is doing?"

"She's hanging in there," I replied. "But her condition is very serious."

"She'll recover, won't she?"

"We hope so. How long have you known my mother?" I asked.

"About two years." He licked his lips. "We had a relationship, but that ended a while ago."

"Why?" Dani asked. "And what do you mean by relationship? Were you sleeping together?"

I gasped at her directness. Tom looked shocked, too.

He cleared his throat and said, "That's between your mother and me. I'll let you go. Please give her my best wishes."

Tom handed me the vase, then walked away. I watched him until he walked up the steps to the house on the corner.

Then I turned to Dani. "I can't believe you asked him if he was sleeping with Mom."

"Well, he didn't say no."

That was true. I frowned. "I met a man at her school who said they were dating. Maybe that's why she broke up with Tom."

"She certainly seems to be popular," Dani said sharply. "I guess she hasn't been living a lonely life away from us."

I understood her resentful tone because everything about my mom's current life annoyed me, too. "It's hard to hear people say how much they like her, how caring she is, how supportive... I keep thinking back to how devastated we were when she died, how alone we felt. And Dad retreated into a world of sadness."

"Maybe she cheated on Dad. She was unhappy in her marriage, and she wanted to get out. She made it look like she died in the hurricane, but it could have all been a ruse for her to leave."

"But why wouldn't she have just left?" I challenged. "She didn't need to pretend to be dead. There has to be more, Dani."

"You're right, and she wasn't scared of Dad. There must be another reason."

"That's what I need to figure out." I paused. "I should put these flowers in the house. Are you leaving now, or do you want to come in?"

"I'll come in for a second."

I took out the keys as I approached the door, then stopped so abruptly Dani ran into me.

"What are you doing?" Dani demanded.

"The door is open. I locked it when we left." I gave her a panicked look.

"I'm calling the police," Dani said. "Let's go back to the sidewalk."

I put the flowers down on the porch and followed her down the steps as she spoke to the dispatcher. But standing on the sidewalk didn't make me feel safer. This was where my mother had been shot. As I turned my head away from the stain of blood, I saw a motorcycle racing down the street. It made a quick turn into the driveway, and I jumped back in alarm.

"What the hell?" Dani said.

The man took off his helmet, his longish brown hair falling over his eyes before he pushed the strands away. I let out a breath. "It's okay," I told Dani. "It's Kade."

"What's going on?" Kade asked, as he strode toward us. His gaze moved from me to Dani. "This must be your sister."

"Yes, this is Dani."

"Hello," he said. "I'm Kade Beckham."

"My mother's tenant," Dani said, giving him a sharp look and a curt nod.

"I didn't realize you rode a motorcycle," I said, drawing his attention back to me. "I thought the truck was yours. Or maybe it's my mother's."

"The truck is mine. I use it when I move my art pieces. Otherwise, I prefer my bike, which I usually keep in the garage. Your mother drives a Honda. It's in the garage. I guess you haven't been inside."

"No, I haven't."

"Are you all right?" he asked. "Why are you standing out here?"

"The door to the house is open. I think someone broke in. We just called the police. Have you been in there since you left this morning?"

"No, I haven't."

As Kade finished speaking, a police car came down the street. As two officers got out, Dani told them that someone had broken into the house and that the owner of the house had been shot and was in the hospital. Dani went into her typical take-charge mode, which was fine with me since I didn't feel like going over the story again. The officers asked us to wait in the driveway and then entered the house with guns drawn.

"Did anyone notice if my door was open?" Kade asked.

"I didn't look. I'm sorry. I was rattled."

"Understandable. I'll find out soon enough. It's good you weren't here. Where were you?"

"At the hospital. Someone attacked my mom this morning. He tried to unplug the machines that are keeping her alive."

Kade's jaw dropped as he removed his sunglasses. "Are you serious?"

"Yes. And he got away. Maybe he came here after that. I don't know." I looked into his shocked dark eyes. "Someone wants her dead, Kade. It wasn't a random attack yesterday or today."

"When did you move in here?" Dani interrupted.

"About a month ago," he said, turning to Dani.

"And my mother got you a show at a gallery?"

"She put in a good word for me, but my work speaks for itself."

"One of his paintings is in Mom's house," I told Dani. "It's beautiful and dark and very emotional. I can see why she was drawn to the piece. She always loved art. Remember all those trips to the museum?"

She frowned. "Of course I remember. I was beyond bored. She made us go the first Saturday of every month. The only part I enjoyed was when she went to buy snacks and we'd get to paint in the kids' room." Dani gave Kade another suspicious look. "How exactly is my mother supporting you?"

"That's between me and her," Kade replied.

"Well, we can't ask her," Dani retorted. "Is it a secret? Is she your sugar mama?"

"Dani," I said, surprised by her callous comments.

Kade's lips tightened and there was anger in his eyes, but he said nothing, and the silence became very uncomfortable. Fortunately, that silence was broken when the police officers left the house.

"We didn't find anyone inside," one officer said. "But the house was torn apart. Someone was looking for something. Do you know what that might be?"

"I have no idea."

"We checked in with Inspector Greenman," the officer continued. "He'll be over to check things out shortly. In the meantime,
he asked if you'd stay out of the house until he arrives."

"All right," I said. "We'll wait out here."

"You can come into my place," Kade said. He turned to the
police officer. "I live downstairs. Was that unit broken into?"

"We didn't go in there," the officer replied. "The doors were
locked."

"Well, that's a good sign." Kade looked at me. "Do you want
to wait inside my place?"

"Sure," I said. "Dani?" I questioned as she took her ringing
phone out of her purse.

"It's Steve," she said. "I'll be inside in a minute."

"Okay." I followed Kade into his unit, which was much smaller
than my mother's flat. The living room looked like an artist's studio
with easels and half-painted canvasses. There were paint supplies
and other materials including wires, metal, fabric, wooden crates, a
basket of bottle caps and another one of metal washers and screws.
A worn couch and armchair filled out the space.

"It's a mess," Kade said with an uncaring shrug.

"It looks like a lot of work in progress," I replied, my gaze
moving from piece to piece. Some were paintings, others were
sculptures, some a mix of paint and other materials. "You have
quite a few ideas."

He smiled. "Always have. Sometimes I don't know when
there are too many ideas."

"Better to have too many than not enough."

"That's what I tell myself. Do you want something to drink?"

"All right," I said, following him into the kitchen.

"Beer or water?" he asked, as he opened the fridge.

"I'll take a beer. It seems like that kind of day."

He pulled out a bottle and handed it to me, then grabbed one
for himself and took a long swig. Then he said, "So your sister
likes to be in charge, doesn't she?"

"Always been bossy," I replied. "But Dani gets stuff done."

"Was she shocked to see your mother?"

"More shaken than I've ever seen her. And after she heard my mom was attacked in the hospital, she got really scared."

"This break-in won't help."

"She wants me to go back to Carmel with her, leave all this to the police to figure out."

He took another drink, then set down the bottle. "Not the worst idea."

"But I can't just leave with so many questions unanswered."

"You'd be safer."

I frowned. "It sounds like you want me to leave."

"I don't have an opinion, just stating the facts. I can't imagine you'll want to stay here tonight."

"No, but on the other hand, whoever broke in might have found what they were looking for. Maybe it's over."

"So, you're an optimist."

"Not really. I usually think that when things get too good, they'll disappear just as fast. Sometimes, I'm right."

Dani's voice rang through the apartment. "Brynn?"

"We're in the kitchen," I called back.

Dani came into the room a moment later.

"Can I get you a drink?" Kade asked.

"No, thank you. You're drinking in the middle of the day, Brynn?" she asked me, a gleam of annoyance in her gaze.

"It felt like a beer moment. Kade also has water."

"I don't need anything to drink. Steve wants me to come home, and he wants me to bring you with me. Jeff is also anxious about you. Now that this has happened, I hope you've changed your mind about staying."

"I haven't. I'm sorry, Dani. I know that's not what you want to hear. But I need to watch over the investigation."

"What on earth can you do that the police can't?" she asked in frustration. "Except put yourself in danger?"

"I can make sure they keep looking for the truth by letting them know I'm watching, and I'm advocating for our mother."

"Who never did the same for you."

Dani's harsh words were delivered out of fear more than anything else, but they still stung.

"She took care of us for seven years," I said. "She was there when we were sick or hurt or scared."

"But where was she for the last twenty years? You're deluding yourself that she's going to wake up and want to be your mother again. It won't happen, Brynn. Even if she wakes up, she'll just be the woman who left us. Don't you get that?"

"I'm still staying." Dani wasn't the only stubborn one in the family. "It's my risk to take. I can take care of myself. I'll get a hotel room. I'll be fine."

The doorbell rang. "That must be Inspector Greenman," I said.

Kade and Dani followed me down the hall. I opened the door to let the detective inside.

"I've looked through your mother's house," he said. "It was trashed. Whoever broke in went through the place in a rage. There's a significant amount of damage. And it's clear that someone was searching for something. The question is what?"

"I have no idea," I said.

"Well, you'll need to have the locks changed as soon as possible. I'd also suggest that you stay elsewhere," the detective said.

"I'm going to get a hotel room," I replied. "But I'll look through the house before I go. Maybe I can figure out what they took. I stayed there last night."

"I can help," Kade said. "I've been in Laura's home several times."

"That would be great." I turned back to Inspector Greenman. "Can you check with the neighbors to see if any cameras caught anyone on the property?"

"I will do that, but watch your back—all of you," he said, his gaze sweeping across the three of us. "This is a dangerous, unpredictable situation. Call me if anything else happens."

"I don't think you should be here when anything else happens," Dani muttered as Inspector Greenman left. "You're being irrational, Brynn."

"I'm going to check out the house and find a locksmith to come out and change the locks," I said, ignoring her comment. "Then I'll go to a hotel."

"I suppose I can stay long enough to help you with that," Dani said.

I didn't like the paleness of her skin or the stress in her eyes. "I can do it on my own. Please, just go, Dani. I'll feel better if I don't have to worry about you."

"And I'd feel better if I don't have to worry about you," she retorted.

"I can help," Kade offered. "I can call a locksmith and stay with you, Brynn."

"I wouldn't say no to that," I told him, relieved by his generous offer.

Dani frowned. "We know nothing about you, Mr. Beckham."

"Well, you should know you can call me Kade," he drawled. "And you should know your mother trusted me."

"Maybe she made a mistake," Dani said.

"Dani, please," I interrupted. "Everything will be fine. Kade is trying to help. And he knows Mom's house better than either of us. I need him to look around with me."

"Fine. I give up," Dani said. "I'll go, but you take care of this, Brynn, and then you go to a hotel and call me from there. I want a photo of your room."

"Got it. Drive carefully and text me when you get home."

I walked with her to her car. She paused before getting inside. "I know you like to believe the best in people, Brynn, but you don't know that man. Kade Beckham could be anyone. He could have an ulterior motive for helping you. You don't know a thing about Mom's life or the people in it. You can't trust anyone."

"I understand what you're saying, but sometimes you have to take a chance, and I think Kade is okay. He's normal."

"He's a crazy, dark artist. I doubt he's anything close to normal."

"Even if you can't trust him, you can trust me. Drive safe." I gave her a long hug and then stepped away as she closed the door and started the engine.

After she pulled out of the driveway, I walked back up the steps. Kade was waiting by the front door. He gave me a grim look.

"What?" I asked, not liking his expression.

"I just took a look inside. You're not going to like what happened in there."

"I haven't liked anything that's happened in the past twenty-four hours, so I'm ready."

"I doubt that."

He was right. When I stepped into the house and saw the ruthless destruction, I felt completely overwhelmed. There was a part of me that wanted to run outside, jump in my car, and follow Dani back to Carmel.

"It's not too late to leave," Kade said, drawing my gaze to his.

I thought about that. "It is too late. It was too late yesterday when I saw my mother for the first time in twenty years. This is an awful, terrifying mess, but I can't run away from it."

CHAPTER TEN

As soon as I saw the destruction in the living room, I wanted to change my mind and run away as fast as possible. The cushions on the couch had been slashed with a knife and tossed to the floor. Pictures had been ripped off the walls. It looked like someone had put a sledgehammer through various sections of the walls. "Why would they do this?" I murmured.

"I'm guessing they thought there might be a safe hidden in the walls."

"Or something hidden in the couch cushions. But what would that be?"

"No idea." He pulled out his phone. "I'll call a locksmith. I'll have my locks changed, too, just to be on the safe side. I don't want my place to end up like this." He stopped, frowned, and then hurried down the hall.

I ran after him. The family room was as bad as the living room. And Kade's beautiful, dark, troubling painting was face-down on the ground. He walked over to pick it up.

I let out a breath when I saw that the canvas was intact. "Thank God, it wasn't slashed," I said.

Kade's lips were hard and tight, the pulse in his jaw beating fast. He nodded and then put the painting back on the wall, covering up the broken drywall.

"I'll make some calls," he said, a rough edge to his voice. He walked out the kitchen door to the back deck.

Looking through the window, I saw him brace his hands on the railing and take several deep breaths before looking at his phone. He'd certainly had a powerful reaction to the possibility of his painting being damaged. I guess I could understand that. It was his art. It was a piece of him. But it also seemed a little extreme.

Dani's warning not to trust Kade rang through my head. But I couldn't distrust him because he cared about his art.

I looked away from the window and saw the violin sticking out from under the sofa. My heart leapt into my throat. I squatted down and pulled the instrument out with trepidation, expecting to find it in pieces, but it was intact. I felt immensely relieved.

Pressing the violin to my chest, I closed my eyes, imagining my mother playing it, hearing the melody in my head, feeling my only real connection to her. There was so much chaos all around me, but in this moment, I could feel a measure of peace. I opened my eyes and put the violin on the coffee table, realizing I'd just had the same reaction to the violin that Kade had had to his painting. It wasn't just the violin I'd been reacting to, but what it represented, the connection to my mother.

As my gaze moved back to the window, I wondered if Kade's reaction had also been about more than the painting. *Was there something between Kade and my mother?* Dani had asked him point-blank about their relationship, and he had told her it was none of her business. That hadn't been a denial.

Shaking my head, I told myself to focus on what was most important, and that was putting some order back into this room and trying to figure out what might have been taken.

I turned toward the pile of books on the floor and started putting them on the shelves. My mother seemed to be a big reader, with well-worn paperback and hardcover copies of popular fiction titles as well as historical non-fiction. Some of the books appeared to have been read several times. I could relate to that. I had a couple of favorite books I'd read more than once. My love of reading had also come from my mother. *Had I gotten anything from my dad?*

Dani had inherited my father's ambitious brain for business as well as his love of sports. My mom and I had usually read books while he and Dani had cheered for their favorite football team. Even now, she and Steve spent their weekends with a football game on the TV.

Dragging my brain out of the past, I returned the slashed cushions to the sofa, wincing again at the evidence of violence. I didn't want to think about someone wielding a big knife throughout this house, but that was what had happened.

The back door opened, and Kade came inside, looking more composed than he had when he'd left.

"I found a locksmith," he said. "He can come at two thirty."

"Great. Thanks."

"You've made progress."

"A little. But I have no idea if something is missing. The things that are broken don't seem that valuable or important. The paintings were ripped from the walls, but they weren't damaged. It doesn't feel like someone was after the art."

"No, it doesn't," he said.

I pressed a hand to my head, as the ache in my temple intensified.

"Are you okay?" Kade asked.

"I have a headache."

"Have you eaten lunch?"

"No. That might help."

"There's a good café about three blocks from here. We have a good two hours before the locksmith will arrive."

"Food sounds good. But should we just leave? The house is wide open."

"I doubt much more damage could be done, Brynn."

"That's true. They must have come in the second Dani and I left for the hospital." I stopped abruptly. "God, maybe they were watching us."

"But they didn't come in until you left. That means you and your sister are not targets."

"That's true. But it would have been better if they hadn't gotten in at all."

It was a nice walk to the Morning Glory café, which was on a cute street of shops and boutiques. There was a patio in front of the restaurant, and I was happy to be outside with the sun taking the chill out of my body.

"This feels much better than my mom's house," I said after ordering an iced tea and a Greek salad with salmon, while Kade opted for a French dip with a side of fries.

"It's going to take some time to put the house back the way it was, if that's even possible," Kade said.

"I know. What do you think they were looking for?"

"We could speculate forever and get nowhere."

"Let's just do it for a few minutes," I said. "Give me some ideas."

"Cash. Jewelry. Maybe something more personal," Kade said.

I nodded. "Like damaging photos of someone. Blackmail material. Or company secrets."

"She works at a school, not a company. I don't think there are any trade secrets there."

I could see the amusement in his gaze. "True, but when we're brainstorming, there are no bad ideas. You think outside the box when you're creating your art, so I know you can do that now."

"All right," he said. "Drugs. She could be dealing drugs to the kids at the school, and she was ripping someone off or double-dealing."

I frowned. "I don't like that suggestion."

"You said to think outside the box."

"That's too far outside. My mother isn't a drug dealer."

"All right. Let's go further back. She ran away from your life. Maybe she took something with her, and someone finally caught up to her. They want it back, whatever it is. It could be something personally damaging, like photos or bank statements, evidence of fraud, something that someone would desperately want back."

"Inspector Greenman seemed to think that there's a connection between her past and what's happening now," I admitted.

"You need to find out more about her past, and you're in the right position to do that. You can talk to your father, your mother's old friends, relatives. There must be someone who can give you more information about her life."

"My dad isn't calling me back, which is odd."

"And also suspicious," Kade said, a speculative gleam in his eyes.

"My father isn't a violent man or a criminal."

"But your mother did leave him."

"Maybe she just didn't love him anymore. Maybe she never loved any of us." That thought was depressing. "What did you and my mother talk about? You said you'd been in her house a few times, that you'd kept in touch the past two years. What was your friendship based on?"

"Art. That's what we talked about ninety percent of the time."

"And the other ten percent?"

Kade shrugged. "She asked about my family, my life, how I'd gotten started in art, what motivated me, that kind of thing."

"Did she give you money?"

His face tightened. "She paid for the painting in her house and another one that she said she gave to a friend. She didn't just hand over cash. I don't take charity, Brynn."

"But you're living in her house, and you're not paying rent," I couldn't help pointing out.

"I offered to pay. She refused. She said she wasn't planning to rent the place, and that it was only for a few months. So, I accepted her generous offer. But I'm not a freeloader."

"I didn't say you were. I'm just trying to figure out your relationship."

His gaze bored into mine. "As I told your sister, it's not your business."

"Yes, it is. Everything about her is my business. Why are you being cagey? You just told me I have to figure out her life, well you're in her life."

He sat back, crossing his arms in front of his broad, muscular chest. "Fine. I'll be direct. There is nothing sexual between us and there never has been. She was a mentor, a supporter, and a friend. That's it."

"Why didn't you want to say that before?"

"Your sister wanted to make me into a problem. I didn't like her attitude. But you're asking for a different reason. You just want to find the truth."

"I can't leave until I do. It would be different if I could talk to her, if I could just ask her what the hell happened. But I have to put the puzzle pieces together without her."

"I get that. I want to make it clear that I'm not part of the puzzle."

"Okay. Thank you for being direct." I sat back as the waiter brought our order to the table. "This looks good."

"Yours looks very healthy," he said, a small smile on his face now, easing the tension that had grown between us.

"I try to eat healthy, but your French fries look better than my greens."

"I'll share," he said, pushing his plate forward.

"Really?"

"Absolutely. Take what you want."

"Maybe just one or two," I said as I stabbed two of his fries with my fork and moved them to my plate. I bit into one and the salty warmth washed over me. "This is delicious."

"You can have more."

"It's okay. I just wanted a taste." I picked up my fork and attacked my salad. The salmon was tasty, too, and in the long run, the salad would probably sit better in my perpetually nervous stomach. "Tell me about your life," I said, as we ate. "You were living in New York before this?"

"Yes, I grew up in the Bronx and then moved to Brooklyn about ten years ago. I work out of my studio apartment there."

"What about family? You mentioned you lost your father— what about the rest of your family?"

"I have a mother and a couple of aunts from my dad's side of the family, a few cousins, but we're not close. My mother still lives in the Bronx, but the rest of them are spread around the country."

"Are you and your mom close?"

"We are. It was just the two of us after my dad died. We took care of each other."

"What is your mom like?"

"She's very sweet, works hard, doesn't ask for a lot, hates when someone has to take care of her."

"Have you had to take care of her?" I asked curiously, picking up on a note in his voice.

"The past couple of years she has been battling breast cancer, and she's had some bad weeks. But she is in remission now and doing much better."

"I'm glad to hear that. Will you go back to New York after the show?"

"I haven't decided yet. The change has been good for my work. I've been getting a lot done the past few weeks. I'm really enjoying the city and the entire Bay Area. I'm glad your mother got me out here."

"It's interesting how she kind of adopted you."

"Interesting or irritating?" he challenged. "I've been thinking about your story, how she abandoned you and your sister, and the look on your face when I told you she was supporting my art. You were hurt."

"You're right. It wasn't easy to hear that the person who ran out on me and claimed to have no family could be kind and generous to a stranger struggling with their passion. Where was she when I was struggling? Where was she when I needed a mother?" I gave a helpless shrug. "It's confusing."

"I can see that. It's difficult for me to understand how the woman I knew could have left her children without a word and pretended to be dead. It has to be impossible for you to wrap your head around it."

"Impossible is an understatement. It's why I have to get to the bottom of it."

"Your sister doesn't feel the same way."

"No. Dani is angry. And she doesn't like it when she's not in control of a situation. It stresses her out, and I don't want her to be stressed. She's had some difficulties the past few years trying to have a baby, and she's four months pregnant now. The last thing I want is for this situation to affect her health or her child. I was relieved when she wanted to leave."

"It sounds like she made the right decision."

"But she believes I made the wrong decision, which isn't unusual. She always thinks she knows better than me. Do you have any siblings?"

"I don't. And I can't imagine having an identical twin, although I noticed a few small differences between you."

"Like the fact that her hair is short, and mine is long."

"Yes, but I was thinking more about the freckle under your left eye. Hers is on the right."

"We're mirror twins. I can't believe you noticed that so quickly. She's also right-handed; I'm left-handed."

"That's interesting." His gaze studied my face with an intensity that I found uncomfortable as well as inexplicably exciting. "Did you ever wear your hair exactly the same? Did you dress the same? Pretend to be the other sister?"

"Yes, yes, and yes. Mostly after my mom died. She wanted people to see us as individuals, so she used to put us in different outfits. She wanted us to pursue our own interests. Once she was gone, that changed. My dad hired a nanny to take care of us. When she took us shopping, she just bought two of everything. That's when we started playing tricks on people, especially my father. He had trouble telling us apart, which seemed weird, because my mother always knew who we were."

"Maybe she was more connected to you because of the mother-daughter bond."

"Probably. She was very loving. She was always hugging us, kissing us, snuggling in bed with us. My dad was much more hands-off. He loved us. He provided for us. But I can't remember having deep conversations with him. Not ever. That's weird, isn't it?"

Kade shrugged. "Everyone is different. Why do you think he isn't calling you back? Is that unusual?"

"It is and it isn't. He doesn't always answer me right away, but he usually answers Dani or his wife, Vicky. The fact that none of us has heard from him is disturbing. What's also weird is that earlier today when I went to my mother's school, I thought I saw him. I probably just imagined it was him."

Kade gave me a challenging look. "Do you really believe that?"

"I want to. With everything going on with my mom, and the suspicion about why she left my dad, I don't think it would be good if he was here when she was shot."

"Maybe he came after she was shot. He could have heard the news, same as you."

"That's true. But why isn't he calling us back?"

"The police can probably track his phone."

"They'll probably do that. He's a person of interest, but he's not a violent, angry person. He wouldn't shoot anybody. He's an executive, a business sales guy. He never even raises his voice. When he gets mad, he gets quiet. I can't imagine he would even know how to shoot a gun." I paused. "I'm sorry to dump all this on you, Kade. You just took a room in someone's house. I'm sure you didn't expect to be caught up in all this."

"Life is full of the unexpected. I've learned to roll with it."

"I thought I had learned that, too. But I'm having trouble rolling with this one."

"I think it's impressive that you want to fight for your mother even though she…"

"Didn't fight for me," I finished. "I'm not just doing it for her, though. I'm doing it for me and for Dani. My dad, too, I guess." I let out a breath. "How did we get back to me? We were talking about you. When did you start painting?"

"After my father died, I had a lot of anger issues. I couldn't sleep at night. I was exhausted during the day. My mom made me talk to a shrink. The doc suggested I write down my feelings so I could get them out of my head. I tried to do that, but it wasn't words that came out—it was art. I could express myself through sketching and painting. It made a tremendous differ-ence in my life, and it just grew from there. By the time I was thirteen, I was painting everywhere, including the buildings in my neighborhood." He smiled. "That wasn't always appreciated."

"You were a graffiti artist?"

"I was. The world became my canvas. If I thought I could add to something, I did. I got myself into some trouble along the way."

I wasn't surprised. Kade definitely had a bad-ass kind of vibe.

"What kind of trouble?"

He shrugged. "It doesn't matter."

He was being cagey again, but I didn't think I could persuade him to open up on his past, so I went back to art. "What themes inspire your painting?" I asked.

"No matter where I start, I always end up with a struggle, a battle against insurmountable odds."

"Like the small boat in the huge storm in the painting on my mother's wall."

"Yes."

"I'm beginning to understand why your art is so dark."

"It comes from inside my head."

I thought about that, wondering just how dark the inside of Kade's head was. He seemed like a good guy. He'd been nothing but kind to me, but his art showed a very different side. *Was he who he appeared to be?*

"What about you?" Kade asked, interrupting my thoughts. "What do you do in your real life? I think you said you were sometimes a musician, but then you said something about a store."

"It's complicated."

"Is anything in your life simple?" he asked with a small, knowing smile.

"No, but it should be. I've played music my entire life. I minored in it in college. It was going to be my major, but Dani said I should be more practical. I should get a business degree with her. My dad had always made it clear that he wanted us to be responsible for ourselves. He paid for the first two years of college, and then we had to pay for the rest. It didn't seem likely that I could pay off my student loans with a music degree, so I switched."

"Interesting."

I found his one-word response to be extremely judgmental, but maybe that was because I was judging myself. "I thought I could still pursue music after I graduated, but that wasn't as easy as I'd thought it would be. A series of events sent me down a different path."

"What kind of events?"

"First, my sister got married in Carmel, and she needed my help with the wedding, so I followed her from LA to Carmel. Then she wanted to open a clothing boutique. Fashion was her passion, and she wanted me to be her partner. I didn't have any other great opportunities at the time, so I helped her open the Two Sisters Boutique."

"Appropriate name."

"She needed me to be the second sister. Everything was always supposed to be temporary, but then weeks turned into years. My sister had trouble conceiving a baby, then trouble carrying a pregnancy. She had multiple miscarriages. She was sick. She was hurting. She needed me to stay in the store, so I did."

"There's something to be said for family loyalty," he said.

"Really? You don't think I've just wasted my talent?"

"Do you think that?" he challenged.

"Sometimes. I've been playing on the side, performing locally, giving lessons, but my dream was to play for a renowned orchestra. Last Thursday, I actually got an incredible offer to be second violin for an orchestra that's going to play in Europe for two months starting in November. I was just figuring out how I would tell my sister that I was going to leave her in the middle of her pregnancy to go after my long-awaited dream when I got the call from the hospital about my mother."

"That was a big curveball."

"It threw everything into a tailspin. I have to give my answer to the orchestra by Monday, and I haven't told Dani yet, because I couldn't do that in the middle of everything else that's going on." I paused. "I think I'm going to have to turn down the job."

"Seriously? Why?"

"I don't know how long I'll need to be here. I don't know what's going to happen with my mom. There's just too much going on."

"You should do it," Kade said flatly. "You should go."

"How can I?"

"How can you not? You've put your dreams on hold for too long. This is your chance. You have to take it."

"What about Dani? What about my mom?"

"What about you?" he challenged. "Your sister has a husband, right?"

"Yes."

"And people who help in the store?"

"A few. But there's still my mother. I know I don't owe her anything, but I still can't imagine leaving right now."

"Well, you don't have to leave now. You said November."

"Rehearsals start in two weeks."

"A lot can happen in two weeks. A lot can happen in an instant. You only get one life, Brynn. If music is what you need to do, then do it. Everything else will work out."

"You make it sound simple, but it feels selfish."

"Your sister will survive. She can find a manager for the store. You can keep in touch with her. You can be supportive."

"I owe her, Kade. I don't think I would have survived after my mom died without Dani. She was everything to me. She was only born twenty-two minutes before me, but she has always been my big sister, my second mother. We are incredibly close. Sometimes, it feels like we're one person."

"But you're not. You're two individuals who can love each other and still have their own lives. Maybe I don't completely understand the bond of twins, but perhaps it's not the bond that makes you want to choose safety over risk. Maybe that's just what you want to choose. And if that's the case, then that's fine. It's your life. You get to decide what you want."

"I don't think I've ever made a decision without thinking about Dani."

He met my gaze. "Maybe it's time to start."

"Maybe." I wasn't entirely sure I could ever be as free to choose as Kade thought I should be. But I didn't want to talk about it any further. "We should probably get back to the house."

Kade nodded and called the server over to request the check. We headed down the street a few minutes later, arriving just minutes before the locksmith showed up.

While Kade worked with him on the locks, I went up to my

mother's bedroom to start cleaning up. The destruction felt even worse in this room, as if a horrible rage had been completely unleashed. Everything was ripped and broken. Devastation was everywhere I looked. I couldn't bear to see my mom's clothes slashed into pieces, especially the dresses she'd bought from our boutique. It felt too personal. I left the closet and moved over to the desk, where everything from inside the drawers had been dumped on the floor.

The file folders were mostly filled with receipts and bills for utilities and online retailers. Nothing seemed particularly important. My eye caught on a folder that had slid under the desk. I opened it to find a half-dozen envelopes, all addressed to the same place in Brooklyn, New York. As I picked up one of the envelopes, it felt like there was something inside. Opening it, I was shocked to discover five one-hundred-dollar bills.

I looked back at the front of the envelope. There was a return address label with the name Children's Support Network and my mother's address. As I read the name of the addressee, my jaw dropped in surprise.

It was addressed to Louise Beckham. Kade's last name was Beckham. That couldn't be a coincidence. Kade had said his relationship with my mother had started through art. *Was that a lie?* My heart raced with more questions. I felt like I was standing on the edge of another cliff.

CHAPTER ELEVEN

"THE LOCKSMITH IS DONE," Kade said.

I jumped at the sound of his voice.

"I have keys for the front and back door," he added as I turned to look at him. "The locksmith gave me two sets. You should keep them both until your mom is out of the hospital. He also changed my locks, and I have an extra set that your mother can have as well."

"Okay."

He walked into the room, his gaze narrowing as he gave me a concerned look. "What's going on? You look shocked."

"I found this." I handed him the envelope, watching his face closely as he read the address. A look of puzzlement ran across his face.

"What is this?" he asked.

"I don't know. But there's five hundred dollars in cash inside." I paused as he opened the envelope to look at the money. "Is Louise Beckham related to you?"

"She's my mother," he said, his frown deepening as he pulled out the cash. He stared at it for a long minute. Then his gaze moved back to the envelope. "I've seen this before when I used to get the mail for my mom. She told me she was getting some financial support from a nonprofit group that helped single mothers."

"The Children's Support Network?"

"I guess that was it. But the address is here. It's this house." He shook his head in confusion. "I don't understand why your mother was sending my mother money."

"Neither one ever told you?" I asked.

"No, never," he said vehemently.

"There are several envelopes in the folder, all pre-addressed to your mom. But you haven't been a child in a long time. What are you—thirty?"

"Thirty-one," he said, his jaw turning to stone. "This makes no sense."

"Welcome to my world, where nothing makes sense."

"I need to speak to my mother."

"Maybe you should call her now."

He pulled out his phone, punched in a number, and then left the room.

I wanted to follow him. But it wasn't my business. *Or was it?* If my mother was sending his mother money, then I needed to know why.

I got up from the floor and walked to the door. I could hear Kade talking in the family room. I moved closer to the stairs so I could hear better.

"I don't understand," he said. "How long have you gotten the money? Do you know the person who sent it to you—Laura Hawthorne?" He paused. "You're seriously telling me you don't know her? No, we can't talk later. I need to know why a woman who has been supporting my art was also sending you money." He paused for several minutes. "You never heard the name Laura Hawthorne except from me? I don't understand." Silence followed his words, then he said, "It matters because Laura was shot yesterday, and someone broke into her house today. They're looking for something. And I don't like that suddenly you're in the middle of this. The police are trying to unravel Laura's life. I don't want you mixed up in whatever she's involved in." He paused. "I'm not going to calm down. This is serious, Mom." He let out a breath. "All right. Call me back."

As he finished his call, I made my way down the stairs. "Well?" I asked.

He looked at me with irritation in his gaze. "My mom said the first letter she received wasn't signed. Nor was there a return address. It just said the group had heard she was struggling. Their nonprofit was made up of single moms who knew what it meant to be alone, trying to support a child. They would help by sending cash that wouldn't be taxed. They wanted her to think of it as a gift in her time of need but not to tell anyone about it, as they couldn't support everyone as much as they wished they could."

"That sounds too good to be true. She didn't question how they heard about her?"

"She'd been applying to loans and grants for months. She assumed that's where they got her name. The money came once a quarter, and it was always five one-hundred-dollar bills."

"That's two thousand dollars a year," I murmured. "How long has it been coming?"

"She said it started when I was about eleven, and it didn't end until three years ago when she found the will to send the money back with a note expressing gratitude but letting them know that her child was grown, and she didn't need it anymore."

"The money started going to your mom twenty years ago. That's right around the time my mom disappeared. That can't be a coincidence."

"It seems unlikely," he admitted, a scowl on his face.

"And if they stopped sending your mother money three years ago, why is this envelope filled with cash still here?"

"I don't know."

"You said there was no return address on the envelope, but there is a tag on the envelopes upstairs."

"My mom said she didn't start seeing a return address until the last few years before she asked them to stop."

"How did she do that exactly?"

"She sent the money back with a note—to this address, I presume."

I thought about that. "We need to find out more about this group, but that might not be easy. It doesn't sound like they operate publicly."

"No, but the money has to come from somewhere," Kade said. "Your mother is a teacher. I don't think she's rich enough to be sending cash to people all over the country."

"And why would she be so committed to helping out single moms? She wasn't a single mom. She had a husband and kids she left behind. If anything, she should have been sending my father money."

"Maybe she did."

I frowned at that suggestion. "I don't think so. I never saw any of these envelopes before. And they were only addressed to your mom. Where were the other recipients?"

"I don't know."

"You said my mom ran into you at a gallery in Seattle two years ago and became a fan. Wouldn't she have known that you were the same kid she was helping to support? You and your mom have the same last name." I shook my head as I tried to piece it together. "There has to be a connection we're missing."

Kade gave me a grim look. "I agree. It doesn't add up. I need to talk to my mother more about it, but she had a dinner to go to with her cancer support group. They're celebrating her friend's remission. She said she'd call me later."

"Maybe she'll be able to tell you more then."

"I hope so." He ran a hand through his hair. "I have to get out of here. I need to paint. I need to work on the pieces for my show. What is your plan? Are you leaving now? Are you going to find a hotel?"

"I might do a little more cleanup first," I said.

"Why don't you just leave it? Take a break. Find a place to stay and then check in on your mom."

He suddenly seemed eager to get me out of the house. I wondered if that was because he wanted to do some searching on his own. "I'm going to keep going for a while longer," I said.

"Do you want me to stay and help you?"

"Help me or hinder me?" I challenged.

"What does that mean?"

"Our mothers are tied together, and now you suddenly want me to leave this house. I have to assume that's because you want to look around here without me."

"Actually, I just want to think about everything that we learned, because it's fucked up," he said, anger burning in his gaze. "Laura never said one word to me about my mother or about sending her money. But she made a point to get to know me, to buy my art, to set me up with a show. What the hell is going on?"

"Clearly, my mother has a lot of secrets."

"Clearly," he echoed, betrayal in his gaze. He blew out a breath. "I won't be able to work now; I'm too pissed off. I'll help you get organized here. I'm in this, too, now, for better or worse."

"The way things are going, I'm expecting worse."

Kade and I worked for a couple of hours, not talking much as we sifted through files and papers and put the house back together. We didn't find anything else of interest. There was no information on the nonprofit, no evidence of a checkbook or bank account in that name. I looked for the group online as well but found nothing.

By six o'clock, I was tired, frustrated and in need of a break. I was thinking about leaving when Dani called. "I'm still at the house," I said pre-emptively. "But I'm going soon."

"You're supposed to be at a hotel, Brynn."

"I had to clean up and change the locks. It took longer than I thought. How was your drive home?"

"It was fine. I talked to Steve, and we think that we should hire a private investigator to look into Mom's death and her sudden reappearance. Steve knows a PI in San Francisco. He called him, and he's interested in working with us. Since you're in the city, he'd like to meet with you as soon as possible."

"Okay." A private detective probably wasn't the worst idea. "Text me his number, and I'll call him. Have you heard from Dad yet?"

"No. I just talked to Vicky again, and she's whipping up all kinds of bad theories in her head, most of them having to do with Dad cheating on her."

"I wish I thought that's what his silence was about, but the longer he stays out of touch, the more I worry."

"I feel the same way. Has anything else happened since I left?" Dani asked.

"I discovered Mom was involved with a nonprofit that sends money to single moms with financial problems. One of those women is Kade's mother."

"What?" Dani shrieked. "Kade? As in the guy downstairs? I told you to be careful about him. I told you there was more to the story."

"Kade was as shocked as I was. He never knew there was a connection between Laura and his mother. His mom said she got the money from a nonprofit, but it never had Laura's name on it. I don't think she was lying, because I saw the pre-addressed envelopes that had been sent to his mother, and Mom's name wasn't on them."

"This is bizarre, Brynn. You need to get out of there. For all we know, Kade could have been the one who shot Mom."

A shiver ran down my spine. "I don't believe that. He wants to find out the truth as much as we do."

"That's what he says, but you don't know."

I needed to get her off Kade. "Let's put him aside for the

moment. The money started going to Kade's mom the year Mom left us. So, there's another coincidence. What happened that year to change everything?"

"Who knows? I don't like any of this, Brynn. I still think you should leave San Francisco and come back here. We can hire the investigator and do this from afar."

"It will be easier for me to talk to the investigator in person. I'll call him now. Don't worry about me, Dani. This new wrinkle isn't dangerous. It's a clue that will hopefully lead to more answers."

"You don't know that, and I can't stop worrying about you, Brynn. Yesterday, I felt like my life was finally going in a good direction, but now it has hit a brick wall. I kind of hate Mom for putting us through all this again. If she hadn't told that nurse to call you, we'd just be living our lives. We wouldn't be dealing with any of this."

"Well, we can't go back in time. I'll call the investigator, and we'll go from there."

"Call me back after you talk to him."

As Dani clicked off, I retrieved the number for the investigator from her text and punched it in.

A moment later, a man's voice came across the line. "Warren Investigations," he said.

"I was given your name by Steve Garfield, an attorney in Carmel. I'm his sister-in-law, Brynn Landry."

"Right. Your mother has come back from the dead."

"She has, but she was shot yesterday, so there's a chance she could die for real this time. I'm trying to figure out why she left twenty years ago and what she's been doing for the past two decades and who might want to kill her now."

"When can we meet?"

"I'm free now."

"Where are you staying?"

"I'm at my mom's house in Haight-Ashbury."

"Got it. Why don't you meet me at McElroy's Bar on Haight Street in thirty minutes?"

"Okay, I'll be there. Thanks for agreeing to help."

"Write down as much pertinent information as you have and bring it with you. We'll take it from there. Twenty years is a long time to trace."

"I know. And we need information fast. Someone is still trying to kill my mother."

"Understood."

"How will I find you?"

"From what I understand, you look just like your sister, so I'll find you."

As I set down the phone, Kade came down the hall and into the family room. "Who were you talking to?" he asked.

"A private investigator that Dani found for me. He works here in the city, and he's agreed to meet me in a half hour."

Kade nodded. "An investigator is a good idea. I'd like to go with you, Brynn."

I hesitated. "I don't know, Kade. Don't you think we're getting too tangled up?"

"Oh, we're definitely tangled up, which is why I need to go with you. My mom is mixed up in this, too, now. I need to know what's going on. You want to protect your mother; I want to protect mine."

He made a good point. "All right. You can come with me, but the priority is finding out who's trying to kill my mother. I don't think she was shot because she was sending money to your mom."

"I hope that's true, but we don't know anything for sure."

CHAPTER TWELVE

MCELROY'S WAS a small neighborhood bar with wood paneling and dim lighting. There were no TVs blaring out sporting events, but there were a couple of tables with chess and checkers built in, as well as a dartboard on one wall. The bar was full, but we snagged a table toward the back.

We ordered drinks from the waitress, who also set down a bowl of party mix in the center of the table. The atmosphere in the bar was one of happy excitement that the weekend had arrived. I wished I could feel that happy, that I could just be having drinks with a good-looking guy in a different city than I was normally in, but that wasn't the case.

"How's your sister doing?" Kade asked.

"She's worrying and trying to figure out how much she can control from Carmel." I gave him a thoughtful look. "What about you? You've been quiet since we found the money and you spoke to your mother."

"I'm...confused."

"Join the club."

"I know why my mother took the money and didn't ask questions. We were very poor after my dad died. She was working two jobs, and neither paid more than minimum wage. She was doing her best, but she'd gone from having a husband who took care of her to having to take care of herself and a small child. I was four years old when he died."

"That must have been difficult. What was your dad like? Do you remember him?"

"I have some memories, but I'm not sure they're mine or if I just heard so many stories about him that I made them memories."

I knew exactly how that felt. I'd done the same with my mom.

"I remember him being big and strong," Kade continued, as he sipped his beer. "He used to take me to Central Park on the subway. When I got too tired to walk, he'd put me on his shoulders and say, 'How's the view up there?' I'd say it was great. He told me it's always good to get a different perspective."

"That's a nice memory. And it sounds like it's yours."

"He also used to cook breakfast on Sunday mornings. He'd tell my mother to sleep in while he whipped up chocolate chip pancakes and a huge platter of bacon and scrambled eggs with cheese mixed in. Sunday was our day for breakfast and the park. I didn't see a lot of him during the week. He worked long hours. After he died, my mom had to go to work. There were a few relatives around who would babysit but no one had extra money to help. I'm sure when that cash started arriving, my mom thought it was a gift from God. She wasn't going to question her good fortune."

"I can see why she wouldn't. She was using the money to raise her child. But over time, it must have added up to something like thirty or forty thousand dollars. That's a lot of money."

"It is." His mouth turned down in a frown, his brown eyes darkening with a mix of emotions. "I don't understand where this group gets its money and why Laura uses her home address for distribution. I looked them up, and I couldn't find anything."

"They must have funding from some wealthy people."

"Maybe. I also keep asking myself, why did they choose my

mother? She was living on the other side of the country. Unless... Did your mother ever live in New York?"

I shook my head. "Not that I know of. She was born in Atlanta. Her parents died early. She lived with her grandmother until she was seventeen. After her grandmother died, she moved to San Diego with a friend to go to community college. And then she went to LA to work. That's where she met my father."

"What did she do for work?"

"She taught music, worked in an office, waited tables...a bit of everything from what I know. But what I know is very suspect now, isn't it?"

"I'm starting to feel the same way. I'm questioning every conversation I had with Laura."

"Did you talk to Laura about your parents?"

"Not in depth, but I mentioned my father had died when I was young, and she said she could relate to that as she'd lost her parents."

"Maybe that part was true then."

"At some point, I told her my mom was being treated for cancer. She expressed concern. But we never talked about money. She certainly never mentioned the nonprofit or the fact that she had been sending my mother money for two decades. I don't think she just forgot that, so why did she keep it a secret?"

"I have no idea. Do you think she met you by accident in Seattle or was it planned? Because it seems like another huge coincidence. She was paying your mom. She had to know who you were when she met you."

"You're right, Brynn. She had to know. Her patronage was pity or charity."

I heard the unhappiness in his voice. He felt betrayed by my mother. I knew what that felt like. "Maybe after your mother stopped accepting the cash, my mom wanted to find another way to help you," I said. "But why would she do that? Why is she so obsessed with your welfare?" Once again, I couldn't quite keep the hurt tone out of my voice.

Kade's eyes softened. "I can't think of any reason."

A crazy idea came into my head. I immediately tried to shove it away, but it wouldn't go.

"What?" Kade demanded, straightening in his chair. "What are you thinking now?"

"I don't want to say it out loud."

"I can guess," he said harshly. "You have an incredibly expressive face, Brynn. Your eyes change colors with your moods. They're blue when you're calm, and purple when you're worried or worked up about something. You also lift your chin like you're fighting some subconscious battle."

I was a little flustered by his close study of me. "You can see all that?"

"I'm an artist. I always see the details. They make up the picture. So, if I had to guess what you're thinking now…"

As his voice drifted away, I studied his face with the same detail in which he'd studied mine. His eyes darkened with emotion, his brows drew together when he was puzzled, and his lips tightened whenever he had something distasteful to say —like now.

"You think your mother has a personal connection to me," Kade continued. "So, just say it."

"Why don't you say it?" I countered.

"You're wondering if I might have been adopted, if your mother is my mother."

I drew in a quick breath, his words spelling out exactly what I'd been wondering. "I didn't want to say that out loud."

"I'm not adopted," he said firmly. "My mother was in labor for eighteen hours with me. My father videotaped the delivery. I've unfortunately seen just about every moment of my birth in far greater detail than I ever wanted to see it."

Relief ran through me. I didn't know what I thought about Kade, but I definitely did not want him to be my brother. "Well, that's good."

"It is good," he said, meeting my gaze. "We're not related. I have no doubt about that. But there is some connection."

"You need to press your mother for more answers, Kade."

"I'll call her tomorrow. I don't think she knows more than she told me, but maybe she does." Kade paused as a man walked up to our table.

"Brynn Landry?" he said. "I'm Jeremy Warren."

I didn't know what I'd expected—probably more of a big bodyguard type guy. But Jeremy Warren was a thin, wiry man, in his forties, wearing jeans, a gray pullover sweatshirt, and a baseball cap.

"It's nice to meet you," I said as he sat down with us. "This is Kade Beckham. He's living in the downstairs unit at my mother's house."

"Good. Sounds like you might have some helpful information, Mr. Beckham."

"Don't get your hopes up," Kade said. "I don't know much."

"I put together what little information I have," I said, sliding a piece of paper in front of Jeremy. "I did a timeline of what I know of my mother's life before she allegedly died in a hurricane in New Orleans twenty years ago, and then a very short recap of what I know about her life now. Inspector Greenman with the SFPD has my mother's phone with her contacts in it. He probably has more information than I do."

"I'll check in with him tomorrow." Jeremy perused the sheet, nodding with approval. "This gives me a place to start."

"There's something else, if you turn the page over," I said. "My mother was apparently involved with a charity—Children's Support Network. She was sending cash to Kade's mother from the charity, but Kade didn't know anything about it until we found the envelopes in my mom's house today."

"My mother didn't even know the money was coming from Laura," Kade interjected. "The envelopes were sent from the charity, but we found several at Laura's house."

Jeremy's eyes gleamed with interest. "There's a tie between your two mothers? That's odd."

"Everything is odd," I said. "Kade and I can't figure out what the connection is. His mother, Louise Beckham, has always lived in New York, and to my knowledge, my mother has never been there, or if she has, it was only for a quick trip."

Jeremy looked back at the information I'd given him, then lifted his gaze to mine. "Your brother-in-law filled me in on the circumstances surrounding your mother's alleged death in New Orleans. But he couldn't provide the name of the friend she went to help."

"I don't know who that is, either. My father would know, but he hasn't been in touch with anyone. We're worried about him, too."

"Steve gave me the information on your dad; I'm going to try to find him as well."

"Good. There's one other thing. My mother was attacked at the hospital this morning. The police have put security on her room now, so hopefully no one else can get in. Also, earlier today, her house was ransacked while I was at the hospital. Someone was definitely searching the house for something."

"Got it." Jeremy said with a nod. "Before I go, getting back to the link between your mothers, Mr. Beckham... How did you end up living in the downstairs unit of Ms. Landry's mother and what is your relationship with Laura Hawthorne?"

Kade's lips tightened. He was probably getting tired of everyone assuming he had a sugar mama.

"We met two years ago," Kade replied. "Laura was an art patron. She helped me get a show here in the city and offered me a place to stay while I was getting ready for it. We've had several conversations in the past month. We had dinner together twice and coffee another time, but our discussions never got too personal. And, no, we're not romantically involved. We're not having sex. We're friends."

"There are a couple of men who've approached me who seem

to be friends with my mother," I interjected. "I noted them on the sheet. Mark Harrison said he met my mother at the Harding School of the Arts, where his stepdaughter goes. Tom Wells is a neighbor who said he dated my mother in the past, but he hasn't seen her in a while."

"I'll track them both down, and I will call you as soon as I learn anything."

I felt a wave of relief at his words. I knew the police were working on the case, but this man was working for me. "Thank you."

He got to his feet. "Take care."

As Jeremy left, I turned to Kade. "I feel like a weight just slipped off my shoulders. He seems like he knows what he's doing, right?"

"I don't know. He said little about his experience or his tactics."

My relief dimmed. "You're right. But my brother-in-law, Steve, knows him. He wouldn't send me to anyone who wasn't good. At least, we have someone digging into things."

"It definitely can't hurt."

As a burst of loud conversation rang out near us, I realized how crowded the bar was getting. "We should go."

"I agree. There's a pizza place on the way back to the house. Should we pick up some food? Or are you eager to find a hotel?"

"I never say no to pizza," I said. But as I followed Kade out of the bar, I wondered if I should start saying no to him. He was becoming very entwined in my life, and he had an odd connection to my mother. I could hear Dani screaming in my head not to ignore the big red flags.

But it was just pizza. And Kade was the only friend I had in the city, the only one who could understand what I was going through, because he was now going through it, too. It wasn't a coincidence that he'd ended up in my mother's house. She'd wanted him there, and we both needed to know why.

CHAPTER THIRTEEN

AFTER PICKING UP PIZZA, we returned home around eight thirty. I walked up the steps with trepidation, seeing several boxes and bags on the front porch. The flowers that Tom Wells had given me were still there, as well as a second bouquet, a plastic-wrapped bag of cookies tied with a bright red ribbon, a fruit basket, and a couple of cards.

"My mom has friends who care about her," I murmured.

"Like I told you the first time you asked, Laura is a really nice person."

The sound of footsteps drew my head around, and Kade stepped in front of me as someone came up the path. Then he relaxed and moved to the side as a middle-aged woman came into view.

"Brenda," he said.

"I was hoping to catch you, Kade," Brenda replied. "Do you know how Laura is doing?" She halted when she saw me. "Oh," she said in surprise. "Who...who are you?"

"I'm Laura's daughter. Brynn Landry."

"Her daughter?" the woman echoed in surprise. "I heard someone was staying at the house, a young female relative, but I didn't know Laura had a daughter."

"She does," I said shortly.

"I'm sorry that I'm staring. You just look so much like Laura. I'm Brenda Palmer. I live a few blocks away. Laura and I are in book club together." She held up a book. "I thought maybe you could take this to her in the hospital. She can read while she's recovering."

I took the book out of her hand. "I can do that, but she's not conscious right now."

Brenda's jaw dropped. "She's not? I thought she was out of surgery and doing better."

"She's holding her own, but she's not awake yet."

"Well, I really hope and pray that will happen soon."

"Me, too. How many people are in the book group?" I asked.

"About a dozen. It depends on the day."

I looked down at the book jacket, which was a beautiful fantasy image. "She likes fantasy, huh?"

"One of her favorite genres. She likes to escape into other worlds."

I smiled somewhat bitterly. "Well, that's probably the truest thing I've heard all day."

Brenda looked confused by my words. "Sorry?"

"Never mind. I'll make sure she gets the book. You said you live nearby. Were you home yesterday when my mother was shot?"

"No. I work at a hair salon a few miles from here. That's how your mom and I met. She's one of my clients."

"And she never told you about her daughters?"

Brenda shook her head. "Daughters? There's someone else besides you?"

"I have a sister, too."

"She never mentioned having children. Or maybe I just wasn't paying attention. Sometimes, I drift away when people are talking. I cut hair all day long. I hear a lot of stories."

Brenda seemed a little flaky and also somewhat defensive.

"Do you know if she was having trouble with anyone—a friend, a boyfriend, a coworker?" I asked.

"Like someone who would shoot her? I thought it was just a drive-by."

"No. The police are looking for someone who might have had something against her."

Brenda thought for a moment. "Laura mentioned that she'd had an unpleasant conversation with Tom's ex, Renee. Laura and Tom had gone out a few times, and Renee showed up at her door one day and told her they were getting back together, and Laura needed to leave him alone. Tom told her it wasn't true, but Laura didn't want to get involved in their drama, so she ended things."

"The police need to know about this woman," I said. "She sounds volatile."

"I don't think Renee is dangerous," Brenda said. "Maybe I shouldn't have even mentioned it. I don't want to get into the middle of any drama, either. You can tell the police about Renee if you want but leave me out of it. I better go."

Brenda practically ran away from the house. My gaze turned to Kade.

"Let's talk about it inside," he said.

I opened the door, happy to see the locks were still intact. I grabbed the bag of cookies and brought it inside while Kade put the pizza in the kitchen and then went back to bring in the rest of the items on the porch.

The cookies looked so deliciously chocolate, I undid the ribbon and grabbed one to eat as I opened the note inside the bag. *Hope you feel better soon. Love, Candice, Mitch, and the girls.*

I set the paper aside, then opened the book that Brenda had given me. There was a note written on the first page: *Thinking of you, Laura. Can't wait to argue about this love triangle at our next meeting. Brenda.*

As Kade set the rest of the items on the counter, he said, "Did she write something interesting in the book?"

"No. Just good wishes and see you soon."

"There are some other notes with these goodies," he said.

"I'll read them after pizza."

"You mean after your cookie appetizer?" he asked with a hint of a smile.

"Yes. The chocolate cookies are heaven. They were apparently made by someone named Candice."

"Candice lives two doors down with her husband and two kids."

I tilted my head as I gave him a thoughtful look. "You recognized Brenda, and you know who Candice is. Who else haven't you told me about?"

"Candice and Brenda came here for a book club meeting one night. I met them in passing. I don't know anything else about them." He frowned. "I'm not holding back on you, Brynn."

I really wanted to believe that was true. "Okay. I'll text Inspector Greenman and tell him about Renee Wells."

I picked up my phone and sent the text while Kade took plates and the pizza box to the table. I joined him there a moment later, feeling marginally more hopeful that we were finally making some progress. Jeremy Warren was going to investigate for us, and I'd sent a new name to Inspector Greenman. I thought about telling the inspector about the connection between Kade's mother and my mother, but I decided to wait until Jeremy had a chance to look into it. I grabbed a slice of pizza and bit into it with delight, the sauce slipping down my chin.

Kade handed me a napkin. "You look happier."

"It felt good to take some action. I hope it pays off." I took a couple more bites of pizza, then added, "Jeremy didn't look like a private investigator, though."

"No?" Kade questioned.

"I thought he'd be more rugged. Someone who looked like he'd been in a few fights, maybe had some scars, some tattoos. Speaking of tattoos," I said, as my gaze ran down his arms. "What do you have going on there?"

Kade pushed up the sleeve of his left arm to reveal a multitude of tattoos that included a lion in mid growl and several black roses entwined around a dagger, as well as a maze of swirls and shapes that felt much like his turbulent paintings.

"Did you design those?" I asked.

"I did."

"What do they mean?"

"A lot of things. Power, strength, courage, fear, heartbreak, death..."

The last word sent a chill through me, reminding me that Kade had a dark side. "Your arm is just another canvas, isn't it?"

"Yes. But I decided a long time ago that less is more. So, I started creating outside of myself."

"Do the dark emotions all come from your father's death?"

"Probably not all of them, but a lot. I felt cheated by his death. Growing up without a father in a rough neighborhood wasn't easy. I had to be the man in the family when I was far too young. My mother didn't want me to take on that role. She wanted to be my protector, but when she was working, I had to protect myself. There wasn't anyone else to do that."

His words resonated within me. "I felt cheated by my mom's death, too. My life wasn't as much of a struggle as yours, but her absence left an immense hole in my life. I've never really been able to fill it." I paused. "I can't stop wondering if she realized just how much pain she gave us when she left, or if she felt any pain herself. I want her to explain it to me."

His gaze clung to mine. "Is that really what you want, Brynn? Because I don't think you want to listen to her as much as you want to talk. You want to tell her how you feel about what she did."

"I need to get that out," I admitted. "I want her to know what she did was wrong. But there's also a part of me that wants to see her with her eyes open, who wants to hug her, and tell her how much I missed her." I shook my head in bewilderment. "I have so many mixed emotions. My thoughts feel as dark and turbulent as your art. I wish I could paint my feelings away."

"Why don't you play them away?"

"What?"

He got up from the table and retrieved the violin and bow. "It seems like you might find some peace with this."

"I don't know if I can play now."

"Why not?" he challenged.

"It's her violin."

"When you're playing, it will be yours. Come on." He held out the violin, and after a moment, I took it. "Don't think, just play."

"Easier said than done."

I pushed back my chair to give myself a little more room and then lifted the violin to my shoulder. The bow was slightly bent, but maybe that was fine, because I felt a little bent, too. I closed my eyes and tried to push all thoughts out of my head.

With the first note, my instincts took over. I played a song my mother had taught me. I hadn't learned it completely before she died, but afterward, I'd made it a mission to perfect it.

As my emotions blended into the melody, I felt a release of anger and frustration, grief and sadness, uncertainty and fear…

The music flowed through me like a warm, healing breeze, and I played a second song, and then a third. When I finally hit the last note of that melody, I felt immensely better.

I set down the violin and lifted my gaze to Kade's. He stared back at me with a gleam of admiration.

"That was beautiful, Brynn. Spectacularly beautiful. You are very talented."

"Thanks. I think you're exaggerating."

"Not even a little. You have a gift."

"I do love to play. And you were right…it helped."

"Sometimes it's just too much to hold the emotions in." He paused. "It's not my place to say this, but you need to play with that orchestra. It would be a crime not to use your talent."

"I tell myself that, too, but it feels selfish, especially with everything else going on. But I don't want to think about it now. For the first time in the last forty-eight hours, I feel calm. How about a cookie?"

"I wouldn't say no," he replied, as I got to my feet.

I grabbed the bag of cookies as well as two cards that had been left for my mom and brought them to the table.

While Kade reached for a cookie, I slid open the first envelope and pulled out the card. It read: *Praying for you, Laura. Feel better soon. Our school needs you!* It was signed by Joanne Hunt, the principal of the school, and several other teachers.

I opened the next envelope and pulled out a card that made me gasp.

"What's wrong?" Kade asked.

"Is this supposed to be a joke?" I showed him the face of the card. A series of tombstones were lined up in a cemetery with the quote: *This is where it all ends.*

"Who's it from?" he asked tersely.

I was almost afraid to open the card, but I finally did. "You know why," I read, then lifted my gaze to his. "It's not signed with a name, but this is definitely personal."

"It feels like there was a betrayal," Kade murmured.

"That's exactly what it feels like," I said, meeting his gaze.

My phone buzzed on the table, and I glanced down at the screen. "It's Inspector Greenman."

"Can you put it on speaker?"

"Sure." I picked up the phone. "Hello? Did you get my text?"

"I did. Renee Wells is a new name. I'll check into that."

"Good. I also got a card. It was left on the porch with other items from my mother's friends and neighbors. It's threatening. It shows a cemetery and says, 'this is where it ends, you know why.' No signature."

"All right. Can you take a photo and send it to me? Then put the card in a plastic bag, and I'll get it from you tomorrow. In the meantime, I have a video I want to send you. Let me know if you recognize the person in the shot."

"Okay," I said warily.

"I'm texting it now."

I set the phone on the table as I waited for his text. A moment later, a video appeared, and I pushed play. Kade got up to take a look over my shoulder.

The video was only eight seconds long, but the shot showed someone getting into a car across the street from my mother's house. They were wearing a hoodie, but when they turned their head, their face was captured by the streetlight. I gasped. "Oh, my God," I said. "When was this taken?"

"Wednesday night. Do you recognize this woman?"

"Yes," I said, my stomach turning over. "It's my stepmother, Vicky Landry. But she would have been in LA on Wednesday night."

"She wasn't."

"I talked to her on Thursday. She said nothing about my mother. She was just upset because she couldn't get my father to call her back. She was worried about him." My mind raced in a dozen different directions. "She thought he might be having an affair."

"With your mother?"

"No," I said. Then I realized I had no idea. "I mean, she didn't say anything about my mother."

"Not even after you told her your mother was alive?"

"I didn't give her that information. I didn't want to tell her before I spoke to my father." I swallowed hard. "Have you talked to either of them?"

"Your father hasn't gotten back to me. We're trying to trace his whereabouts. I'll give your stepmother a call now."

"Do you want me to talk to her first? Maybe she would tell me something before she'd tell you. I think she'll clam up and call her lawyer before she'll answer any of your questions."

"All right. See what you can find out. Then call me back."

"Also, I hired a private investigator."

"He's already been in touch with me. But believe me, Ms. Landry, we're doing everything we can to find the person who shot your mother."

"I understand. I'll call Vicky and then I'll call you back." As he clicked off the line, I played the video one more time. "I can't believe this," I murmured.

"That's your stepmother, huh?"

"Yes."

"How long has she been married to your father?"

"Since I was eleven. She happily stepped into my mom's shoes, which felt really weird, because she'd been one of my mom's best friends. They met at a yoga class. They both loved live music, and they'd go out together when my dad was traveling on business. Vicky was in and out of our house so much, I called her Aunt Vicky. After my mom died, Vicky was very comforting to me and to Dani. But that changed fast. When she would come over, she would just want to talk to my father. Four years later, they got married and six months after that, Dani and I went to boarding school."

"Seriously? She sent you to boarding school?"

"Well, it was a school specializing in artistic programs, so she sold it like it was a great opportunity for us. To be honest, we were okay with it. We didn't like living with them. Our dad retreated from us after our mom died, even before Vicky moved in. But once she became Mrs. Landry, he had even less to do with us. He thought we'd love her, because we'd loved her when she was our mother's friend, but we could see that she didn't have much use for us."

"What's your relationship now?"

"We tolerate each other. We're polite. They live in LA, and Dani and I live in Carmel, so we don't get together much."

"But she calls you when she's worried about your dad?"

"Sometimes. She hasn't been worried until lately, or if she has been, she hasn't said anything to us about it."

"But now, at the same time she's worried about your father having an affair, she shows up in San Francisco near your allegedly dead mother's house."

"It's damning," I murmured. "She had to know my mom was alive, but when did she find out? Was it the whole time? Or was it recently?"

Kade's lips drew into a tight line. "You need to call her."

"I know. I'm just not sure I'm ready for any more truth."

"Isn't that what you came here to get?"

I let out a sigh. "Yes. Fine, I'll call her."

"Can you put it on speaker? I'd like to hear her story."

"Why not?" I punched in Vicky's number and turned the speaker on. She answered on the third ring.

"Brynn," Vicky said, her voice rushed and a little thick. "Have you heard from your father?"

"No. Have you?" I asked.

"I haven't. It's so unlike him to be out of touch this long."

"Do you think something has happened to him or are you worried he's with someone else?"

"I don't want to believe he'd turn to anyone else, but things have been a little off between us the last few months."

"If you think there's someone else, do you have an idea who that would be?"

There was a long silence at the other end of the phone.

"Vicky?" I pressed.

"I don't know," she said. "And I shouldn't even be talking to you about this. It's between me and your father. I'm just worried about him. I'm going a little crazy."

"I'm worried, too." I licked my lips and said what I needed to say. "Do you think Dad is having an affair with someone in San Francisco?"

Vicky couldn't hide her quick intake of breath. "What do you know, Brynn?"

CHAPTER FOURTEEN

I THOUGHT about how to answer Vicky's question for a long moment. "I know you were on Dunbar Street in San Francisco on Wednesday night."

"Oh, God, Brynn. You know, don't you?" Vicky muttered.

"That my mother didn't die twenty years ago? Yes. How long have you known she was alive?"

"About two weeks," Vicky replied.

Her answer surprised me. "Two weeks? What happened two weeks ago?"

"I saw a video online, and she was in it. I thought it had to be a mistake. But there were still photos, too, and in each one, her features were so clear. She'd cut her hair, dyed it a lighter shade of brown. But it was still her, with those same blue-violet eyes that you and Dani have."

"What was this video? Was it a music performance?"

"No, it was a news clip. She was at a school concert and that blues singer, Miguel Rodriguez, made a surprise appearance and had a heart attack onstage. Your mother did CPR and saved his life. There were news crews there to film his performance. It was all over the internet. I thought with your music connections, you might have seen it."

"I had no idea. I assume you told my father."

There was another long pause. "I didn't tell him," Vicky said, a note of defiance in her voice. "I didn't see the point."

"You didn't see the point of telling him that his wife hadn't died? You didn't see the point in telling me and Dani that our mother hadn't drowned in a storm?" My voice rose with the force of my emotions until I was almost yelling.

"I wasn't completely sure if it was her," Vicky replied.

"You're lying. You just said it was her. That's not why you didn't tell us," I said flatly.

"No, you're right, it's not," Vicky said, her voice louder now, too. "I didn't want her to be alive. If she didn't die, that meant she left; she ran out on her family. I didn't want to put you back into that place of grief. So, I didn't say anything."

"But then, Dad suddenly went out of town and became unreachable."

"He left Tuesday. He said it was a last-minute business trip. I talked to him Tuesday night. He told me he was in Portland. But I called his hotel the next morning and they had no record of him being a guest. I called a bunch of other hotels, too. I checked in with his office, and his admin said he'd made his own travel arrangements."

"So you figured he'd seen the video and gone to San Francisco."

"Yes. In fact, I wondered if that video wasn't why he went to New Orleans two weeks ago. I thought maybe he was trying to find information on how she died. I tried to reach him, but he didn't answer his phone. I got desperate, so Wednesday afternoon I flew to San Francisco. I went to the Harding School. Your mother was conducting some after school concert rehearsal. I waited for her to leave around six and I followed her home."

"Did you talk to her?"

"No. I was going to. But then a man walked up to her door, and she let him in. I got back in the car and waited for another twenty minutes, but the man didn't leave. I started to realize how crazy I was acting. Your father wasn't with her. She had someone else in her life, so I left. But I'm still waiting to hear from your dad. I think he knows your mother is alive and is having some kind of breakdown."

Everything she said made sense. It fit the timeline, but she'd also raised questions about my dad. *Why had he suddenly stopped all contact with us?* She'd last talked to him on Tuesday evening. It was Friday night. That was a long time to be out of touch, especially in light of everything that had happened.

"How did you know I was at her house, Brynn?" Vicky asked.

"The police have been looking at security footage from the neighborhood."

"Why?"

"My mother was shot on Thursday afternoon. You didn't know that?"

"What? No!" Vicky exclaimed. "I had no idea. Who shot her?"

"The police don't have a suspect. She's alive but in critical condition. The hospital called me on Thursday, shortly after my mother was admitted. Apparently, my mom asked the nurse to contact me."

"Are you in San Francisco now? Have you seen your mom?"

"I have. But she hasn't seen me; she's unconscious."

"Oh, honey, I'm sorry."

"Don't pretend to be sorry, Vicky. You could have told me two weeks ago. You could have shown me the video. You had plenty of chances to tell me she was alive. You didn't want me to know."

"I was protecting you."

"You were protecting yourself. I think Dad is also here in San Francisco. Have you called hotels in the city?"

"I contacted a couple of the chain hotels that he normally uses, but I couldn't find him. I honestly don't know where he is."

"Do you know why my mom would fake her death? Twenty years ago, you were one of her best friends. Was she having problems with Dad? Was she scared of him? Was there some other problem in her life that she talked about?" I asked, the questions rushing through my lips.

"I can't imagine why she would have done what she did. She was in love with your dad, and she certainly wasn't scared of him. That's not why she left. How could you even suggest that?"

"Because the police are suggesting that. And they're interested in you, too. You and Dad have a lot of explaining to do. You were at my mom's house the night before she was shot, and Dad was in the city the day after. Inspector Greenman will be calling you shortly. I suggest you be completely honest with him."

"The police are going to call me?" Vicky asked nervously. "Can't you just tell them what I said?"

"No, I can't. And I wouldn't avoid answering their call. It will only make things look worse for you."

"Well, I'm not talking to any cops without a lawyer."

"Whatever. Do what you want. I can't talk to you anymore, Vicky. I can't." I ended the call, feeling overwhelmed by emotion. I sat back in my chair feeling drained. I blew out a breath.

Kade gave me a compassionate look. "That was rough."

"For her or for me?"

"Both of you."

"What do you think? You heard everything she said, and you're probably more objective than I am when it comes to her."

"I think...you need a cookie." He handed me a cookie, and that made me smile.

"You're very intuitive," I said, as I took a bite of the sweet chocolate.

"Haven't heard that one too often," he said dryly. "As for what I think about your stepmother...she sounded scared and desperate, like she was afraid of losing someone she loves."

"I get that, but she acted so oddly. She didn't tell anyone about the video. She flew to San Francisco to confront my mother, but then says she didn't do that. I don't know what to think."

"When she realized your mother was alive, she became terrified that she was going to lose her husband, her stepdaughters, and the family that she loves. That's why she didn't tell anyone. She was probably hoping no one would ever know that your mom was alive."

"That's true," I murmured. "I still don't know if Vicky was telling me the entire truth about her trip up here, though."

Kade pulled out his phone and started scrolling.

"Am I boring you?" I asked with annoyance.

He gave me a pointed look. "I'm searching for the video your stepmother was talking about."

"Oh. Sorry."

"Got it," he said.

"That was fast."

"Miguel Rodriguez is a big star," he muttered.

I moved my chair closer to his so I could watch the video. There was a lot of activity on a stage, with people rushing to aid the man on the ground. Then a woman took charge, giving CPR, barking out commands to others. She worked relentlessly on the man until the EMTs arrived. And then she stepped back and looked at the camera.

It was like I was looking at myself. It was different seeing her now, with her eyes wide open. She was alive. She was real. She was a freaking hero.

"Do you want me to play it again?" Kade asked.

I shook my head. "No. I've seen enough. I need another cookie."

He pushed the bag across the table. "What now?" he asked.

I devoured the cookie in two bites. "I need to call Inspector Greenman back."

"You should send him the link to the video. It's possible that the video didn't just bring your father and Vicky to the city. It also brought the shooter."

"You're right. The note left on the porch said: *You know why*. Whoever she ran away from twenty years ago must have found her because she was caught on the news saving someone else's life. That's tragically ironic."

"Yes, it is. And I hope that someone isn't related to you."

"I don't think it's my dad or Vicky, even though I don't like her. It has to be someone else."

"It probably is. I hope that video showed you another side of your mother, one that is generous, brave, and strong."

"It brought her back to life in a different way," I admitted. "The woman in the hospital bed is lifeless. She almost doesn't seem real. But my mom was alive on that video." I blew out a breath. "I'm suddenly exhausted."

"You should find a hotel. It's almost ten."

That idea felt like it would require too much energy. "I'm going to stay here. I'm tired. The locks are new, and it doesn't seem like someone would come back tonight."

"You can't be sure of that. But if you want to stay here, I'll sleep in the guest room."

"I can't keep letting you do that. This isn't your problem, Kade."

"It is my problem. I still need to know how our mothers are connected."

"The mattress in the guest bedroom was slashed."

"I'll throw a blanket over it. Torn-up things aren't a problem for me. You've seen my art and where I'm living."

"Which feels more like an artist's studio. Is that how your place at home looks?"

"Yes. But working where I live is fine for me. I don't sleep a lot, anyway. I do my best work at night."

"Can't get your brain to shut off, huh?"

"Always been a problem," he admitted.

"Then let's go downstairs to your place. I'll sleep on the couch. You can work."

"You wouldn't be comfortable."

"It won't matter. These days I'm lucky to sleep at all. And I'll feel less guilty if you're in your own bed."

"Downstairs works, but you can take my bed. The couch in the living room pulls out. I'll get some work done and crash when I'm finished."

"Are you sure?"

"Yes. For whatever reason, your mother helped support my mom during a rough time, and she supported me. Let me help you get through the night." He paused, frowning. "That didn't come out exactly right. You can trust me, Brynn. I hope you know that."

"I want to trust you, but I'm feeling like a fool for trusting anyone."

"Well, I can promise that you'll be safe with me."

I could hear Dani's voice in my head screaming at me not to be stupid, but Dani wasn't here, and I wanted to believe him, so I said, "Okay. I'll come downstairs. But first I need to call Inspector Greenman and fill him in."

Thirty minutes later, I walked around Kade's living room, looking at the various stages of his art pieces. It felt even more chaotic than the last time I'd been here. I picked up a strand of copper wire. "What do you do with the wire?" I asked.

"Depends," he said, taking the wire out of my hand. "The bedroom is in there."

"I know. But I was thinking I could watch you work."

"No one watches me work."

"What is this going to be?" I asked, looking at the splashes of paint on a nearby canvas.

"Not sure yet."

"Really? You don't know where you're going with this?"

"Have you ever written music?" he asked.

"Yes, or at least, I've tried, but I've never been able to finish anything. I get random ideas, but I can't finish them."

"Why do you think that is?"

"I don't know."

"Try again."

I shrugged. "Maybe I'm scared to finish because then I'll have something that can be judged and when it's judged, it will probably be bad."

"Why does it have to be bad?"

"I can play music, but I don't know if I'm good at creating it. How do you find the confidence to be so bold?"

"It developed over time. The first few things I painted got laughed at by kids who didn't understand."

"Or maybe they were jealous."

"I told myself that to feel better," he said with a small smile. "But I was also just trying out stuff. I didn't start out to be provocative. I was playing it safe, attempting to give people what I thought they wanted. Eventually, I realized I could only create what made me think or gave me an emotional reaction, what felt right, even if it looked all wrong."

"That's brave."

"It's just who I am. I'm stubborn, and I like to do what I want to do. I'm probably not going to get rich doing it."

"But you'll be proud of it."

"In the end, that's what matters. When you make art or music, it's subjective. It goes out in the world. Some people love it. Some hate it. But that's not the worst thing that can happen."

"What is the worst thing?" I asked curiously.

"That people don't care. Then it's like you did nothing."

I thought about that. "That makes sense. But it still doesn't feel easy to create something."

"It's not supposed to be easy. What would be the fun in that? Give me the keys for the upstairs."

"Why?" I asked suspiciously.

"I forgot something."

"What?"

He held out his hands. "Keys, please."

I handed him the keys, and he headed out the front door.

While he was gone, I looked more closely at his pieces. I was particularly interested in some of the sculptural designs where the paint was part of the materials being used. I didn't really understand some of it, but it made me think. Maybe that was all that mattered.

A few minutes later, Kade returned with the violin, and I knew what he wanted.

"No way," I said. "I'm not going to write music, not tonight, anyway. I'm spent."

"You're wired," he said with a smile. "Exhausted but amped up. No way you're going to sleep any time soon."

"Well, I'm not in a music-making mood."

"You don't wait for a mood. You just do it. I'll make you a deal. I work for an hour. You work for an hour. We'll see where we end up."

"I'll end up with nothing."

"Well, at least you'll be quiet while I'm working," he said with a laugh.

"Funny."

"Take the bedroom. I'll work out here. And don't think, just play. Take your feelings to the violin and see where it leads you."

I took the violin into the bedroom and sat down on the unmade bed. I wasn't going to play. I'd just give Kade his time to work. But there wasn't much to distract me in the bedroom. Aside from the bed, there was a dresser with a pile of clothes on top of it. That was it. No television. I did have my phone. I could waste an hour on that.

I scooted onto the middle of the bed, resting against the backboard as I took out my phone. I searched for the video of my mother again and found it quickly. As I watched my mother spring into action to save a man's life, an odd feeling ran through me. It felt like pride.

I didn't want to like anything about her, not after what she'd done to me. But she was a hero, at least in that moment.

Setting down the phone, I grabbed the violin. Maybe it was

time for me to find a little courage of my own. I held the instrument for several minutes, played a few chords that didn't go together, and almost quit. But it was just an hour of trying. I could do that. I didn't have anything else to do.

Taking Kade's advice, I stopped thinking and just let my fingers play my emotions. All the fear, anger, and pain came out in notes that felt clashing but also cathartic.

When Kade came into the room, I looked at him in bemusement. "Has it been an hour?" I asked.

"It has been two." He sat down on the edge of the bed. "What were you playing just now…was it your music?"

I nodded. "Yes. But I don't even remember all the notes. I was just playing."

"How did it feel?" he asked, his gaze intent on mine.

"It felt good. It felt like me. Now, tell me how it sounded to you."

"Amazing. Did you write anything down?"

"No," I said, gazing into his beautiful dark eyes. "But that doesn't matter. Thank you, Kade. Thank you for making me try."

The air between us suddenly seemed electric. I became very aware of where we were and the anticipation running through my body. This man had somehow gotten into my head in a way that no one else had.

Kade suddenly cleared his throat and got up. "Goodnight, Brynn. I hope you can get some sleep now."

He was gone before I could say a word.

I stretched out on the bed, my feeling of peace having already evaporated, replaced by other, more complicated emotions. My body was tingling from the heated look we'd just exchanged, and I had a feeling that sleep had just gotten further away.

CHAPTER FIFTEEN

I WOKE up Saturday morning completely disoriented. It took a moment for me to realize I was sleeping in Kade's bed. But at least I was alone. That was a good thing, I told myself. My life was complicated enough. I didn't need an unexpected attraction to a sexy painter to tie me up in even more knots.

It was very quiet in the apartment. I got out of bed, realizing I'd once again slept in my clothes, although I had managed to kick my shoes off. At some point, I needed to find a real place to stay. I just couldn't seem to take myself away from my mom's house. This was the farthest I'd gone, and it was just downstairs.

I moved to the door and opened it quietly, peeking into the living room. I expected to find Kade asleep. I'd seen the light under the door until late into the night.

But Kade wasn't on the couch or anywhere in sight. I moved into the kitchen and once again found a fresh pot of coffee and a note: *Gone to the gallery. Will check in later.*

I felt a little too disappointed by his absence. I'd gotten used to him being nearby, sharing every shockwave that hit me, but he had a show to do, and it wasn't fair to keep putting my problems on him. Although, his mother had had an odd relationship with my mom. And if I were being honest, Kade had an odd relationship with her, too. I didn't understand either of those connections—another missing piece in the puzzle that was my mother's life.

It was probably good that Kade was gone. Things had gotten a little heated last night. By forcing me to make some new music, he'd opened up a part of me that hadn't seen the light of day in a while. And the music had unleashed feelings in me that I preferred to keep buried.

That was probably why I'd felt so emotional when he'd come into the room, so on edge when he'd looked at me. I'd felt bare, vulnerable, stripped of my defenses, and somehow, I'd let this stranger in when I was very good at keeping everyone out.

But that was last night, and today was a new day. Nothing had happened between us, mostly because Kade had left the room in a big hurry. Whatever moment we'd had was long over. I needed to go to the hospital to see my mom, check in with my sister, and follow up with the PI, as well as Inspector Greenman. I also still needed to find my father. I wondered if he might show up at the vigil tonight at my mom's school.

The list of things I had to do drove thoughts of Kade out of my head, and I was grateful for that. Unfortunately, they came flying back when I saw a box of freshly baked donuts on the counter.

Damn him. He'd gotten me donuts before he'd left. *Why did he have to be so nice?*

I lifted the lid on the box, and my mouth watered at the sugary glazed, chocolate, and vanilla donuts. Something for everyone. I grabbed a glazed donut and felt immediately soothed by the warm, sugary pastry.

Kade was an interesting mix of toughness and kindness. I felt continually thrown off by him. Just when I finished forming one opinion, he did something that changed that opinion, made me think of him differently. Dani would tell me I was getting too close too fast, and she wouldn't be wrong. As if on cue, my phone vibrated, and Dani's name flashed across the screen. She must have been reading my mind.

"Hi, Dani," I said.

"I'm still waiting for the picture of you at a hotel."

"I'm at the house, but everything was fine last night."

"I knew you weren't going to leave. Was it really fine? I just got off the phone with Vicky. She told me about your conversation, about the video, about her going to San Francisco. Why didn't you call me?"

"It was late. I was going to call you this morning. Did you watch the video?"

"Yes. It was eerie. I can see why Dad has gone off the deep end. He must be confused, heartbroken, and angry," Dani said. "His wife faked her death and left him with two small children. It's not surprising he'd be overwhelmed and need space."

Dani was eager to make excuses for our father. She'd always given him more breaks than I had, but then they'd had a closer bond. I had felt more connected to my mother than him. "Well, whatever the reason for his absence, we need to find him before the police do."

"Jeremy said he's going to make finding him a priority."

"I thought I was working with Jeremy," I said.

"Steve just wanted to check in. With Jeremy on the case, you can come home, Brynn."

"I can't do that, Dani. I need to stay close to Mom. I'm going down to the hospital shortly."

"Are you sure you want to keep seeing her, Brynn? It can't be easy."

"It's not, but that video of her saving that man's life made her seem real again. It made me remember she was a good person. Maybe she still is."

"Is she getting any better?"

"I haven't heard anything different."

"You should give Jeff a call, Brynn. He's worried about you."

I hadn't given Jeff one single thought since I'd seen him on

Thursday, right before the bottom of my world had fallen out. "I can't talk to him now. Tell him I'm busy and when this is all over, we'll have a conversation."

"That doesn't sound promising."

"It's not, Dani. I'm not in love with Jeff. To be honest, I think I've just been dating him as a distraction."

"But you two have fun together."

"He's fine. It just isn't going to be anything."

"You don't have to decide now. You're upset. Jeff is a good guy, someone you can count on."

"We'll talk soon," I said, hanging up before she could sing any more of Jeff's praises. I'd known there was no future with Jeff weeks ago, and I'd just let things drift along, because that's what I'd been doing in every part of my life. That had changed now. I wasn't drifting. I was caught up in a rip current, a current I wasn't sure I could survive. But that current was also bringing out a strength in me I hadn't known I had.

Grabbing my purse and keys, I left Kade's apartment and went upstairs to the main house. Everything was still locked up nice and tight. I took a shower, changed clothes, and then headed to the hospital.

The doctor was with my mother when I arrived, and the nurse asked me to wait until she had completed her examination. I tapped my foot impatiently on the floor as I looked around the hallway. There was still a security guard outside my mom's door, which I was happy to see. But what I really needed to see was some improvement in my mother's condition.

Finally, the door opened, and the doctor came out. Dr. Elizabeth Ryker was an attractive blonde with her hair pulled back in a French braid.

"How is my mother?" I asked.

"Unfortunately, there hasn't been any change," Dr. Ryker

replied. "But she's holding her own."

"Do you have any idea when she'll wake up? Is she still heavily medicated?"

"We have her on pain medication, but it's no longer enough to prevent her from waking up."

"Then why isn't she awake?" I asked in frustration.

"Her body is healing. We should know more within the next forty-eight hours."

"You said that before," I couldn't help pointing out.

"I know it's difficult but try to stay positive. If there's any change, we'll notify you."

"Thanks."

After the doctor left, I entered my mother's room. The nurse had just finished taking some blood. She gave me a smile and then left us alone.

I walked over to the bed and gazed down at my mom once more. It seemed like there was more color in her face. Maybe that was just my imagination.

"I need you to wake up, Mom," I said. "It's Brynn. I'm here. I'm staying at your house. I'm trying to find out who hurt you, but I need your help." I wanted to say I needed her, but that would make me feel too vulnerable. I'd needed her when I was a child, and she'd left me. *Why would it matter now how I felt?* My needs hadn't stopped her from leaving me the first time.

"You owe me," I said instead. "You owe me and Dani answers. Dad, too. We loved you. You can make things better if you wake up, if you talk to us. I can't imagine the truth will be worse than this terrible void of information."

As I finished speaking, I wondered if what I'd just said was true. Maybe the truth would hurt even more.

I put my hand on hers, almost recoiling from the coolness of her skin. My mom had always felt so warm, so safe. I wrapped my fingers around hers. "Your daughters need you," I said. "Come back to us. Please, come back."

I caught my breath, feeling her fingers move, but when I

looked at our hands, they were still. I turned my gaze to the machines keeping track of her vitals, and there was absolutely no change. I must have imagined the movement because I wanted it so badly.

I had to leave. I couldn't stay here and drive myself crazy. The answers weren't coming from my mother. I needed to go out and find them.

I let go of her hand and backed away from her bed. Then I left the room, walking quickly down the hall, sickened by the smells, the fear, and the uncertainty. It was too much.

The elevator took me down to the lobby. I felt immensely relieved when I got outside, and the air hit my face. I walked across the semi-circle drive in front of the building, heading to the parking lot. As I turned the corner and moved across the ramp to get to my car, I heard a sudden squeal of tires. I froze, as a vehicle sped straight toward me.

He wasn't going to stop.

That shocking realization jolted me into action, but I wasn't fast enough. The fender of the car caught me and threw me several feet in the air. I hit the ground hard as a woman screamed and the car raced away.

A man and a woman ran toward me.

"Are you all right?" the woman asked, dropping to her knees beside me.

I was shaking so badly I couldn't answer. I heard the man on the phone with 911. And then others were racing toward me.

They all had the same question: *What happened?*

I heard it asked more than once as I was taken into the hospital. The man and the woman said someone had hit me, that they were speeding, and they didn't stop.

I knew why they hadn't stopped. Because it hadn't been an accident.

The truth hit me harder than the ground I'd landed on. *Someone had tried to kill me. They weren't just after my mother. Now, they were after me.*

CHAPTER SIXTEEN

AFTER GETTING CHECKED out in the ER, it turned out that while I'd scraped both knees and jammed a few fingers when I'd hit the ground, I hadn't broken anything, which was a blessing, considering the alternative. The nurse told me she would have the doctor sign my release and be right back. I was waiting for her when Inspector Greenman came in.

"Ms. Landry. How are you doing?" he asked, concern in his gaze.

"I'll be all right. I just got banged up."

"From what I hear, you were lucky."

"I know."

"We found the car," he said. "It was stolen a few hours ago and abandoned a mile away. Did you see the driver?"

"I think he was wearing a baseball cap, but I didn't have a good look."

"It was definitely a man then?"

I stared back at him, my mind replaying that moment when the car sped toward me. I thought it had been a man, but all I'd really seen was the ball cap. "I don't know," I murmured. "I assumed it was a man."

"Okay."

"It's not okay," I said in frustration. "Someone tried to kill me. And I'm pretty sure it's the same person who shot my mother, so please tell me you've figured something out."

"Your father checked into the Hillcrest Hotel on Nob Hill on Thursday afternoon. He hasn't checked out yet, but he was not in the room when we went to find him."

My heart flipped over. "Oh. I wasn't expecting you to say that."

"There was an open suitcase in the room, so it doesn't appear that he's left town."

I straightened. "Well, my father didn't try to run me over. He wasn't driving that car."

"You're absolutely sure about that?"

"He's my dad," I said, my stomach churning. "Of course, I'm sure. He would never hurt me. He would never hurt my mother. It's someone else." I felt almost desperate to convince him.

"We're not just focused on your father," the inspector reassured me. "But we need to talk to him. You still haven't heard from him?"

I gave a negative shake of my head, then said, "What about my stepmother? Did she tell you anything she didn't tell me?"

"No. She said she'd only speak to me with her lawyer on the call. We've set that up for later today. In the meantime, I've asked patrol to keep an eye on your mother's house. I'll have security escort you to your car when you're ready to leave, but you should watch your back. And you might want to consider leaving the city."

"I'll think about it," I murmured.

"Security will be waiting for you when you're discharged."

"Thank you."

The nurse returned a few minutes later. I signed the release forms and then left the ER with a security guard by my side as I made my way to my car. I didn't take a full breath until I was locked in and driving out of the lot.

It felt marginally better to be back in control. But now what?

I didn't know where to go, what to do. I needed to talk to someone, and the only person I could think of was Kade. I pulled over and called him. He didn't answer his phone. He was probably still at the gallery. I went on the internet and searched for an upcoming show by artist Kade Beckham. I found the name of the gallery and then started the car.

The gallery was only a couple of miles away, and with each passing minute, I questioned what I was doing. Kade was working. I had no right to interrupt that. But I couldn't seem to make myself turn around.

When I arrived at the gallery, I parked in the adjacent lot and then walked toward the front door. On the window was a flyer for Kade's show that would be starting in two weeks, with a special preview in a week. There were samples of his work on the flyer and a short bio about his incredible rise in the art world. This was going to be a big deal for him, and I really didn't need to get in his way.

I was about to turn around when the door opened and Kade walked out.

"Brynn," he said in surprise. "I thought that was you. What are you doing here?"

"I'm not entirely sure," I admitted. "I called you, but you didn't answer."

"Sorry. I was in a meeting with the owner." His gaze narrowed. "What happened?"

His concern brought tears to my eyes. I furiously blinked them away. "I shouldn't have come."

"Hold on," he said, moving closer to me. "What's going on? And don't say nothing."

"Someone tried to run me down when I was leaving the hospital. I'm okay. I just didn't know where to go, what to do next. I shouldn't be here. You're busy."

"Someone tried to run you down?" His gaze swept the street. "Come in. Let's talk inside."

"I don't want to bother you. We can talk later."

"It's fine. I was about to take a break, anyway."

He ushered me into the gallery. There were a few people perusing the main showroom, but Kade moved past them, taking me into a large workroom where I could see multiple pieces, one of which had been in his apartment the night before.

"This is what you were working on last night," I said, looking at the sculpture that was a mix of bottles, caps, and wire, with crushed pieces of glass glued to wood. "You got so much done." I paused. "But I don't really know what it is."

"What does it feel like?"

"It feels like someone smashed up a bar in anger."

"What does it make you want to do?"

"Break some glass," I said.

He smiled. "Maybe I'll let you help me do that later."

"I can't think of anything better right now than breaking a few things." I looked back at the piece. "I thought you said you were stuck last night, but you got unstuck."

"Your music helped me figure out what I wanted to do."

"My music?"

"It's a small apartment. It played through me, and it inspired me. I wasn't really thinking about breaking glass in anger, though. I was thinking about how the pieces of glass create a different picture than the bottle. It's like the sum of the parts doesn't always add up to the end result."

He'd gone much deeper than I had. "So, you can make lots of different things with the same pieces," I murmured.

"Exactly. Kind of like life."

"You really are talented, Kade, and a deep thinker."

"You're talented, too. But you're also guarded. You didn't show me who you were until you played."

He was right. "It's where I feel the safest." I drew in a breath. "But then the music stops, and there's no more safety, especially now."

"Did you talk to the police about what happened?"

"Yes. Inspector Greenman came to the hospital. They found

the car. It had been stolen and abandoned, so I doubt they can trace it to anyone. It feels like another dead end. Whoever is doing this is smart."

Kade put his hands on my shoulders and looked into my eyes. "You're sounding hopeless, Brynn."

"I feel that way," I whispered. "Inspector Greenman found my father's hotel room. He wasn't there, but his clothes were. My dad is definitely in San Francisco. But he's not calling me back, and that can't be good." I ran a hand through my hair as I drew in a ragged breath. "I'm sorry. You need to get back to work, and I need to...I don't know—do something else."

"Let's go," he said.

"Where?" I asked in surprise.

"Out of here."

"You have to work."

"Like I said, I could use a break. Come on."

As Kade led me to the back door, I said, "My car is out front."

"Let's take my bike."

"Really? A motorcycle?" I asked doubtfully.

"It will be fun. You could use some wind in your face. It will help you clear your head." He led me into the back alley and then handed me a helmet. "You'll be safe, Brynn."

I wasn't sure about that but being with Kade felt better than being alone. "Where are we going?"

"Wherever the road takes us."

"That's all you're going to tell me?"

His smile was his only answer, and it sent butterflies through my stomach. I was probably making a mistake, but I wanted to escape, and he was offering me a ride. *How could I say no?*

The road took us across the Golden Gate Bridge and up through the North Bay cities of Sausalito, Mill Valley, and San Rafael. I had never ridden on the back of a motorcycle, and it took me about twenty minutes to loosen my death grip on Kade, but gradually I began to relax, especially as the traffic thinned out.

Kade got off the highway when we hit the Sonoma wine country, driving us down lonesome roads lined with vineyards and ranch houses. With the wind at my back and the sun heating my face, I felt my stress ease, and I started to enjoy the ride. I loved the feel of the bike and Kade's body so close to mine. I had never ever imagined that riding a motorcycle could be so hot, but it wasn't just the bike, it was the man who was driving it. With my arms wrapped around him, I could feel the muscles in his abs, the power in his body, and I felt not only safe but also charged up. I thought I could ride like this forever. I could forget about everything that we'd left behind us.

But as the afternoon shadows lengthened, Kade got back on the highway, and headed south toward the city. As we neared San Francisco, I felt tense again. I was dreading what I had to go back to, all the secrets I still had to unravel, the danger I had to avoid. So when Kade took the exit right before the Golden Gate Bridge, I was happy to put reality off for a few more minutes.

He drove up into the hills and parked the bike in a small lot. As I got off the motorcycle, I took off my helmet and shook out my hair. Kade did the same, giving me a questioning smile. "Fun?"

"More fun than I've had in a long time," I said. "I thought you were taking me back to the gallery."

"I am taking you back, but not yet. This is the best view of the city. Have you seen it from these headlands?"

I shook my head. "No."

"Come with me."

I didn't think I could ever not go with him. He was a magnet, and I was caught up in his pull. Or maybe I just wanted to be caught up, so I didn't have to choose to do something else, something that would be a lot less fun.

We walked down a sloping hill just above the bridge. Kade was right. The view was magnificent. The city was directly in front of us. Off to our right was the Pacific Ocean where a thick bank of fog was making its almost daily entrance into the bay. Off to our left was Alcatraz, the once famous prison, and Angel Island. In the distance was the Bay Bridge leading over to the East Bay.

"What do you think?" Kade asked.

"It's stunning." I shivered as the wind lifted my hair and the fog grew thicker as it blotted out the sun. "But this also feels like a metaphor for my life. Everything was so clear a minute ago, and now it's hazy. What I could see before is now disappearing into the mist."

Kade nodded, digging his hands into the pockets of his jeans. "I can relate to that feeling. I talked to my mother again," he said, surprising me with his words. His gaze moved from the view to me, and there was an unhappy light in his eyes.

"What did she say?"

"She wasn't completely honest with me on the phone yesterday. After she sent the money back to the foundation, she got a call from a woman who said that she'd received the money but wanted to make sure that we would be all right without it. My mother told the woman that she'd taken the money for too long, but that it had been a lifesaver, and she was grateful. It had helped her pay for me to go to college."

"You went to college?" I asked, surprised by that.

"For two years. It wasn't for me. But that's not the point."

"Was the woman's name Laura?"

"My mother thought the woman's name was Claire."

"Claire? That's a new one. Unless it wasn't my mother who called her."

"I feel certain it was Laura. My mom told her I was an artist. She mentioned that I had an upcoming show in Seattle."

"And then my mother went to your show. Why? Why was she so interested in you?" I asked.

"I don't know. I asked my mother flat out if I was adopted. I told her she had to tell me the truth. She said I was not adopted.

I was her son. She didn't know why the woman was so interested in me, but she thought it might have had something to do with the way my father died."

"The way he died? How did he die?" I had assumed it was an accident or an illness that had taken Kade's father.

"He was killed."

"You didn't say that before."

"It's not a secret," Kade said with a frown. "I wasn't trying to hide anything."

"What exactly happened?"

"My father was a security guard. That night, he worked a party at a mansion on Long Island, the home of a very wealthy man who was a real-estate investor and well-known art collector. All was well during the party, but afterward, my father was making one last sweep through the home when he interrupted a robbery in progress. He was shot, and he died in that house in the middle of the night. A house manager found him the next morning."

Kade's voice was stoic, but I could feel the fire burning within him. Now I knew where the rage and dark nightmares came from.

"I'm so sorry, Kade."

"I don't remember anyone telling me he was dead," Kade continued. "I'm sure my mom said something to me, but I was only four. It bothers me that I don't remember that night. That there was a specific point where my life went from good to bad."

"You're lucky, Kade. I remember the exact moment that everything in my life changed. I remember the rain on the windows, my sister and I playing when we were supposed to be asleep, the phone ringing, my dad's hushed voice, and then his yell of disbelief. I'd never been so scared in my life."

"That's rough."

"We didn't know right away that she was dead. It took a week before they were sure, but I knew in my heart that my mom was gone, even if I didn't want to admit it. That night haunts me as well as the night my dad finally told us she was gone, that she'd gone to heaven." I swallowed a knot of emotion. "But getting back to you. Did the police ever figure out who killed your dad?"

"No, and I don't think they ever will. My mom made her peace with it. I've tried to do that by painting every negative thought that moves through my head. That works for a while. But then the anger comes back."

"Would it make a difference if you knew who had done it?"

"No, but it would make a difference if there was justice, if they had to pay for what they did."

I thought about that, remembering what else he'd said. "You suggested that my mom was interested in you because of the way your dad died. Why? I don't see the connection."

"My mother said that the woman she spoke to told her that she wasn't a stranger to violence, that it was always the kids that suffered the most, the innocent children. She was making it her life's work to help children who were affected by violence."

"That makes no sense. She didn't have a history marred by violence."

Kade gave me a long, pointed look.

"I don't really know, do I?" I said with a sigh. "She could have had violence in her past, long before she married my dad."

"Or while she was married to your father."

"That's difficult to believe, but I have to stop defending what I don't know. I have to find out the truth." I looked out at the city, now barely visible through the fog. "There's an answer somewhere."

"There might be an answer, but there's also danger," he reminded me. "Someone tried to run you down. If you continue to ask questions, they'll keep coming after you. You can leave now, go back to your life, the life you were living before your mother came out of the shadows. You don't owe her anything."

"Even though she left me, she's still my mother. She gave me life. I have to find out who she is—if she's a victim of violence or if she's a horrible, evil person."

"The truth is probably somewhere in between. It may not bring you peace."

I looked into his eyes. "If you could find out what happened to your dad, would you do it?"

"I've tried to find out. I've never gotten anywhere. The case is a dead end."

"And if you got a clue?"

"I'd chase it down until I hit a brick wall," he admitted. "Even then, I might try to crash through that wall. But there might be a big cost."

"I know I'm taking a risk, Kade. But I can't stop, not yet. There's a vigil tonight at my mom's school. I said I would go, and I want to do that. I don't know if it will provide a clue to who shot her, but it might tell me more about her life, and I'm hungry for those clues as well. Maybe I won't find out who tried to kill her, but I need to at least know who she is."

He nodded. "I get it. I admire your persistence, Brynn. You're a lot braver than you think you are."

"Thank you for this afternoon. For taking me away for a little while. I never thought I'd enjoy riding a motorcycle. I thought I'd be too scared, but it was wonderful. I enjoyed it."

"When you weren't holding on to me in sheer terror," he teased.

"I got better," I said defensively.

"You did. You definitely eased up your grip on me. Not that I was complaining about you holding on to me so tightly."

A light simmered in his gaze now, the one that made my stomach do a little dance every time it appeared. I needed to ignore it. At least, for now.

Kade cleared his throat, as if he'd come to the same conclusion. "I'll take you back. And I'll help you find the truth, Brynn. You were right when you said your mom has an unusual attachment to me. That keeps gnawing at me, and I need to understand why Laura made a choice to meet me after my mother turned the money away. Laura was eager to encourage me, to support my art, to get me this showing. I need to know what was motivating her to do that. And I hope..." His voice drifted away as his gaze moved back to the city view.

"What do you hope?" I asked, worried about the change in his demeanor. He'd stiffened, lost his teasing smile.

"That we don't end up on opposite sides," he said finally, looking back at me.

I knew what he was thinking, but I didn't want to accept it. "She couldn't have had anything to do with your father's death," I said. "It was a robbery on Long Island. She was living on the other side of the country."

"Maybe she was. Maybe she wasn't. I hope she didn't have anything to do with what happened to him, because I like your mother. Or I did. I'm not sure how I feel about her now."

"I wish she'd wake up so she could tell us what's going on."

"I hope that happens. Until it does, we're on our own."

"On our own together," I said, wanting to keep him on my team as long as possible.

CHAPTER SEVENTEEN

AFTER WE GOT BACK to the gallery, Kade walked me to my car and told me he needed to wrap up a few things before he went back to the house. As I drove home alone, the fog had thickened, adding an eerie atmosphere to the darkening day. I'd felt safe with Kade on his bike, riding up the coast, leaving all my worries behind, but they were back now.

I pulled into the driveway behind Kade's truck and ran up the steps to the front door. My hand shook as I put the key into the lock, but I got inside without any problems and immediately turned the dead bolt. I moved through the rest of the house, feeling completely on edge, but there was no one there, and nothing had changed in the hours since I'd left. I let out a breath of relief.

My hand was aching a little, my fingers still swollen from my fall, and I was feeling a soreness in my knees, back, and hip, more reminders of what had happened in the hospital parking lot. But I'd survived, and I'd be more careful in the future.

I sat down on the couch in the family room and propped my feet up on the coffee table. I'd no sooner taken a deep breath when my phone rang. I groaned as I saw Dani's name, but not answering wasn't an option.

"Hi," I said wearily.

"You don't sound good, Brynn."

"Just tired."

"What's going on? You haven't called me in hours."

I didn't want to tell her about the hit-and-run. It was too upsetting to talk about. "Dad has a hotel room here in San Francisco. The police went by, but he wasn't there."

"I know. Vicky told me. She just spoke to the police."

"What else did she say?"

"She said the police are trying to frame Dad for Mom's attack."

"Which is why Dad needs to call someone back," I said in frustration. "He could be in serious trouble, Dani."

"I know. I keep calling, but he doesn't answer." Dani blew out a breath. "Did you see Mom? How was she?"

"The same. No change. I talked to her, but she didn't respond."

"Did you tell her you love her no matter what she did?"

I could hear the edge of anger in her voice, and it bothered me. Dani and I didn't fight that much, mostly because I usually went along with her plans, but it was also because we'd always been on the same side. Now, our mother was putting a wedge between us. "I told her I needed her to wake up and talk to me. That she owed that to us."

"She owes us more than she can ever repay."

"That's true," I murmured.

"I think Dad found out Mom was alive, and he fell apart. That's why he's not talking to any of us."

"I don't know if that's why," I said slowly, the doubts about my father growing more with each minute that he stayed away.

"It is," Dani said confidently. "You remember how he got when Mom died. He couldn't talk to anyone. At the funeral, he disappeared halfway through the reception. He drove up to the cabin and didn't come back for two weeks. He doesn't like to be with anyone when he feels weak."

"He likes to disappear, doesn't he? When things get rough, he's nowhere to be found."

"But he always comes back."

"He better come back soon," I said heavily.

"What are you doing tonight?" Dani asked. "Can I at least persuade you to finally go to a hotel?"

"I'm going to the concert at Mom's school tonight. They're going to have a vigil for her before it starts. The principal thought it would be nice for me to be there."

"I guess you can't get into too much trouble at a high school concert. But I hate that you're alone."

"Kade is going with me." I steeled myself for Dani's negative reaction.

What I got was a big sigh. "What are you doing, Brynn?"

"You know what I'm doing."

"You like this guy too much. It's weird that he's letting himself be supported by Mom. It's weird that he's living downstairs. We don't really know what their relationship is."

"They weren't sleeping together," I said.

"I wouldn't believe anything he says."

"Mom has a connection to him, but it's not about sex."

"Then what is it about?" Dani asked.

"Well, it turns out that Mom was working with a charity group that was looking out for kids who had been hurt by violence. Kade's father was killed in a robbery, and Mom was sending money to his mother all these years through that group. Kade knew nothing about it until we found the information last night. He thought she just loved art. She never told him about the charity or the donations to his mom, nothing."

"That's a bizarre story," Dani said. "Are you sure it's true?"

"I found the evidence. Kade didn't come up with this story. He's as shocked as we are about it. Now, he's questioning everything he knows about Mom."

"Well, he can join the club. Our mother had a lot of secrets, Brynn. I don't think we ever knew her."

"I don't think we did either. But I'm going to find out who she is now. On another note, how are you feeling? How's the baby doing?"

"All is well. I just feel guilty that I'm not with you. Whenever I bring it up, Steve shuts me down. He doesn't want me to take any risks."

"He's right. You should stay put." I inwardly shuddered at the idea of someone going after Dani the way they'd gone after me today. "You keep my nephew safe."

"I will. Be careful, Brynn. And come home as soon as you can."

"I will be exceptionally careful. I'll call you tomorrow." I ended the call and then went upstairs to change my clothes. I put on a pair of black slacks and a silver sweater, thankful I'd tossed something into my suitcase other than jeans. Not that the school concert would be fancy, but I wanted to honor my mother at the vigil.

At a quarter to six, Kade texted me that he was on the porch and didn't want to scare me by ringing the bell. I smiled to myself, thinking that he was already starting to know me a little too well. I hurried down the stairs to answer the door.

Kade had changed clothes, too, wearing black jeans and a dark-brown leather jacket over a black shirt. His hair was still damp, and he smelled really good, but I wasn't going to think about that. "I'm ready to go," I said.

"Good. You want to go on the bike, or…"

"I'll drive. I just got the wind out of my hair."

"I liked the wind in your hair," he said, his gaze sweeping across my face and down my body. "But this is a good look, too."

"Thanks," I said, feeling suddenly nervous. I'd slept in the man's bed the night before, but this moment felt even more intimate. I grabbed my bag from the table by the door. "We should go."

"Let's do it."

We walked out to my car, and I was happy to have Kade by my side. I felt like there were eyes on me everywhere I went.

The vigil was just getting started when we arrived. There was a sizable crowd, probably over a hundred people. Two local news stations had parked their vans in front of the school, with their spotlights on the gathering.

We walked over to a table where the principal, Joanne Hunt, was handing out candles. She smiled when she saw me.

"Ms. Landry, I'm so glad you came."

"It's much bigger than I thought it would be," I replied.

"The concert usually draws a big crowd, and your mother has been such a big part of it that everyone wanted to come early to participate in the vigil. We'd love for you to say a few words."

"Oh, I don't know," I said, flustered by that idea.

"It would mean so much to the kids to hear from Laura's daughter. Please."

"Uh, all right."

"Good. We're ready to start now." Joanne grabbed my hand and led me to the front of the crowd. She picked up a microphone and asked for attention. As the crowd hushed, she said, "I'd like to thank you all for coming. Laura Hawthorne is a beloved member of our school community. Without her, our concerts would not be as magnificent as they are, and I know we are all praying for her to have a quick recovery." She paused. "We have someone very special here tonight—Laura's daughter, Brynn. She'd like to say a few words."

I heard a murmur float through the crowd at my introduction. I suspected most people had no idea that Laura had a daughter.

Joanne handed me the microphone. I looked over at Kade, who gave me a nod of encouragement. Then I turned to the people who had come out to support my mother. I couldn't see their faces as the news crews had turned up their lights now that I was about to speak, which only made me more nervous. I didn't know who was in the crowd. Maybe the person who'd shot my mother was there. Maybe I was now a huge shining target. I forced myself to breathe. I just had to say a little something and then I'd be done.

"Hello," I said, my voice cracking a little. I cleared my throat. "Thank you for organizing this vigil for my mom. I am touched by how much love she has in her life. I know she is fighting hard to come back to you. Thank you."

I handed the microphone back to Joanne, as my eyes welled with tears. I knew what I'd just said was true. My mom was fighting to come back to them, not to me, and that realization stung.

Kade's arm came around my shoulders, and I was grateful for the support. "That was perfect," he murmured.

I glanced up at him. "They really love her."

He nodded with understanding. "Yes. But don't forget this— the last person she was thinking about when she got to the hospital was you."

I bit down on my lip as his words filled me with emotion. I couldn't speak, so I just nodded and sent him a silent thank-you.

As Joanne announced that the vigil walk around the school would begin, Kade and I moved into the crowd. One of the other teachers lit our candles, and we walked with the kids and parents as several students with flutes and guitars played songs of hope and healing.

The vigil was very moving and made me think about how many people whose lives had been touched by my mom. It also made me wonder why I was here, why I was trying to find out who she was when she'd been so determined to make sure I never found out.

When the walk ended where it had started, Joanne announced that the concert would begin in thirty minutes, and she hoped everyone would attend.

"Ms. Landry, may I speak to you?" a female reporter asked, sticking a microphone in my face, her cameraman right behind her. "Can you tell us what your mother's condition is?"

"She's fighting for her life," I said.

"Do the police know who shot her?"

"No."

"We've heard rumors that your mother may have been involved in a love triangle."

My jaw dropped. "What?"

"When did your mother divorce your father?" the reporter continued. "We haven't found any records about your mother being married."

As she called out more questions, each one more personal and distressing than the last, I backed away.

Kade stepped in front of me. "That's all she has to say." He grabbed my arm and walked me toward the school.

We were almost at the front door to the auditorium when a man approached me. "Are you all right?" he asked, concern on his face.

I looked into his blue eyes, recognizing the man who'd dropped off the flowers—Tom Wells. "I'm okay."

"I heard what that reporter said to you, and it's not true."

"It's not? Because someone mentioned that your ex-wife had a confrontation with my mother."

"It was a conversation, not a confrontation," he said. "Renee was confused. She's had a difficult time since we separated, but I made it clear to her that your mother had nothing to do with our marital problems, which she did not. We didn't go out until after Renee and I had split up."

"Did my mother break up with you after this conversation?" I asked.

Tom nodded. "Yes. She didn't want to have any part in what-ever was going on between Renee and myself. It was very sad. I really cared about her, but I understood why she felt we needed time and space for things to settle down." He paused. "I thought they had quieted down, but I suspect Renee is the one who told that reporter that we were in a love triangle. She used to be a news producer, and she still has contacts in the industry."

"Well, that's great," I said with a sigh.

Tom gave me an apologetic look. "I'm sorry."

"You need to do more than be sorry," I told him. "You need to talk to the police. And so does your ex-wife."

"Renee had nothing to do with what happened to your mother."

Despite his words, I could see a cloud of uncertainty in his gaze. "You're not sure, are you?"

"I am sure. She's a loose cannon, but she's not violent."

"Then you don't have to worry about talking to the police, do you?"

He squared his shoulders. "No, I don't have a problem. I will clear this up."

"Good."

Tom's gaze narrowed on my face. "I have to say that I don't understand why Laura didn't tell me she had a daughter. I thought we'd gotten close. To leave out something so important seems unimaginable."

"She left my life a long time ago," I said.

"We should go inside," Kade interrupted, and I was happy for that. I didn't want to talk to Tom. I was too confused about who he was to my mother and what had happened in their relationship.

"Please talk to the police," I said to Tom. "If you still care about my mother, then you should do everything you can to keep her safe, because the person who shot her might not be done trying to kill her."

Tom's face paled at my words, but he didn't respond.

I turned away as Kade put his hand on my back and ushered me into the auditorium. It was a relief to be inside and away from the reporters. As we waited in line to go to our seats, I turned to Kade. "Do you think it's possible that this love triangle is the motivation for my mother being shot? I've been working under the assumption that the danger came from her distant past, but maybe it didn't."

"I think the police need to look into Tom and his ex-wife."

"I'll follow up with Inspector Greenman after the show."

"And get Jeremy on it, too," Kade said.

"I'll text him when we sit down." As I finished speaking, another one of my mother's male friends came up to me. Mark Harrison wore a black suit with a gray tie, and he looked quite handsome. I could see why my mother might have been interested in him, maybe more than she'd been in Tom. She might not have broken up with Tom because of his ex-wife, but because of this guy.

"Hello," he said, giving me a kind smile. "I don't know if you remember me. We met the other day."

"Yes. You're Mark Harrison."

He nodded. "Your words about your mother were very sweet."

"Thank you." I waved my hand toward Kade. "This is Kade Beckham."

"Nice to meet you," Mark said.

"Likewise," Kade replied as they shook hands.

"Is your stepdaughter in the concert?"

"Yes. Sylvie will play the clarinet tonight. Hopefully, she will sound much better than she does in her mother's house," he said lightly.

"I'm sure she'll be great. Performances usually bring out the best in a musician."

"I hope so. How is your mother? Is she awake yet?"

"Not yet, no."

"That's too bad. But soon?"

"Hopefully. They tell me she's healing and to stay positive." Before I could say anything further, Joanne interrupted us, a look of distress on her face.

"Is something wrong?" I asked.

"Your mother promised one of our students that she would play with her in the concert, and now this girl is backstage, crying. It's a bass and violin duet, and she can't do it without a good violinist. Didn't you tell me you play the violin?"

"I do play the violin, but I hurt my hand earlier." I flexed my fingers at the end of my statement.

"Oh, I didn't know," Joanne said, her gaze drifting to my hand. "But are you sure you couldn't just play this one song? This student lost her mom in an accident a few months ago. The music is the only thing that keeps her going. We don't have anyone else who can play the violin at her level. This girl is gifted. It would mean a lot to your mom if you took her place."

I debated for another second, but Joanne's words tugged at my heartstrings. I wasn't going to do it for my mother; I would do it for another motherless girl who had found an escape in music. "Okay. I'll play. I'll do my best."

Relief flooded Joanne's eyes. "I'm sure your best will be more than enough. I'll take you backstage."

I nodded and turned to Kade. "I'll see you afterward."

"Break a leg," he drawled, a smile of encouragement in his eyes.

"I'd actually prefer if you wished me good luck," I said dryly.

"Good luck."

CHAPTER EIGHTEEN

I FOLLOWED Joanne backstage to find a trembling, sobbing girl who was so thin it looked like a strong wind would blow her over. Standing next to her was a double bass that was almost as tall as she was.

"Mila, this is Brynn," Joanne said. "Laura's daughter."

"I know," Mila said with a sniff. "I heard you outside."

"Joanne said you don't want to play your duet, Mila," I said.

"There's no one who can play with me," she replied. "I was only going to do it because Ms. Hawthorne said she'd be there with me."

I moved closer to Mila as Joanne faded into the background. "What grade are you in?"

"I'm a sophomore."

"How long have you been playing?"

"A couple of years. My mom used to play the bass. She taught me how to play, but she died, and I don't know why I keep playing, because she can't hear me anymore."

"I used to think the same thing."

Mila gave me a confused look. "But your mom is alive."

"She is," I said, not wanting to confuse the girl. "She taught me to play the violin, and I would love to play the duet with you, if you'd let me. I know my mother would want you to take the stage. What song were you going to play?"

"Autumn from *The Four Seasons*."

"One of my favorite pieces by Vivaldi. I think we'd make a great team, Mila."

"Are you…good?" Mila asked hesitantly.

I smiled. "I'm pretty good."

"Okay, I guess."

That was one problem solved, but I realized I had another. "I need a violin."

"The one your mom was going to use is in the music room. I'll get it."

As Mila left, I peeked through the curtains and saw the first group taking the stage, a trio of saxophone players. As the brassy music lit up the auditorium, I realized how talented they were. This high school for the arts was filled with gifted kids. Mila was one of them. I didn't want to let her down. And I wouldn't, I told myself firmly. I knew the piece she was going to play very well. It was going to be beautiful.

———

Twenty minutes later, after warming up backstage, Mila and I waited to be introduced. When I looked over at Mila and saw the panic in her eyes, I quickly reassured her. "You'll be fine, Mila."

"There are so many people out there."

"You're not playing for them; you're playing for you. That's all you have to think about."

"That's what your mom always says."

My gut clenched at that remark. Maybe my mom and I were still alike in ways that mattered. "My mother taught you well. You're ready."

"I hope so," she muttered.

We walked out to enthusiastic applause and took our places

on the stage. We looked at each other and locked into the moment. Then we began to play.

Mila's first few notes were shaky, but as I accompanied her, she got stronger, gained confidence and trusted herself and me. I loved watching her blossom right in front of me, and I wanted to do everything I could to make this moment special, to help her take her music to the highest point it could go. My energy inspired hers, and our playing was filled with passion, the melody flowing through our minds, our bodies, and our fingers.

Our performance ended with a crescendo and then abrupt silence.

We smiled at each other and then the applause came, with people jumping to their feet and clapping as hard as they could.

I urged Mila to take a step forward, and she shyly did that, basking in the glow of her achievement. Then we walked off the stage together.

As soon as we put our instruments down, she threw her arms around me and gave me a tight hug. "Thank you," she said. "That was the best I've ever played."

"Me, too. You were terrific, Mila. My mother will be so proud of you when she hears about this."

"And proud of you, too."

Her words put a knot in my throat. I'd often thought about my mother when I played, thinking she was up in heaven watching me make music and feeling proud of me. But she hadn't been in heaven; she hadn't been watching over me at all. She'd been focused on other kids when she'd had two daughters who had been left with huge holes in their hearts.

Mila turned away as her dad came backstage to congratulate her. I let out a breath, relieved that it had all gone well. The concert had three more acts, and I could go out front and watch them, but I felt emotionally drained after the performance, so I headed for the nearby stage door and stepped outside.

There were two girls in the quad, practicing a song.

I moved a few feet away and leaned against the wall. The fog had broken over this part of the city, and a few stars were peeking through. It was cold, but I didn't feel it. I was still coming off the heated high of the performance. It had all been for Mila, but I had to admit it had felt good being on the stage.

While I'd played in local, community concerts off and on for most of my life, it had been more than a year since I'd performed, and I'd loved every second of it tonight. Which reminded me that my future was going to contain a lot more nights like these. I had one more day before I needed to get back to Ray with my decision. Twenty-four hours to resolve all the problems in my life seemed overly optimistic, but I would like to have a few more questions answered before I committed to the job. Not that I could possibly turn it down. I had to say yes. This was the life I needed to have. But to really move on, I also wanted my mom to wake up, to talk to me, to stop lingering in the world between life and death.

Although, in some ways, she'd been lingering in that space for a long time. She'd killed off her previous life to start another one. She'd become someone else, made new friends, invented a life that had no connection to the past until now. Until her worlds had come crashing together by a gunshot.

So far, I hadn't run into anyone who hated her. On the contrary, everyone loved Laura. She was a great friend, an excellent teacher, someone who inspired others. She'd saved a man's life, too. But someone wanted to kill her. I didn't know if that person came from her past or her present, but I did know that they weren't done. At that reminder, my stomach churned, and goose bumps ran down my arms. My sweater wasn't nearly warm enough now that the adrenaline was wearing off. I also suddenly realized I was alone. The girls had gone inside.

I pushed myself off the wall, turning toward the door to the auditorium when I heard a noise behind me. I started to turn, but I was too slow. Someone grabbed me, one arm going around my neck, as a smelly towel was pressed against my nose and mouth. I struggled, but my assailant was big and strong, and I was feeling faint.

Whatever I was breathing in was making me dizzy. My limbs felt heavy. When he dragged me across the ground, I tried to kick and to scream but nothing was working. I almost felt paralyzed. I'd been so stupid to go outside by myself.

I heard a car door open. He was going to push me inside and take me away. Once I got in that car, no one would find me. From somewhere down deep inside, I found the strength to kick out at him. He grunted and lost his grip for a second. I tried to scramble away, but I couldn't get anywhere.

Through the recesses of my mind, I heard a shout. The man tried to pick me up. I made myself as heavy as I could. And then someone came up behind him, and he let me go. My head hit the ground as I was finally released from his grasp.

I tried to roll away, but I could barely move. Each new breath was a struggle, a fight to stay awake. Through my blurry gaze, I realized there were two men now, and they were fighting.

Kade slammed the guy against the car, so hard the glass shattered, raining down all over me.

And then there was a scream, more shouts, people rushing toward us. Their faces swam before me. They were asking me questions, but I couldn't make out the words. And then Kade barreled through the crowd surrounding me, his dark hair falling over one eye, a darkening bruise on his face.

"Are you all right?" he asked.

"Think so," I said, still having trouble focusing. "Is he dead?"

"No. I just knocked him out," Kade said. "Did he drug you?"

"Smelled something."

I saw Kade grab something white off the ground. "Don't worry," he told me. "It will wear off. You'll be okay."

I heard sirens as I fought to keep my eyes open. Minutes later, the police arrived, along with an ambulance. The EMTs strapped me onto a stretcher. "Kade," I said, not wanting to be alone again.

"I'll meet you at the hospital. I have to talk to the police. You'll be safe."

"I don't trust anyone but you."

"Then trust me." He gazed into my eyes. "They're just going to take you to the hospital and get you checked out. I'll see you soon."

I hoped he wasn't lying, but his face was blocked by the EMT and then they loaded me into the ambulance. I closed my eyes, tired of the struggle. I really hoped I was safe because I couldn't stay awake any longer.

After a blurry ride to the hospital, I was taken to the ER and put through a series of tests by a young male doctor, with a reassuring older nurse standing nearby. With each passing minute, my mind became clearer, allowing me to answer questions to the doctor's satisfaction. At the end of the exam, I was told I had a mild bump on the back of my head but no evidence of a concussion. The effects of the drug I'd inhaled would be short-lasting, and I should feel better by the morning.

As the doctor and nurse left to get my release papers ready, Inspector Greenman and Kade entered the room.

"We have to stop meeting like this," I said.

He gave me a brief, tense smile. "I agree. How are you feeling, Ms. Landry?"

"I'll feel better if you have the guy who attacked me in custody."

"We do. Thanks to Mr. Beckham. The man's name is JR Beatty. He's muscle for hire, takes assignments off a dark web app. Said he was paid two thousand dollars to try to run you over earlier today. He was then paid another five thousand to grab you tonight. He was supposed to drive you to Golden Gate Park and drop you off by the windmill. He claims he has no idea what was supposed to happen to you next."

My stomach turned over at the thought of being dumped in the park, unconscious and helpless. "Who hired him?"

"He doesn't know anything other than the name on the app, which was Jerdog27. We're getting into it."

"Did he shoot my mother, too?"

"He says no," the inspector replied. "We'll continue our interrogation when he's done getting his face stitched up."

"It feels like another dead end," I said wearily.

"No. This is a good lead. We'll find out who hired him. Did he say anything to you?"

"Not one word."

"All right. I'll be in touch when we know more. Try to stay out of trouble for at least the rest of the night."

"I will do my best."

As Inspector Greenman left, Kade moved forward, putting his hand on my arm. "How are you really feeling?" His gaze searched mine for the truth.

"Achy, tired, terrified."

"That sounds about right."

I looked back at him, noting his swollen left eye and the purple bruise on his cheek. "You're hurt."

"It's nothing. The other guy looks worse than me."

"It's not nothing. You saved my life, Kade. How did you know I was in trouble?"

"I had a bad feeling when you didn't come back after your performance. I went backstage and someone told me they saw you go outside. When I went through the door, I saw him trying to put you into a car." His lips tightened. "I'm glad I got there in time."

"Another few minutes, and you wouldn't have. I was trying to fight, but whatever he made me breathe made me so weak. I tried to kick him."

"I saw that. You distracted him enough that he didn't see me coming. We make a good team."

"You shouldn't be on my team. I'm trouble. And when you're with me, you're in trouble, too."

"I've been in trouble before. You don't need to worry about me." He paused. "So, do you have to stay here?"

"No. They're going to discharge me. I should be fine by morning. Will you take me home?"

"That's good to hear. We'll stay together in the house tonight. I won't let anyone get to you."

"I don't know why you're sticking around, Kade."

"I want to find out the truth about your mother, and we're getting closer."

"Why on earth would you think that? Every lead ends in nothing."

"Not this one. The police have a man in custody. They'll find his employer."

I shook my head in bemusement. "When did you get to be optimistic?"

"Someone needs to think positive. As difficult as this whole night was, the police have someone to talk to now, and a trail to follow. That's more than they had before."

"Well, I'm happy to help by almost getting kidnapped," I said dryly.

He smiled. "I'm glad you can joke about it."

"I'm trying to stay in the light," I said. I didn't think I could function if I let myself think about how bad things could have gone.

The door opened and the nurse walked in. "I have your discharge papers if you're ready to go. However, we strongly suggest that you have someone stay with you tonight, until you get your feet back under you."

"I'll stay with her," Kade said.

"Good."

For the second time that day, I checked myself out of the ER. But this time when we went into the parking lot, Kade was right next to me. He got me into the passenger seat and then slid behind the wheel.

When we got back to my mom's house, it was almost eleven. The street was very quiet, and the house was dark, but as we walked up the steps, I froze, seeing a man in the chair on the porch.

As the man stood up, Kade rushed past me and threw him up against the wall.

"Who are you? What are you doing here?" Kade demanded, giving the man a hard shake.

That's when I saw the man's face for the first time. "Stop," I said, shocked once more.

Kade threw me a questioning look. "Do you know him?"

"Yes. He's my father."

CHAPTER NINETEEN

KADE IMMEDIATELY LET my dad go. "Sorry," he muttered.

My father gave me a bleary look. "Is that you, Brynn?"

As I moved closer, I was overwhelmed by the smell of alcohol. "Are you drunk?" I asked in surprise.

My dad never drank more than two glasses of wine. He always had a hard limit on alcohol, but tonight he was wasted. His slacks were wrinkled, his shirt untucked and stained. He didn't appear to have shaved in several days, a white grizzly beard covering his jaw. His eyes were red and puffy, his skin pale, and he seemed to be having trouble staying on his feet and keeping his eyes open.

"Let's go in the house," I said, taking the keys from Kade. "Can you help him?"

"I think that's the only way we're getting him inside," Kade replied.

I opened the door and stepped back as Kade put my dad's arm around his shoulders and then helped him into the living room. He got him as far as the couch and then my dad fell back against the cushions.

"I'll make some coffee," Kade said.

I sat down on the sofa next to my father. "Dad, where have you been?"

He gave me a bemused look. "This is her house, isn't it?"

"Yes."

His gaze moved around the room, and he frowned. "It's a mess."

"Someone broke in here and trashed it. I put it back together as best I could." I licked my lips. "When did you find out Mom was alive?"

"Last week," he bit out. "I couldn't believe she faked her death. She betrayed me. She betrayed you and Dani. She left us. She made us grieve for her. I hate her." He paused, then gave a helpless shake of his head. "I want to hate her."

"I know." I completely understood his conflicted feelings. I put my hand on his arm. "It's hard to hate someone you used to love."

"Love," he spat out. "I don't think she ever loved me. She just used me. That's all it was. I thought we had this great love affair, that we'd be together forever. I was a fool—stupider than I've ever been in my life."

"Did you see her before she got shot?" I asked, wanting to know more about the last week than the more distant past.

"I saw her."

"What did she say?" I prodded.

He stared back at me and then blinked a few times, as if he could barely stay awake.

"Dad, what did she say?"

"Said she was sorry." He shook his head in frustration and anger. "Like that makes any difference. I don't care if she's sorry. I'm sorry. I'm sorry I ever met her."

"Where have you been, Dad? Why haven't you called anyone back?"

"I didn't know what to say. I needed to think, but everything I thought just made me furious. So, I decided to stop thinking and start drinking. But then, I saw you on the news tonight. I was in a bar and there you were. You were talking about your mom, acting like she was still in your life. It didn't make sense. I came to find you, to tell you that you're not making sense."

"You're the one who isn't making sense," I said wearily. "You're drunk."

"She's not good. Not good at all, Brynn."

"You need to sober up. I'm going to check on that coffee." I got to my feet and headed toward the kitchen. Kade met me in the hallway, a mug in his hand.

"Thank you," I said. "He's rambling on and on. I can't make much sense out of him."

"Hopefully, the coffee will help."

I took the coffee and headed back into the living room, only to find my dad had stretched out on the couch and was fast asleep, his breathing heavy. "Dad," I said.

He didn't move.

"I think he's out for the night," Kade said.

"It looks that way." I set down the coffee mug and grabbed a blanket from a nearby chair and put it over him. As I stared at him, I felt like he was a stranger, too. Not in the same way my mom was. But he had never looked like this before, and he'd certainly never acted so out of control. Hopefully, in the morning, he'd be back to a version of himself that I recognized.

I followed Kade into the kitchen, taking the coffee with me. I didn't usually drink caffeine this late at night, but one sip made my head feel clearer, so I took another.

"There's leftover pizza," Kade said, reaching into the fridge. "Hungry?"

"Not really."

"You should try to eat something. There are still cookies."

"Maybe I'll try one slice of the pizza," I said.

"I'll heat it up for you."

I slid onto a stool by the counter. "You're being so nice to me, Kade."

"You've had a rough night."

"You, too," I said, noting that the bruising on his face had only gotten darker. "Maybe you should put some ice on your eye."

"Don't worry about me."

"Does anyone worry about you?" I asked curiously.

"I hope not," he said, as he heated up the pizza in the microwave.

"That's a vague answer."

"Do you want to make your question more specific?" he countered.

"All right. Do you have someone in your life besides your mother who you care about, who cares about you?"

"I have plenty of friends, just not in San Francisco. But I don't have a girlfriend or a wife, if that's what you're asking. What about you? Do you have a significant other?"

"I've been dating someone for a few weeks, but to be honest, I've just been using him as a distraction, which isn't fair to him. I need to end that when I get back."

"Why didn't he come with you?"

"I didn't ask him to. In fact, I told him not to. He's best friends with my sister's husband, so it's a little complicated."

"Did your sister fix you up?"

"She threw us together a lot. There's nothing wrong with Jeff. He's a nice guy."

"Just not the guy for you."

"No. He would be another Dani in my life, warning me not to try anything too different, not to reach too high. It's fine coming from my sister, but I don't need someone else telling me what not to do. I need someone who pushes me outside of my comfort zone." I didn't want to say I needed someone like him, but the idea had crossed my mind.

Kade took the plate out of the microwave and put it in front of me, then slid the remaining slices onto another plate to heat up for himself.

"It sounds like you need to let him go," Kade said, folding his arms as he leaned back against the opposite counter and gave me a thoughtful look.

"I'm going to do that when this is all over." Seeing the contemplative expression on his face, I said, "What are you thinking about?"

"Just wondering what it would have been like to grow up with a twin, someone who looked exactly like me, who made me feel like I was part of a duo instead of a single."

"Dani didn't make me feel that way. It's just a fact. Twins are together before birth and forever after that. It's a bond that's impossible to describe to anyone who hasn't experienced it. It's like I can feel her in my heart, and the same goes for her." As I finished speaking, I took a bite of pizza. I was relieved that it tasted normal and drove away the metallic taste that had been lingering in my mouth since I'd been drugged.

"But you and your sister are different people," Kade said.

"Yes, and that's where it gets tricky. Because it's easier to be the same. People expected us to be the same. Dani was good in math, and the math teacher had high expectations for me that I could not meet. Same thing for music, but in reverse. Because I played an instrument, everyone thought Dani should, but she had no talent or interest in music."

"What about your dad?" he asked, as the microwave began to beep. "What was his relationship with you both?"

I thought about his question while I finished chewing. "It's not easy to answer that. When we were young, before my mom died, I thought we were all close. After my mother died, my dad withdrew from Dani and me. It started the day of my mother's funeral when he disappeared and didn't come back for two weeks. After that, he couldn't seem to tell us apart, which we both found annoying. Even now, when I call him on the phone, he gets irritated if I don't say who I am right away. I guess we do sound alike, but my mom could always tell us apart."

"Where did he go when he disappeared during the funeral?"

Kade asked, his brows drawing together as he gave me a questioning look.

"He drove up to a cabin we had in Big Bear. A neighbor took us in until he came home."

"That seems odd. He should have been comforting you, not running away from you."

"That's what I always thought. When he came back, he hired a nanny to take care of Dani and me and buried himself in work. He made sure we had everything we needed, and he'd occasionally show up for an open house at school or a soccer game. But he also missed a lot, and we stopped expecting him to show up. Then he married Vicky, and it was all about her and their life."

"It doesn't sound like you were close at all."

"Dani was closer to him than I was. She usually leans into whatever he has to say. I talked to her earlier, and she was defending him for not getting back to us without even knowing why he was out of touch. She wanted to give him the benefit of the doubt. Now that he's shown up drunk and a mess, I probably should cut him some slack, too. He was clearly shocked to find out my mother was alive."

"Your father said he talked to Laura, that she said she was sorry. I wonder when that happened. There's no video footage of him here at the house."

"That's true. Only Vicky was caught on camera. Maybe it was at the school. I thought I saw him there on Friday when I went by. But my mother was already in the hospital by then, so why would he have been at the school that day?"

"You'll have to ask him."

"When he wakes up," I agreed.

"You said your father isn't a man with a lot of rage, but when he said your mother betrayed him, the anger was burning right through him."

I met his gaze, seeing the question in his dark eyes. "He didn't shoot her, Kade."

"I hope not."

"He loved her."

"Love and hate can be two sides of the same coin."

"Even if he hates her, and maybe he has a right to hate her, I know he wouldn't hurt her. He just wouldn't. I'm sure of that."

"You know him best."

I let out a sigh, knowing I didn't know my dad the best. That was Dani or Vicky, but neither of them was here. I wiped my mouth with my napkin. "Thanks for the pizza and the coffee. I feel better."

"I'm glad."

"I don't remember everything that happened after you saved me. There were a lot of people around, weren't there? I hope the kids weren't scared."

"The parents kept the kids back."

"That's good."

"By the way, your performance tonight on the stage was incredible."

"I just wanted to do everything I could to make Mila shine. She is very talented. And she loves my mom so much. My mother inspired her to play even when she felt too sad." I shook my head. "It makes me think again how kind and generous my mom is to other people."

"But where was she when you were sad?" he asked.

"Exactly. How could she never look back?" I sighed. "You don't have to say anything. Only my mom can answer that question." I paused. "I went outside tonight because I was feeling emotional after the performance. I should have stayed more alert. I don't know what I was thinking."

"It's hard to keep your guard up every second."

"It could have gotten really bad for me tonight. God knows what was going to happen to me in that park."

"You're not thinking about that, remember?"

"Maybe I should. Isn't it cathartic to face your fears?"

"You might need time before you can do that. It's too fresh."

"Who knows how much time I have before something else

happens? This isn't over, Kade. The police have the guy who jumped me, but he's not the one in charge. He didn't shoot my mom. There's someone else out there pulling the strings, like some sick puppeteer. I have no idea what's coming next."

"That's something to worry about tomorrow."

"It's hard to turn off the questions in my head."

"You need to rest, Brynn. Why don't you go upstairs and get some sleep? You'll be safe tonight."

"I'm not sure I'll feel safe until this is over, but I am in your debt, Kade. For everything you've done. I don't know how I can pay you back."

"No payback required."

I slid off the stool. "I'm going to check on my dad before I go upstairs."

He nodded, following me down the hall to the living room.

My father was right where I'd left him, but he'd kicked the blanket off, and it would get colder tonight. I put it back over him.

He rolled onto his side, his eyes flickering open. "Brynn? Or is it Dani?"

"It's Brynn," I said, sitting on the edge of the coffee table. "Are you okay?"

"Where am I?"

"Mom's house."

"Right." His mouth curled into a sneer. "Her house. Her life. I hate her, Brynn. I hate her for what she did."

"Did she tell you why she left you?" I asked.

"She didn't just leave me, she left you," he reminded me. "She left her precious girls. After everything I did to make us a family. She betrayed me."

My gut twisted into a painful knot. "Did she tell you why?"

"Why she left her daughters with a man who wasn't even their father?" he asked. "No, she didn't tell me why. I'm so tired," he said, his eyes closing.

"Dad, wake up," I said, my heart jumping. "What do you mean? Mom left us with you. You're our father."

I shook him by the shoulder, but his eyes remained closed, and a snore escaped his parted lips. My blood was racing once more. I looked over at Kade. "Did you hear what he said?"

"I'm not sure," Kade said carefully.

"He said my mom left me and Dani with a man who wasn't even our father. But he is our dad." I pressed my hands to my suddenly throbbing head. "I had to have heard him wrong. He's drunk. He's confused. He's always been my father. Wake up," I shouted.

"He's out, Brynn," Kade said quietly. "You're not going to get anything out of him tonight." He held out his hand to me, and after a small hesitation, I took it. He pulled me into his arms, and I wrapped my arms around his waist. I rested my head on his chest and closed my eyes, trying to calm my racing heart.

"It's going to be okay," Kade said. "You'll get your answers in the morning."

"I don't think it's going to be okay." Lifting my head, I looked into his eyes. "For the first time since I got here, I don't want the answers. I thought I knew everything about my life, but I knew nothing. If he's not really my dad…"

"He might not have meant it the way it sounded. You'll know more tomorrow."

"That's what I'm afraid of," I whispered.

He shook his head as he gazed at me. "I wish I could say it was going to be all right."

"I wish you could, too. But you can't. It's too much, Kade."

"You need to go to bed, Brynn."

"I won't be able to sleep now."

"Then take the violin with you."

I stared back at him, thinking I'd rather take him with me. But he was already letting go of me, adding a chill to my fevered body. He looked at me, then shook his head, his jaw tight. "Go to bed, Brynn. I'll keep an eye on your dad."

I wrapped my arms around my body, feeling cold without his arms around me. Then I walked down the hall and up the stairs. As I laid down on my mother's bed, my mind started to spin once more, and it wasn't just the drug I'd inhaled making me dizzy, it was everything else in my life. Maybe Dani was right. I should have gone home before I'd gotten hurt. But it was too late to go back. I'd gotten hurt, and I had the feeling there was a lot more pain headed my way.

CHAPTER TWENTY

I WOKE up Sunday morning with a pounding headache. As I'd predicted, I hadn't slept well, tossing and turning most of the night as my dad's words ran around on a loop in my head. Now it was time to get some answers. It was only eight and the house was quiet, so I took a shower and changed into jeans and a sweater before going downstairs. As always, Kade had made coffee. This morning, he was also making breakfast.

"Morning," he said, as he scrambled eggs. "I decided to use up what your mom had in her fridge."

"You cook. That's impressive."

"Not really. I cook just well enough not to starve."

"Have you seen my father?"

"Checked on him a few minutes ago; he was still asleep."

"Well, I guess that's better than finding out he snuck out in the middle of the night."

"I thought about that," Kade said. "I looked in on him a couple of times, but I didn't think he was in any condition to leave, and he didn't."

"I'm going to see if he's awake." I walked down the hall into the living room. As Kade had said, my dad was asleep and snoring heavily. I returned to the kitchen and sat down at the counter as Kade put a plate in front of me. "He's still out."

"Then you can eat."

"You're very good at feeding me," I said with appreciation.

"I was hungry, too."

I didn't have much of an appetite, dreading the conversation that I knew was coming, but I managed to eat my eggs and sip some coffee. And then my phone buzzed. "It's the investigator," I said, putting the call on speaker as I answered. "Hello, Jeremy. Do you have any news?"

"Yes. The charity that was sending Mr. Beckham's mother money doesn't exist. There is no nonprofit group by that name anywhere in this country. No evidence of a business license, a bank account, nothing. It's a fabrication."

"My mother was just sending his mom cash on her own?"

"That's the only explanation I can come up with. However, I've also gone through your mother's financial accounts, and there is no evidence that she has any money beyond what she takes in from her job. The purchase of her house sixteen years ago was made with a cash down payment, of about three hundred thousand dollars, but I have no idea where she got that, unless she took it from your father. The life of Kim Landry ended in that hurricane in New Orleans. The life of Laura Hawthorne began about nineteen months after that."

"Who was she for those nineteen months in between?"

"No idea. But at some point, she purchased a new identity. And this identity was incredibly detailed. She was given new identification that matched new fingerprints, a fake history that included a degree in music from a university in Colorado. That's how she was able to get a job at the school where she works."

His words blew me away. "How does one even do that?"

"If you have enough money, and/or powerful connections, it can be done." Jeremy paused. "I also don't think it was the first time she changed identities. I looked up her past before she married your father. You said she went to community college in San Diego, but I can't find any record of her at any school in that city. In fact, Kim Cooper came to life about a year and a half before she married your father. I was able to trace some credit cards in that name, but then that life ended after she disappeared in New Orleans."

"That's crazy. How can she keep changing identities? And why does she do it?"

"Good questions. I checked with a friend of mine who is with the US Marshals to find out if it's possible your mother was in witness protection."

My heart leapt against my chest. "That would explain how she could become someone else."

"Yes. Unfortunately, I couldn't get anyone to confirm that she was. I did point out that she's now lying unconscious in a hospital, so if she is supposed to be under protection, someone has messed up. I was told again that they couldn't provide me with any information."

I thought about that. "If she were in witness protection, that would explain why she faked her death, why she stayed away all these years, why someone tried to kill her now," I said. "People go into protection when they testify against someone, right?"

"That's one of the reasons. Their life is usually in danger by something they do to aid the government. I'm going to keep digging," Jeremy said. "Any word from your father? He hasn't come back to his hotel room. I know the police are keeping an eye out for him as well."

I hesitated, not sure what I wanted to reveal at this moment. "I'm still waiting to talk to him," I said. It was partly true. "Is there anything else, Jeremy?"

"I did some research into the death of Kade's father."

I licked my lips as I looked across the counter at Kade, whose expression had turned to stone. "What did you find out?"

"The robbery occurred after an event at a private estate, owned by billionaire real-estate developer James Holden. The crew took jewelry worth about ten million dollars at that time, probably double that now, two paintings valued at over a million dollars each, and about five-hundred thousand dollars in cash."

"That's a lot of cash."

"It is. The police believe the crew got access to the estate before the party started and hid away until after the event ended, as there was no evidence of forced entry. It was also believed that it could have been an inside job as the private security firm had the alarm codes. There was some speculation that Kade's father was part of it, since he was supposed to have left with the other security personnel. One theory suggested he gave the crew access, but there was a disagreement, and he ended up getting shot."

"No fucking way," Kade said loudly.

"I guess Kade is there. A heads-up would have been nice, Brynn," Jeremy said dryly.

"That didn't happen, Jeremy," Kade said, moving closer to me and the phone.

"I'm just telling you what I saw in the police report," Jeremy said. "Apparently, your father had been arrested for petty theft when he was in his late teens and was involved in a gang."

"That was when he was a kid, running with a bad crowd. He got his life together. He did not let that crew into the house."

I saw the anger in Kade's eyes, as well as a hint of uncertainty. We both wanted to believe in our fathers, but now we had questions.

"I'll keep looking into it," Jeremy said. "Anything new on your end?"

"A lot," I said with a sigh. "Someone tried to kidnap me last night. The police have him in custody, but he was hired off the dark web. Maybe you can check in with Inspector Greenman and see if you can help."

"Of course. Are you all right? I just spoke to your brother-in-law; he didn't mention anything about a kidnapping."

"He doesn't know. I'd appreciate it if you would let me talk to my sister and brother-in-law about what happened."

"All right. Take care of yourself."

"I'm trying," I said, ending the call.

"Jeremy is wrong," Kade told me. "My father was a good man. He tried to stop that robbery. He wasn't there to participate in it. I would bet my life on that."

"It was just a theory, Kade."

"Because the police were looking for an easy scapegoat," he said bitterly. "Just because he had some problems when he was a kid, he became a person of interest."

"It never went further than someone's idea," I reminded him.

"I'm not so sure about that. Maybe they stopped looking for my father's killer because they thought he was involved."

I didn't know what to say. "Maybe my mother knows something about it," I finally said.

"I wish to hell she'd wake up."

"Me, too." I paused. "I liked Jeremy's theory about her being in witness protection. It makes sense how she could have changed her life so many times. But I guess that's just an idea, too." I got to my feet. "I'm going to wake my dad up. He needs to start talking."

I marched down the hall and into the living room. My father was beginning to stir.

"Dad," I said loudly.

He opened one eye, squinting at me. Then he closed his eyes and groaned.

"I know you probably have a massive hangover," I said. "But it's time to talk."

Kade came into the room with a mug of coffee. "Maybe this will help," he said.

My father opened his eyes again and struggled to get into a sitting position. When he'd managed that, Kade handed him the mug.

My dad took a sip, then said, "Who are you?"

"Kade Beckham," he replied.

My father looked at me. "Is he your boyfriend?"

"No. Drink some more coffee," I ordered.

He did what I suggested, probably because he was also trying to buy some time.

"I can leave you two alone," Kade offered.

"I'd rather you stay, if you don't mind," I said.

"I don't mind." Kade settled into a nearby armchair.

"I think we should talk alone, Brynn," my dad interjected.

"And I don't think it's up to you. Where have you been?" I asked, needing to leave out the part about him not being my father until after I had more information. "When did you know Mom was alive? Did you talk to her?"

"Slow down," he said, grimacing with pain. "My head is about to explode."

"I don't care about your head. I've been calling you for days. Everyone is worried about you. Vicky even flew here to find you."

"What?" he asked in surprise.

"It was last Wednesday, the day before Mom was shot. I know you must have heard about that."

"What did Vicky do? Did she confront your mother?"

"No. She claims she saw Mom with some other guy, not you, and she just left the city and went home. She felt stupid for thinking you and Mom were having some secret affair."

"Vicky knew she was alive? She thought we were having an affair?" he asked in bemusement.

"Yes. She saw Mom on the news, saving a man's life. I'm assuming you did, too?"

"I couldn't believe my eyes," he said, his gaze distracted, as if he were reliving that moment. "I was working late in my office, and I had the TV on. I was waiting to hear the sports scores, and there was a news clip about Miguel Rodriguez having a heart attack, and there she was. I thought I was dreaming. I watched that clip a thousand times. I had to find out for sure. So instead of going to Portland for business, I came to San Francisco."

"When did you get here?"

"Tuesday night. I went to her school on Wednesday and caught her when she was going to lunch. She was smiling, laughing with someone, and then she turned around and saw me, and her smile vanished. I thought she might run away. But she didn't. She walked over to me and told me to meet her at a coffee place nearby. Then she got in her car and drove away. I ran to my rental car, thinking I was going to lose her again. But she went where she said she was going to go. We sat down at an outside table and stared at each other. I didn't know what to say."

"What did she say?" I prodded as he once again got lost in his thoughts.

"She told me she was sorry, that she did it to protect me and you and Dani. She'd gotten into some trouble that she couldn't get out of unless she faked her death. She wouldn't give me any details."

"And she couldn't at any point in the last twenty years tell us the truth?"

"I asked her the same thing. She said it wasn't safe. That she knew I'd do a good job raising you and your sister, and it was the only comfort she allowed herself."

"The only comfort?" I questioned. "She made another life for herself, one with friends, coworkers, a job, a house. It's not like she's been in jail all this time. She's been living life."

"I know. It's unthinkable. It's unforgivable. I told her that she'd betrayed me. That I hated her. She leaned in and said she was sorry again, and I saw red. I slapped her. I'd never ever hit a woman before. I was stunned. A couple at the next table came over to ask if she was all right. They said they were calling the police. She told them not to, and then she got up and walked away. I went in the other direction. I didn't want those people to think I was following her." He took a ragged breath. "I shouldn't have hit her, but I never felt so angry in my life. I couldn't see straight. I got drunk that night and slept most of the next day. Then I heard there had been a shooting and I saw her picture on the news again."

"I thought I saw you at her school on Friday."

"I went there to see if I could get any information on the shooting. I didn't want to go into the office or anything official, so I asked some of the teachers, pretending to be a concerned friend. They told me she was in a coma." He shook his head. "I went to the nearest bar and started drinking again. I haven't been back to my hotel in two days. Every time I tried to sober up, I couldn't stand the pain. I got your messages, but I couldn't handle talking to you or anyone. I didn't know what I would say."

"What you just said," I told him. "We've been worried about you, Dad. The police found your hotel room. They've been waiting for you to come back."

"The police? Why? Shit! Did someone report the fight we had?"

"I don't think so, but when I told the inspector that Mom had run away from her life and now you were nowhere to be found, they came up with the idea that she'd left you because you were violent and, perhaps, you'd found her again."

His face paled. "All I did was slap her, Brynn. I swear that's all I did. It was wrong. I feel sick about it. I don't hit people. You know that. You know me."

I swallowed a quickly growing knot of emotion. "I thought I knew you, Dad. Although now I wonder if I should be calling you that."

"What are you talking about?" he asked in confusion.

"I'm talking about what you said last night before you fell asleep."

His lips tightened. "I don't remember what I said last night. It's hazy."

A part of me wished I'd forgotten it, too. But I hadn't. "I'm going to tell you what you said, and you're going to give me the truth."

"The truth about what?"

I drew in a breath of courage and then said, "Last night, you told me that Mom left you with two kids who weren't even yours. You wondered how she could do that."

The blood drained from his face. "Brynn," he whispered.

"If Dani and I are not yours, then who is our father?"

CHAPTER TWENTY-ONE

"God!" My father ran a hand through his hair, his eyes jumping all around. "I—I shouldn't have said that. You're my daughters. You've always been mine."

"Then why would you say such a thing?"

"I was drunk."

"You're not drunk now, but you're lying, aren't you? Are you my biological father or not? It's a yes-or-no question."

He drew in a ragged breath, then said, "No. I'm not your biological father."

I'd been expecting that answer, but it still shook me up. "Why would you pretend you were? And who is my father?" I asked in bewilderment.

"I don't know who he is."

"So Mom cheated on you? Is that it? Did you find out before or after we were born?" The raging anger inside of me drove me to my feet. "Well?" I demanded when he didn't say anything.

"Your mother didn't cheat on me," he replied. "I didn't meet your mom until after you were born. You were three months old when I met you."

I shook my head in disbelief. "Are you serious?"

"Yes. I met your mother at a coffee shop where she was working. I fell for her the first time I saw her. But she wouldn't go out with me. She said she had two babies, and she didn't date. But I couldn't take no for an answer. I kept asking and eventually we went out. It was magic. We fell for each other, hard and fast. I told her I loved her on our third date. And a month later, I asked her to marry me. I wanted to be her husband. I wanted to be your father. I wanted us to be a family."

"Where was my biological father during all this?"

"She said he'd left her before she knew she was pregnant. She told me it was just as well, because he was a mean drunk, and it was better if he didn't know about you at all. She was going to raise you on her own. I didn't care about her past. I had lost my parents young, and I missed having a family. Kim was alone in the world, too, struggling to make ends meet. It seemed like fate had brought us together. We got married right away, and I officially adopted you and Dani."

"How could I not know this?" I asked in confusion. "I've seen my birth certificate. It doesn't say I was adopted."

"In California, they seal the original birth certificate, and the new one looks like the old one with the last name changed. Kim didn't want you to know you were adopted, and I didn't want you to know, either. I wanted us to be a family. I loved her more than I'd ever loved anyone." He drew a heavy breath. "I thought we were happy. For seven years, I had exactly what I wanted. And then she died."

"You left the day of the funeral. You didn't come back for two weeks. And when you did, you weren't the same. You didn't really love us, did you?" I asked. "You loved her, and we were just part of the package deal."

"Of course I loved you. I just felt helpless and weak after she died. She was my world, and she was gone. And she was always so good with you. She knew what you needed before you could say you needed it. I didn't."

"It actually makes sense," I said. "Finally, something makes sense—why you drifted away from us. Once Mom was gone, the bond was broken."

"I loved you girls; I still do," he argued. "I've been around your whole lives. I'm sorry I said what I said. I never wanted you to find out, especially not like this."

"Does Vicky know?"

He gave a guilty nod. "Yes. I told her after your mom died."

"Probably why she found it easier to suggest boarding school."

"I thought the school was good for you. You both seemed happy there, not as sad as when you were at home. And you had each other. You always had each other. Sometimes, I envied the connection you had. I felt like the outsider."

"You just told yourself that so you could be the outsider," I said harshly. "I—I can't do this anymore." I felt overwhelmed with emotion. "I need to be alone." I ran down the hall and up the stairs, locking myself in my mother's bedroom. But as I looked around her room, I found little peace. Instead, I was reminded of all the lies she'd told. Everyone in my life had lied to me. Except Dani. Even that wasn't true. Dani had lied about seeing Mom at our high school graduation.

That was a small lie, I told myself. *And she'd done it to protect me.*

But hadn't all the lies been excused by the idea that someone was trying to protect me?

It was wrong—all of it.

And I couldn't do it alone anymore. I took out my phone and called Dani. As soon as she answered, I started to cry.

"What's wrong, Brynn? Talk to me," she said with concern.

"Everything is wrong, Dani. Every damn thing."

"Start with one."

I decided not to start with me almost being kidnapped. That would scare her too much. "Dad showed up last night. He was very, very drunk. He looked awful, like he'd been sleeping on the street in his clothes."

"What did he say? Where has he been?"

"He's been here in San Francisco since last Tuesday. He had a brief conversation with Mom on Wednesday. She attempted to apologize, but Dad got so angry he slapped her, and some other people tried to intervene—"

"What the hell?" Dani interrupted. "He slapped her?"

"He was blinded by rage. Anyway, she left. He was going to go see her the next day but then she was shot, and he fell apart. He started drinking and he couldn't stop. He said he was so heartbroken and angry that he couldn't talk to any of us. He couldn't believe the woman he'd loved so much had lied to him and deserted him, leaving him with her children."

"We were his children, too."

I drew in a breath. "That was a lie, too, Dani. We aren't his kids."

"What are you talking about, Brynn? We are his kids. I know you didn't always feel close to him, but I did."

"Which is why this is going to hurt you," I said, wishing I didn't have to tell her. "Dad told me that he's not our biological father. He didn't even meet Mom until we were three months old. He said he fell in love with all of us at the same time, and he wanted us to be a family, so they got married, and he adopted us. He and Mom agreed that they would never tell us the truth."

"Why would he tell you now?" she challenged.

"He didn't mean to. It came out as part of his drunken ramblings last night. I brought it back up this morning, and he told me everything. He said he was sorry that he'd let the secret out, that he'd loved us like his own. But we are not his biological children."

"Who's our father?"

"He doesn't know. Mom told him the guy wasn't a good guy and she didn't want him to know about us. He apparently didn't ask any more questions."

"This is unbelievable."

"I know. It's one shock after another."

"Does he know why Mom left?"

"He doesn't seem to know, but to be honest, after he dropped this bomb on me, I couldn't talk to him anymore, and I came upstairs. I needed a minute to regroup."

"Does Vicky know that he's not our dad?"

"He said he told her a long time ago." I paused, tensing as another question ran through me. "You didn't have any idea, did you?"

"Of course not," Dani said sharply. "How could you ask me that, Brynn?"

"You just seem a little quieter than I thought you would be."

"I'm trying to process everything."

"I told Dad that the police want to talk to him. He's not eager to do that, and I know why. The public fight he had with Mom right before she got shot won't look good. And the fact that he's been drunk and missing ever since then will lend more credence to the idea that he got angry and shot her."

"But he didn't do that."

"I don't think he could have. He was a slobbery mess last night. As much as I hate him for keeping this secret from us, seeing how devastated he is, I think he really loved Mom."

"I always thought he did," Dani said. "Have you learned anything else?"

I still didn't want to tell her about my kidnapping, so I went with Jeremy's theory of witness protection. After I'd filled her in on that idea, there was another long silence.

"Well," Dani said finally. "There's a lot to think about, isn't there?"

"Yes. And a lot to still be discovered. We have a father out there in the world."

"Who is not a good guy. Maybe he's the one who shot Mom. Maybe he's the one she's been running away from this whole time."

I hadn't made that connection, but it was a big one. "That's true," I said slowly. "But the problem is trying to find someone who can actually give us information. Mom's life has been lived in three parts: before she married Dad, her life with us, and what happened after she faked her death. I'm pretty sure she used a different name for each of those parts. Which is why witness protection makes sense. But no one will admit that she's in it."

"She had to have some help in starting her life over so many times."

"Maybe the friend she went to see in New Orleans. I need to ask Dad who that was. Because I get the feeling that person knows about her past."

"Can you give the phone to Dad? I want to talk to him, too."

"Are you sure? It's just going to stress you out."

"I'm already stressed."

"All right. He's downstairs. Hang on."

I left my mom's room and jogged down the stairs. Kade was in the kitchen, talking on his phone. I moved down the hall and into the living room, my jaw dropping as I saw the blanket on the floor and absolutely no sign of my dad.

"Dad," I yelled, checking the bathroom. It was empty. So was the guest room. I ran back to the front door and yanked it open. There was no sign of my father. I put the phone to my ear. "He's gone," I told Dani. "He left the house, and I have no idea where he went." Disappointment and more anger ran through me. "He had to know what disappearing would do to me. I just got through telling him how much it hurt when he didn't call any of us back, but he left anyway."

"I'll try calling him," Dani said. "Maybe he thinks you're pissed off at him."

"I am pissed off at him. In fact, my blood is boiling."

"I know. I get it. But let's not forget who we should really be angry with. That's not Dad— it's Mom."

"Maybe it's both of them," I muttered, feeling very much alone as I ended the call.

It wasn't just the distance between my parents and me that hurt—it was the growing space between Dani and me. She was so quick to jump to Dad's defense. I used to think we were on the same side. It was the two of us against the world. But right now, it felt more like me against the world.

CHAPTER TWENTY-TWO

"WHAT'S GOING ON?" Kade asked, as he came up behind me.

"My dad is gone." I stepped back into the house and shut the door. "Did you see him leave?"

"No, I got a call from the gallery, and I went into the kitchen to take it." Kade gave me a regretful look. "Sorry, I didn't think he was going to bail. He was feeling bad after your conversation. He said he never should have told you he wasn't your father, that he never wanted that to come out. He wanted me to know that he really loved you. I said he didn't have to convince me. It was between you and him."

"Anything else?"

"No. That was it." He paused. "I need to go to the gallery. There's an issue with an installation that I need to resolve. It shouldn't take more than an hour. Do you want to come with me? I don't want to leave you here alone."

I hesitated. After everything that happened, I didn't want to be alone, but I also wanted to be somewhere my dad could find me. "I don't know. My dad might come back, and I'd like to be here if he does."

"I don't know that he'll be back, Brynn."

"You're probably right, but you should go do what you need to do."

"It won't take long, no more than an hour."

"I'll be fine. I'll keep everything locked up tight, and while you're gone, I'll make some calls. I want to follow up with Inspector Greenman and Jeremy as well."

"If you talk to Jeremy, can you ask him to send the police report on my father's murder? It sounded like he had a copy."

"Of course. You haven't seen it before?" I asked.

He shook his head. "I was a little kid when my father was killed, and years later when I asked about it, I got stonewalled. The police assured me that the case was still open, that they hadn't given up, but it didn't seem that way."

"I'll text Jeremy now," I said, as I typed out the request. When I was done, I looked back at Kade. "I'll let you know when I hear from him. I'll call the hospital, too. Maybe today will be the day my mother wakes up."

"I hope so. I'll be back as soon as I can."

"Okay." I tried to look unconcerned by his departure, but I'd become very attached to him the past few days. My anchor was leaving, and I felt suddenly adrift.

Kade gave me an odd look. Then he moved forward and wrapped his arms around me.

I drew in a breath, soaking in the warmth of his embrace for a long minute. I looked up at him. "How did you know I needed a hug?"

"Because I needed one, too," he said, his gaze clinging to mine.

Something between us shifted. The hug no longer felt comfortable or friendly. It felt like something else, something exciting, tingly...

When Kade lowered his head, I couldn't resist. I wanted his mouth on mine, and it was everything I'd imagined and more. His kiss was hot, purposeful, and demanding. Kade always pushed me out of my comfort zone, and this was no exception.

One kiss led to another and another. I couldn't seem to let him go, even though I knew I should.

Finally, Kade pulled back, the mix of our breath enveloping us in a sexy, warm cloud of passion.

As he opened his mouth to speak, I cut him off. "Don't say anything. Don't ruin it."

He gave me a long look, then stole another kiss and left the house. I watched him get on his motorcycle and speed away. Then I closed and locked the door, my lips still tingling, my breath a bit ragged. We'd just made things more complicated, but it was worth it.

And it was so much better to think about kissing Kade than anything else. I wanted to lose myself in a beautiful daydream about the sexy Kade Beckham and pretend for just a few minutes that my life was like it used to be, when no one had betrayed me, when I didn't have questions, when I wasn't afraid for my life.

And then my phone buzzed.

The number came up as St. Mary's Hospital.

Reality came back, hard and fast.

"Hello?" I said warily.

"This is Nurse Redding at St. Mary's. Is this Brynn Landry?"

"Yes, it is. Are you calling about my mother? Is she all right?"

"She's waking up," the nurse said.

My pulse leapt in excitement and relief. "Oh, my God. Does that mean she'll recover?"

"The doctor is examining her now."

"I'll be there as soon as I can." I couldn't believe it. My mother was opening her eyes. Maybe she could finally tell me what the hell was going on.

I ran into the kitchen to get my purse and keys and then left the house in a hurry. I jogged out to my car and jumped in, locking the doors as soon as I was inside. I wished Kade was still around, but I couldn't wait for him to come back. I needed to see my mom, and I was probably safer at the hospital anyway.

Although, first I had to get from the parking structure to the building...

When I arrived at the hospital, I parked as close as I could to the entrance and then waited for a father and daughter to walk by my car before getting out. I stayed close to them, thinking there was safety in numbers, but my gaze darted in every direction as I made my way into the hospital. I didn't take a full breath until I was stepping off the elevator and walking to my mother's room.

The doctor came out of the room just as I got to the door.

"How is she?" I asked.

Dr. Ryker gave me a smile. "Much better. We removed the tubes. She's still very weak, and her mind is muddled. But all that is to be expected with a head injury such as hers. We'll run more tests over the next day or two. As the swelling goes down, she should continue to improve."

"Does she know where she is?"

"She's aware she's in the hospital. She doesn't remember being shot."

My hopes dimmed at her words. But even if my mom didn't remember the shooting, she should be able to tell me about the rest of her life.

"I spoke to Inspector Greenman," the doctor added. "He's on his way over."

Which meant I probably only had a few minutes to talk to my mother alone. "Thanks for everything. I really need to see her."

"Go ahead," the doctor said. "But take it slow. She can speak, but her throat is sore and dry from the tube. I'm sure you have a lot of questions for her, but don't throw them all out at once."

"Okay." I drew in a deep breath and then opened the door.

As I stepped inside the room, it appeared that my mom's eyes were closed. I felt a wave of disappointment. She'd fallen asleep again. I probably should let her rest, but I couldn't do that. I couldn't go one more second without looking into her eyes, without hearing her voice.

I moved closer to the bed. "Mom," I said.

Her eyes fluttered open.

I caught my breath. They were the same dark-blue purple eyes that I remembered, that I saw in the mirror every time I looked at my own face. My father might not be my father, but this woman was definitely my mother.

"Brynn," she whispered.

I was shocked that she recognized me right away, that she didn't question if I was Dani or Brynn. She saw me. *She knew me.*

That realization set off a deep, almost agonizing pain of happiness. I hadn't felt like this in twenty years. I was with my mom. Whatever she'd done, she was still my mother, and there was a bond there whether I liked it or not.

"It's me," I said.

"You're so pretty, so grown up."

"It's been a long time. I thought you were dead."

"Your sister didn't tell you I wasn't?"

I drew in a sharp breath at that reminder. "No. She didn't tell me she saw you at our high school graduation until a few days ago. She said she thought she'd just imagined it was you."

"I waved to her on impulse. I shouldn't have done that. I thought she realized it was me, but then she turned away, so maybe she did think I was a ghost. I shouldn't have gone to the graduation. I should have left it alone, but I missed you both so much." Her gaze ran across my face. "You must be angry with me."

"I am angry. But I don't want to talk about my feelings right now. Someone is trying to kill you, Mom."

"The doctor said I was shot. I can't remember."

"Do you know who would want to shoot you?"

"I—I don't," she stuttered, but there was an odd flicker in her gaze.

"Are you sure? Because someone tried to get to you here in

the hospital, too. They're not going to stop trying until they succeed."

"Here?" Her gaze darted to the door.

"Yes. There's a guard outside now. The police are investigating, but they haven't had much luck. You must know something that will help, Mom. You've clearly led a life of secrets. One of those secrets caught up to you, didn't it?"

"You should go back to Carmel, Brynn."

"How do you know I live in Carmel?" I asked.

"I bought some things from the store you and Dani started. The clothes are beautiful. Although I was surprised you didn't do more with your music. I went to one of your shows at the community center. You were so good."

"You went to my show? Why? Why did you leave us?" I asked, knowing that was the real question I wanted answered. "How could you do that? Losing you was so painful. We were all devastated." I blinked back tears. "We loved you so much."

"I loved you, too. I had to leave, honey. It was the only way to protect you all."

"How could it have been the only way?"

"I can't tell you why. You have to go home. You have to forget you ever saw me."

"It's too late for that," I said, shaking my head. "Someone tried to grab me yesterday."

Fear sparked in her eyes. "No. You must leave, Brynn. Get out of this city. And make sure Dani is far away, too."

"Tell me what's going on."

"I can't," my mom said, struggling to sit up. As she did so, the machines in the room started beeping in alarm. "I have to protect you. It can't all be for nothing," she said, her speech starting to slur as her breath came too fast.

"Mom, stop. Breathe."

My mom couldn't seem to catch her breath and a second later, Dr. Ryker and a nurse came into the room. "You need to leave," Dr. Ryker told me, as she attended to my mother.

"What's wrong?" I asked.

The nurse waved me into the hall. "Please, step outside."

I had no choice but to do as they asked. As I moved into the corridor, Inspector Greenman came down the hall.

"Is your mom awake?" he asked.

"She is, but something is happening. I don't know what. She was talking to me. Then she got upset, and the machines started beeping. The doctor and nurse are with her now."

"What did she tell you?"

"She didn't see who shot her. But she knows something. She begged me to leave. She said she disappeared to protect us. Then she got so upset, everything went haywire, and that's all I know."

"I'm sorry," he said, compassion in his gaze. "You've had a rough time."

"I thought I was going to finally get answers, but I made things worse. She was getting better. Now...I don't know." I turned around as the doctor came out of the room. "How is she?" I asked. "What happened?"

"Her blood pressure was skyrocketing. I had to give her a sedative. She'll be asleep for several hours. I'm sorry. I know you both wanted to ask her questions, but it will have to wait."

"Is she going to be all right?" I asked. "I didn't mean to upset her."

"We'll know more in a few hours."

I was so tired of hearing that response, of hoping I would know more in a few hours. But those hours came and went, and I still knew nothing. I should have kept my mom focused on talking about who was trying to kill her instead of getting caught up in the past.

"I'll be back," the inspector told me.

I thought about telling him that my dad had shown up, but I'd just be throwing my father under the bus, and I still didn't know if he belonged there, so I let him go.

I debated on what to do next. My mother would be asleep for

a long time, and I didn't want to spend all day at the hospital. I might as well go back to the house. Maybe my father would return, and we could talk some more.

Before heading to the elevator, I stopped in the restroom. As I opened the door, I ran straight into a woman.

"Sorry," I said, then caught my breath as I stared into the woman's face. "Oh, my God," I said in shock. The woman pushed past me and ran down the hall.

I couldn't let her get away. I chased after her, following her down the stairwell, our heels clamoring on the steps as we raced toward the bottom. I caught up to her just before she could leave the building, throwing myself in front of the door.

We stared at each other for a long minute. Her hair was a dirty blonde, but her eyes were the same as mine, her face the same as mine, but years older. She didn't look just like me; she looked like my mother.

"Who are you?" I whispered.

CHAPTER TWENTY-THREE

"No one," the woman said. "Get out of my way." Her voice also sounded familiar.

"You're her sister—maybe her twin sister," I said in amazement. "How is that possible?"

"You need to move and forget you ever saw me."

"That's not going to happen." I blocked her way as she tried to move around me. "Mom said she didn't have any family. She was an only child. Clearly, that was a lie, too. *God!* Was everything she told me a lie? Was any of it true?"

"She loved you. That wasn't a lie."

"How do you know?" I asked.

"Which one are you? Brynn or Dani?"

"So, you know more about us than we know about you. I'm Brynn. What's your name?"

She licked her lips. "It's Rachel."

"Is that your real name?" I challenged.

"How's Laura?" she asked, ignoring my question.

"Don't you mean Kim?"

"Is she alive?" Rachel pressed.

"Yes. She opened her eyes, but when we started talking, she got agitated. Her blood pressure rose so high, the doctor sedated her." I paused. "You know she was shot, right? That someone is trying to kill her?"

"I saw it on the news. What did she tell you about it?"

The way she crafted the question made me more suspicious. There wasn't any actual proof that the person who shot my mother was a man. It could have been a woman. It could have been this woman. But she was my mom's sister. It seemed unimaginable that she would try to kill her.

"Did she see who shot her?" Rachel pressed.

"No, but she didn't want to talk about it. She was more interested in telling me to get out of the city. She did say that she disappeared to protect me and my sister. What do you know about that?"

Rachel stared back at me. "I know it was the most difficult thing she ever did in her life. You need to do what she asked you to do, Brynn. You need to leave San Francisco as soon as possible. It's not safe for you here."

"I know it's not safe. Someone tried to run me over the other day and last night, a man tried to drug me and shove me into his car."

Her eyes widened. "Where did this happen? Who was the man?"

"It was at the school where my mom works. The man claims he was hired off the internet to kidnap me and deliver me to Golden Gate Park. He didn't know what would happen after that. And he doesn't seem to know who hired him." I wondered if I was giving her too much information. I needed to do a better job of getting her talking. "If you know that I'm in danger, then you have to know why. Tell me, so I can protect myself. So we can both protect Laura."

"Telling you would only make the danger greater. If you leave now, you'll be safe."

"You can't guarantee that." I tilted my head, giving her a considering look. "You were going to try to see her, weren't you? That's why you're here."

"I was, until I saw the guard outside her room. I thought I might be able to claim that I was family, although I wasn't thinking anyone would realize so quickly how much alike we are."

"I'm not just anyone. Your eyes are like mine, like hers, like my sister's. You have the same freckle under your eye."

"You grew up to be a beautiful woman," Rachel said, her gaze softening.

Her words confused me. "It sounds like you saw me when I was younger. Did we meet?"

"No. But one time when you were a little girl, I thought maybe you saw me at the museum."

"At the museum?" I echoed.

"Your mother and I used to meet there every couple of months, while you and your sister were in the children's room."

"Was that why she took us there, so she could meet you away from our house? My father didn't know about you, did he?"

"No. We agreed a long time ago that it was better if no one knew that either of us had a sister."

"Why was it better? What were you involved in?"

Before she could answer, we heard someone coming down the stairs. "We have to get out of here," she said.

I nodded, then pushed open the door behind me. We exited the building near the parking structure and ran inside, ducking behind a truck. As we watched the door we'd just come thru, a young woman exited the building. She was on her phone and didn't look at all threatening.

I blew out a breath. "We're okay," I said.

"We're not okay. Where's your car?"

I led the way to my vehicle, flipping the locks so we could get inside.

She put on her seat belt and said, "Drive."

"Where?"

"Somewhere that isn't here. We need to get away from this hospital."

I started the engine and pulled out of the space, keeping an eye out as I left the lot. I drove a few blocks, not sure where to go next.

"Turn left at the next street," Rachel said.

I followed her directions, realizing we were heading toward Golden Gate Park, and my misgivings came back.

"I'm not going to the park," I said flatly.

"No, we're going to the beach. Just go straight. We'll run right into it."

I had a million questions to ask her, but they were all jumbled up in my head, so I drove to the end of the road and entered the parking lot next to Ocean Beach. The fog was just off the coastline, the waves large and wild.

I turned my gaze away from the sea to Rachel. "Tell me why my mother is in danger."

"There was trouble a long time ago," Rachel said, turning to face me. "Actually, Laura and I were born into trouble."

"What does that mean?"

"We lost our parents when we were young. A neighbor took us in after that. Mrs. Hursh was really good to us. She was a music teacher. That's when Laura learned how to play. She started with the piano and then moved to the violin. She was a natural. I had zero talent. But then the county caught up to us being on our own and we got split up for three years. It was the longest three years of my life."

"How old were you?"

"Fourteen. After high school, we managed to find our way back to each other. Laura got a scholarship to NYU to study music, and she told me to come with her. I could sleep in her dorm room and go to community college, get a job."

"So, you were in New York," I said, another piece of the puzzle falling into place.

"It was probably the worst place we could have gone. More trouble found us, and we had to scramble to survive."

"Did that trouble involve a robbery and the death of a security guard?"

Rachel started at my question, her gaze narrowing on mine. "Why would you ask me that?"

"Because Mom was sending cash to the guard's family for a long time. They didn't know why, but I think it's because she had something to do with that robbery."

Rachel shook her head. "That's not true, Brynn. Your mother didn't have anything to do with that."

"Then why would she have been secretly sending money to the security guard's widow and child?"

"She met the widow and the little boy at a community center where she was performing. She heard their story and thought it was incredibly sad. When she had some extra cash, she decided to help them."

"Really? That's the connection?"

"Yes."

I wasn't sure I bought her story, but I needed to know more. "Getting back to New York, when did you leave the city?"

"After Laura graduated from college. We decided it was time to start over somewhere new."

"Why? What happened?" As she hesitated, I added, "My father told me yesterday that he isn't my biological father, that when he met my mom, she had two kids who were three months old at the time. My mom said she had me when she was twenty-two, so that seems pretty close to the time she'd be graduating from college and living in New York."

"She was living in LA when you and Dani were born," Rachel said.

"Were you with her?"

"For some of the time, but not when she met your father. I remember how happy she was when she called to tell me about him. She said she was making a new family, and I was really happy for her."

"She was happy in her new family until I turned seven, until she faked her death and disappeared," I said. "Then she changed her name. She built a life away from her own kids. And I don't understand why. What happened in New York? What happened with my biological father? Why did my mom fake her death when I was seven years old?"

"Trouble," Rachel said, repeating what appeared to be her favorite word. "She thought she'd escaped it, but then it found her again. She didn't want to put you or your sister in danger, so she made the difficult decision to leave. She had to protect you."

"Why are you being so vague? Why didn't she go to the police? Why didn't you? What exactly is the trouble you're talking about?"

"It's complicated."

"Well, I'm sure when the police talk to you, they'll find a way to uncomplicate it."

"You can't go to the police. You can't tell them about me."

"Why shouldn't I?"

"Because it could get your mother killed. You have no idea what's going on."

"Because you're not telling me," I said in frustration.

Rachel's lips tightened. "The last thing your mother would want me to do is tell you the truth and put you in danger. You need to go home."

"I'm not leaving without knowing the truth, without making sure she's safe."

"Where's your sister? Where's Dani?"

"She's in Carmel. She's pregnant, and she can't be stressed out. She can't be here."

Rachel nodded, a gleam in her eyes. "You're protecting her the way your mother always protected me."

"You are twins, aren't you?"

"Yes. It's been the two of us against the world almost since we were born. We'd do anything for each other, no matter the cost."

"Do you have kids?"

"No. I wouldn't have made a good mother."

"My mom was a good mother until she left."

"It broke her heart, Brynn."

I shook my head, telling myself not to care about my mother's broken heart. "She doesn't get to be the victim. She's the one who caused the heartbreak."

"I know she hurt you and your sister. She knows it, too. But it was to protect you."

"Well, I'm old enough to protect myself now. We need to go to the police. Or at least to the PI I'm working with. He can help us. But you have to tell us where to start. You have to give us a name."

Rachel gave me a long look, then turned her gaze back to the ocean. "I always seem to end up at a beach," she said.

I frowned at the odd comment. "What does that mean?"

"Just thinking how many times I've run to the ocean before making a momentous decision. I've seen a lot of water in my life."

"I've actually done the same thing," I said, feeling an odd connection to her.

"Some things pass from generation to generation."

"Like twins. I don't know how my mother didn't talk about you. Have you been with my mom since she went from Kim to Laura?"

"No. We weren't together. It wasn't safe. But we did keep in touch."

"Well, at least you had the opportunity to do that," I said bitterly.

"Are you and Dani close?"

"Extremely. She hates not being here now, but she has her own baby to protect."

"Is she having twins?"

"No. She's having one—a boy."

"Well, that's something wonderful, isn't it? Is her husband a good man?"

"Very good. He adores her." I started the car. "As much as I want to hear more about you and my mom and share stories about me and my sister, we need to move forward. Will you talk to the PI with me?"

She hesitated, then said, "All right. But I don't want to go back to your mom's house."

"I'll ask him to meet us for coffee."

"That should be okay," she said slowly. "Maybe he can help me find out where someone is."

"You're not going to tell me who that someone is, are you?"

"I'll tell you both at the same time."

"All right." I texted Jeremy that I needed to see him; I had some new and urgent information. I asked him to meet me at the café. He texted back almost immediately that he'd meet me there. Then I pulled out of the lot.

As we drove across town, I looked at Rachel and said, "Do you know who my biological father is?"

Her body stiffened. Then she shook her head. "Laura refused to tell me. He wasn't a good person, and she didn't want me to know who he was. She didn't want you to know, either. Don't go looking for him, Brynn."

"I can't believe she didn't tell you who he was. You're twins. You told each other everything, didn't you?"

"Not everything," Rachel said quietly. "And we weren't always that close. There was a time in our lives when we went our separate ways, when we were angry with each other. That was a mistake. If you and Dani ever have problems, try to work them out. Don't let anything divide you."

"I won't. But I can see the need for us to have our own lives. I don't want us to be each other's crutch or each other's anchor— you know what I mean?"

Rachel sighed. "I know exactly what you mean."

My phone started buzzing, and I saw Kade's name. When I stopped at a light, I grabbed the phone and sent him a quick text that I had a lot to tell him and if he was free, to join me, and

Jeremy, and my AUNT—in capital letters. He texted back he was on his way.

"Who's that?" Rachel asked. "Boyfriend?"

"No. That's Kade Beckham, the man my mother has been sending money to since he was a child. The son of the security guard that was shot in New York."

Her lips tightened. "He's in San Francisco?"

"Yes. My mom let him stay in her downstairs flat while he was getting ready for a show at an art gallery."

Rachel's gaze turned toward the window, but her profile was hard and a little angry.

"You didn't know?" I asked her.

"No," she said in a clipped voice. "That was a mistake."

"Why was it a mistake?"

"The light is green," she said, ignoring my question.

I drove through the intersection. "I don't believe my mom met Kade's mom at a community center by chance. There's no way anyone supports a complete stranger for twenty years because of a brief meeting. I need to know the truth, Rachel, so I can protect myself and my mom, and maybe Kade, too."

"I understand. I said I'll talk to your investigator."

"And Kade," I said. "He deserves to know the truth."

"Fine, but I don't want to have to go through it twice," Rachel said, a hard note in her voice. "You'll have to wait."

I didn't want to wait, but I didn't have a choice.

We arrived at the café a few minutes later. Jeremy was seated at a table but got up to greet us.

"This is Rachel," I said. "She's my mom's twin sister."

Jeremy looked more than a little surprised. "Well, that is not the new information I expected to hear. I never saw any trace of a sister in your mother's life."

"That's the way we wanted it," Rachel said.

"Can I get you some coffee?" Jeremy asked.

"No thanks," I said, as I sat down at the table.

"I could use a coffee. I'll get it," Rachel said, heading toward the counter.

"Where did you find her?" Jeremy asked as he took his seat.

"I ran into her in a restroom at the hospital. She hasn't told me much," I said, my gaze moving toward the counter where Rachel was ordering coffee. "I'm hoping that will change now." I paused as Kade came into the café.

"I was worried about you when I got back to the house and saw you weren't there," he said. "I thought you were going to stay home."

"A lot has happened," I told him, as he sat down next to me. "My mom woke up, and I spoke to her for a few minutes. And then I ran into my mom's twin sister in the hospital restroom."

"Twin sister?" he echoed. "Are you serious?"

"She's right over there." I turned toward the counter and then realized Rachel wasn't there. "Wait, where is she?" I jumped to my feet as my pulse began to race.

"Maybe the restroom," Jeremy suggested.

I ran down the hallway toward the restrooms. Both were empty. Right across from them was a back door, leading out of the café. I ran outside, my gaze scanning the parking lot, but there was no sign of Rachel.

Kade and Jeremy joined me outside.

"She's gone," I said. "Dammit. I thought we were finally going to get some answers."

"Do you think someone grabbed her when she went to the restroom?" Kade asked.

I met his gaze, wishing that were true. "No. I think she left so she wouldn't have to tell me the truth. I should have kept a closer eye on her, but she seemed willing to meet with you both..." My voice faded away. "But she lied, and I shouldn't be surprised, because she and my mom have been lying their entire lives. Maybe nothing she told me was true."

CHAPTER TWENTY-FOUR

"WHAT DID SHE TELL YOU?" Kade asked.

"Let's go inside," I said. "I'll fill you in."

We moved back into the café, where the barista was calling out Rachel's name. I decided to get her coffee, since I could use a shot of caffeine. Along with the drink came an iced cinnamon roll. I took that to the table, too.

"Maybe something happened to her," Kade said. "She did order coffee and food."

"I think that was just part of her plan. She went along with me until it was easy for her to slip away." I sipped her coffee, which was delicious and probably exactly what I would have ordered. That was weird. I shrugged that thought out of my mind as I focused on the men at the table. "I ran into Rachel at the hospital. I knew instantly she was related to me. Our eyes are the same. She tried to run away from me. I chased her down the stairs and made her talk to me."

"What did you learn?" Kade asked.

"Not that much. She said she didn't want to tell the story twice so when she agreed to speak to Jeremy, she said she'd explain it all then."

"How did you get her to agree to talk to me?" Jeremy asked curiously.

"I told her it was you or the police, that she owed it to me because someone wasn't just trying to kill my mother but also me. Rachel said maybe you could help her find someone. Before you ask, she didn't say who that someone was." I took another sip of coffee as that thought made me feel stressed. "Here's what she did say about the past she shared with my mother. Their parents died when they were young. They lived with some neighbor named Mrs. Hursh. I don't know where that was. Mrs. Hursh taught my mother music. But she couldn't take care of them at some point, and they were split up for three years and put into foster care. They reconnected after high school. My mother got a scholarship to NYU for music and convinced Rachel to go with her."

"They were in New York," Kade said, his mouth tightening.

"Yes. I asked her why my mom was sending your mother money. Rachel said that my mom met you and your mom at a community center in New York shortly after your dad died and that she felt a strong connection to you. She wanted to help."

"By sending a stranger money?" he challenged, a gleam of disbelief in his eyes.

"That's what I asked. Rachel stuck to her answer, but she was surprised and annoyed that my mother had invited you to stay in her downstairs flat."

"There's more to that story," Kade said.

"I agree." I looked at Jeremy. "Maybe you can find some evidence of my mother at NYU. My mom told me that she had me when she was twenty-two. That could have been a lie as well, but if it's not, you might be able to figure out what years she was there."

"Definitely worth a shot," Jeremy said. "But she was probably registered under a different name."

"I think she would have taken music classes. That might have been her major."

"That helps to narrow it down."

"Wait a second," Kade said suddenly. "Did you say your mom woke up?"

"Oh, right, I kind of buried that, didn't I? Yes. She woke up, and they removed the tubes, so I was able to talk to her. She looked right at me and said she was sorry. She also said she doesn't know who shot her and doesn't remember anything about that day."

"But she remembered you, and surely she knows her past," Kade said.

"She wouldn't tell me anything except she left to protect me, and she didn't want it to be for nothing. She started shouting at me to go home, to leave, to stop asking questions. Then her blood pressure went up, and the machines went off, and the doctor told me to go. My mother was sedated. I hope I didn't mess up her recovery by pressing too hard."

"You're trying to help her stay alive," Kade said. "Did the doctor say it was a setback?"

"She just said my mom needs time to rest and heal. I'm afraid she won't have that time if she doesn't tell us where to find the person who is trying to kill her."

"You don't think it's her sister, do you?" Jeremy asked.

"I can't believe it would be, but I have to admit it crossed my mind."

"We don't know if the person hiring muscle on the web is a man or a woman," Kade added.

"But Rachel is my mom's twin sister. I know what that bond feels like, and I don't believe Rachel went to the hospital to hurt her sister. I think she went there to try to help her." I paused, frowning. "Maybe I'm being naïve."

"I'm going to go see what I can dig up on the NYU connection," Jeremy said. "If your mother was there on a music scholarship, I should be able to narrow it down. Hopefully, I'll know exactly who she is by the end of the night."

"That would be amazing."

"One more thing," Kade said. "I need the police file from my father's murder."

"Right. Brynn asked me for that," Jeremy said. "As soon as I get back to my computer, I'll send it to you. I have to warn you, there's not much in the way of evidence."

"I understand, but I would like to see it."

"I'll get it to you as soon as I can."

As Jeremy left, I tore off a chunk of the cinnamon pastry and popped it in my mouth. "This is good. Do you want some?"

"I'm amped up enough without adding any sugar." He paused. "You should have told me you were going to the hospital, Brynn. When I got back from the gallery, and you weren't there..." He ran a hand through his hair. "I know you don't answer to me, but damn—"

"I'm sorry you were worried. I was so shocked when the hospital called, I jumped in my car. I couldn't think about anything but talking to my mom."

"I get that. I'm glad you're all right."

"I'm fine, but I let Rachel out of my sight for a second, and I lost our best lead. I wish I'd gotten more information from her."

"Did she say where she was staying?"

"No. She did say that the police can't help, but she didn't say why. Only that I didn't know what I was dealing with, which is true."

Kade stared back at me, and I could see the wheels turning in his head.

"It looks like you have an opinion," I said.

"Just thinking. If they can't go to the police, then they either don't trust the police or they have something to hide."

"But why would the San Francisco police be a problem? I think their trouble, as Rachel called it, started in New York."

"With the robbery," Kade said, nodding in agreement. "There's a connection."

"I think so." I blew out a breath, shaking my head in bemusement. "I can't believe my mom has a twin that she never talked about. Apparently, they'd meet every few months when my mother took us to the museum, but it wasn't safe for them to be together."

"Perhaps Rachel is the person your mom met with in New Orleans."

I started at that suggestion. "She had to be. That makes sense."

"Did she say anything about your biological father?"

"Only that he was allegedly a terrible person, and my mom didn't want anyone to know who he was. Rachel warned me not to go digging into that secret. She was extremely agitated at the thought of me trying to find him." I paused. "Which makes me wonder if he's the guy at the center of all this now. He could even be a cop, which makes them reluctant to trust the police."

"Do you think your father knows about Rachel?" Kade asked.

"I doubt it. I think my mom left him in the dark about her past. But if he hadn't run away, we could ask him." I frowned. "Every single one of them is good at running, aren't they? No one wants to stay and face the music."

"Except you, Brynn."

"Which makes me brave or stupid; I don't know which."

"Let's go with brave."

I smiled. "I would prefer that."

Kade glanced down at his phone. "I just got the police report from Jeremy. It looks like a sizable file. I need to get back to the house and download this on my computer."

"I'm ready to go," I said, taking one last bite of the cinnamon bun before following him out of the café.

CHAPTER TWENTY-FIVE

I DROVE my car back to the house while Kade followed on his motorcycle. He pulled into the driveway, and I parked behind his truck. Kade grabbed his computer from his apartment and then we went into my mom's house, setting up in the family room.

As Kade downloaded the file, his movements were jerky, and he appeared to be very tense.

"Are you sure you want to do this?" I asked.

"Yes. You're risking your life to get the truth about your mother; I'm just opening a file."

"You're opening a window to the past. It's not just a file."

"I doubt it will tell me that much. I already know that no one was charged with my father's death, and Jeremy said there's no bombshell clue in here."

"That's true." As Kade settled in, I said, "I need to call Dani and fill her in on our aunt. I'll do it upstairs."

"Okay," he said distractedly, his gaze on the computer screen.

I moved up the stairs to my mother's bedroom. I sat down in the middle of the bed and called Dani. "Are you sitting down?" I asked.

"Why? What's happened now?"

"A couple of things."

I drew in a breath, then related what had happened when I got to the hospital. Telling Dani that our mother had woken up, that she'd recognized me, that she'd apologized and then had required a sedative because I'd worked her up too much made me feel like I'd done something wrong. Dani didn't exactly reassure me that I hadn't, instead suggesting that I needed to let Mom recover before I asked any more questions. The important thing was that our mother was awake and that I could come home.

A little irritated with her attitude, I said, "There's more, Dani. Mom has a sister—a twin sister named Rachel. I ran into her at the hospital."

"No way. That's impossible."

"Her hair is dyed blonde, but her face and her eyes are the same as Mom's, the same as ours."

"Mom has a sister?" Dani murmured in wonder. "How is that possible?"

"I don't know how or why she kept that fact to herself, but it is true. They are twins. I don't know if Rachel is the name our aunt was born with, but it's the name she gave me."

"What else did she tell you?" Dani asked.

"Very little. She alluded to some trouble that they'd run into in their lives. She said Mom left us to protect us. I thought she was going to tell me more, but she ran out on me, just like Dad did. No one wants to tell me the truth."

"Because it's all bad," Dani said. "Everything you find out just makes it worse. Did our aunt say who our biological father is?"

"Mom didn't tell her his name, only that he's a bad guy, which also isn't great to think about."

"Brynn, come home."

"You need to stop telling me that," I said wearily.

"I want to protect you. I want our lives to be normal again."

"It's not your job to protect me. And I don't want to come back to Carmel. I don't even want to be normal again."

"What does that mean?" Dani asked, annoyance in her voice.

I knew I was making a mistake. This wasn't the right time, but I had to say it. "When I went to LA a few weeks ago, I auditioned with the Pacific Coast Orchestra for second chair violin. The orchestra is going on tour for two months throughout Europe, starting in a month and lasting through the New Year. They offered me the job on Thursday. I have to give them my answer tomorrow."

"I can't believe this," Dani said in shock. "Why would you audition without telling me? We have the store, our business. I need you, Brynn."

"It's not our business; it's your business."

"Our store is called Two Sisters. Of course it's ours."

"It's your vision; it always was. My dream was music. You know that."

"And what happens after this job? I'm just supposed to wait three months for you to come back?"

"No. You shouldn't wait. You should find someone to help you manage the store."

"So, you're never coming back?" Hurt entered her voice. "I can't believe you're doing this to me with everything else that's going on."

"I'm sorry. I wasn't going to say anything until this problem with Mom was resolved, but I don't know if there's an end in sight."

"What about when I have the baby? Where are you going to be, Brynn? I need you. And not just in the store. You're my sister. You can't miss this important time in my life. I'm going to have your nephew."

"I'll be back before the baby is born," I assured her.

"But you'll miss all the little moments...the first flutter, the first kick, my belly getting bigger."

"We'll talk all the time."

"It won't be the same. This is a scary time for me. I can't believe you'd do this now."

My guilt grew with every word that came out of her mouth, but I had to stay strong. "I've been putting it off for too long. If I don't take this opportunity, I don't know if there will be another one. I need you, too, Dani, but I also have to have a life."

"I've been stopping you from having a life?" she asked angrily. "I have been there for you every second of our lives. I have always looked out for you, Brynn. When Mom died, and you fell apart, I picked you up. I made sure you were okay."

"Yes, you did. But somewhere along the way, I started living your life, instead of mine."

"This isn't you, Brynn. You're just upset about everything that's going on, and you're all alone there. Please come home, and we'll talk about everything."

"I'm not leaving until I figure out what's going on with Mom and her twin sister. They're our family, Dani."

"You and I—that's our family."

"We're still a team, Dani."

"It doesn't sound that way. You're making decisions without me. So, do whatever you want. You're going to, anyway."

I sighed as Dani hung up on me. That conversation had not gone well, but it was done. I punched in Ray's number and got his voicemail. "I'm taking the job, Ray," I said. "But I'm out of town for a few days. Let me know who I need to talk to and what I have to do, and I'll do it. Thank you again for this opportunity. I owe you."

As I ended my message, I let out a sigh of relief. Despite Dani's negative reaction, at least I'd told her the truth, and I'd made a decision. I had one less problem weighing me down.

I took my phone and went downstairs.

Kade was engrossed in whatever he was reading on his computer. He didn't even look up when I sat next to him on the couch.

"Have you found anything?" I asked.

"Maybe," he said, turning his gaze to mine. There was a gleam of excitement in his eyes.

"What?" I asked.

"The owner of the house where my father was shot, the wealthy private collector—his name was James Holden."

"Okay," I said slowly. "Jeremy said that name before, but you look like it means something to you now."

"James Holden doesn't mean anything to me, but he has a brother, Ian Holden. And Ian was a professor of music theory at NYU for almost two decades. Some of those years would coincide with the time your mother was in college on a music scholarship."

I sat up a little straighter. "That is interesting. Why is he in the police report?"

"James and his brother hosted the charity event together, and the NYU music department was the recipient of the money raised that night. The party was held at James's house, but he left before the event was over to fly to London. Ian was the last person on the scene. He said goodbye to my father about thirty minutes before my father was shot."

"Where did Ian go?"

"Home. He lived in a condo in Manhattan," Kade said.

"Ian might have known my mother. How old is he?"

"It doesn't say here, but it probably does online."

I took out my phone and looked him up. "Got it. Ian Holden is fifty-nine years old, and he still teaches at NYU." I paused. "My mom is forty-nine. At least, I think she is, if she was actually twenty-two when she had me. Ian would have been ten years older than her." I looked at some of the images that had come up in my search. "Ian is a good-looking man. There's a bunch of stuff here about his music and his brother the billionaire." My jaw dropped as I read through the headlines of some other articles. "Wait a second. Here's something interesting. He took a job as a guest professor at UC Berkeley this fall." I looked back at Kade. "He's in the area. He's been here since August. We need to find him. I'm going to text Jeremy and see if he can get us an address."

"If he can't do that, we can see what class Holden is teaching at Berkeley and try to find him there," Kade said.

I sent Jeremy a text and then looked at Kade. "This could be the break we've been looking for."

"Maybe. But if Ian knew who killed my father, he didn't say anything at the time. I can't see why he'd talk now. But he is a link to your mother's past."

"And your mother is connected to mine," I reminded him. "This might not be everything, but it's something."

"Something," he echoed. "We'll see."

"He was also the last person to talk to your dad." I paused. "I wonder if Ian was involved in the robbery. The police suspected an inside job. Maybe Ian was supposed to get a cut. Maybe he didn't like living in his brother's shadow."

"He could have been involved with your mom, too. A professor-student relationship."

"It's possible. Rachel warned me against trying to figure out who my biological father is. She said he's a dangerous person. Could he be Ian Holden?"

Kade held up a hand. "Hold on. That's a big leap, Brynn. All we know is that Ian taught at the university where your mother went to school—allegedly. Let's not get too far ahead."

"Far ahead? I feel like I'm constantly behind." I paused as the doorbell rang. "Who could that be?"

Kade jumped to his feet, and I followed him down the hall. I looked through the window and saw my father and a woman on the porch. "My dad and my stepmother," I said, my stomach sinking.

"Your father came back."

"Yes, but he came back with her. That can't be good."

Kade gave me a small smile. "Only one way to find out."

"I know."

I squared my shoulders as Kade opened the door. After letting my father and Vicky into the house, Kade headed down to his apartment. I couldn't blame him. I was getting tired of all my family drama, too.

Vicky looked stylish as always, wearing black jeans, boots, and leather jacket, her dark hair pulled back from her face. But there were shadows under her eyes. The last few days hadn't been easy for her.

My father looked better than he had earlier in the day. He'd obviously taken a shower at some point and changed into dark slacks and a long-sleeve gray sweater. Only his bloodshot eyes gave evidence of the stress of the last several days.

Vicky looked around the room, taking note of the broken walls and damaged furniture. "What happened in here?" she asked.

"Someone trashed the place right after my mother was shot," I answered.

"I didn't realize it was so bad," my father said, as his gaze swept the room.

"You weren't in any condition to notice much of anything."

"I'm sorry about that, and I want to apologize for running out on you this morning."

"Why did you?" I asked.

"I couldn't stand the look of betrayal in your eyes." He paused. "It's still there. I never wanted you to find out you weren't my daughter, Brynn. I shouldn't have said anything to you."

"It's the secret, the lie, that bothers me more than the fact you're not my biological father. I can see why you didn't say anything when I was younger, but I'm twenty-seven, and it was long past time to tell me something that important."

"Your mother never wanted you to know. I couldn't imagine breaking that promise after she died. You'd already lost her. I couldn't let you lose me, too."

I stared back at him. "I feel like we lost a big part of you when Mom died. You were never the same after that. Maybe you didn't want to tell us that you weren't our father, but I feel like deep down, it played a role in our relationship. You might have tried to stay closer if we were your blood. But Mom left you with two kids who weren't yours."

"You were mine," he said fiercely. "And I've always loved you. I just didn't know how to show it. Your mother was better at that. She was loving and nurturing. I always felt awkward and uncomfortable. I never said the right thing, and I knew I wasn't the father you wanted me to be." He let out a breath and sat down on the sofa.

Vicky sat down next to him, putting a comforting hand on his leg.

I took the chair across from them, thinking that this was the way our relationship had played out since they'd gotten married —the two of them together and me on the opposite side.

"When did you get here?" I asked Vicky.

"Your father called me this morning, and I got on the first plane out."

"Have you spoken to the police yet?" I asked.

"I spoke to Inspector Greenman briefly," Vicky replied. "But he wants to have a longer conversation at some point."

My gaze moved to my father. "What about you?"

He shook his head. "Not yet. Did you tell him you saw me?"

"No," I admitted. "But you need to call him and tell him exactly what happened. I don't know why you're afraid to do that. You didn't shoot, Mom, did you?"

"Of course I didn't shoot her," my father said vehemently. "I've never shot a gun in my life."

"Then you shouldn't be afraid to talk to the police."

"I slapped your mother the day before she was shot. If that was caught on camera anywhere, I'm going to be a suspect," he said. "I don't want to get railroaded because of a fight. I shouldn't have hit her, but my God, what she did to me—the lies, the deception—I had a right to be angry." He paused, his gaze narrowing on my face. "I don't know why you're not angry, too, Brynn."

ver, but obviously I can't change your mind. I'm surprised
olice didn't catch up to you before now. I thought they were
hing your hotel."

 haven't been back to the hotel. Vicky brought me a change
othes."

is actions only made me more suspicious. It was one thing
t want to talk to the police and another to actively avoid

dad rose to his feet, his gaze pleading as he looked at me.
e you, Brynn. Maybe I haven't told you that enough or
ed you that I care, but I do. I was thrown when your mom
 I admit that. I let you down. I hope you'll give me a chance
ke it up to you."

is what it is," I said as I stood up. "But running away from
olice doesn't make me proud. It makes me worry that
 hiding something else."

 drew in a quick breath, glanced at Vicky, then back at me.
ot hiding anything, Brynn."

ur actions say otherwise."

 thought for a moment, then turned to his wife. "She's
 should talk to the police inspector before we leave."

u can call him from LA," Vicky said. "With our attorney on
."

, I'll call him now, from the car." He turned back to me.
u can believe that I'm not hiding anything."

ould have believed it more if he was willing to make the
 front of me, but I could always find out what happened
spector Greenman.

father moved toward the front door, then paused, looking
 me. "Your mother has told so many lies, how will you
ow what's the truth, Brynn?"

know it when I find it. I'm not counting on her to tell me
h. But it's out there, and I'm going to get it."

safe," he said. "I couldn't stand to lose you, Brynn. And

"Oh, I'm angry. I have been through every emotion there is since I found out she was alive. I can't believe she left us. She said she did it to protect us. But there had to have been another way."

"When did she say that?" he asked.

"She was awake for a few minutes this morning, but she didn't tell me much except that she'd had to disappear to save our family from some danger she was in."

"Is she going to be all right? Does she know who shot her?"

"Mom said she doesn't know who would shoot her, but I don't believe that's true. While we were talking, she got agitated, and the doctor sedated her. I can't talk to her again until tomorrow."

"What kind of danger was she in?" Vicky asked.

"I don't know. I think her whole life was a series of secrets. Mom wasn't who she said she was. She got into trouble when she was young, and it followed her to our family, and then came back around now." I paused. "Did either of you know that she had a sister?"

"What?" my dad asked in surprise. "No way. She was an only child."

"She wasn't. She has a twin sister, an identical twin sister."

"That's unbelievable," my father said. "How did you find out, Brynn?"

"I ran into my aunt at the hospital. She said her name is Rachel. She didn't have much else to say, except alluding to the fact that they were in danger and had been for a long time. I thought we were going to talk it all out, but she ran out on me, too. Seems to be what people do these days."

My father tipped his head at my pointed comment. "It's been a difficult time for all of us."

"I can't believe she had a sister," Vicky murmured, shock apparent in her eyes. "I guess I really didn't know her at all."

"Probably not," I said. "So, what now?"

"Vicky and I are going back to LA," my father replied.

"I don't understand how you can just leave. Don't you want to see Mom? Don't you want to talk to her?"

Before my dad could answer, Vicky cut in. "Why should he see her? Why should any of us see her? She betrayed all of us, me included. I was her best friend. She left me, too."

"Don't you want to know why?" I challenged.

"If she won't tell you, she's not going to tell us," Vicky said.

"She might tell you, Dad. You were her husband."

"I gave her a chance to explain; she didn't take it." He shook his head. "Vicky is right. We are not a part of her life anymore. She made sure of that. I'm glad she has survived the shooting, and I hope she can stay alive, but it's not our problem. You have your own life, Brynn. Focus on that. I'm certain that's what your mother would want." He paused, giving me a sharp look. "She told you to leave, too, didn't she?"

"Yes," I admitted. "She said she didn't want it to all be for nothing. She wanted me to be safe, and she was sorry she ever told the nurse to call me."

"I can't believe she had your number."

"She was watching over us." I paused. "Didn't you wonder if she might be alive when Dani told you she saw her at our high school graduation?"

"Wait, what?" Vicky asked in surprise.

"I thought Dani imagined it," he said. "I told her that her mom was always watching over her. I had no idea she was alive, although maybe deep down it did give me pause. Your mother's body was never found, and that part always haunted me. But I couldn't imagine how she could be alive and not with me or her children." He let out a breath. "I've spent the last week in complete turmoil since I learned she was alive, but I realize now that there's no going back. She isn't the woman I fell in love with, and I'm no longer that man. She moved on and so did we. I hate that she's pulling you back into the past. Don't let her do that, Brynn. Go home, live your life, and forget about her."

It wasn't the worst advice. But the thought of never know-

ing… "I can't," I said. "I have to know why it we ended up here. And I have to try to save h

"Why?" Vicky asked. "She left you, Brynn.

"You don't have to keep saying that. I kno I loved her, and I think she loved us. If this us, then don't we owe her some protection, t

"There's nothing we can do," my father us enough information to help her. And th into it. They'll find who did this to her."

"They haven't found them yet."

"Well, the longer you stay here, the mor my father said. "If you still love her even a do what she wants you to do—go home."

Silence fell between us, then Vicky clea want to rush this, but we need to leave no she said.

"Why did you come here, Vicky?" I ask

"Your father called me this morning, ar couldn't leave him here alone." Vicky pau that your mother loved your dad, and mother, but their marriage ended a lon husband. I love you and Dani, too. We're

"We've never been the family," I said us to the side as soon as you got Dad t your fault. He let you. He let Dani and m

"That's not true," my father said.

"It's not true," Vicky added. "I loved own."

"You know what? It doesn't matter. you. I just want us to be honest. You sho that flight. But the police will catch u don't you?"

"I'll talk to them," my father sai attorney."

I shook my head. "I don't see w

Dani would die. Think about that when you're deciding how long you should stay here."

His words sent a shiver down my spine. After they left, I turned the dead bolt and leaned against the door, wondering if I was being fair to Dani to put my life on the line. We'd been born together. I couldn't imagine living without her, and I knew she couldn't imagine living without me.

As I thought about our twin bond, I wondered if that's the way my mother and my aunt felt, if that's why trouble had found them both, because one couldn't stand by while the other was in danger.

My mother said she'd done everything to protect us.

Had she done it for us or for Rachel?

I pushed myself off the door and walked back to the family room. Then I called Kade.

"Everything all right?" he asked.

"Yes, my father and stepmother are flying back to Los Angeles. They're done with this whole situation."

"Just like that, huh?"

"My dad said he'd been through enough hell with my mother. I can't say I totally blame him. He wasn't going to talk to the police or even go back to his hotel, but I think I persuaded him to call Inspector Greenman. We'll see if he actually does it."

"I don't understand why he's avoiding the police."

"It's because he slapped my mom in their public meet and he's afraid someone will try to pin the attempted murder on him."

"Which only makes him seem more suspicious."

"I can't disagree," I said wearily. "But deep down, I think he's just protecting himself. I don't believe he shot her. Anyway, what are you doing? Working?"

"No. I've been reading up on Ian Holden. I looked up his classes, and he's teaching one at ten o'clock tomorrow morning. If we can't get an address for him before that, we should check out his class."

"Sounds good."

"I'm going to do a little work now, unless you need me," Kade said.

I wanted to tell him I was starting to need him every second of the day, but that would sound more than a little desperate. "I'm fine. I can do some cleanup around here."

"All right. Why don't I put in a few hours of work and then pick up some Thai food to share? Interested?"

"Absolutely," I said.

"If you need anything before then, call me. I'm right downstairs."

"I'll be fine," I said, hoping that was true.

CHAPTER TWENTY-SIX

THE DOORBELL WOKE ME UP, and I sat up on the family room couch in bemusement. I checked my watch as the bell rang again. It was after seven and it was dark outside. I'd apparently fallen asleep.

I grabbed my phone and saw a couple of texts from Kade, including the last one, which said he was outside. Jumping up, I moved quickly down the hall, checked to make sure it was him, and then let him in.

Relief filled his gaze when he saw me. "I was beginning to worry about you," he said, as he stepped inside, carrying a large paper bag that smelled delicious. "You didn't answer any of my texts."

"I fell asleep on the couch. Everything caught up to me." I tucked my hair behind my ear, feeling a little self-conscious about my appearance. I had no idea what I looked like, but it probably wasn't good.

"Good. I'm sure you needed the rest, and I'm glad that's why you were ignoring my texts." He led the way into the kitchen. "I wasn't sure what you liked, so I ordered a variety of dishes."

"It all smells great, and I'm not that picky."

"Neither am I," he said, as he pulled cartons out of the bag. "Especially when I'm hungry. I worked up an appetite."

"Sounds like you were productive," I said, seeing the lightness in his gaze.

"I was very productive until the end when I got stuck on how to finish one of my pieces. It was time to take a break."

"Does that happen to you often—getting stuck?"

"More often than I'd like. It usually means I've gone wrong a step earlier, and I have to figure out where that was."

"What do you do when you're blocked?"

"I push through it. When that doesn't work, I take a long ride somewhere on my bike, or I get in the shower. That seems to free my brain up."

The picture of a naked Kade getting inspired in the shower inspired all kinds of thoughts in my head. I wouldn't mind losing myself in Kade for a while. He was not only incredibly sexy, he was also incredibly kind. I hadn't come across that combination in a very long time, maybe ever.

Kade gave me a quizzical look. "Something wrong?"

I cleared my throat, knowing I could not tell him where my thoughts had gone just now. "Just thinking," I said vaguely.

Fortunately, Kade didn't press the question as he filled up his plate with Thai noodles, yellow curry, and shrimp. I took a little of everything as well and then we sat down at the table to eat.

"Thanks for picking up the food," I said.

"I didn't think you'd want to go out."

"No. I'm starting to feel more comfortable here in the house, even though it's probably not the safest place in the world for me. But no one has tried to get back in again, so that's a good sign." I paused. "I wonder where Rachel went after she left me. She must have a hotel room somewhere."

"Probably under a name we haven't heard of yet," Kade said dryly.

"I'm sure you're right." I paused as Kade pulled out his phone to read a text. "Everything okay?"

"Just a friend wondering when I'm coming back to New York." He sent a quick reply, then set down his phone and continued eating.

"What did you tell him?" I asked curiously.

"That I have no idea."

"Do you still have an apartment there?" I asked, curious about the rest of his life.

"I sublet it for six months. I'm not sure if I'll go back there, stay here, or go somewhere else."

"I'm sure your friends miss you."

He shrugged. "My friends have their own lives."

"Are they mostly artists?"

"Some are. Some aren't. It's not a requirement."

I suspected he wasn't the kind of man who needed a lot of people in his life. He could probably be on his own and be perfectly happy. "Tell me something about yourself that has nothing to do with our parents, Kade. I know you got started in art early. What else did you do? Were you a sports guy? Were you good in school?"

"I played pick-up basketball in the park growing up, but that was about it for sports. As for school, I was more of a trouble-maker than a student. I found school completely irrelevant to my life. My mom was struggling with two jobs and very little money. She didn't have time or energy to push me to do well academically, although she did try. But I didn't see how most of the subjects I had to learn were going to help me."

"I bet you were good in art."

"Spent most of my days drawing instead of taking notes," he admitted. "What about you? Was it always music?"

"Yes. It was the one thing I was good at."

"I'm sure you were good at more than one thing."

"Not really. I was an okay student. I didn't care that much about my grades. I never did extra credit, while Dani always did anything she could do to get extra points. She was a serious overachiever. If there was something to win, she won it."

"Did you like to compete, too?"

"No. I didn't need to win, and I didn't want to fail, so it was easier to just stay in the middle."

"Except when it came to music."

"Except then," I agreed. "That's where I excelled."

"We both knew early on what mattered to us. That's not a bad thing. We didn't waste our time on subjects or activities that didn't matter to us."

I thought about that. "I didn't go after music the way you went after art, though. I always played, but I never really believed music could be my career. I couldn't think that big or that far in the future. I'd get anxious when I tried. I was afraid to want too much, because I knew how bad it would feel if I didn't get it. I think some of that insecurity goes back to losing my mom at an early age. But maybe that's not true, because Dani didn't become insecure, she actually grew in confidence. She had ambition and drive, and I was happy to follow her. I let her take over my life."

"And then you got mad about it," he said, a perceptive light in his eyes.

"I did. But it was my fault. I gave her the control." I paused. "That's not exactly true. I didn't have to give her control because she always had it. Our relationship started before we were born, and she was born first, which made her the oldest. She never let me forget that."

"By a few minutes, I'm guessing."

"Those few minutes were all it took," I said with a smile. I finished my last bite and wiped my mouth. "Thanks for dinner. I should pay you."

"You can buy the next one."

I liked the idea of another dinner. I liked the idea of spending more time with Kade. But at the same time, I felt like we were coming perilously close to the edge of a cliff, and future time was not guaranteed.

"You just lost your smile," Kade said, his gaze turning speculative.

"Just thinking how impossible it is to make future plans when the future seems very unpredictable."

"Well, I've always thought too much planning is a bad idea anyway, even when it's not life and death. Sometimes, you just have to make choices as they come and roll with the consequences."

"I'm getting pretty banged up from all the rolling. So are you," I couldn't help pointing out. "You have a nasty bruise on your face."

"Doesn't it just make me look hot?" he teased.

Butterflies danced through my stomach at his words. "I don't think I need to tell you that you often look hot. You already know that." I cleared my throat and then got up to take my empty plate to the kitchen. "Are you done? I'll put the leftovers in the fridge."

"I'm done," he said, bringing his plate to the sink. "And I didn't mean to make you uncomfortable, Brynn."

"You didn't," I said, not quite looking him in the eye as I put the cartons in the fridge. I wanted to get out of the kitchen, because he was way too close, so I left the dirty dishes in the sink and walked over to the couch.

I should have picked one of the chairs, I thought, as Kade sat down next to me a few minutes later.

"You're still uncomfortable," he said, a knowing gleam in his eyes.

"It's been an uncomfortable day. I had a rough conversation with Dani earlier."

"Oh, yeah? About Rachel?"

"Yes, and about the orchestra job. I told her I was going to take it."

Surprise and approval mixed in his gaze. "That's good. How did she respond?"

"She was hurt, angry, and disappointed. She told me to do

whatever I wanted because I was going to do that anyway. Then she hung up on me."

"Did that make you want to change your mind?" he asked.

"No. It's the right move for me professionally. It wasn't the best time to tell her, but I needed to make a decision by tomorrow, so I made it. It was probably crazy to say yes to the job with everything going on with my mom. But she did wake up earlier today, and I think she's going to recover, so..."

"You need to move on with your life," he finished.

"I do." I paused. "To be honest, Kade, you helped me make up my mind, too, when you pushed me to make some new music. I hadn't done that in a long time. It opened my mind back up, not just to this new job, but to other possibilities. You're so free. You do what you want, live where you want. I want to feel like that, like I'm in control."

"You should feel like that. You should live like that, Brynn."

"Do you ever feel like you're being selfish?"

"No, but I don't have a twin that I'm in business with," he said with a smile.

"That's fair."

"But you only get one life to live. This is your life. You have to make the most of it."

"You're right. I just don't know what path to take."

"That's what makes life exciting. I feel the most alive when things are uncomfortable, when they're hard, when I'm out of my element. It's so much better than boring."

"I can barely remember what boring feels like."

He smiled. "That's good, Brynn."

"Is it good?" I asked, completely captivated by the glittering look in his eyes.

"It means you're living, not just existing."

"Am I living or am I running?"

"Does it matter? Your blood is pumping. You're taking action and making decisions. That's what counts."

"I could have died last night," I reminded him.

His smile faded. "I'm very aware of that. I'm not saying that you don't have to take precautions right now, because you're in danger and that comes with some limitations. But later, when all of this is resolved, you should live your life on your own terms."

"I don't know if I'm going to have a later," I said. "Which is why I don't want to wait, because if I wait, I might miss out on something amazing."

His gaze darkened. "What are you afraid of missing out on?"

I licked my lips. "I'm…I'm not sure," I lied, losing my courage at the last second. I'd never been good at asking for what I wanted or just taking it.

"You're sure, Brynn. Go for it. Ask for what you want."

Kade wasn't making it easy. He knew what I wanted, but he was forcing me to choose, to act, to own it. And I was ready to do that. "What if the answer is no?"

"That's the risk you have to take. Is what you want worth the risk?"

His husky voice made the answer to that question incredibly clear. I leaned forward, putting my hands on either side of his handsome face. His dark gaze burned with the heat growing between us, and I wanted that heat everywhere.

"I want this," I said, pressing my mouth against his. "I want you."

He responded immediately, our hot kisses freeing me from whatever lingering doubts I might have. I wasn't going to think tonight. I wasn't going to judge myself or anyone else. I was just going to feel. I wanted to live wildly, recklessly, passionately. Thankfully, Kade was on the same page.

Within minutes, we were tearing off each other's clothes. The bedrooms were too far away. The need was too great. I didn't know what tomorrow would bring, but I had tonight, and I wanted to make it count.

I threw caution to the wind when I threw myself into his arms, and Kade made me feel alive in a way I'd never felt before. I was going to savor every last second of it.

CHAPTER TWENTY-SEVEN

I WAS DISAPPOINTED to wake up alone in bed in the guest room on Monday morning. At some point, we'd wanted a bed and making love to Kade in my mother's bed had seemed wrong, so we'd gone into the guest room. I thought I'd wake up in Kade's arms. Now, only the delicious smell of coffee made me feel better.

Kade was gone, but he'd once again been nice enough to make coffee. Although maybe he'd just made it for himself. Maybe I kept giving him credit when he was just taking care of himself. I frowned at that thought.

Wrapping a throw blanket around my naked body, regrets and doubts crept into my mind. I forcibly pushed them out of my head. I wouldn't regret the night we'd had, the passion we'd shared. I'd never felt so free, so very much like the woman inside my head, not the woman I often pretended to be. Kade had opened something up inside of me that I'd been suppressing my whole life. I would always be grateful for that.

I got out of bed and walked down the hall, hoping to find Kade in the kitchen, but while the coffeepot was full, there was no sign of him. I gathered my clothes from the floor in the family room, heat burning my cheeks as I remembered all that had gone on between us. I'd had sex before, but not sex like that. I'd never felt so wild or so brave. Nor had I ever felt so well-loved.

But it wasn't love; it was sex. And I shouldn't confuse the two. With that reminder, I went upstairs to shower and dress.

When I came back down thirty minutes later, Kade was in the kitchen, looking incredibly sexy, and a wave of heat ran through me when he gave me a very intimate smile.

"Morning," he said huskily.

"I thought you might have gone to work."

"Nope. Just went downstairs to change."

"You get up early, don't you?"

"Always have." He gave me a smile. "Why are you standing so far away?"

I drew in a breath. "I wasn't sure…"

He breached the distance between us in three short steps and kissed me before I could get another word out of my mouth. "Last night was fun," he said. Then he kissed me again.

My heart was already pounding too fast. "It was very fun," I agreed. "A good…escape. From everything that has been going on."

He tilted his head, giving me a speculative look. "What are you thinking? That I'm expecting something from you, Brynn?"

"No, of course not. And I'm not expecting anything from you. It was just a great night. That's all it was. And it was good. And now I'm rambling like an idiot."

He smiled. "You overthink things, Brynn."

"I know," I said with a sigh. "It's a bad habit. So, what's the plan for today?"

"If we want to make Professor Holden's class, we need to leave in about thirty minutes. Unless you got an address from Jeremy?"

"No. I checked my phone when I was getting dressed. He hasn't gotten back to me yet. I also called the hospital. My mom is still asleep, so I'll check in with her after we see Professor Holden."

"Okay. Do you want coffee and something to eat before we go?"

"Yes. And Kade, I want to say one thing…"

He met my gaze. "Then say it."

"Whatever happens in the future, I don't have any regrets."

"Me, either."

———

We arrived at UC Berkeley a few minutes after ten and managed to slip into the back of the auditorium where Ian Holden was teaching. The room was packed with over a hundred students and within minutes, it was clear to see why the professor was so popular. Ian Holden was a charismatic and entertaining speaker. He was also a handsome older man, who looked younger than his age. His brown hair was thick, and wavy. He was fit and dressed in jeans and a button-down shirt. He had an engaging smile and a way of looking around the class that made it feel like he was looking right at you. I could only imagine how handsome and interesting he must have been twenty-seven plus years ago.

"He was good," I murmured to Kade as Ian finished the lecture.

"Was he?" Kade asked, stifling a yawn.

I laughed. "Were you bored?"

"I told you last night I was never much of a student. Also, I didn't get a lot of sleep last night."

His wicked smile sent a tingle down my spine. "Maybe we can take a nap later."

"I like the way you think."

"But right now, we need to talk to the professor."

We got up and made our way down the steps to the stage. The line of students wanting to talk to Ian was ten deep, so we waited off to the side.

I was impressed with how interested he appeared to be in

each student's question. He gave all his attention to the person he was talking to. It was very charming.

Finally, the last of the students walked away, and he turned to look at us. His jaw dropped when he saw me, an audible gasp coming through his parted lips.

"My God," he murmured. "Who are you?"

"Brynn Landry," I said. "This is Kade Beckham."

Ian barely gave Kade more than a cursory look before his gaze swept my face once more. "You look just like someone I used to know."

"What was her name?"

"It was Kim," he said. "Kim Larimer."

I made a mental note of the last name. I had no idea if it was her real name, or one she'd bought, but it would help us track down her past. "Kim is my mother," I said.

He shook his head in bemusement. "I can't believe it. Your mother? I always wondered what happened to her. I had no idea she had a child. How old are you?"

"Twenty-seven." I stiffened when I realized he was adding something up in his head. *Was he trying to figure out if I was his daughter? Was he my biological father?* That thought shook me. Aside from his dark hair, I didn't feel like we looked very much alike, but then I had clearly gotten my mother's genes. "Did you and my mother have a relationship?" I asked. "When she was a student at NYU, and you were her professor?"

"Is that what you came here to ask me?" Ian challenged.

"It's one question, and you didn't answer it."

"Why are you here?" he countered.

"My mother was shot last Thursday," I replied. "Did you know that? It happened outside her house in San Francisco in the middle of the afternoon."

He stared back at me. "I don't know anything about Kim's life. I haven't seen her since before you were born."

"You didn't know she's living in San Francisco? It's just a coincidence that you took a guest lecturer job very close to her?"

"Yes. What is going on? Why are you asking me about your mother?"

"Because we think she might have been involved in the robbery at your brother's estate," Kade answered. "That robbery happened while Kim was a student at NYU. The thieves were never caught. They got away with a lot, including murder. A security guard was killed."

"Yes, I know," Ian said.

"Did you know that that guard was my father?" Kade asked.

Ian straightened, shifting his feet, his gaze darting around the room as if he was looking for an escape hatch. Finally, it came back to us. "I'm sorry about your father, but I don't know why you've both come to talk to me after all this time. I don't know anything about the robbery except that my brother was the victim." Ian turned to me, his mouth no longer smiling. "And your mother was definitely not a victim. She did exactly what she wanted."

I stared back at him, hearing anger and pain in his voice. "She hurt you, didn't she? You had a relationship with my mother. Admit it." I could see by the flinch in his shoulders that I was right.

"I don't have to tell you anything," Ian said.

"But you should," I urged. "Look, someone is trying to kill my mother, and it has become clear that it's tied to her past. I'm desperately trying to unravel that past. I believe my mother might have been connected to what happened at your brother's house. Please, just tell me what was between you."

He drew in a breath as he wrestled with my request. "I can't say I'm surprised she's in trouble, because she was nothing but trouble."

"So, you did have a relationship?"

"One that she started. She came to my office after class. Then she tracked me down at my apartment. It was completely inappropriate, but she was beautiful and sexy, and I couldn't say no.

It was a wild, torrid affair," he said, his gaze somewhat distant now, as if he'd gotten lost in the past.

"What happened?" I asked.

"It ended as fast and as abruptly as it began."

"Did it end before the robbery or after?" Kade asked.

"The two events were not connected," Ian said, then paused, frowning. "Were they connected?"

"Did Kim ever ask you anything about your brother, about his collection of jewelry and art, about his party?" Kade asked.

I watched in fascination as Kade's questions seemed to start a whole new train of thought in Ian's head.

"She did ask me about my brother," Ian admitted. "I didn't think much about it. He was a self-made billionaire. Everyone asked about him. She wanted me to take her to the party that night, but I said no. There would be other people from the university there. She said she was dying to see his estate." He cleared his throat. "I wanted to make her happy, so I took her to his house the week before the party, so she could see it."

I started at that piece of information. "You took her to the house?"

"Yes."

"What did you do there?" Kade asked.

"We just walked around."

"Was she ever alone?" Kade pressed.

"Maybe for a short time, but not for long."

"Why do you think she wanted to go to the house?" I asked, directing my question to Kade.

He met my gaze. "Maybe to get inside information on the layout, the security system." He turned to Ian. "Did you have access to the security system?"

"I had my own code to get in. My brother didn't care if I used his house when he wasn't there, mostly because I never did. I didn't love going there. I wasn't impressed by his wealth or by him. We were very different people. He only cared about money. He valued himself by how many dollar signs he had after his name." Ian paused. "After I took Kim to the house, I realized that her passion wasn't really for music. She barely looked at the violin my brother had purchased from Solomon Hasher."

"Really?" I asked. "That seems strange. Solomon is a renowned violinist."

"I thought it was odd, too," he admitted.

"Kim used you to get into your brother's house," Kade said harshly.

"I don't know that that's true," Ian said slowly.

Despite his words, I could see that he was starting to realize that was exactly what had happened. I felt immense disappointment in my mother's behavior, too. I had never thought she was that mercenary.

"Why didn't you tell the police you took Kim to the house a week before the robbery?" Kade asked. "That wasn't in the police report."

"I didn't believe it was relevant. She wasn't at the party. The police only asked me about that night. It never occurred to me that our trip had had anything to do with the robbery. Kim a twenty-one-year-old girl who played the violin. She wasn't dangerous."

"But you were at the party," Kade said. "And you were the last one to leave, the last one to speak to my father. Isn't that correct?"

"Yes. I went to that party because it was a fundraiser for the college. When it was over, I said goodbye to the security guard, and I left. I don't know what happened after that."

"Did you see my mother after the party?" I asked.

"No. She called off our next date. She was sick. I wanted to take care of her, but she lived with roommates, and we couldn't let anyone know about us. I kept waiting for her to get better and call me, but she never did. The next thing I knew, she dropped out of school, and her number was disconnected." He paused at the sound of voices.

I turned my head to see several college kids entering the auditorium.

"There's another class starting soon," Ian said. "We need to leave."

"Wait," I said. "Can you give me your number? I might have more questions."

He hesitated. "I really don't want to talk about this anymore. I'm sorry Kim is hurt, but we ended a long time ago. Good luck."

He walked away as the next teacher came down to the stage. As they exchanged a few words, Kade and I headed up the steps and out of the auditorium.

Kade was tense and silent as we walked across the parking lot to my car. When we got inside, I turned to him. "What do you think?"

"I think your mother helped the robbery crew get into the house, and she used her professor to do it."

"But she felt guilty when your father was killed and sent your mother money."

"Blood money," he said coldly. "I'm sorry I sold her my art. I'm sorry I moved into her house. I'm sorry I ever met her."

I could understand where his anger was coming from, and I suddenly realized where this might all be going. Kade was done with my mom, and he might be done with me, too.

CHAPTER TWENTY-EIGHT

"Let's go back to the city," Kade said. "I need to get to work."

I started the engine and pulled out of the lot. On the way back to San Francisco, I thought about what I could say to him that might make him feel better, but nothing came to mind. If my mom had helped that crew, then she was tied to the murder of Kade's father. And whatever she'd done to help Kade had come from a place of guilt.

I'd felt jealous of her interest in Kade's life, in her willingness to support a complete stranger over her own daughter. Now I just felt incredibly sorry that he'd been hurt again, that her actions had brought him more pain.

I should have gone home a long time ago. I wasn't the only one getting hurt, and Kade didn't deserve any of this.

While the thoughts spun around in my head, I couldn't get any words out. And Kade didn't seem interested in talking, his gaze turned out the window as we crossed over the Bay Bridge and headed back into the city.

When we got to the house, Kade followed me inside, then stopped in the entry. "Why don't you make sure everything is okay here?"

"And then what? What are you going to do?" I asked.

"I need to get some work done, Brynn."

"I get that, but do you want to talk about what we learned?"

"No. I'd rather not talk about any of it," he said harshly.

"You're upset."

"I'm pissed. I'm more angry than I've been in a long time, and I don't want to take that out on you."

"I appreciate that, but I think we should talk it out."

"I can't. I'm going downstairs and…" His lips tightened. "You know what? I'm not going to work. I'm going to pack up my things and find a hotel. I cannot stay in your mother's house."

A wave of disappointment ran through me. "Okay. I understand."

"It's not you," he said. "I can't stay here knowing she…" He shook his head. "Do you realize that she might have actually killed my father, Brynn? We keep thinking she let the crew in. Maybe she was part of the crew. Maybe she pulled the trigger."

"I can't believe that, Kade."

"You didn't know her. You were a little kid who loved her mother, but you didn't know who she was, what she did."

"That's true, but—"

He cut me off with a hard shake of his head. "Where do you think she got the money to pay my mother all those years, Brynn?"

"I don't know."

"Where do you think she got the money to buy this house?"

"I don't know," I repeated.

"Yes, you do know. She used what she stole to finance her life. It's the only answer that makes sense. No one ever found the diamonds or the cash or the art that went missing that night. And think about what happened here, all the holes in the walls. It's obvious that someone was looking for something. I think it's what she stole all those years ago. She probably took it from whoever is trying to kill her, from whoever else was in the crew."

His words painted a horrifying scenario, but there was a lot of truth to them.

"You should go home," Kade continued. "Your mother was lost to you a long time ago. Even if she recovers, you'll never get back the person you lost, because that person doesn't exist. Let her live in your memories. It's safer."

"I thought you were the one who never chose safe," I reminded him. "And I need to hear my mother confirm everything you just said."

"You think she's suddenly going to confess to crimes she committed more than twenty years ago?"

"Yes, because I'm her daughter, and I think she loves me enough to tell me the truth now."

He shook his head. "You're living in a world of delusion." He moved toward the door, then turned back to me. He blew out a breath. "I'm sorry. I just said I wasn't going to take out my anger on you and that's exactly what I'm doing. I'm not walking out on you. If you're staying here, then I'll stay, too. I don't want you to be alone."

"I don't want you to stay here if it's going to make you crazy. You don't deserve that. I can take care of myself, even though it might not look that way."

"Why don't I take you to a hotel?"

"Why don't you just do whatever you need to do, Kade. I need time to think about what we've learned and what I want to do next."

"Are you going to stay here?"

"Until my mom wakes up. Then I'll go to the hospital. After that, I'll see."

"Touch base with me before you leave. I'll go with you."

I shook my head. "I don't think that's a good idea. I've already lost a day of talking to my mom because I got her agitated. If you try to talk to her in this mood, she'll probably freak out again."

He frowned. "Well, call me before you go. We'll figure it out."

I turned the dead bolt after he left, feeling more alone than I had since I'd arrived. Whatever had been brewing between us had been instantly snuffed out by the knowledge that my mother was probably involved in his father's death. He would never be able to look at me without being reminded of the tragic loss of his dad.

The sound of an engine revving took me to the window. Kade sped out of the driveway on his motorcycle. Apparently, he'd decided not to work but to take his anger for a ride.

Letting the curtain drop, I walked slowly down the hall, debating my next move. The open door to the guest room and the messy bed reminded me of the passion we'd shared, which now felt like a million years ago. I moved inside, stripped the sheets off the bed and then took them into the laundry room. I started the wash and then returned to the family room.

Kade had left his computer on the coffee table. It was still open, and as I hit the space bar, it lit up with the pages from the police report. I sat down and started reading, eager to see again exactly what the police had found on the scene and where their investigation had led. I was particularly interested in what had been stolen, and I zeroed in on that section.

James Holden had reported the loss of stones that included diamonds, sapphires, and opals as well as several pieces of jewelry, with a combined value of ten million dollars, and that had been more than twenty-seven years ago. It would all be worth a lot more today. The two stolen paintings had been valued at another two million dollars, Holden had reported missing a half-million dollars in cash.

Who kept that much cash in their house? I couldn't even imagine.

If my mom had been involved in the robbery and gotten some or all of what had been taken, she would have never had to work again. Maybe my mother was a criminal and not an innocent victim. Perhaps her shooting had been retribution for betrayal among thieves.

As I thought about that, I had to wonder about Rachel, too. She'd been in New York with my mother. *Had she been part of the*

*crew, too? Had they been in on it together? Was that why they'd gone
on the run and why they couldn't go to the police now?*

Putting those disturbing thoughts on hold, I read through the
rest of the report, but nothing else jumped out at me. We'd
already found the link between my mom and the Holden broth-
ers. The theory that Kade's father was in on the job wasn't
backed up by anything but speculation. There was no link
between him and the Holdens. Kade's father had worked for the
private security company for more than two years with no inci-
dent. The only clue that had led to the speculation was that he'd
told the other security personnel he was going to stay behind to
take one last pass through the house. They said they didn't know
why he'd done that because they'd all done their checks thirty
minutes earlier.

*Why had he stayed behind? Had he seen something or heard
something?*

Sadly, I didn't think we'd ever know. I looked up as the sound
of bells from the washing machine pierced my reverie. I got up
and moved the bedding into the dryer, then I returned to the
couch, thinking about what I'd put together so far.

I couldn't begin to figure out who had robbed James Holden
and killed Kade's father, but my mother and possibly her sister
had had some involvement. Ian had taken my mother into his
brother's house a few days before the party. That wasn't a coincidence. She'd learned something while she was there. It was
possible someone had used my mom's connection to Ian Holden
at NYU to coerce her into helping the robbery crew. But I could
be giving her too much credit.

Closing my eyes, I drew in a breath and slowly let it out, my
mom's image floating through my brain. I didn't try to chase it
away. I wanted to see where it would take me. I wanted to
remember not just the good times, but the bad times.

But there weren't any bad times, I soon realized. She'd been a
great mother. Maybe she'd used the museum as a way to meet
up with her sister, but she'd taken us a lot of places where we

could learn about art and history and music. She'd taught me to play the violin. She'd read us stories. She'd watched movies with us. She'd taught us how to garden. Every spring, we would do a new planting. Watching her putter around that garden, tending to each plant with nurturing love, had made it feel magical. The flowers had practically shimmered in the sunlight. I remembered the dirt slipping through her fingers as she dug down deep into the planter box. And then everything was so shiny when the sun hit her hand.

My eyes flew open, and I abruptly sat up, my heart beginning to race. There hadn't just been dirt in her hands—there had been stones, shiny stones. I'd asked her once where she'd found them. She'd just laughed and said she'd gotten them a long time ago. The shiny stones helped the plants grow.

But they hadn't been magical stones to grow plants. They'd been real stones, clear, sharp-edged brilliant rocks that looked like diamonds, blue stones that could have been sapphires, and green ones that could have been emeralds.

I jumped to my feet and paced back and forth, wondering if I could possibly be on to something. As my gaze moved toward the window, I saw the garden on the back patio and the colorful flowers planted along the back fence.

I threw open the back door and dashed down the stairs.

When the person had broken into the house, they'd turned over the patio chairs and tossed around the gardening supplies in the small shed at the back of the property, but they hadn't dug into the planter boxes.

As I stared at the garden options, I wondered if I was crazy. *Would my mother have really planted priceless gems in dirt?*

I didn't even know if she actually had any of the stolen items. But as Kade had pointed out, she'd paid for things that cost far more than she would make on a teacher's salary.

I picked up a spade from the shed and walked over to the flower garden. Getting down on my knees, I put the spade into the earth and started to dig.

Thirty minutes later, I'd ripped apart most of the flower bed and had found nothing. My hands were dirty, and my knees and arms were aching. I thought about giving up, but there wasn't much farther to go. I might as well finish it.

As I ripped up the last bunch of flowers, my spade hit something hard, and my heart jumped. I dug down deeper, tossing away the garden tool to use my hands. Finally, I pulled out a metal box that was about eight by ten inches in size. I could hardly believe it. There was a small combination lock on the box and for a moment, I thought that would stop me. But I put in my birthdate, and it popped open. I sat back on the ground and opened the lid, my heart beating very fast.

Inside the box was a stack of baby and toddler photos from the first seven years of my life. She must have had them in her wallet when she'd disappeared. There was also a stack of postcards from random places, none of which had been written on, which made me frown. I wondered if my mother had been to those places over the years, but why hide them away?

I set them aside. I'd think about what those meant later. Underneath the cards was about ten thousand dollars in cash, and a large, black velvet pouch. I pulled open the strings on the pouch and poured the contents into my hand, staring in amazement at the beautiful and brilliant stones. There were mostly diamonds, with a couple of sapphires and a shockingly red ruby. There was also a large square-cut emerald ring surrounded by diamonds, a diamond choker necklace, and another sapphire and diamond ring.

I couldn't believe what I was looking at. These had to be from the robbery. I needed to compare what I'd found to the inventory list in the police report. This didn't seem like everything, but what was now in my hand was probably worth millions of dollars.

And they'd been hidden away in a flower bed by my mother.

More realizations hit me. My mother had had these stones when I was a kid. She'd probably had them since the robbery, which happened before I was born. My mom was a thief, maybe a murderer. She was a criminal. Even if she'd done what she'd done in the heat of the moment, that was years ago. And all this time, she'd kept the stolen property. She must have sold some items off to buy this house and to build her life.

I wondered about Rachel. *Had my mom been supporting Rachel, too? Had they split the stolen goods? Had they been in on it together?*

Maybe that's who they were—thieves, criminals, con artists.

There certainly wasn't anything in my hand that led me to believe otherwise.

What the hell was I doing here?

I was risking my life for a woman who might have been good to me for a while but had disappeared without a trace, leaving me to be raised by a man who wasn't even my father. No wonder my dad had fallen apart when he'd realized the depth of her betrayal.

As I thought about my dad not being my biological father, I couldn't help but wonder about Ian Holden. *Was Ian Holden my father?*

The timing fit, but the description Rachel had given me of my bio dad being a dangerous man did not. Or maybe I didn't know Ian any better than anyone else.

Was it just a coincidence that he'd shown up in San Francisco a month before my mother was shot? Maybe he was the one who'd shot her. Or he was the one who'd hired someone to do it, to try to kill her, to grab me. He had money and connections. He worked at universities; he probably had access to plenty of students who could guide him onto the dark web or wherever people went to hire hitmen.

A buzzing in my pocket made me slip the stones back into the pouch as I grabbed my phone.

"Hello?" I said.

"Ms. Landry? This is Nurse Miller from St. Mary's. I have good news. Your mother is awake, and she's asking for you."

My heart flipped over. "That is good news, because I really want to see her, too. I'll be down there as soon as I can."

I ended the call, then took the pouch and the metal box into the house. I debated where to put them. I couldn't just leave the box on the table, so I took everything upstairs and buried the box under a pile of clothing. I went back into the bedroom to grab a jacket.

As I put it on, I had second thoughts about the stones. I went back into the closet and removed the velvet pouch from the box. I took out the emerald ring and slipped it into the inside zippered pocket of my jacket. I wanted something to put in front of my mother to force her to tell me the truth. I was about to put the pouch back into the box when I thought it might be smarter to separate the items.

Debating for another moment, I took the pouch into the bedroom and looked for a better hiding place. There were several holes still in the walls. I'd covered some with the pictures that had originally hung in those spots. It seemed doubtful that someone would look where they'd already looked, so I took down the painting over the bed and tucked the pouch into the broken wall, then replaced the painting.

As I stepped back, I thought I should probably just take everything to the police station on my way to the hospital, but I wanted to talk to my mother before the police took over, and I probably only had a short window of time in which to do that.

I grabbed my bag and jogged down the stairs. When I headed outside, there was no sign of Kade's motorcycle. Who knew where he was now? He could be anywhere. He had a lot of anger to ride off. I sent him a quick text that my mother was awake, and I was heading to the hospital. He didn't answer by the time I'd gotten in the car and started the engine. He was probably still on the road. I wanted to tell him what I'd found, but I didn't want to leave it in a text, so I set down my phone and headed to St. Mary's. I felt more optimistic on this drive to the hospital than any other.

I couldn't wait to talk to my mother about what I'd found. She wouldn't be able to lie to me, not with the proof in my pocket. I was finally going to get the truth. I just hoped she wouldn't get so agitated that the doctor would kick me out again. I'd have to approach things as calmly as I could, which wouldn't be easy, because adrenaline was racing through my body.

My phone buzzed, and I glanced down at the console to see Dani's number. We hadn't talked since she'd hung up on me the night before. I needed to speak to her, but not right this second. I couldn't get into a long conversation now when I was about to turn in to the hospital parking lot. I'd call her back after I spoke to our mother. Hopefully, I'd finally have a complete story to tell her.

The parking lot was crowded, so I had to park on the top floor of the parking structure. Too impatient to take the elevator, I raced down the stairs. I was nearing the ground level when I heard someone coming down behind me, moving fast, making a lot of noise. I was about to turn around when I felt an enormous weight come down on my head. I tumbled down the last few steps as pain ripped through me, along with the fatalistic thought that I wasn't going to get away this time.

CHAPTER TWENTY-NINE

I DON'T KNOW how long I was out but as I became aware of noises around me, I realized that I was still alive—at least, for now. I was laying on something hard and cold.

As I opened my eyes, pain swept through me, made worse by the light coming through the slits in the blinds above me. I squinted as my eyes tried to focus through the throbbing ache that seemed to get worse with each breath, each beat of my heart.

I heard someone crying. As I tried to sit up, I realized my hands were tied behind my back. It took me a minute to roll over, but I managed to get onto my side. I was in a storage room. There were dusty shelves filled with Bibles. I blinked at that odd realization. There were also boxes of candles and pamphlets, some music stands and containers that smelled like incense.

My gaze moved across the room, stopping abruptly when it came to the figure lying on the floor across from me. My heart skipped a beat. Her hands were tied, and there was a blindfold around her eyes, but I knew her like I knew myself.

"Dani," I said, finding new energy to get onto my knees and scoot across the floor. "Oh, my God! How did you get here?"

"Brynn?" she asked between sobs as she rolled over onto her back.

"It's me. What happened?"

"I don't know. I was grocery shopping. I put the bags in the back of the car and then someone hit me over the head. I woke up, blindfolded, in the trunk of a car. I was there for hours. Then some guy carried me in here and dropped me on the floor. Where are we? Can you see anything?"

"Yes. We're in a storage room. It kind of feels like we're in a church. There are shelves with

Bibles and candles."

"A church? How can we be in a church?"

"I don't know. I was knocked out, too. I just woke up a few minutes ago."

"You're the person they dropped in here a little while ago. I heard the door open. I asked who was there, but no one answered. I heard footsteps and then a thud. I thought someone was in the room with me, but I couldn't tell."

"Let me see if I can get your blindfold off. My hands are tied behind my back, but maybe there's a way to pull it down. Can you try to sit up? There's a wall right behind you."

It took Dani several minutes, but she finally managed to prop herself up against the wall. I moved forward and using my mouth and teeth on the edge of the blindfold, I managed to pull it down around her neck. Our gazes met.

"Oh, God!" Dani said as tears slipped down her cheeks. "What's going to happen to us, Brynn?"

"I don't know. Are you okay? Does anything hurt?"

"My head hurts and my hip, from where I landed on the ground." Her eyes filled with more tears and more fear. "I hope the baby is okay. I can't tell."

"That's a good thing. If you don't feel anything bad, then it's probably fine," I reassured her.

"It has to be."

"I'm so sorry, Dani. This is my fault. I should not have looked into Mom's life. I should have come home when you asked."

"It might not have mattered. They grabbed me a couple of blocks from my house."

"How could they know where you live?"

"Who knows?" she asked wearily. "I shouldn't have left you alone here in the city. I should have stayed. We've always been better together."

At her words, I pressed my forehead against hers, the skin-to-skin contact immediately soothing. This was Dani, my sister, my best friend, my other half. She was right; we had always been better together. We'd find a way out of this. We had to.

I lifted my head and looked around the room. There was a small window with blinds, but it was at least five feet off the ground. I didn't see anything to stand on.

"There's no way out," Dani said, echoing my thoughts. "Our hands are tied, and even if they weren't, I'm sure the door is locked."

I listened for a moment. "It's very quiet. This could be the back room of a church or maybe it's a religious school."

"Wouldn't a school be filled with people on a Monday afternoon?"

"I would think so. You know what's weird, I got a call from you right before I was knocked out. It couldn't have been you. You would have already been here."

"They grabbed my phone, made me give them the password. I think they took a photo of me to send to you."

I thought about that. Maybe they weren't sure they could get me alone and had planned to lure me here with Dani as the bait, but instead I'd entered an empty stairwell in my hurry to see my mother.

"Did the man say anything to you besides wanting the password?" I asked.

"He just said I wouldn't be alone for long. His voice was deep and menacing but it also sounded happy, like he was excited about what was happening. Do you know what time it is? I've lost track of everything."

"It was probably around one thirty when someone grabbed me." I turned around. "Can you see my watch?"

"It's two," Dani said.

"Then I wasn't out that long, and we can't be that far away from the hospital," I mused.

"Do you know what they want?"

I thought for a moment. Only one answer came to mind. "I think we're leverage."

"What does that mean?"

"Mom was part of a robbery crew before we were born. Maybe our aunt, too. I don't know. They stole diamonds, cash, and art from some wealthy collector. A security guard died during the robbery. I think Mom and Rachel have been running ever since then."

Dani's eyes widened in shock. "Mom was a thief?"

"I think she was a lot of things, and that was one of them. I was going to the hospital to talk to her, to finally get answers when they grabbed me." I paused, trying to think through the pain in my throbbing head. "But even without talking to her, I know a lot more now. Mom and Rachel went on the run after that robbery. At some point, they split up. Mom had us and married Dad. For seven years we had normal lives. Then something happened to change that. Mom went to New Orleans, probably to meet Rachel, disappeared, and faked her death. She couldn't come back to us without putting us in danger, too. She was able to stay hidden for a long time, until she saved a man's life, and her picture was on the news."

"What do they want now? Why are we even still alive? Why didn't they just kill us to get back at her?" Dani asked.

"Because they want the diamonds and the other stones. That's why they tore Mom's house apart. But they didn't find what they were looking for, so they needed incentive. They're going to use us to get Mom and Rachel to talk, to tell them where the jewels are," I said, as more pieces of the puzzle fell into place.

"And then they'll let us go?" Dani asked hopefully.

I couldn't dash that hope, even though it seemed incredibly unlikely. "Maybe, but we need to try to escape before they come back."

"How the hell are we going to do that?"

"We can stand up. We can try to jump whoever comes through that door next."

She looked at me in shock. "Seriously? That's your plan? We can't use our hands, Brynn."

"Do you have any better ideas?"

"No. But that's not going to work."

"It might. We have the element of surprise. They could think we're still unconscious."

"They know I'm not."

I struggled to get up, rolling onto my knees and then propelling myself to my feet. I hadn't counted on a shocking wave of dizziness, and I backed into the wall to try to steady myself.

"Are you all right?" Dani asked with alarm.

"Feeling a little dizzy," I said.

"Me, too. Every time I move my head, it hurts." Dani paused. "I can't jump anyone, Brynn. I can't risk the baby. Even though, it doesn't look like I'm going to be able to have this baby."

"Don't say that. You're going to have your baby—your boy," I said fiercely. "I will make sure of that."

She looked at me in bemusement. "You've changed. You're like a ferocious tiger. You're not hiding behind me or looking for me to lead."

"I let you lead for a long time, and you did an incredible job. In fact, if I'd listened to you, we'd both be in Carmel right now, but we're here, and I'm not giving up without a fight. You saved me when Mom died. You were my rock. I wouldn't have survived without you, Dani."

"You would have been okay. You've always been stronger than you think. And I've always been weaker than you thought."

"That's not true."

"It is true. I always needed you, Brynn. I just let you believe you needed me." She gave me an apologetic look. "I kept you from going after your own life, because I couldn't stand the idea of us not being together. I had to have you there when I got married, when I started the business, when I tried to get pregnant. You were right the other day when you said you had to live your own life. I didn't realize I'd been forcing you to live mine. I'd told myself you wanted everything I wanted, but you didn't."

"Force is a strong word. I stayed because I loved you, Dani."

"You should have been playing in orchestras years ago, but I persuaded you that music was an impractical career choice when, really, I just couldn't stand the thought of you going out on tour. I didn't want to be alone. I know Dad was around, but I always thought of you as my family. You were the only one I could count on."

"Same goes for me. I always counted on you, and we are going to get ourselves out of this mess, because this is not the end of our story."

Despite my strong words, I wasn't at all sure how to get out of this situation. I couldn't even move away from the wall. *How was I going to jump someone with my hands tied behind my back and my ability to move hampered by debilitating waves of dizziness?*

A door slammed somewhere—the noise a long, loud echo. I straightened.

Dani shot me a panicked look. "He's coming back."

I heard more than one voice, and one of them belonged to a woman—a woman who sounded exactly like Dani and me. She was arguing, demanding to be let go. And then the door opened, and she was shoved into the room so hard she fell to her knees. I caught a glimpse of a tall, bearded man, and then the door closed.

She looked up and met our gazes, her hands also tied behind her back.

"Oh, my God," she whispered. "He got both of you."

"Yes," I said. "He went all the way to Carmel to get Dani."

Rachel stared at us, a look of pain and sorrow in her dark-blue, violet eyes. "I'm so sorry, girls. I never wanted this to happen."

"What is happening exactly?" I asked.

Before she could reply, the door opened again, and a different man walked into the room. He wore black jeans and a gray sweater, and his brown hair and eyes were very familiar. I gasped in surprise once more.

"You?" I asked, shocked at the man facing me. "Mark Harrison? My mom's boyfriend? You kidnapped us?"

"That would have been one of my associates," he said smoothly.

"His name isn't Mark Harrison," Rachel said, a fiery anger in her eyes. "It's Max Davino, and he is not your mother's boyfriend. He's a criminal. He's a murderer."

My stomach clenched. I'd thought Mark was a nice, older man who had a crush on my mom, but he looked far from that now. The façade he'd shown me before was gone. He looked younger, sharper-edged, and ruthless.

"Look who's talking," he said to Rachel, his tone laced with anger. "You're right where you belong—on your knees."

Rachel immediately sprang to her feet. "Never," she said defiantly.

He slapped her hard across the face, her head snapping back, the horrifying sound echoing throughout the room.

Dani cried out in alarm.

"Stop," I said, as he looked like he was going to hit her again, if for no other reason than to destroy the defiant expression on her face. "What do you want? Why are you doing this?"

His hard gaze swung to me. "To get what's mine," he replied. "I have to admit you were a surprise. I couldn't believe it when I saw you at the school. I had no idea there were daughters—twin daughters. But I soon realized I could use that to my advantage." His gaze swung back to Rachel, whose left cheek was burning red from the imprint of his hand. "Did you think I'd forgotten about you? Or your sister?" he asked.

"No," she said coldly. "I just didn't think you'd find us. But then, Laura had to go and be a hero."

"Laura—nice name," he drawled. "What are you calling yourself now?"

"What does it matter?" she challenged.

"It doesn't matter. What matters is that you betrayed me, not just once, but twice. You stole from me. You put me in prison."

"You put yourself there," Rachel said sharply.

"I'm not stupid. I know you were behind the setup. You thought you won, but you didn't. I've been waiting a long time for this moment. You will pay for what you did to me. The question is—who else is going to pay? Your sister? Your nieces?" He pulled a gun from the back of his waistband. "I want it all back. And you know exactly where it is. So, tell me."

"It's gone," Rachel said defiantly. "We got rid of it years ago. We sold everything and gave the money to charity. There's nothing left."

"You're lying. You've lied about everything from the first day we met. You said you were an only child. You said you wanted in on my business. You said I could trust you. You said you loved me."

I was shocked by his words and by the anger and betrayal I saw in his eyes. This was about more than just stolen jewels.

"That was before I knew you were part of a crime family," Rachel said. "That was before I saw you shoot someone in the head without a second thought."

"That was your fault. You were supposed to make sure security had left. You fucked up."

"The guard wasn't supposed to be there," Rachel said defensively. "But you didn't have to kill him."

"And you didn't have to run away with my bag, but you did."

I realized they were talking about the robbery now, about killing Kade's father. Clearly, Max had pulled the trigger. At least I knew my mother wasn't guilty of that.

I frowned, wondering where my mother had been the night of the robbery. The way Rachel and Max were talking, it almost sounded like she wasn't there. Maybe her only role had been to get the access codes from her professor while Rachel and Max pulled off the heist.

"Let the girls go," Rachel said. "They're not part of this."

"Yes, they are. They're your blood. You'd do anything for family." He paused. "I've been waiting for this moment for a long time. You hid your tracks very well. But I turned on the TV one day, and there you were. Only it wasn't you; it was your sister. I shouldn't have been surprised it was her. She was always better than you, wasn't she?"

"Yes, she was," Rachel said. "And you shot her."

"She was uncooperative, and I had to do something to get your attention. I knew you'd come for her. Just like she came for you twenty years ago in New Orleans," Max said. "If it hadn't been for her, this would have been over a long time ago."

"What happened in New Orleans?" I asked.

"Brynn, stop," Dani implored. "You don't need to know any of this."

"Yes, I do. Look where we are. I have a right to know what happened in New Orleans."

"Tell her," Max said. "Tell her how you and your sister killed a man."

"It was self-defense," Rachel said tersely. "It was him or us. I'm just sorry we didn't kill you, Max."

I sucked in a breath as her words fanned the fire in his eyes.

"No, but you did your best to destroy me and my business," he said. "That's over now. I want what's mine. Where are the stones?"

"I told you—they're gone," Rachel said.

He lifted the gun and fired it in our direction. Dani screamed, and I ducked as the bullet hit the wall between us. My breath came hard and fast as I saw the intent in his eyes.

"Next one goes in her head," he told Rachel, pointing the gun toward Dani.

I scrambled toward Dani, wanting to protect her. Rachel did the same, moving in front of both of us.

"You can't kill either one of them," Rachel said fiercely.

"I can, and I will, unless you give me what's mine."

"It's not yours. It was never yours."

"And never yours," he retorted.

"Well, you can kill me, but you can't go after them. Because..." She drew in a deep breath.

As I waited for her to finish that sentence, I felt a nervous tingle shoot down my spine. There was something else coming. Something bad. Something shocking.

"Because why?" Max demanded. "I'm curious what you think you have over me."

"You're their father."

Rachel's words sent me reeling. I backed into the wall again as I tried to stay on my feet.

Max's gaze narrowed as it moved past Rachel to me and to Dani. "No way."

"It's true," Rachel said. "You're their father."

"I can't be. You're lying."

I wanted her to be lying. I didn't want this horrible man to be my father. I looked back at Dani. She was shaking with fear, her gaze unfocused. I wasn't even sure she'd heard what Rachel had said.

"I'm telling you the truth," Rachel said. "If you kill them, you're killing a piece of yourself. They're your blood, Max." When he didn't answer, Rachel pressed on. "They're twenty-seven years old. I'm sure you have their IDs. You can check the birthdate."

"That could have been faked, like everything else about your life."

"Look at them. They're yours," Rachel said.

"Stop!" I interrupted with a desperate shout. "Stop saying he's our father. He can't be our father."

Rachel gazed at me through sorrow-filled eyes. "I'm sorry, Brynn. Unfortunately, he is your father. I never wanted him to know about you. I was afraid he would use you, just like he is now. But he has to know that you're his blood."

"You're just saying that, so I won't kill them," Max said, but there was a note of uncertainty in his voice now.

"It's the truth. I was pregnant the night of the robbery, but I didn't know it until a week later," Rachel turned to me once more.

I shook my head in the face of whatever was about to come out of her mouth. "Don't," I said, knowing where she was about to go. "Please, don't. Don't take away my mother, too."

Rachel drew in a shaky breath. "I'm sorry. I gave you to my sister because I couldn't take care of you. I was a mess. I've always been a mess. But my sister was strong and nurturing, and she loved you from the minute you were born."

"And you didn't," I said dully, as I sank to the floor, unable to stand against this last horrific truth.

"I did love you," Rachel said. "That's why I gave you away. You needed a mother who could take care of you, and that wasn't me. I also thought that one day Max might find me, and you'd be safer with my sister. And you were safer," Rachel reiterated. "She loved you like you were her own children. It tore her apart when my problems caught up with us, when we had to run again, but it was the only way to keep you safe. We couldn't allow Max to know about you, which meant we couldn't stay close to you."

My gaze moved to Max, who, for the first time, seemed a little off-balance. As his gaze met mine, I sensed I had a small opportunity. There was a crack in his armor. He was rattled, and

I needed to take advantage of that. I didn't know if Rachel's plan was going to work, if he would spare us because we were his daughters, so I had to try something else, something that could buy us time if nothing else.

"If you let my sister go, I'll tell you where the stones are," I said.

His gaze sharpened.

"Brynn, stop," Rachel implored.

I ignored her, focusing on Max, on the gun in his hand. "It's a fair trade," I told him.

"No," Dani interrupted, suddenly coming back to life. "You're not trading yourself for me, Brynn. I'm not going anywhere without you."

"You have to go," I said, looking back at her. "You have other people to think about. They need you."

"And I need you," she said, her voice filled with emotion.

"Let them both go, and I'll give you what you want," Rachel said. "This is between the two of us, not them, Max."

"They'll run to the cops," he said.

"We won't," I told him, as I got back to my feet. "Do you think I want anyone to know my real parents are terrible people?" I saw Rachel's face whiten at my words, but I needed them both to believe that my hatred was real. Actually, it was real. At this moment, I hated them more than I'd hated anyone in my life. "We just want to leave. We don't care about anything you stole."

"She's definitely your kid," Max sneered. "She thinks she can lie her way out of this. But she can't. Here's what's going to happen. One of you will tell me where the stones are, and then my guy is going to get them. If he doesn't come back with anything, then I'll shoot someone." He paused. "You won't be first, Rachel. Because I don't think these girls know anything, but you do. You know where your sister hid the stones. So, if you don't want to see your girls die, then start talking."

I saw Rachel hesitate. Clearly, she didn't believe that telling him the truth would save our lives. I didn't believe it, either. I also knew that the stones were no longer buried in the garden. But sending someone to the house would buy us time. I didn't know what we were going to do with that time since our hands were tied, and Max had the gun. But I did know that we couldn't just do nothing.

"I know where they are," I said. "I found them earlier."

"Brynn, don't," Rachel pleaded. "It won't matter. He'll kill us anyway."

I turned back to Max. "Will you let my sister go if I tell you?"

"No. But I'll let you both go once I get the stones."

"He's lying," Rachel said. "Don't give away our only bargaining chip."

"You can't bargain," he told Rachel. "It's too late for that."

"They're in the master closet in a box under a pile of clothes at my mom's house," I said. "I found them earlier. They were buried in the garden. I hid the box in the closet when I left." I didn't mention that I'd taken the pouch and put it in the wall, because I didn't think we'd survive once he had everything.

Max stared at me, as if weighing my words, then walked out of the room.

Rachel shook her head. "You've made a mistake, Brynn."

"We need time, and I bought us some," I said harshly. "And I don't think I'm the one who's making the mistakes, Rachel. Or should I call you Mom? No. I can't call you that," I said with a shake of my head.

"I'm sorry you had to find out this way. But I still hope that knowing you and Dani are his daughters will stop Max from killing you."

"I'm not sure it matters to him at all, or if he even believes you. I'm not sure I even believe you. You've told so many lies."

Rachel's expression turned grim. "It doesn't matter what you believe. Giving him the jewels won't save us."

"He's not going to get them. I hid the box in the closet, but the jewels are somewhere else."

"Then he'll kill one of you for sure when he sees the box is empty. Where did you put them?"

I thought about telling her, but then Max returned to the room, cutting off our conversation.

He left the door partially ajar, and I could see a hallway and stained glass in the distance. My first impression had been right. We were in a church. But where was everyone else? *Shouldn't there be a priest or a minister somewhere? Office people? Cleaning staff? Someone?* It felt too quiet.

"One of these days, God is going to strike you down for all the evil dealings you've done in church," Rachel said.

He offered up an evil smile. "God isn't calling the shots. I am."

"How did you two get involved?" I asked, wanting to break up their conversation, which was filled with so much anger it made the situation more volatile.

"Do you want to tell her our love story?" Max asked, as he waved the gun at Rachel.

"It wasn't a love story. It was a nightmare," she retorted.

"It didn't start out that way," he said. "You wanted me so badly you couldn't stand it."

"I was stupid. I didn't know who you really were." Rachel turned to me. "I met Max in a bar in Brooklyn. I had just turned twenty-one and was working as a waitress while my sister was at NYU getting a degree in music. She was the smart one. I was anything but smart. Max and his friends would come into the bar, and I couldn't see past his charm."

I could understand how she'd been taken in. I'd thought Max was charming when I'd first met him, and he'd lied to me very convincingly about having a stepdaughter in the school and having dated my mother. "Go on," I said when the silence in the room lengthened. I needed to keep them both talking. Maybe buying more time wouldn't buy me and Dani a ticket out of this horrible situation, but at least I could find out more about why we were in it in the first place.

"Tell her how you begged me to let you make a few extra bucks," Max said.

"That's true," Rachel replied. "I knew Max was doing more than working for his aunt's travel agency, which was just a front, providing cover for a smuggling operation that had been run by his family for decades. He always had a lot of cash, and I wanted some." Rachel kept her gaze focused on me, as if she couldn't stand to look at Max. "It started out so simply. I just had to take an envelope to church with me and leave it in the confessional, under the kneeler."

"What was in the envelope?"

"I don't know," she said. "I didn't ask. The job was easy, and it paid well."

"Then she got greedy," Max cut in. "She wanted to do bigger jobs."

"So did you," Rachel said, flinging a hard look at Max. "You were more ambitious than I was. You hated that your cousins kept getting bigger jobs than you. Your family only got the crumbs. So you came up with a plan to make a big score for yourself, start your own operation on the side, by stealing from James Holden, who was as dirty as you were, just a lot richer and a lot more polished."

"You loved the idea," Max reminded Rachel. "You couldn't wait to help me. When I told you the target, you came up with a way to help me gain access to the house, through the target's brother."

Another piece of the puzzle fell into place. "You slept with Ian Holden," I said. "It wasn't Mom, was it? You were the one Ian took to his brother's estate."

Rachel gave me a surprised look. "How did you know about that?"

"I talked to Ian. He told me he had an affair with his student, and that student was my mother, but it was you who had the affair. You pretended to be her, didn't you?"

"Yes," Rachel admitted. "But my sister did have a crush on

him. She talked about how brilliant and handsome Ian was, and how she thought he might like her. When I found out he was related to James Holden, I saw a way to help Max, to prove my value to him."

Not one word that came out of her mouth made me like her more. I was beginning to think she was as bad as Max was.

"I made a horrible mistake," Rachel continued. "I knew it that night when the reality of what we were doing sank in. Everything before then had seemed like a risky gamble, a game. Stealing from James Holden, who was a billionaire who had been accused of shady business practices and harassment of women, made me feel like we were Robin Hood, stealing from a bad guy who didn't deserve what he had anyway. But then the guns came out. And a man went down, and his blood was very, very real. Max told me to get the car. I had one of the tote bags we'd filled up from the safe, and I ran."

"But you didn't get the car," Max said. "You drove away and left me and Jonah to take the fall."

"I didn't kill that man. You and Jonah did," Rachel snapped. "And you didn't take the fall. You got away with the art and half the cash."

"What happened after that?" I asked.

"I ran to my sister," Rachel replied. "I begged her to help me. I told her that Max and his family would come after me."

"Why didn't you leave the stolen items behind?" I asked.

"I thought I might need insurance. I didn't tell my sister what was in the bag until after we were far away from New York. She didn't know about any of it for a couple of weeks."

I thought about that. "Why didn't you give it back then?"

"Good question," Max said.

"I wasn't talking about giving it back to you," I said, sending him a disgusted look. "It belonged to James Holden."

"It didn't really belong to him, either," Rachel said. "James Holden was also a thief. He liked to collect stolen goods and show them off to his friends. That was another reason why I decided that robbing him was a good idea."

"Sounds like you were good at rationalizing," I said coldly.

Rachel stiffened. "You wanted the story, I'm telling it. My sister and I needed the cash to survive, to buy new lives for ourselves, and I didn't think there was a way to return anything without compromising ourselves with the police or bringing attention to us."

"So you ran away, had two babies, then gave them to your sister and ran away again. For seven years, everything was good. Then you met up in New Orleans. Why?" I asked.

Rachel licked her lips. "It doesn't matter. It was another mistake. I've made a lot of them. And I'm sorry for all of them."

"I don't think sorry will help us right now," I said harshly.

Max smiled. "That's cold. Maybe you are my daughter."

"I'm not your daughter," I said. "I don't care what my DNA says. My father is not a murderer."

His eyes darkened into hard points.

"Brynn," Dani implored. "Stop."

I turned to look at my sister. She'd been so quiet I'd almost forgotten that she was there.

Dani pushed herself up into a standing position. "If you're our father, you need to let us go. We don't have anything to do with any of this, and you know that. You have Rachel. She's the one who betrayed you."

Rachel paled at Dani's unforgiving words. I was pissed at Rachel, too. But I didn't want her to be hurt or, worse, to be killed. I couldn't leave her behind. But it didn't matter what any of us thought or wanted. The only one calling the shots was Max.

"You're all staying. Until I get what's mine, I'm not letting anyone go. Where the fuck is he?" Max muttered as he checked his watch. Then he left the room.

Dani gave me a worried look.

"It's going to be okay," I said.

"I don't think so," she told me.

I didn't think so, either, but I had to stay positive. There was no other option.

Max strode back into the room, his gaze focusing on me. "Did you send him into a trap?" He raised the gun. "Your sister was right. I don't need all three of you. So, let's see who I should take out first."

I moved in front of Dani, as she started to cry once more. Rachel looked at both of us with sorrow and desperation.

Before any of us could move, a loud crash came from somewhere nearby. As Max looked toward the door, Rachel ran forward, barreling into him so hard she knocked him off his feet and the gun went off with an ear-splitting blast.

"Run," I told Dani, as Rachel and Max got tangled up on the floor.

We raced toward the door. I had no idea what was waiting for us in the hallway, but it couldn't be any worse than what was behind us.

CHAPTER THIRTY

I RAN down the hall and through another open door, Dani right on my heels. We found ourselves in a small room next to the altar where the families with babies would stay during the service. Hearing Max coming after us, we ran into the church. Crossing the altar, we headed for the side door, but before we could get there, a gun went off, and a bullet whizzed past my ear.

We dove into the nearest pew as more shots sprayed the air. I looked at Dani, seeing the panic and fear in her eyes. "I'm sorry," I said, realizing we were trapped. There was nowhere to go.

"I love you," she said.

We pressed our heads together once more as Max's voice grew louder.

"No way out, girls," he said, a triumphant note in his voice.

I broke away from Dani and lifted my gaze. Max was standing at the end of the pew, his gun pointed at us. "Are you really going to kill your own children?" I asked. "What kind of monster are you?"

"That bitch was probably lying," he said. "And I can't let you go. It's you or me."

"And you always choose you, don't you?"

I shifted in front of Dani, but there was no way to really protect her. I wanted to close my eyes, but I also didn't want to show him that I was afraid. I couldn't give him that satisfaction.

For a split second, I thought I saw a gleam of admiration in his eyes. But then he lifted his arm.

I jerked and ducked as a shot rang out. Dani screamed. I waited to feel something, but there was nothing. As I lifted my gaze, I saw Max fall to the ground.

Oh, my God! He hadn't shot us. Someone had shot him.

A man came running down the aisle, and I let out a breath of terrified relief.

"Kade," I said, shocked to see him. I jumped to my feet. "You shot Max? Where did you get the gun?"

"From the guy I took out in the parking lot," he said grimly. "Are you all right?"

"Thanks to you." I looked back at Dani, who was still cowering on the floor. "It's okay, Dani. Kade shot Max." When my gaze returned to Kade, I saw him checking Max for a pulse.

"Is he dead?" I asked.

"No, but his pulse is faint." He stood up, his gaze sweeping across me and Dani, who was now sitting on the edge of the pew, tears streaming down her face. "The police are on their way. Is anyone else here?"

I started at his question. "Yes. Rachel. Max shot her. We need to get to her." I ran to the aisle, and stepped over Max, who was bleeding profusely from the back of his head.

Dani and Kade followed me back to the storage room. Rachel was on the floor, her eyes open, as blood poured from her shoulder.

"You're alive," she gasped, her face white, her eyes huge with relief. "I heard shots. I thought he killed you."

Kade ripped off his jacket and pressed it against Rachel's wound. "Hang in there. Help is on the way."

"How did you know where we were?" I asked Kade.

"I was in my apartment when I heard someone in the house.

You'd texted me that you were at the hospital, so I knew it wasn't you. When I looked out the window, I saw a man leaving with a box in his hands. I had a bad feeling. So, I jumped on my bike, and I followed him here. I confronted him in the parking lot and took him down. The box he'd been carrying had photos of you and your sister inside. I called you, and your phone was in his pocket. That was the worst moment of my life," he said, his eyes burning as he looked at me. "I called the police next. They told me to wait outside the church. But then I heard shots, and I knew there was no time to wait. I grabbed the guy's gun, and you know the rest."

"We're so lucky you were home," I said. "I told Max that I had found the jewels and they were hidden in a box in the closet. I wanted to buy us some time."

"What jewels?"

"The ones that were stolen from Holden's house. My mom had at least some of them. But my strategy wouldn't have worked if you hadn't been there. Max knew there was a problem when his partner didn't come back. He was going to kill Dani and me."

"But he didn't," Kade reminded me.

His words helped stem the shaking fear running through my body. We were all still alive. And as sirens rang out, followed by shouts and footsteps, I finally believed it was over, and we were safe.

Within minutes, the storage room was filled with police, followed by EMTs, and eventually Inspector Greenman made his way in.

Rachel was stabilized and whisked away to the hospital, along with Max and the man who had been working for him. Dani and I were finally released from our cuffs, and we immediately reached for each other. After a long hug of gratitude and love, we broke apart. I gave Inspector Greenman a statement and then the paramedics took us to another ambulance for a trip to the hospital to get checked out.

Kade stayed behind to continue his discussion with the inspector.

As Dani and I sat together in the ambulance, she slid her hand into mine and our eyes met. That connection took away the last of my fear.

"We survived," I said.

"Because of Kade. I'm sorry I ever doubted him."

"He's a good guy."

"He seems that way." Dani gazed at me through exhausted, bloodshot eyes that still held the terror we'd been through. "I thought we were going to die, Brynn. You put yourself in front of a bullet for me more than once. How could you do that?" she asked in wonder.

"How could I not?" I countered. "You're my sister."

"I didn't put myself in front of you." Guilt ran through her eyes.

"You're pregnant. You have to protect your child. He comes first."

"But you've always come first," Dani said, tearing up again.

"Well, now I come second, maybe third. I might let Steve go ahead of me, too," I said lightly. "But our relationship is as close as it ever was. We're two halves of a whole."

"You're my better half."

"You're mine," I said, feeling emotional as it was starting to sink in how close I'd come to losing her.

"I can't believe that man is our father or that Rachel is our mother. I don't know what to think about either one of them. They both seem horrible," Dani said.

"Rachel did try to save us. She took that bullet, so we could get away."

"But all the other things she did..." Dani shook her head in bemusement. "And what about Mom? What was her role in all of it?"

"We still need to find that out. I'm pretty sure it was Rachel who brought the trouble and Mom who kept trying to save her and save us."

"But Mom had stolen jewels in her house," Dani said. "Right?"

"Yes, she did. We'll figure it all out. What's important now is that we're safe, and Mom and Rachel are safe, too."

"You don't think there's anyone else who's going to come after us?"

"I really hope not," I said.

When we arrived at the hospital, we were checked out by an ER doc who ordered brain scans for both of us as well as an ultrasound for Dani. My tests were done about an hour later. I was diagnosed with a mild concussion and told to take it easy for the next forty-eight hours. After being released, the nurse wheeled me into the lobby of the ER, and I found Kade pacing by the window.

He immediately came toward me, taking my arm and ushering me into another chair, his gaze filled with concern. "What's the prognosis?" he asked.

"I'll be fine. I just need to rest for a few days. Dani is getting the baby checked out. Hopefully, she's all right. Do you know anything about Rachel?"

"She's in surgery. Her wound is not life-threatening."

"That's good. What about Max?"

"I thought his name was Mark," Kade said.

"That's the name he gave me, but it was a lie. His real name is Max Davino. He's part of some criminal organization in New York."

"New York, huh?" Kade's lips tightened.

"Yes. Is he in surgery, too?"

"No. He didn't make it. He died in the ambulance."

I let out a breath at his words, not even sure how to feel about that news. The man would have killed me if it hadn't been for Kade. But that man was also apparently my biological father.

"Okay," I said, the word seeming woefully inadequate, but it was all I could come up with. "What about the other guy?"

"He was arrested and taken down to the station."

"Good. I have a lot to tell you, Kade. Max and Rachel were part of the robbery crew at James Holden's house. Max was the one who killed your father."

He sucked in a sharp breath, his dark gaze filled with emotion. "Then I'm even more glad I shot him and that he's dead." He paused. "Was your mom part of the crew?"

"Yes, but that's where it gets more complicated." I drew in another breath. "Laura isn't my biological mother. She's just the one who raised me for seven years. Rachel is my real mother. And my biological father was Max."

His jaw dropped in amazement. "Seriously?"

"Don't make me say it twice."

"I'm sorry." He shook his head in confusion. "That's a lot to process."

"I know. It all came out in a rush. Rachel thought telling Max that he was our father would stop him from killing us, but Max didn't care. He would have killed Dani and me if you hadn't shot him. It's difficult to comprehend how someone could kill their own children."

"Max is not your father. Your dad is the guy who raised you. And he's not a criminal."

I appreciated the reminder. "You're right. And my mom is the one who raised me until I was seven. And Laura didn't break into James Holden's house. She didn't even sleep with Ian Holden. That was Rachel. She approached Ian outside of class. She pretended to be my mom. My mother knew nothing about it until after the robbery, until Rachel begged her to save her. And Laura did. They left everything behind, got new identities, and started over." I drew in a breath. "I need to hear my mother's side of the story to fill in some of the gaps."

"We can talk to her now. We're in the same hospital."

I thought about that, but that conversation would have to wait. "Not until I know how Dani is. She might want to come, too. Or she might have had enough. Her husband is on his way here now. I'm praying her baby is okay. They knocked her out and kidnapped her from the store by her house. They put her in a trunk for the drive here. She's had a lot of trauma, and it's my fault."

"It's not your fault, Brynn. All you did was try to find out who shot your mother."

"Only to find out she's not my mother at all. My biological parents are horrible people. What does that make me?"

"Your own person. You're not either one of them. You're just you, and from what I've seen, you're amazing."

I smiled at his words. "Right back at you. You saved my life again."

"I should have been with you when you went to the hospital. I never should have left you alone."

"You were shaken by what we found out about Laura, about why she helped you. I knew why you left, and it wasn't the wrong thing to do. You needed time to think."

"That time could have cost you your life. It was selfish."

"Oh, Kade," I said, shaking my head. "You are anything but selfish. I've seen a lot of bad in the last few days, but not with you. You might be a dark artist, but you have been a very bright light in my life. I know you hate that Laura lied to you and supported you out of guilt, but I am very glad that you were staying at her house when I arrived. I don't think I would have made it through the past several days without you. I know it's not the same for you. You made my life easier and safer—I made yours harder and more dangerous."

"Well, we both survived. Some days that's enough."

I nodded, then jumped up as I saw a nurse wheel Dani into the waiting room. We moved over to meet her.

"I'm okay," Dani said, as she got up from the wheelchair and sat down next to me. "The baby is fine. I have a bump on my head, but it's not serious. My blood pressure is going down. Steve will be here in about forty-five minutes. What about you, Brynn?"

"I'm also fine. Rachel is in surgery, and Max is dead," I added. "The other guy is in jail."

"Good." Dani said. "I know that I was there for everything, all the shocking revelations, but I feel like I missed some stuff. My fear was so great I think I was blacking out even though my eyes were open."

"It's okay. I can fill you in when you're ready. I don't know everything, though. That's going to involve Mom."

"I knew you were going to say that," she said with a sigh.

"I can talk to her on my own. I just might need a minute before I do that."

"You don't have to rush it," Kade said. "Why don't we all go back to Laura's house? It will be more comfortable waiting for your husband there than here."

"I like the sound of that," I said. "Dani?"

She hesitated, then nodded. "I'll call Steve and tell him to meet us there."

When we got back to Laura's house, it was after seven. Dani and I curled up on the couch in the family room while Kade went out to pick up food for all of us. Steve arrived before Kade returned, and the happy, joyous relief that flowed between Dani and her husband filled me with emotion. I would not have been able to face Steve if anything had happened to Dani.

Dani had already asked me not to go into detail with Steve about what had happened at the church, and while I didn't completely agree, I understood that not only did she not want Steve to realize how close he'd come to losing her, she also didn't want to relive it. I didn't want to relive it, either.

When Kade arrived with pizzas, salads, beer, and wine, Steve and Dani decided to stay the night. We all agreed that we would talk to Laura in the morning. Hopefully, Rachel would be recovered enough to join us, because we really needed them both to be in the same room and the same conversation.

While we ate, we kept the conversation light. Kade asked Steve and Dani questions about their lives, their businesses, the baby. He was very good at distracting them from the horror of the day, and I was grateful to him again.

As we finished eating, Dani said, "I know we're not talking about what happened earlier, but I'm aware that you suffered some trauma tonight, too, Kade. And I just wanted to say again how grateful I am that you came when you did and that you didn't let me run you off days ago with my big mouth."

Kade smiled. "You were just looking out for your sister."

"I didn't appreciate that you were looking out for her, too. I thought you had an agenda, but I was wrong. I'm sorry."

"No need to apologize," he said.

"Have you spoken to your mom?" I asked.

"Not yet. I want to hear what Rachel and Laura have to say first."

"Wait a second," Dani interrupted. "I just remembered something, Brynn. You told Max that you found the stolen items, the jewelry, and the cash. Where is it? Do the police have it?"

"They have the box that the guy got from this house," Kade said. "I don't know exactly what was inside."

"I do," I said. "And the jewels weren't in the box. There were photos of me and Dani as kids, a weird stack of blank postcards, and about ten-thousand dollars in cash."

"So the jewels weren't there?" Dani asked.

"Nope." I unzipped my jacket and then pulled out the ring from the inside pocket and set it on the table. "But here's one of the pieces of jewelry that was stolen from James Holden."

Dani gasped at the shimmering stone as it caught the light. "Oh, my God," she said. "That's beautiful and enormous."

"I know. Hold on one second." I got up from the table and ran up the stairs. The pouch was right where I'd hidden it in the wall. I took it back to the kitchen table and dumped the contents out.

"Whoa," Kade said. "That's a lot of diamonds."

"I've never seen anything like it," Dani muttered. "Mom had these all this time?"

"Yes. I don't know if there were more. Maybe they sold off some stones over the years."

"How did you find them, Brynn?" Dani asked.

"I was reading the police report on Kade's computer about the robbery and the missing stones, and I had this weird memory. Mom was in the garden, and she had something shiny in her hand. It was a blue stone. I asked her why she was planting the stone. And she said that stones made the flowers grow." I paused. "I looked out the window at her flower bed and I just had this feeling I should dig."

"You used to tell me that stones made flowers grow, and I didn't know what you meant," Dani said, a gleam in her eyes.

"I don't think I understood what I saw when I was little. But it suddenly clicked into place." I paused as Dani stifled a yawn. "You're exhausted. You and Steve can have the guest room. I washed the sheets earlier. They're still in the dryer. I'll make the bed up."

"I'll make the bed up," Kade said, waving me back into my seat. "You sit."

"I'll help," Steve said, as he got to his feet.

As the men left the table, Dani reached out her hand to me. "Kade is a better man than I thought. You figured that out earlier than I did. I guess I should stop questioning your instincts."

I smiled. "You should, but I'm not sure you can."

"I will try. I have some habits that need to be broken when it comes to you, Brynn. I meant what I said earlier—I pretended that I was the strong one, the one you needed so much. But it was really the opposite. I needed you to need me. You gave me the strength to do everything. I took over your life because I couldn't make a decision without you. It wasn't fair to you."

"I let you take over because I needed your bossiness. It made me comfortable, sometimes too comfortable." I took a breath. "We don't know Mom and Rachel's story, but I think maybe they are a mirror we need to look at."

Dani cocked her head to the right as she gave me a speculative look. "What do you mean?"

"They seem to have had a very close, twisted, secretive, co-dependent relationship. I can see how easily they fell into that, because being twin sisters is different than being sisters. It's easy to feel like you're living one life instead of two. I'm not saying I don't want us to be as close as we have been, because I do. I love you more than I love anyone else in this world, but we need to have our own lives, Dani. You're going to have a baby. You have a husband who adores you, and those two people need to be your priority."

"They will be, but I'll still be loving you, Brynn, and worrying about you no matter what you're doing. I'll also be rooting for you every step of the way, and I better get good tickets for your shows."

"First row, I promise." I looked up as Steve and Kade came back into the room.

"Your bed is waiting," Steve told Dani.

"I'm ready," Dani said as her husband helped her to her feet. "Thank you again, Kade."

"Get some rest," he replied.

"I will." She turned to me. "You'll be upstairs?"

"Yes. Sleep well."

"You, too."

As they moved down the hall and into the guest room, I took our plates to the sink.

"You're not cleaning up," Kade told me, as he blocked me from doing any more clearing. "Why don't you go upstairs and lay down?"

"I am tired. Where are you going to be?" I asked.

He hesitated. "I'm going to clean up and then I'll go to my apartment."

As our gazes met, there seemed to be a lot of unspoken words between us, but neither one of us opened our mouth. Finally, Kade cleared his throat, and said, "I'd like to go with you to the hospital tomorrow. I want to hear what Laura and Rachel have to say."

"You should be there. Their story is part of your past as well as mine. I'm sorry they had anything to do with what happened to your dad."

"I'm sorry, too," he said heavily, a deep sadness in his gaze. "But it has nothing to do with you."

As I headed upstairs, I wished that was true, but I had a feeling it wasn't.

CHAPTER THIRTY-ONE

MY MOTHER HAD BEEN MOVED out of the ICU, and there was no longer a guard at her door when Dani, Steve, Kade, and I arrived at her room just before eleven o'clock on Tuesday morning. We'd all slept in after the exhausting, traumatic events of the day before. But now our break from reality was over.

I entered the room first, the others following close behind. My mother was sitting up in bed, a bandage on her shoulder and another on her head, but her face had more color in it. A mix of emotions ran through her gaze as she looked at us. I saw pain and guilt, but also a steely resolve. She'd clearly been mentally preparing herself for this moment.

Before any of us could speak, the door opened once more, and a nurse wheeled Rachel into the room. A thick bandage was visible on her shoulder, and she looked tired but also resigned.

"I asked the nurse to tell me when you got here," Rachel said. "I thought we should all be together."

"How are you feeling?" I asked.

"I'm fine," Rachel said, with a dismissive shake of her head. "And that's not what you came here to talk about, so let's get down to it."

My gaze moved from Rachel to my mom. "What do you know about what happened yesterday?"

"Rachel filled me in earlier," she replied. "I'm so sorry you and Dani went through all that. I never thought you would ever have to face that evil man."

"That evil man is our biological father," Dani said, a hard note in her voice. "Isn't that right?"

My mother gave a regretful nod. "Yes. Unfortunately, that is true."

"Let's back up," I said. "I want to know how we got here. What are your real names? The names you were given when you were born?"

"We were born Claire and Elaine Thompson," my mother said. "We lived in Chicago. Our father was never in our lives. Our mother had problems with substance abuse. She was in and out of rehabs. We lived with a neighbor when she would disappear. Mrs. Hursh saved us for as long as she could. She taught me how to play music. It was my escape."

I could relate to that. "So you lied about your parents dying young."

"It was simpler that way," my mom said. "It wasn't a complete lie. They were pretty much dead to us. Mrs. Hursh made sure we had food and a place to sleep. We were safe with her until our mom came back one day with a new boyfriend. She demanded that we go with her, and we couldn't say no." My mom's voice faltered. "We'd only been there a day when the worst happened." My mom drew in a breath and reached out her hand to Rachel.

Rachel squeezed my mom's fingers, reminding me of how many times Dani and I had done the same thing.

"What happened?" Dani asked impatiently. "It was something bad, wasn't it?"

When my mother didn't answer, Rachel said stoically, "I was raped by my mother's boyfriend, while my mother was passed out. I was fourteen."

"Oh, my God!" I murmured. "I'm so sorry."

"It was my fault. I shouldn't have left her," my mother inter-rupted, guilt and pain in her eyes. "But I didn't want to miss my music recital. I had been practicing for weeks. I was selfish."

"You didn't know what was going to happen," Rachel said.

"I should have." My mother drew in a deep breath. "When I got back to the house, I took Rachel to Mrs. Hursh's, and she called 911. We thought they'd let us stay with her, but they said she wasn't an approved home. The social worker split us up and put us into foster care." She paused, more guilt running through her eyes. "My situation was better than Rachel's. I had foster parents who made sure I got to school and helped me pursue my music. I tried to convince them to take her in, but they said they weren't licensed for another child."

My gaze moved to Rachel. "What happened to you?"

She shrugged. "I was in a group home. It was survival of the fittest and a lot of manual labor for people who didn't give a shit. They'd lock us in the basement when we created problems for them. I ran away a bunch of times, and tried to report them, but I was always sent back or sent somewhere else. Finally, when I was seventeen, I found my sister again."

"I was a few weeks short of high school graduation when she showed up," my mom continued. "I hid her away for a couple of days and then talked my foster parents into not turning her in. Since I was moving out soon, they agreed. I had a scholarship to NYU, so we went to New York. I started school and my sister got a job as a nanny."

"One of my many jobs," Rachel said. "I couldn't settle into my life. I took classes at the community college, but I was a terrible student. I didn't have a talent for anything except getting into trouble, and the older we got, the more I envied my sister's life. Laura was doing exceptionally well. She had so much to brag about. It was probably the first time in our lives we were at odds. And that was on me. I felt like I was falling behind, and I was. I dropped out of school. I started looking for jobs that were more exciting, more money. Eventually I began waitressing at a bar in Brooklyn."

"We already know what happened there," I said. "You hooked up with Max and got swept up in his criminal activities. I know you ran away after he killed Kade's father, but I don't know what happened after you changed your identities. Where did you go?"

"We took a bus to Atlanta," Rachel said. "We became Kim and Megan Cooper. And eight months later, Kim Cooper had two little girls."

"And you were Kim Cooper?" I asked, even more confused. "But Mom's name was Kim."

"She had to become Kim because I went into the hospital as Kim. When I left her with you and your sister, we switched IDs, so hers would match the birth certificate."

"I can't keep track of all your names," I said in exasperation. "What should I even call you now?"

They exchanged a quick look and then my mom said, "You can call us Laura and Rachel if you want. That's who we've been for the last twenty years."

"I still think of you as Mom," I murmured.

Laura's lips trembled and she blinked away tears. "I still think of you girls as my daughters. I always will."

"Why didn't you want us?" Dani asked, turning to Rachel. "Why did you give us to your sister to raise?"

Rachel drew in a quick breath as Dani went on the offensive. "I had problems with depression and anxiety, issues that got worse during my teen years. But I also think there was post-partum depression, too. I didn't really know what it was, I just knew I felt bad, and I couldn't be a good mother. You deserved better. There was no one better than my sister, no one I would trust with my kids."

"How did you feel about that?" I asked Laura.

"I was furious when Rachel left. I thought she'd come back, but she didn't, and she made it clear that I was to be your moth-er." She gave me an emotional smile. "I loved you both from the first minute you were born. It was an honor and a blessing to be your mother. You and Dani gave me so much love, joy, and purpose. I felt like it was a new start. And I hoped that Rachel would find happiness, too."

"Did you love our father?" Dani asked. "I'm not talking about Max Davino; I'm talking about Ross Landry."

"I did love him," my mom said. "Ross was so good to me and to you girls. He was solid and kind and caring. He'd lost his family, and he was happy to take on a woman with two little babies. He wanted you to be his daughters. That's why we never told you that you were adopted. When I had to leave you, I knew you would be all right with your dad. I wasn't leaving you in a bad situation. I was giving you a chance to have a normal, happy, and safe life."

Her words hung in the air for a long moment. I didn't want to say our dad hadn't been the hands-on father she remembered. In fact, I didn't want to talk about him at all right now.

"What happened in New Orleans?" I asked. "Did you leave knowing you were going to fake your death? Or did something happen there?"

"Something happened," my mom said.

"Because of me," Rachel added. "I'd been living in New Orleans, working at a café, trying to stay out of trouble when I made friends with a woman in my yoga class. I thought she was a travel agent, but it turned out that she and her boyfriend were helping to set up a smuggling pipeline of drugs and guns from the Gulf Coast up to New York."

"And that tied into Max's family?" I asked.

"Yes. My friend never said exactly what she was doing, but her boyfriend drank too much one night, and he had a whole lot to say about his friends in New York, which gave me an idea."

I could see by the gleam in Rachel's eyes that it wasn't a good idea.

"I thought," Rachel continued. "That if I dug up dirt on this smuggling operation, I could send Max to jail and get him off my trail and make him pay for killing that guard, even if he didn't go to prison for that crime. I started asking questions and spending more time with my friends, and I got too close to the group. Someone recognized me and told Max. I was shocked when he showed up in the city. I called your mom and told her Max was in New Orleans, and I needed to get out, but I was afraid to leave my apartment. She said she'd be on the next plane."

"I couldn't let her face him alone," my mother said.

"I told her to bring the stones that I'd left with her in case I needed to barter them," Rachel continued. "When your mom got into town, we were supposed to meet someone to get me a new identity. The meet was at an old cemetery, which seemed perfectly ironic for starting a new life, but Max caught up to us. He had his friend, Jonah, with him, and I ended up killing him in self-defense. I hit him over the head with a shovel. It gave us time to get away."

"For the next few days," Rachel continued, "there was nothing but chaos in the area. Rising waters were everywhere. The place where I'd been staying was flooded. We couldn't go back there even if we wanted to. I said something like someone will find my stuff and think I'm dead." Rachel looked at my mom. "And then we both realized that was the only way out. We had to die in the storm. There was no going back. Max had seen both of us."

"So you faked your deaths," Dani said heavily. "It seems like you had other choices."

"Maybe. But we had to decide fast," Rachel said.

"And protecting you girls was my priority," my mom said. "I couldn't risk going back to you, to your father, to the life I'd led. I would have put everyone in danger."

"Wait a second," I said, looking at Rachel. "Max didn't know you had a twin before New Orleans? How is that possible?"

"I met Max when I was pissed off at your mom. I told you that I was angry and envious of her life," Rachel said. "I didn't talk about her to anyone. I didn't tell Max I had a sister. I told him I had no family, and that's why I needed money."

"Okay," I said, trying to keep up with the story. "What happened after you left New Orleans?"

"We started over," Rachel said. "I told your mother I'd never ask her to come to me again. We had to stay apart, but we'd send each other postcards whenever we were thinking about each other. It would be our way of saying I love you."

"The postcards in the box," I said. "Now that makes sense."

"I made a new life in San Francisco," my mom continued.

"And I went to Phoenix for a while," Rachel said. "While I was there, I got in touch with a cop in New Orleans who I knew had been working on taking down the smuggling operation. I told him everything I knew about the organization and the Davino family. Eventually he, along with some cops in New York, busted Max and his family for at least some of their criminal operations. Max was sent to jail for ten years."

"That's why Max said you set him up," I said.

"Yes. I had to do something. When he was locked away, it was the first time I could breathe."

"Did you tell that cop you were involved in the robbery at Holden's estate, that Max had killed Kade's father?" I asked.

Rachel shook her head. "No. I focused on the other information I had gotten on his current operations. I didn't have any proof for the other."

"And you didn't want to get yourself in trouble," Kade said sharply.

"That's true, too," Rachel admitted. "After Max went to prison, the cop I'd become friends with helped us get new identities again. We weren't officially in witness protection, because I hadn't testified publicly, but we were able to get new social security numbers, fingerprints, IDs, and fake histories. We became Rachel O'Connor and Laura Hawthorne."

That explained Laura's fake background that had allowed her

to teach. "Okay. But why didn't you come back when Max went to prison, Mom?"

"It had been three years since I'd died," Laura said. "It was too late."

"It wasn't too late," I protested. "Dani and I were ten years old. We still needed our mother."

My mom looked at me with sorrow in her eyes. "I actually did go back to see you a year later, but your father was about to marry Vicky, and you all looked so happy, I couldn't ruin that."

"You saw us when we were eleven?" I asked in amazement.

"I was nearby at other times in your life, too. I had to let you go, but I still needed to see you."

"What about what we needed?" Dani demanded, her voice rising with the level of her agitation. "Did you ever think about that? I'm guessing the answer is no. Because you and your sister are selfish. You only think about each other."

"Dani," Steve said. "Maybe we should go. This is too much for you."

"You're right," Dani said. "It is too much. And I'm not sure I even believe half of what either of you are saying. I'll wait outside for you, Brynn. Unless you're ready to go now?"

I could see the challenge in her eyes. Dani wanted me to leave with her, to walk away, but I couldn't, not yet. "In a few minutes," I said, seeing the unhappy gleam in her eyes, but she followed her husband out of the room.

"I don't blame Dani for being angry," my mother said. "I'm sure you feel the same way, Brynn."

"I feel a lot of things." Drawing in a breath, I turned to Kade, who had been standing by throughout their story. "Kade needs to know the truth about his father and why you started sending his mother money," I said. "I've told him some of what I know happened that night, but you need to give us the details."

"I was in Holden's house with Max and this other guy, Jonah," Rachel said. "When Ian took me to the estate days earlier, I was able to get the alarm access codes. When we entered, security was supposed to have gone. But your dad showed up unexpectedly, and Max panicked. He shot your father in the head. I think he died before he hit the ground. Max yelled at me to get the car and bring it around. We'd filled two tote bags with things we'd stolen from the safe. I had one of them in my hand, and I ran. But when I got into the car, I didn't bring it around. I drove away."

"You could have called for help," Kade said harshly.

"Your father was already dead. No one could have helped him."

"That's what you say now. But you didn't want to call for help. You didn't want your boyfriend to get caught and implicate you."

I wondered if Kade was right.

"I was in a panic," Rachel admitted. "But I knew your father was dead."

"And you thought that by doling out some cash to my mother that you would somehow exonerate yourself for what happened?" Kade challenged.

"I never thought that," Rachel said, not backing down from his direct glare.

"She didn't," Laura said. "It wasn't Rachel's idea to send your mom money; it was mine. I couldn't live knowing that my sister had been involved in something that led to a man's death, that there was a widow and a child who were struggling. I came up with the foundation idea to protect our identities, and I sent the money for years until your mother sent it back."

"Why didn't you let it go then?" Kade asked. "Why seek me out? Why pretend to love my art?"

"I didn't pretend. I did love your art. I do love it," Laura said. "When your mom asked me not to send any more money, I thought okay, it's done. But then I saw your art and I wanted to support it. It was so raw and real. I grew up in a world of pain and turmoil, too. Your art spoke to me, and I wanted to help you reach your potential."

"But you weren't even at the robbery, Laura," Kade said. "Why did my dad's death bother you so much?"

"Because it was wrong. Because it was horrible. And because my sister blamed herself, too. Rachel was a wreck for months. Her anxiety about that night led to her giving up her children. She couldn't live her life because she'd been there when an innocent person had lost his."

Kade's gaze moved from my mother to Rachel. "Did you feel that way? Or is your sister making you out to be a better person than you are?"

"The answer to both questions is yes," Rachel replied. "I was messed up when I met Max. I was stupid and reckless, and I didn't think I had anything to lose, but it turned out I had a lot to lose—my babies, my name, my life. I wish I'd never met Max, never gotten involved with his crew. I had no idea how dangerous he was until that night. That doesn't excuse what I did, but it's part of the story."

"I just wonder if it's a true story," Kade said. "You and Laura appear to be very good liars. And the fact that you kept the jewels for twenty-seven years and never turned yourselves in tells me that you never had enough guilt to want to come clean about everything."

"We always thought the stones were our insurance policy," Rachel said. "That Max could never kill us until he got them back."

"Did you sell any?" I asked.

"Only a couple small diamonds," Rachel replied. "To pay for some things we needed, but we were too afraid to sell more. We thought they might be traced back to us." She paused, her gaze moving to me. "How did you find them?"

"I remembered my mom telling me that she had magic stones that made the flowers grow."

Laura gave me a sad smile. "You caught me one day, and I had to make up a story. I can't believe you remember that."

"I remember a lot of things. This past week, when I met Kade and your students and your friends, I got angry, Mom. I resented the fact that you were there for so many other people, but not for me or for Dani. You were nurturing other peoples' dreams, but not ours."

"I shouldn't have told the nurse to call you. I just had this feeling I was going to die, and I wanted you to know that I loved you, that I was sorry. It was selfish of me to do that. When I left you, I should have cut the ties completely, but I kept going back to punish myself with glimpses of you and your sister and your dad. I got your number from a flyer at a music school where you gave violin lessons, and I put it into my phone, pretending we still had a relationship."

"Why didn't you put Dani's number in there?"

"After she turned away from me at graduation, I thought it was best that I never show my face near her again. I thought she'd told you that she'd seen me. And then I felt horrendously guilty and afraid that you'd both start looking for me."

"Dani didn't want to believe you were alive, nor did she want to upset me, so she stayed silent. The first time I knew you were alive was when I got the call from the hospital saying my mother was dying." I paused. "Did you talk to Max before he shot you?"

"Yes. He confronted me after I left school on Tuesday. He had found me through the video that went viral. I'd always stayed out of the limelight, but that night I'd had no choice but to do what needed to be done. I never imagined the clip would spread to so many news outlets."

"What did Max want?"

"The stones and Rachel," Laura answered. "I said I didn't know where the stones were and that I hadn't seen my sister in twenty years. Max made a lot of threats, but I was able to get away when some of my students interrupted our conversation. I sent Rachel an emergency text. She didn't get back to me, and I didn't know what to do. I needed to warn her. I also needed to leave. But then your father showed up the next day and I had a really unpleasant scene with him. It was all starting to unravel. I decided I would leave town after the concert. I didn't want to leave the kids in the lurch. I thought I could find a way to stay away from Max for a few days, but he wasn't having that. I was told he shot me in front of my house."

"You're lucky he didn't kill you," I said.

"I know."

"Is it over now?" I asked. "If Max is part of some crime family, won't there be others who want the jewels? Who will want revenge for Max's death?"

"Max and his friend Jonah did the Holden heist on their own," Rachel said. "If it had gone as planned, Max would have bragged about it and used it to bolster his position in the organization. But because it was a total screw-up, he couldn't tell anyone that he'd killed someone and had lost the stones. It was better for him to stay quiet." Rachel paused. "To answer your question, we're safe now because both Max and Jonah are dead. There's no one else who knows anything about the robbery."

"But the family will know that Max is dead," I pointed out. "Couldn't they want revenge just for that alone?"

"They won't care," Rachel said. "Max went to jail for ten years and he completely destroyed their business operations. His death won't matter to anyone in that family. I made it look like he sold them out. In fact, I hoped he'd die in prison, that one of them would kill him, but somehow that didn't happen. Max always seemed to come out on top."

"Well, he didn't today," Kade said.

"Thanks to you," Rachel said.

"We don't want the stones," my mother put in. "We'd happily give them up if we could finally be free."

"Then give them up," I said.

"It's not that easy," Rachel said. "If I come clean to the police, I might take Laura down with me. She wasn't at the robbery, but she helped me hide everything, and she was with me in New Orleans when I killed Jonah. I don't want to see her go to jail for my crimes. I don't want her to lose you again because of me, but that could happen."

She made a good point. I didn't feel emotionally connected to Rachel. In fact, if I felt anything, it was dislike and anger, but my mom…I really didn't want to see her go to jail. I saw the worry in both of their eyes—eyes that looked exactly like mine. *How on earth could I turn in my mother and aunt?*

"The police don't know that I found the jewelry," I said slowly. "All they have is the box of photos, the postcards and the cash. None of that ties you to the robbery. The cash could have come from anywhere. I don't want you to have to run away again. But I also don't want to hang onto stolen jewels. I think we should get them back to James Holden. I know you don't think he got them legally, Rachel, but two wrongs don't make a right. My mom once taught me that."

Laura's eyes brimmed with tears at my words. "I wanted to be a good role model for you, but I wasn't."

I turned to Kade. "What do you think? Your father died during the robbery. It's as much your call as it is mine."

Kade didn't answer right away. Finally, he said. "We'll send the jewels back to Holden anonymously. Then this will be over. My father's murderer is dead. Rachel did some good trying to tear apart Max Davino's criminal enterprise. I don't think anyone has to run again."

I let out a breath at his words. He was being far more generous than I'd expected. "That works for me," I said. "But Inspector Greenman might dig deeper into your lives. He's very curious about why Mom ran away twenty years ago. Can the police officer from New Orleans, the one who helped set you up with new lives, talk to the inspector about how you helped take down the mob? Seems like that should get you off the hook for the fake identities."

"Possibly," Rachel said. "I haven't been in contact with him in sixteen years, but I can tell Inspector Greenman about that part."

"Then that's what you should do." I blew out a breath. "I want you both to be free. I really do."

"Thank you, Brynn," my mom said. "But there's still Dani to consider. She may want something different."

"Dani will be happy to let all this go. She won't want to drag our family skeletons through a public spotlight." I took a breath. "And I don't think anyone needs to know that Max is our biological father."

"They don't need to know I'm your biological mother, either," Rachel said.

I thought about that. "It's so strange. You're my mother, but you feel like my aunt." I turned to Laura. "And you're my aunt, but you feel like my mother."

"Maybe we can just be two people who love you," my mom said.

"Maybe. I guess we'll see."

When Kade and I stepped into the hallway, Inspector Greenman was waiting. "Thanks for giving me the time alone with them," I said.

"Are they ready to talk?"

"Yes. They're going to tell you everything."

"I may follow up with you to make sure what they tell me is the truth," he said.

I nodded. "That's fine. Did the man you arrested at the church have information to share?"

"Yes. He said Max Davino shot your mother. He drove him to and from the scene."

I nodded. "Max admitted that when we were in the church. What about the man who kidnapped me? What will happen to him?"

"He'll be charged with a number of crimes. We were also able to trace his transaction to Max Davino. Since Mr. Davino is deceased, we should be able to wrap up this case quickly. We know who did what, but I'm not as clear on the motivation, which is what I want to find out today."

"My mother and my aunt are waiting to speak to you."

He gave me a small smile. "I have a feeling that's going to be quite a story. I'm glad you're all right, Ms. Landry."

"Me, too."

As Inspector Greenman went into the room, Kade and I walked down the hall to the waiting room. Dani and Steve got up when they saw us. I could see the strain and guilt in Dani's eyes.

"I'm sorry," Dani said. "I just couldn't listen to them anymore, Brynn. Maybe another time when I'm less tired."

"I completely understand. It's a lot to take in."

"Steve and I are going to drive back to Carmel from here," Dani said. "I'd love for you to follow us, but I know that you still have your things at the house. I can't go back there. I can't stand being in her home for one more minute. But we can wait in the car outside while you get your bag."

"It's fine. You and Steve should leave from here. I have some loose ends to tie up."

Steve cleared his throat. "Kade, do you want to walk downstairs with me? We can get the cars, give the women a minute."

"Sure," Kade said, as they left the waiting room.

"You are coming back tonight, right?" Dani asked, a question in her eyes. "Or is there someone else you want to spend time with? Kade did save our lives, and you two seem like you've gotten close."

"We've gotten close, and we've also gotten further apart. Our mother played a part in his father's murder. Even if she didn't pull the trigger, she also didn't go to the police and turn herself in or tell anyone that Max killed Kade's dad. I have a feeling that when he looks at me, he's going to remember all the lies and the tragedy of his father's death."

Dani gave me a sad but understanding look. "I wish I could

say you were wrong, but I don't know. It's a big hurdle to get over."

"Yes, it is. And besides all that, we've only known each other a few days."

"Life can change in an instant. We've certainly seen that."

"We have. It was funny, watching Mom and Rachel together. They went back and forth like we do, finishing each other's sentences. They spent their whole lives trying to protect each other."

"You said they would be a mirror for us, but I think they're a broken mirror," Dani said. "Of what can go wrong when you don't live your own life."

"They're also a mirror of what can go right when you love with your whole heart. Their love for each other is the most honest thing about them, and it's incredibly strong. They made a lot of mistakes but loving each other wasn't the worst of them."

"Well, thankfully, we are not as messed up as they are," Dani said. "We're not broken, Brynn. We're just a work in progress."

I smiled. "I like that description. And we won't stay close because of guilt or fear or duty, but because we love each other, and we're going to push each other to be better, right?"

"I don't think I can ever stop pushing," Dani said with a self-deprecating smile. "I know I can be bossy."

"And I can be too eager to please, so we'll both make some changes. Now, you should get out of here. I want you to go home, put your feet up, and just love the hell out of your husband."

"I can do that," she said.

When we got out front, Kade was standing by his truck, and Steve was next to him, his vehicle parked in front of Kade's.

Dani and I gave each other a long, tight hug, and then I stepped back as she and Steve got into their car. When I joined Kade in his truck, he gave me a questioning look.

"What?" I asked.

"I'm not ready to go back to the house. Do you feel like taking a walk on the beach?"

I was thrilled to do anything that would put off saying goodbye to him. "Absolutely."

It was only a short drive to the beach. There were things I wanted to say to Kade, but the words weren't ready to come. After parking at Ocean Beach, we walked out onto the sand and sat down. The wide expanse of beach was empty, which was not surprising for midday on a Tuesday. The weather was brisk, the wind blowing back my hair as we looked out at the waves.

"It's funny," I said. "Five days ago, I went to the beach near my store and took a call from my friend about the orchestra position. I looked at the waves and thought about how turbulent my life was about to get. A few hours later, I got another call, and that one made a mockery of the first one. My life wasn't going to just get complicated; it would be turned upside down. Everything I thought I knew was a lie." I gazed over at him. "Now I know what's true, and…"

"You feel calm?" he suggested.

"Hardly. I feel overwhelmed. I have answers, but I don't like a lot of them."

"The truth doesn't always set you free."

"What about you? How has the truth made you feel?"

He didn't answer right away. Then he said, "I feel like I got some justice by killing my father's killer. I wanted revenge for most of my life. I thought it would ease the pain. It didn't do that, but it brought me some closure. I'm still sad that my dad's gone, that he didn't have a chance to live his life, to love his family. That will never change."

"No," I agreed. "You'll never get back what you lost. The truth didn't put my family back together, either. It just explained why it fell apart. But I learned a lot about myself through all this. And you helped with that."

"How so?"

"You showed me what it looks like to go after your passion,

to be free, to take risks, and I'm going to make some big changes going forward."

"That's good."

"Do you think you'll be able to let go of the rage, the darkness in your soul now?"

"Possibly. But then what will my art be like? I guess I'll find out," he said with a small smile.

"Your art will be amazing, whatever direction it takes." I paused. "Changing the subject. How do you think we should get the stones back to Holden?"

"I've been thinking about that. I want to give the stones to Ian," he said.

"Ian?" I questioned in surprise. "Really?"

"Ian is not his brother. I did some reading on him the other day. He's very philanthropic. He gives back to the community, and he's passionate about music and the arts. I'll tell him he can give the stones to his brother, who probably stole the jewels in the first place, or he can find a way to make something good come from them."

"I like that idea. Will you say where you got the jewels?"

"Don't worry. I won't throw your mother and aunt under the bus. Although, I think Ian deserves to know that it wasn't Laura he slept with; it was Rachel. And he's the reason that crew was able to access the house. I don't want him to think he has no guilt in this situation."

"He was just stupid and fell for the wrong girl. I don't dislike your idea, but are you sure you don't want to use the stones to make your mother's life better, to make your community better? What about just selling one of the diamonds and doing something in your dad's name?"

"It feels like blood money to me. I'd rather honor my father by living my life in the right way, making him proud, and I'll take care of my mother myself."

I liked his pride, his strength, his sense of right and wrong.

"That sounds like a good plan. Have you spoken to your mother yet?"

"No. I wanted to hear the full story first. I'm not sure the details will matter that much to her. She made her peace with my father's death a long time ago. I will call her at some point, but the first thing I'm going to do when I get back to your mother's house is move out. I'll find somewhere to stay until after my show, and then who knows? I'll see where the road takes me."

I was a little sad that he wasn't including me in his future, but I couldn't make plans with him, either. I had no idea where my life was going to go, and I had to figure that out on my own. I couldn't fall into someone else's life. I couldn't let someone else's dreams overtake mine. I had to make something for myself.

"Do you think our roads will ever intersect again?" I asked.

His eyes sparkled in the sunlight. "I wouldn't mind if they did."

"I wouldn't mind, either." I leaned forward to give him a kiss. His mouth was warm, his lips a little salty, and I savored the connection for as long as I could, because it might be the last one.

"Let's walk a little before we go back," Kade said as we broke apart.

I got to my feet, and when he reached out his hand to me, I took it. We walked down the beach until we couldn't go any farther, and then we returned to the house.

I turned over the velvet pouch to Kade and we said goodbye on the porch. It didn't take long for me to pack my suitcase and exit the house. There was really no reason to linger.

When I got in the car, I texted Dani that I was leaving San Francisco. Then I drove down the road, forever changed by my past, but looking forward to my future, whatever that might be.

EPILOGUE

Four months later...

The Grande Salle at the Philharmonie de Paris was completely full, with over two thousand people gathered to hear the concert put on by the visiting Pacific Coast Orchestra. I took my seat in the second row of violins, feeling tingles of excitement race through my body as I prepared for the last concert in our European tour, a concert that was taking place on New Year's Eve, which seemed symbolic. This past year had been filled with so many challenges, discoveries, lies, truths, and emotions. It was ending well, but I wasn't sorry to see the calendar change.

I didn't know what the new year would bring, but hopefully more of the joy I'd been experiencing the last two months as I had toured the world and played in front of many audiences in many different cities. Each concert had made me a better musician and more appreciative of the opportunity that had been given to me.

I already had a couple of job offers for next year, but I hadn't made any decisions yet. I was saving those until midnight.

Turning my attention to the conductor, I got into position, and then I began to play. I had always channeled my emotions through the violin, but in the past, I'd sometimes run from those feelings. Now, I reveled in them. I let myself feel everything and then let the emotions flow through my fingers and through my instrument.

We played for over an hour, but it felt like minutes, and I was sad when it ended. But the thunderous applause perked me up, and when I walked backstage, I was still humming from the performance.

"Great job, Brynn," Ray said with a smile. "Can you believe our tour is over?"

"I can't," I said, looking at the man who had changed my life by pushing me into auditioning in the first place. Ray had also been a great support the past few months as I'd found my confidence in my role with the orchestra.

"Have you decided what you're going to do next year?" he asked. "Please don't tell me you're going back to the clothing boutique."

"No. Dani hired a full-time assistant manager and has been taking time off to enjoy her pregnancy. She has five weeks to go and is happy as can be. I will be doing something in music, but I haven't decided yet."

"That's right. You're giving yourself until midnight. I assume I'll see you at the party?"

I nodded. Our orchestra was celebrating New Year's Eve on the rooftop of a nearby restaurant. "I'll see you there." I left my violin with the orchestra manager and walked out of the concert hall. It was a beautiful, cold winter's night, and I felt like walking the streets of Paris before I said goodbye to the year and to this beautiful city.

I had barely taken a step when my phone buzzed. I took it out of my bag and saw that Dani was calling on a video chat.

"Happy New Year!" Dani said as I answered.

I smiled as Dani raised a champagne glass. "It's too early for champagne where you are. You have hours to go."

"It's sparkling cider," Dani said. "And I didn't want to miss you today. How was the concert?"

"Perfect. The best I've ever played."

"That's great. What are you doing tonight? Do you have a date?"

"No, but I have a party to go to."

"Well, maybe you'll find someone to kiss."

I hadn't found anyone I wanted to kiss since Kade. He should have faded from my mind by now. It had been four months since I'd seen him, but he kept coming back into my head. "I'm not worried about a midnight kiss," I told Dani. "I'm just looking forward to the new year. What are you doing tonight?"

"Dad and Vicky are in town, so we're going to have dinner with them, but it will be an early night. It's starting to feel more normal when we get together now. We don't talk about the past anymore."

"That's good. I'm glad you're staying in touch. Dad has been sending me texts as well. He's trying hard to be more engaged."

"He really does love us, Brynn."

"I know," I conceded. "And Mom loves us, too. I think Rachel does as well."

"I got texts from them wishing me Happy New Year," Dani admitted. "I decided to text them back."

"I'm glad. It's not that I want you to forgive or forget anything. I just want us all to move forward, to know each other again, to share our lives. I don't want to look back anymore."

"I don't, either, and I'm trying to get to where you are," Dani said.

"You'll get there," I said confidently. Dani might be more suspicious and wary than me, but she also had a lot of love to give.

"Well, have fun tonight, Brynn. I can't wait to see you. When are you coming home?"

"I'm not sure yet. I might travel for a week or so while I'm in Europe."

"You sound so carefree."

"I feel that way," I said with a happy smile. "I'll be in touch. Love you."

"Love you, too."

As I put my phone away, I stiffened as a man came out of the shadows. He wore slacks and a black wool blazer over a dark-gray shirt. His brown hair was thick and wavy, his jaw strong, his dark eyes gleaming with a sexy smile that flipped my stomach over. My wariness turned into pure joy.

"Kade! What are you doing in Paris?"

"I thought I'd catch a New Year's Eve concert," he said.

"You heard the orchestra?"

"I heard you, Brynn."

"I was just one of many." My body tingled under his hot gaze.

"Really? I could have sworn you were the only one playing, and it was…magical."

"It felt magical," I whispered. "You being here feels magical, too. Why are you here?"

"I wanted to see you. I wanted to see where your road had taken you. How has it been?"

"Everything I dreamed of and more."

"I'm glad. The dream doesn't always match up to reality."

"This one did. I found myself, Kade, and I like this version of me. I'm so happy I took the risk."

"Has Dani been supporting you in your new endeavor?"

"Very much so. We talk almost every day. She sends me reviews of our shows. She's trying to be very supportive."

"And her pregnancy is going well?"

"Yes. She's going to have a son in five weeks, so there will be a lot of change, but all good change. What about you? What have you been doing?"

"Well, I had an amazing show in San Francisco. Then I went down to Los Angeles and created some art by the beach. I made a trip back to New York to see my mom and talk over everything."

"How did she respond?"

"She was okay. She didn't really want to talk about it."

"Did you see my mom while you were in San Francisco?"

"Yes. Laura came to the show. We went out for a drink after-ward. She said you had texted with her a few times. She hoped that someday you'd be able to have a relationship. I don't think she had heard from Dani."

"Dani holds a grudge longer than I do, but she told me tonight that she wished Mom and Rachel a Happy New Year. So, there's progress."

"How is your father doing?"

"He's keeping in touch with us more frequently. He and Vicky seem to be happy again. I think in some ways the ghost of my mom was always hanging over them. Now, that ghost has been exorcised."

"And Rachel?"

"She was staying with my mom for a while, but she realized that she needed to make a life for herself, not just live in limbo or watch what my mother was doing. So, she moved to Seattle and joined a real-estate firm. Apparently, at some point, she got a real-estate license. Rachel and my mom are finally free of the past, and I'm glad about that. They made some big mistakes, especially Rachel, but they also went through some dark times." I paused. "To be honest, I still have conflicted feelings about them, but I'm not letting those feelings derail me. I have my own life to live."

"Yes, you do."

"And that's enough about the past. I was going to take a walk to the Eiffel Tower and then there's a party…any chance you want to join me?"

"I do want to join you—for the walk, for the party…and for whatever else you might want to do." His beautiful dark gaze swept across my face. "And I'm not just talking about a night, Brynn. I want more than that, but I don't know how you feel. It's been some time since we saw each other."

"I wasn't sure you'd ever want to see me again, Kade. My mother's life and your dad's death are tied up together. Can you get past that? Can you see me and not see that?"

"Yes. It was a shock at first, but I've moved past it, and I don't blame you for anything. I like you, Brynn," he said, holding my gaze. "I liked the woman I met in San Francisco, who was just about to stretch her wings and learn to fly. Now, I'd like to get to know the new you. If you'll let me."

"I liked the man I met in San Francisco, too, his passion for his art, his utter confidence in himself, his desire to make his own rules. I don't know if there's a new you or just a new me, but I'd like to find out how we might go together, Kade."

"I've gone through some changes," he admitted. "I defined a lot of my life by my father's death. I've spent the last several months trying to figure out a new definition."

"Were you successful?"

"Still working on it," he admitted with a small smile. "But I'll never change all the way, Brynn. I'm always going to be a free spirit."

"There's nothing wrong with that. In fact, it's one of the things I like most about you."

"What else do you like?"

"I like the way you push me to be the best version of myself. I need someone who is willing to challenge me but not try to control me."

"I would never do that."

"I wouldn't do that to you, either. I don't want to change you, Kade. Maybe I'll become a free spirit, too."

He laughed. "We'll see about that. So, we skipped a few steps when we first met."

"I remember," I said, flushing a little at the heat flowing between us now.

"How about we start over, and I take you out on a date?"

A wave of happy joy ran through me. "Yes. Absolutely. Can

we start now? Because it's going to be midnight soon, and I really want to kiss you again."

He put his hands on my waist and looked deep into my eyes. "I don't see any reason why we have to wait until midnight."

"I do like your no-rules lifestyle," I said, as I leaned in for the kiss I'd been wanting ever since the last one.

WHAT TO READ NEXT...

Ready to read another mystery thriller?

Check out my new standalone novel

ALL THE PRETTY PEOPLE

Other Suspense Titles Available

Off the Grid: FBI Romantic Suspense Series

PERILOUS TRUST
RECKLESS WHISPER
DESPERATE PLAY
ELUSIVE PROMISE
DANGEROUS CHOICE
RUTHLESS CROSS
CRITICAL DOUBT
FEARLESS PURSUIT
DARING DECEPTION
RISKY BARGAIN
PERFECT TARGET

ABOUT THE AUTHOR

Barbara Freethy is a #1 New York Times Bestselling Author of 76 novels ranging from contemporary romance to romantic suspense and women's fiction. With over 13 million copies sold, twenty-nine of Barbara's books have appeared on the New York Times and USA Today Bestseller Lists, including SUMMER SECRETS which hit #1 on the New York Times!

Known for her emotionally compelling and thrilling stories of suspense, romance, and page-turning drama, Barbara enjoys writing about ordinary people caught up in extraordinary adventures.

Visit her website at http://www.barbarafreethy.com

CPSIA information can be obtained
at www.ICGtesting.com
Printed in the USA
BVHW030944150223
658563BV00012B/353/J